Before You Go
The Mother's Secret

DEAR GRACE

CLARE SWATMAN

For Betty and Basil, Hazel and Gordon.
My beloved and much-missed grandparents

Chapter One

Anna stood in front of the frosted-glass door and hesitated. She was surprised at how nervous she felt. It had been a while since she'd had a new client, and she was never sure what to expect. It didn't help that rainwater was dripping from her motorcycle helmet down the back of her neck and running in a slow but steady stream down her spine and under the waistband of her trousers.

She sighed. So much for it never raining on The Island. That had been her grandma's favourite saying, repeated often in a voice that very much emphasised the capital letters in this description of her beloved Lowestoft – only really an island because it was sandwiched between the River Waveney on one side and the North Sea on the other. 'I know, Grandma,' Anna had always faithfully replied. And although she had often laughed, later, when recollecting it with her mother or some other family member, Anna did have to admit that the old woman had had a point. Lowestoft was so far east – 'the most easterly point in England, I think you'll find,' her grandma had liked to point out, absurdly proud of the town's claim to fame as though she'd had something to do with its positioning – that the rains that perpetually battered Cornwall, Wales and Manchester were usually so worn out from rolling and bumping and tipping themselves all over those parts of the country that by the time they'd limped as far as the opposite coast they were hardly more than a squall, a drizzle, or simply a dampness that hung despondently in the air.

Today, though, the weather seemed blissfully unaware of the fact that it wasn't supposed to rain on the island and was busying itself expelling the entire contents of the thick grey clouds that hung over the town onto the pavements, the rooftops and the choppy slate sea with wild abandon.

It was, Anna had concluded as she'd squinted through the smear of her flat window at the bank of dark grey clouds earlier that morning, most certainly not a day for being out on a motorbike. She'd reluctantly grabbed her helmet and pulled her folder out of her bag one more time to double-check her rota for the day. Her first stop this morning had been Mrs Baggs, who she didn't mind too much – unlike the other carers she worked with, who thought the woman was a right old dragon. But Anna liked her. Yes, she was forthright, didn't suffer fools gladly; but why should she? Anna would be bossy and intolerant too if she'd been alive for almost one hundred years. God only knew some of the youngsters needed a bit of shouting at now and then.

She'd dragged her finger slowly down the list, images of the old men and women springing to her mind as she read the line-up of old-fashioned names: Elsie Wilkinson, Betty Lewis, Basil Bird. Finally, right down at the bottom of the page, was Grace Winterton. Today was Anna's first day with Grace, and despite her nerves now, as she was standing in front of Grace's back door ready to enter, she was really looking forward to meeting her. All she knew about her was that she was ninety-four years old and lived on her own. Who knew what else she'd find on the other side of this door?

She glanced at her bike, parked just inside the iron gates of Grace's driveway. It wasn't the ideal way to travel in this weather; the rain had continued to fall in sheets all day so that before she'd even left the car park of her block of flats she'd been soaked to the bone. But she'd had to get rid of the car a few months before as a concession to her cheating husband, and this had been all she could afford. Which was fine, when the weather behaved. But on a day like today, when there was so much water running down the front of her helmet that the world looked like a watercolour – huge strokes of pastels turning the landscape into an impressionist painting, people becoming blobs of paint, smudges of charcoal, streaks of chalk – she longed for the comfort and dryness of her car.

Anna looked skywards. The rain had finally eased as she'd pulled into the driveway of Grace's home, the clouds that had formed a dank grey ceiling over the town all day parting now to reveal thin chinks of light, slices of late-evening sunshine scattering themselves across the shimmering pavement. She wondered if it was a sign. Of what, she wasn't quite sure.

Glancing down at her instructions one more time, Anna carefully typed the code into the box on the wall and extracted the key. She knocked on the door and then pushed it open onto the kitchen. There, a single glass and a single plate were upturned on the draining board by the sink, and she noticed that the cream worktop and 1960s orange cupboards were immaculate. It was like stepping back fifty years.

'Hello, Mrs Winterton, are you there?'

'In here!' came a tremulous voice, which, after pulling the back door shut behind her, Anna followed into the front room, overlooking the street.

The TV was on, the picture playing silently, and a ball of

pale yellow wool and some knitting needles were propped on the arm of Grace's chair. Two bars of an electric fire glowed in the corner and the room felt like a sauna. Anna stripped off her jacket and popped out briefly to hang it at the bottom of the stairs, straightening out her overall and slipping off her boots at the same time.

'Hello, Mrs Winterton, I'm Anna,' she said, stepping into the room in her socked feet and holding out her hand. 'I'm your new carer.' But since Grace didn't extend her own hand in response, Anna pulled it away again awkwardly.

'Hello, Anna,' Grace said, her watery eyes appearing to slowly focus on her visitor from behind her metal-rimmed glasses. 'It's nice to meet you. I hope you're going to be more competent than the last one.' Her pale lips stretched into a smile, revealing improbably straight, white teeth.

'I hope so too, Mrs Winterton,' Anna replied.

'Oh, please, call me Grace. Mrs Winterton always makes me feel ancient. I might *be* ancient but I don't need reminding.' She grinned again and Anna felt herself relax. Something in that smile told her they were going to get on just fine.

'All right, Grace. Now, what would you like me to do? Have you eaten?'

'No, not yet. Well, I had a plate of beef casserole that Good Old Gerald brought round earlier – he lives next door with his wife, Barbara, and they're ever so kind but, well, Barbara's not the best cook in the world and they do insist on foisting tasteless food on me several times a week. I can't complain, of course, but it was terribly bland.'

'Would you like me to make you something for tea now, then?'

'Yes please. There's some sliced white in the bread bin and a lovely piece of cheese in the fridge if you wouldn't mind making me a sandwich. Oh, and a cup of tea, please – milk, no sugar. I could do it myself, of course, but there's not much point in having a dog and barking yourself, is there?'

'Well, no. Quite. Anyway, that's what I'm here for.' Smiling to herself, Anna made her way to the kitchen, filled the kettle, then rummaged around for the bread and cheese.

'Just one slice,' Grace's voice rang out from the front room. 'I don't want to overdo it.'

Anna buttered a single piece of bread, cut some cheese and folded it over. She found a flowery plate in the cupboard above her head and dutifully took the half-sandwich through, along with a cup of tea, to Grace in the front room.

'Not in here, I'm not a heathen,' Grace said, pulling herself up slowly from her chair. 'Blimey, I'm stiff as a board.' Finally upright, she grabbed her stick and started shuffling towards the door.

'In here,' she said, indicating that Anna should follow her. They made their way into the back room, where a couple of patterned armchairs and a huge, imposing dark wooden dresser loomed over a folding dining table covered in a green cloth. The sun, putting up a good fight out there now, flooded through the patio doors and made the room feel stifling. Anna could see a long, well-maintained garden outside and wondered how Grace kept it so neat and tidy.

Grace lowered herself into a dining chair and Anna set the plate and cup in front of her.

'I always eat at the table,' Grace explained. 'It was never the done thing to eat on your lap when I was younger, so I never have. It's not a bad habit to keep.' She took a bite of her sandwich and, as she chewed, Anna couldn't help admiring her. At least keeping standards meant that Grace would never slide into slovenliness like her, shovelling family bags of Doritos into her mouth in front of the TV rather than cooking a depressing meal for one.

While Grace ate her sandwich and sipped her tea Anna tidied up around her, straightening newspapers, clearing away a glass, flicking a duster she'd found under the kitchen sink around the frames on the mantelpiece. One photo in particular caught her eye – a black-and-white one in a gold frame of a much-younger Grace and a tall, broad man, both of them smiling happily into the camera. She wondered who the man was.

'Oh, do stop flitting around,' Grace said, waving her hand as Anna moved behind her to dust the dresser. 'Have a cup of tea and sit down for a few minutes instead.'

Anna paused. 'But I'm meant to be helping you.'

'Yes, I know you are, but there's not much to do really. Most days I'm fine on my own, but it's nice to have someone coming in to see me, even if I do have to pay them.'

Sliding into the chair opposite, Anna felt a stab of pity. 'You don't have any family nearby, then?'

'I did. But most of them died ages ago, I'm afraid. My brother Ernest had a good innings but he went five years ago and most of his children and grandchildren are scattered all over the country now. All over the world, some of them. So, there's only really my great-nephew Tom left. He's a good boy, pops by when he can and keeps my garden tidy for me. I'm luckier than most my age.' She peered at Anna through the thick lenses of her glasses. 'Do you know how old I am, Anna?'

Anna shook her head. She did in fact know exactly how old Grace was because it was written in her notes, but she also knew how much old people liked to shock you so she let Grace have her moment. 'No, I don't.'

'Well, I still feel like I'm about twenty-five, but I'm ninety-four. Can you believe it?' Grace ran her hand over the tight curls of her pure-white hair and sighed.

'No, I can't.' And actually, this time, she really couldn't. Grace seemed so lively, so alert. She didn't seem to have given up on life like so many of the old people Anna had cared for over the years. Despite the white hair and the deep lines that made her crepey skin resemble a piece of paper that had been screwed up and flattened out again, her eyes still shone with mirth.

Anna stood and picked up Grace's empty plate. 'Would you like anything else to eat?'

'No thank you. But there's some carrot cake in the pantry – the Tesco man brought it a couple of days ago. Make sure you cut yourself a piece to take home with you, won't you?' She nodded in Anna's direction. 'You look as though you could do with a bit of fattening up.'

'I will do, thank you.'

Anna took Grace's dirty plate and cup into the kitchen and rinsed them both under the tap. She watched a sparrow bob about on next door's washing line and water drip from the gutter above the garage, splashing onto the path below. Even though the grey clouds still hung stubbornly over the town, Anna could see that Grace's garden was lovely. It was May now, and tulips bobbed their heads, roses were beginning to bloom on the side wall of the adjacent garage, the lawn was lush and green. Wiping her hands on a tea towel, she went back into the dining room, from where Grace was watching the same sparrow.

'Your garden's beautiful,' Anna said.

'Thank you. I do love sitting here looking at it.' She smiled. 'The garden was always Roy's domain – he was my husband. When he fell ill I was worried it would go to pot, that all his years of hard work would be swallowed up and forgotten within months. But then Tom – my great-nephew, if you remember – offered to come and help me out with it all. I'm ever so lucky he's so green-fingered.'

'Well, I think it's gorgeous.'

The two women sat in silence for a few moments watching the clouds scud across the sky behind the pale green tower of St Margaret's Church.

'I do miss him, though.' Grace's voice was so quiet Anna wasn't even sure she'd heard her properly.

'Who?'

'My Roy.' She coughed, her tiny body shaking with each hack. Anna reached out her hand and laid it on Grace's arm. 'Are you all right?'

Grace nodded, her coughs slowly subsiding until she was still again.

'Yes, I'm fine. Just a little chest infection, it's nothing to worry about.'

'Do you need anything? A glass of water? Medicine?'

'No, no, dear, I'm fine, really. It's nothing, nothing at all.'

'OK, if you're sure.'

'Absolutely sure. No need to fuss. I'm just old.' Grace looked back out at the garden. 'You know, sometimes when I sit here I can almost see Roy out there still, pottering around in the flowerbeds, clipping the roses.' She pointed towards the end of the garden. 'He used to grow vegetables over there. Rows and rows of them there were – peas, lettuces, cabbages. A greenhouse full of tomatoes and cucumbers. You couldn't bloody move for them some summers, could have fed the whole street.' She sighed heavily. 'It's been two years since he fell ill and couldn't get out there anymore, six months since he died, and I still sometimes forget he's gone, keep expecting to see him out there, skulking around with his secateurs. Silly, isn't it?'

'It's not silly at all. How long were you married?'

'Sixty-five years. Gosh, doesn't that sound like forever?'

'Sixty-five years.' Anna shook her head in wonder. 'No wonder you miss him.' She thought of something then. 'Is that him, in the photograph?' She pointed at the picture she'd noticed earlier as she was dusting.

Grace nodded slowly, her eyes fixed on the black-and-white photo. 'Yes, that's him. He really was lovely.' She turned back to look through the window again. 'That's why I'm so glad Tom looks after the garden for me. Roy loved it so much, I'd hate to see it go to ruin.' She stopped talking and after a while Anna wondered whether she'd dropped off to sleep. But then she spoke again.

'Do you have someone to love, Anna?'

'Sorry?' Why were old people so blunt? Was it a privilege earned over the years that freed you of any requirement to filter what you said?

'Do you have a young man?' Grace said, loudly and clearly so there was no doubt.

Anna shook her head. 'No, not right now.'

'Oh, that's a shame. A lovely young girl like you ought to have someone to love her.'

'It's a long time since anyone called me a girl. I'm forty next year.'

Grace shrugged. 'Thirty, forty, fifty, it's all young to me.' She turned her head to look at Anna. 'You remind me of me, you know, many, many years ago.'

'Oh? In what way?'

'Long before I met Roy, I got my heart broken.' She sighed, lost in the memory. 'I was supposed to marry someone else, you see, only he turned out not to be quite the man I'd thought he was. Anyway. I was sad for quite some time, and I see that in you. It's your eyes. They look beaten.'

'They do?'

Grace nodded. 'I know we only met half an hour ago, but when you've been alive as long as I have you learn to recognise things in people. I'm also a very good judge of character and I like you, Anna. I think we're going to get along famously. So maybe one day you might like to talk to me about what's bothering you. That's all.'

Anna stood, almost knocking the chair over. 'Thank you, but I'm fine, honestly.' She plastered a smile on her lips and felt her cheeks ache with the effort. She certainly wasn't going to start talking about her love life – or lack of it – right here and now with someone she'd only just met. Despite the eighteen months that had passed, everything that she'd been through with Daniel was still too raw to move on from and so she tried not to think about it most of the time. 'I must just be a bit tired.'

'All right.' Grace turned her face back to the garden with a knowing look. Honestly, old people really could be quite infuriating.

'Right, well, I suppose I'd better be off now, unless there's anything else you'd like me to do?'

'No, nothing else, thank you. But make sure you don't forget that cake.'

'I won't.' She stepped forward and held out her hand and this time Grace took it, her skin warm and dry against Anna's softer skin.

'It's been lovely to meet you, Anna. I think we're going to get on just fine.'

'Me too.' Anna pulled her hand away. 'See you tomorrow.'

And, remembering to cut a slice of cake, Anna turned and left, a frown puzzling her forehead as Grace's words turned over and over in her mind.

* * *

Anna stepped into her flat and hovered in the hallway for a moment, listening. There was the distant sound of the TV from the flat next door, muffled voices drifting through the paper-thin walls. She could hear children's shouts from somewhere, and someone hammering. But inside the coolness of her flat, it was silent. There was no one to greet her – just the empty coffee cup and the crumb-covered plate that had been cast aside when she'd left earlier that day, still sitting there waiting for her to clean them away. There was something about the solitary feeling of her flat that reminded her of Grace's house. She'd always felt melancholy, walking into the houses of the people she cared for, to find single teacups, single plates, single cooking pots lined up in the kitchen. It had felt like the personification of loneliness.

But the truth was these people had lived their lives. They'd had people who'd loved them and lived with them and shared their lives with them. At the end those people might have died and left them, in person. But they were still there, in spirit, in their hearts and their minds; their voices still echoed in the corners of the houses they'd shared.

In contrast, Anna's flat was just empty. There was no one there but her, and there never had been. There was no one who had once cooked up a storm in her kitchen as a surprise, or who had sat on the cheap IKEA sofa waiting for her to get back from work; no one had shared her bed, or snuggled up beside her while they watched TV together, or helped her paint or choose wallpaper for the living room. There were no happy memories here hidden in the shadows. Instead, as she looked around the flat and saw the blank walls, the beige and pine furniture, the cheap carpet, she felt overwhelmed with sadness. This shouldn't have been her life. She should have been living in her lovely Victorian home with its wide windows overlooking the green of the park and, beyond, the wild North Sea and the enormous, far-reaching East Anglian sky; she should have been curled up with the man she loved on the sofa laughing at some silly sitcom while they shared a takeaway and a bottle of wine, a cat snoozing at their feet. She should have had children upstairs in bed, wandering through sleepily in the middle of the night after a bad dream to be rocked back to sleep in her arms.

Not this.

She dumped her helmet and keys on the side table and walked into the tiny galley kitchen overlooking the small car park, where she could see her bike squeezed between a van and a Mini.

She sighed. She was lucky, really. She might be living in this soulless flat while she and Dan tried to sell the home they'd bought together – the home she'd loved from the moment she'd seen it, in all its faded glory – but at least she had her friends and family: her mum and dad, who she saw several times a week and who, even though they drove her mad, she loved spending time with; her brother Adam, who lived down the road in Great Yarmouth and who she saw regularly; and Julia, her oldest friend, who lived ten miles down the road in the market town of Beccles with her husband Al and her children and her great job, and who she should be jealous of but couldn't be because she'd known her forever and loved her like a sister. Not to mention her friends and colleagues from work who she liked to share a cheap glass of wine with when they clocked off every Friday night. She couldn't have got through the last eighteen months without them.

Anna shook her head and pulled a ready meal out of the fridge. Macaroni cheese for one. She jabbed a fork through the plastic covering several times and shoved it in the microwave, then poured herself a glass of water and a large glass of red wine and glugged back both, feeling her shoulders relax as the liquid slid down her throat.

The microwave pinged and she tipped the scorching-hot contents onto a plate and sat down heavily at the tiny pine table shoehorned into the corner by the window. As she shovelled forkfuls into her mouth, she thought about Grace. Anna got on well with most of the people she looked after, as a rule. Well, apart from Mrs Strong, whose house was so cluttered she could barely get through the door, and who snapped at Anna every time she tried to suggest she might want to get rid of a few things for her own safety. But there was something different about Grace. Something she connected with. She'd felt it from the moment she'd first spoken to her, and it wasn't just what the old woman had said about seeing her sadness. Just like Grace, Anna had a feeling the two of them were going to get on.

Her plate empty, she stood and rinsed it under the tap and stuck it on the draining board, then picked up her bottle of wine and took it through to her bedroom and flicked on the TV. As she pulled on her pyjamas – the lovely old-fashioned ones with a proper collar and thick, fleecy trousers that Dan had hated and now she slept in every night – she caught sight of herself in the small mirror stuck to the magnolia wall. She stood in front of it, scrutinising her face. She scrunched her nose up and observed the lines that radiated out from under her eyes, then she raised her eyebrows and watched the skin fold in gentle waves across her previously smooth forehead. She smiled and studied the deepening lines that crept out from the corners of her eyes towards her hairline. It had been some time since she'd last taken a proper look at herself, and her reflection surprised her. When had she started looking like a middle-aged woman? Where had the young woman gone, the one that had met Dan, bought a dream house, been full of hope and plans and excitement for the future? And where would she be by the time she was Grace's age – assuming she got that far? Would the lines and wrinkles that shaped her face then reflect a happy life, or a sad, lonely one?

Climbing under the duvet, she picked up her wine glass with one hand, her mobile with the other, and, using her thumb, tapped out a message to Julia. She'd know what to say to cheer her up. She was lucky to have her as a friend. And she wondered, as she waited for Julia to reply, whether she might just have made a new friend, in Grace. She really hoped so.

Tugging her nightdress over her head that evening, Grace smiled to herself. She'd enjoyed meeting Anna today. She had a feeling they were going to be friends, despite their fifty-five-year age difference. Age didn't matter a jot. But she hadn't been able to stop thinking about the look of sadness in the younger woman's eyes. She'd seen it before, more than once, and not least in the mirror many, many times over her ninety-four years.

'You don't get to my age and not learn a thing or two,' she said out loud to her reflection as she studied her face in the mirror above the bathroom sink. Who was this ancient woman looking back at her? Where had she come from and what had she done with Grace? The Grace who loved to climb trees, who got told off for being such a tomboy; the Grace who loved to dance, whose eyes crinkled gently when she laughed – which was often – and who was, surely, no more than about thirty years old. How had the years passed so quickly without her even noticing?

She ran the tap to fill a glass and walked carefully back to her bedroom. She was lucky, she knew, that she was still pretty independent even at her age. A large majority of her friends were dead now, and those that weren't were in homes festering away, or in hospital being pumped full of drugs to keep them alive. These days the only people she saw on a regular basis were at least twenty years younger than her – Good Old Gerald and his wife Barbara from next door; the people she met at the Scrabble club, who, she was sure, let her win out of sympathy from time to time; and her great-nephew Tom, who helped her out with her garden and came to see her much more often than he needed to.

But she couldn't deny that it was nice to have someone else to get to know. There was something about Anna that she'd liked immediately, maybe because she reminded Grace of her old friend Susan. She and Susan had been joined at the hip as teenagers, had survived the war together and been friends for almost a lifetime until she died of cancer more than fifteen years ago. She missed Susan more than she cared to admit, and now she'd met Anna, with whom she was already beginning to feel a connection, Grace was looking forward to getting to know her better over the coming weeks and months. She just hoped Anna felt the same, and would talk to her. Because Grace definitely saw something of herself in Anna. She saw the Grace who had been left heartbroken all those years ago, the Grace who'd assumed she would never be happy again, who'd believed she didn't deserve to be.

And she wanted to help Anna.

She just hoped Anna would let her.

Chapter Two

Grace was lying on the floor, face-down, her cheek pressed into the rough carpet. She was staring at the underside of the bed and, quite frankly, she wasn't entirely sure whether she was ever going to be able to get up again. In fact, if Anna didn't turn up soon she'd be in danger of lying here in a puddle of her own wee until she died. What a tragic way to go, after all these years.

She could see the box she wanted, right at the other side of the bed, against the wall, but even when she stretched her arm out fully and pressed her face into the side of the bed, she couldn't quite reach it and her fingers flailed uselessly in the air in front of her.

She dropped her arm and let out a puff of air, disturbing the dust in the carpet that floated up her nostrils and made her sneeze. She wished she'd never started this. What was she thinking, getting down on her hands and knees like this and climbing under the bed at her age? What a ridiculous thing to do.

It's just there had been something she wanted to find.

There was something under here she wanted to have a look at and, most importantly, that she wanted to show Anna.

They'd been getting to know each other better over the couple of weeks since Anna had started as her carer, and Grace now realised her first instinct had been right. They *were* going to be friends. But with ninety-four years to catch up on, it was going to take some time to get to know each other properly. It had occurred to her this morning, as Phil and Holly were chatting on the telly about something or other to do with smacking children, that if she could just find these old photographs it might help speed things up a bit. She could show Anna who she really was behind all these wrinkles and this dilapidated old body – it might help her understand.

Right now, though, she was in a bit of a dilemma. Because she couldn't reach the box of photos, and she couldn't get up either. Shuffling herself across the carpet and away from the bed slightly, she closed her eyes and decided to wait. Anna would be here soon. She would help her, Grace was sure.

* * *

Grace was Anna's last port of call every day, and she always looked forward to seeing her. The sun had been shining all afternoon and it felt warm as she let herself in. The kitchen was immaculate as usual. There was a small pile of recycling on the side near the back door waiting to be taken out, a dustpan and brush on the floor, and Anna saw tiny particles of dust dancing in the sunlight that streamed through the small window and reflected off the stainless-steel pans that hung in a row from the little shelf above her head. She wondered how Grace reached them.

'Grace, it's me, Anna,' she called, pulling her helmet off and placing it on the worktop. There was no answer and Anna stopped for a moment, listening. But the house was silent and revealed nothing.

'Grace? Are you there?'

She tried to still her heart, taking slow, deep breaths. She'd been doing this job for most of her working life and yet she still dreaded walking into someone's house and finding them collapsed, or worse. Sadly, it was part and parcel of the job most of the time; she'd recently found an old man on his bedroom floor having suffered a heart attack, and an old woman at the bottom of the stairs after falling several hours before. At first she'd assumed it was something she'd get used to, that she'd learn to detach herself, but she hadn't, and now she heard her heart roaring in her ears. She couldn't help thinking, as she slipped off her boots and stepped across the cool terracotta tiles into the hall, about the persistent cough Grace had been suffering from. Could it have been worse than she'd admitted?

Anna poked her head round the door of the dining room but the air was still, undisturbed, as though no one had been in there for several hours. She carried on along the hall to the front room, where Grace was usually to be found, but it was empty. She swallowed heavily and ran to the bottom of the stairs.

'Grace?' she called, trying to keep the panic out of her voice. 'Grace, are you there?' Hurrying up the stairs, she called out again. 'Grace! Where are you?'

No answer. Anna pushed open the door to the loo, the bathroom door and Grace's bedroom door. Nothing. Where was she? And then she spotted a flash of Grace's hair on the floor behind the door of the spare room, stark white against the green of the carpet, and her heart leapt into her throat.

'Grace!' She pushed open the door tentatively. Grace was lying face-down on the floor and Anna crouched beside her to check whether she was breathing. But just as she placed her hand on Grace's back, the old woman's eyes pinged open.

'Oh, hello, I didn't hear you come in. I seem to be in a bit of a pickle.'

'Oh, thank goodness,' Anna said, her legs shaking beneath her. 'What on earth are you doing down there?'

'Help me up and I'll tell you.'

Taking Grace's arm with care, Anna helped her sit up and then pulled her gently to standing, using the walking stick that had been lying beside her to help take her weight. Grace's face was pale and she had the pattern of the carpet stamped into the spongy skin of her cheek. Anna sat her on the bed and waited as Grace got her breath back under control.

'You gave me a real fright,' Anna said.

'I am sorry,' Grace said eventually, untucking a hanky from the sleeve of her cardigan and dabbing it under her eyes.

'It's all right. But what were you doing down there?'

Grace sighed. 'I was just trying to get something out from under the bed. I sometimes forget this ancient body doesn't work as well as it used to, and I – well, I got stuck, which is a bit embarrassing.'

'Oh, Grace. You should have just waited for me, I could have got it for you.'

'I know, I know. But I just don't like to admit how old and useless I've actually become.'

'You're not useless. You just need to know your limits.'

Grace nodded, a smile on her lips. 'You're not wrong there.'

Anna sat down next to Grace on the bed and felt the old woman tip slightly to one side so that their shoulders were touching. She shivered and looked round the room. It was cold, as though nobody had been in here for many years. A patch of damp had spread across the corner of the room and boxes were piled up next to a sturdy mahogany wardrobe. 'So, do you want me to get it, whatever it is you were looking for?'

'Yes please, if you wouldn't mind. It's a box.'

Anna got down on her hands and knees and peered underneath the bed. There were a few boxes. 'Which one are you trying to get?'

'The pretty one, the one covered in forget-me-not paper. Can you see it? I didn't want to rip the paper on it.'

'I can see it. Hang on.' Anna lowered herself onto her stomach and stretched her hand out towards the box right at the other side of the bed. She reached it, curled her fingers round the top and pulled. It was an effort to slide the box across the carpet towards her. 'Blimey, it's quite heavy, what have you got in here, bricks?' She turned her head to look over her shoulder.

'Not quite,' Grace said, smiling.

Anna continued to inch the box forwards until it reached the edge of the bed, then she stood and picked it up. It was a square box with a lid, and the plain cardboard had been covered, clearly some time ago, in a pretty blue-patterned thick paper, like wallpaper, just as Grace had described. It was quite heavy and she brushed the dust off the top.

'I can't believe you tried to get this yourself.'

'I know, a bit silly really. I thought it would be easier than that.' She glanced down at her knees, encased in smart blue trousers with a crease down the front, and sighed. 'I suppose I need to accept that these legs are old and worn out.'

'Well, I've got it now. Do you want me to take it downstairs for you?'

'Yes please, it's much warmer down there. Thank you.'

The pair walked slowly down the stairs, Grace gripping the banister tightly with both hands, her stick tucked under one arm, and taking one step at a time, Anna following behind with the blue flowery box. She was curious about its contents but she wouldn't ask. She'd wait for Grace to tell her if she wanted to.

At the bottom she followed Grace into the dining room. 'Will you put it on there for me, please?' Grace said, pointing to the table and lowering herself into a chair. 'Phew, I'm exhausted after all that.' Grace's breath was wheezy and she coughed a few times to clear it.

'Shall I make you a cup of tea?' Anna suggested, placing the box gently on the table.

'That would be lovely. And could I trouble you for a small sandwich as well? There should be some shrimp paste in the fridge.'

'Of course. One slice or two?'

'I'll have two today, please. Lunch wasn't all that. I made it myself and the cabbage tasted of feet.'

Anna grinned as she buttered the bread and poured tea into the pot. Grace loved to be as independent as possible, but she was a terrible cook. Perhaps it meant she'd always had someone to cook for her, which Anna loved the idea of. Maybe she'd ask her about it one day.

The tea made, she went back into the dining room. Grace was gazing out of the patio doors into the garden, where a chaffinch was flapping around the bird feeder, pecking its little beak through the holes trying to reach the seeds.

'I love watching them feed,' Grace said. 'There's something extraordinarily calming about it.' Anna placed the sandwich and the cup of tea down. 'Thank you, dear. Will you sit with me for a bit?'

'Don't you want me to do anything else?'

'Not right now. Go on, sit.'

Anna sat and followed Grace's gaze back to the bird feeder.

'Roy used to love birdwatching,' Grace said. 'He'd go out

for days at a time tracking a bird he was hoping to spot, and I'd hardly see him. He tried to get me interested but I wasn't having any of it. Can't be doing with traipsing round the countryside staring at the sky for hours on end. But this – this is lovely. Just sitting here in the warmth of my own house watching the birds come to me and enjoy a lovely meal. This I understand.'

The two women sat for a few moments, watching, until the bird fluttered away. The sun was still warm through the patio doors and Anna closed her eyes, allowing herself to imagine for a moment that she was on the beach somewhere hot, not a care in the world.

'I wanted to show you something.' Grace's voice broke her reverie and she looked round. 'It's in this box.'

Intrigued, Anna leaned forward. 'What is it?'

Grace delicately prised the lid off the box. Inside were yellowed pieces of paper, gathered together with elastic bands. Grace plucked one bundle off the top and carefully picked the dried-out elastic band off it. She dropped it on the table and opened up the package. Within the outer paper were photos – black-and-white and sepia, with curled edges and faded images, white borders with crimping round the outside. Grace spread them out across the green floral tablecloth and handed one to Anna, who took it gently, careful not to smudge it with greasy fingerprints. Two people – one clearly an impossibly young Grace, only recognisable from the glint in her eyes, the curl of her lip when she smiled – stared back at her from the depths of time. Grace was standing, her hair curled and pinned back neatly, her lips dark. She wore a jumper, a straight skirt to just below the knees, and flat shoes. Beside her an unfamiliar man half-sat on black railings, his arms snaked around Grace's waist, his legs stretched out in front of him. He wore a suit jacket over a jumper and his dark hair was slicked back with Brylcreem. Behind them was the familiar sight of the South Pier, and Anna knew immediately where this picture had been taken. But who was the man?

'This is Arthur and me,' Grace said.

Anna looked up. 'Arthur?'

Grace nodded. 'Do you remember the other day I mentioned a man who broke my heart?'

'Yes…'

'Well, this was him. Wouldn't know it, would you, to look at him? Appears perfectly nice.' Grace sighed. 'And he was, to be honest.'

Anna studied the photo, not knowing what to say. She wasn't entirely sure why Grace was showing her this picture. But before she could respond, Grace passed her another one. This time Grace was a bit older, and a different man stood beside her – the man from the photo on the mantelpiece.

'Oh, this is Roy,' Anna blurted.

'Yes, that's right.' Grace smiled, lost in memories. 'This is just before Roy and I got married. He was such a wonderful man, my Roy – you'd have loved him. Everybody did.' She smiled sadly. 'It was just me they weren't so keen on.'

'Oh, I don't believe that for one minute.'

'Oh yes, it's perfectly true, but I don't mind one jot. Roy was the man everyone adored. I was known for being a bit opinionated, which wasn't the done thing for a woman in those days – could get people's backs up, a woman with something to say about things. I was a reporter, you know. On *The Lowestoft Journal*. Quite a thing back then when women were more likely to be found gossiping in the typing pool than reporting in the newsroom.'

'Were you? That's amazing.'

Grace gave a small nod. 'It was. Father disapproved, of

course, but I loved it – the excitement, the fast pace, the sense of making a difference.'

Anna leaned forward, fascinated, enjoying the brief glimpse into the life of this woman she'd only known for a couple of weeks but who she'd already begun to realise had been a bit of a firecracker in her time.

Grace coughed. 'It was different in those days, of course. Frowned upon, for a woman to want a career. But I think that's exactly what Roy loved about me, in the end. My stubbornness. My independence. My refusal to conform.' She shrugged. 'It's just the way I was. Still am, if I can be.'

'So, what happened?'

'What happened when?'

'With this Arthur.'

'Oh yes. Well. It was all rather awful, to be honest. He left me at the altar.'

'What?'

Grace nodded, looking at the photo in front of her wistfully, the light from the patio doors reflected in her glasses. Anna waited for the memories to filter through the years. 'Well, we'd met before the war started, you see, and then Arthur got sent away to fight. I missed him terribly, pined for him almost, but then I was terribly young and didn't really know any better. Most of my friends had either married their husbands before they went off to war or had spent the war years flirting with the soldiers stationed in the town. I couldn't do either of those things because I had Arthur, but he hadn't asked me to marry him.' She coughed, and delicately dabbed her mouth with a hanky, leaving a trace of peach lipstick behind.

'So, anyway, when he came home, afterwards, he was different. He'd always been full of fun, cheeky, game for anything. But when he returned, he was serious and withdrawn. I tried to pretend it wasn't happening, and then when he finally asked me to marry him, I was so thrilled I ignored all my worries.' Grace stopped, as though she'd lost her train of thought.

'So, what happened next?' Anna prompted gently.

Grace glanced up, her eyes shimmering. 'Our wedding day arrived and for the first time since Arthur had returned from the war, I felt hopeful for the future. I was happy, hopeful, anxious. Maybe this would be the beginning of the rest of our lives.' She sighed. 'My flowers were so beautiful. Pink and white they were, green tendrils all the way down to the ground. Funny, the details you remember. It was only a few months since the war had ended so how Mother got hold of them I'll never know – or the tiara and long veil I was wearing. It felt like a miracle. Anyway, Mother was there in her Sunday best, and Father in his faded suit with a patch on the left elbow. A few friends and family were waiting inside the church.'

Grace removed her glasses and wiped her eyes, then replaced them. 'I knew something was wrong the minute the vicar came outside and spoke to Father. Mother took my bouquet from me and led me to a nearby bench and we sat down. Then Father came over and sat next to me, and the look the vicar gave me will stay with me forever. Pity.

'Time kept ticking on and it was clear soon enough that Arthur wasn't coming. I don't know how we decided how long was long enough to wait, but it *was* decided, somehow. So, before anyone could come outside and find me sitting there in my wedding dress, all alone, Mother and Father led me back to the wedding car and we drove home.'

Grace stopped and Anna realised she'd been holding her breath. 'So, what happened with Arthur?'

'Nothing.' She looked at Anna, her eyes huge behind her glasses. 'I never saw him again.'

'What?'

'What I say. He disappeared.'

'But...' Anna was lost for words. 'Someone must have known where he'd gone.'

'I'm sure they must have, but they never thought to tell me.'

'But did...did you try to find him?'

'Oh yes. The day after, once the shock had subsided and turned to pure fury, I stormed round to his parents' house, banged on their door and demanded to know where he was. They were clearly embarrassed to have this raving lunatic on their doorstep and ushered me inside quickly. But it soon became quite clear they had no idea where he was or why he'd disappeared either. In fact, his mother was close to tears and kept saying how sorry she was, how she'd have his guts for garters when he got home.

'I asked a few of his friends, of course, but apart from one person who said maybe he'd gone home to the North East where they'd moved from a few years before, it soon became obvious that nobody knew what had happened to him, and even if they did, they weren't about to tell me. So that was that. I had no choice but to put it behind me.'

'But how did you live with that? I mean, you'd loved him.'

'Yes, I had, deeply. But what else could I do? It wasn't easy to find people who didn't want to be found in those days. There were no computers, and there was certainly no Goo-goo, or whatever it's called.' Anna hid her smile, not wanting to embarrass Grace. Besides, the old woman had a point. The internet made it much easier to find people these days. But back then, if someone didn't want to be found, then, it seemed, it was pretty easy for them to simply disappear.

'God, that must have been heartbreaking. All that wondering.'

'Yes, I suppose it was. And it put me off men for quite some time, I can tell you. It's probably why I focused on my career so much, truth be told. I wasn't about to be hurt like that again, so working seemed to be the best thing for it. So I have that to thank him for at least. My career.' She smiled.

Anna thought for a minute, possibilities whirring through her mind. 'Have you never thought about trying to find him since?'

'Whatever for? What good would that do anyone? He's probably got his own life, and I had a good life too. Besides, he'll be dead now. Everyone is.'

'He might *not* be.'

'Oh, come on, Anna. Practically everyone I know is dead and buried, and if they're not then it's because they're years younger than me. Hardly anyone is as ancient as I am.'

'You're not ancient.'

'I'm ninety-four, Anna. That's pretty decrepit.'

'But you're not decrepit at all.'

'Maybe not, but the point remains that by my age people have either karked it or lost their marbles, so the likelihood of Arthur still being alive *and* compos mentis is minute. And anyway, even if he were, why on earth would I want to see him?'

'To ask him why he left.'

Grace sighed, puffing her cheeks out. 'Oh, why does it matter now? It was a million years ago.'

'I don't know. I just think it would be good to know. I'd want to know.'

'Well, I don't.' Grace folded her arms across her chest and sat back, looking out of the window. For an old woman she could behave surprisingly like a small child having a tantrum.

'All right.' Anna picked up the photo of Roy, deciding to change the subject for now. 'Tell me more about Roy, then.'

Grace tried to ignore her but Anna pushed the photo in front of her face and, slowly, Grace's lips curled into a smile.

'Do you mind if I don't today? I'm wiped out from all that talking about the past.' She picked up the photo of her and Roy and the love was clear in her eyes. 'But to go back to my point, which is the reason I dug these ancient photos out, the thing you need to know is that we've all been there. Heartbreak, I mean. And we've all come through it. Look at me – head-over-heels with the wrong man in one picture, and a few years later even happier in this one with the love of my life. I'd never have imagined back then that that could happen.' She took a sip of her cooling tea and bit into her fishpaste sandwich, chewing slowly.

In the silence that followed, Anna's eyes were drawn to the two pictures in front of her. Old photos told such a story; it was a shame people rarely got any printed these days, just ended up with hundreds and hundreds of snaps on phones – throwaway moments, disposable memories. These photos, printed and carefully stored away – they meant something. She thought about her wedding photo that she'd thrown out along with Daniel's clothes and his beloved vinyl collection and felt a pang of regret.

Grace swallowed and coughed. 'So, what about you?'

'What about me?'

'What's happened to you?'

Anna slid her eyes away from Grace's gaze and watched the distant black dots of birds soar in the pale blue sky, the leaves rustle in the gentle breeze and a tabby cat prowl elegantly across the fence dividing Grace's house from next door.

'Is it that obvious?'

Grace shrugged. 'Only if you know what you're looking

for, I suppose.' She pressed her papery hand on top of Anna's and gave it a small squeeze. 'I'm good at reading people.'

Anna swallowed. She didn't like talking about what had happened with Dan, not even with her best friends or her mum and dad. And, to be honest, she'd bored herself with it all, trying to work out where things had gone so wrong, what she could have done differently. Did she really want to go over it all again? But something about Grace, about the kindness in her eyes, the gentle tilt of her head, and the story she'd just shared, meant Anna found herself telling her new friend what had happened before she'd really had a chance to think about it.

'My husband cheated on me,' she said, picking a loose flap of skin from the side of her nail and wincing as it tore the skin and started to bleed. She kept her eyes trained on her hands as she spoke. 'We'd been together for more than twelve years. Dan was a couple of years younger than me, had always been a bit of a womaniser – a bit of a Jack-the-Lad, apparently – but he seemed to change when he met me. Everyone said it.' She shrugged. 'It seemed true, too. For a while at least. We got married, started trying for a baby, the usual thing. But nothing happened. We went to the doctor, got referred for IVF, but still nothing. And all this time we were drifting further and further apart and pretending it wasn't happening.' She glanced out of the window, focusing on nothing in particular but not wanting to meet Grace's eye. 'Then Dan started staying out late, going out drinking with his friends. I stopped wanting him to be near me, was glad of the space to be alone. I still loved him – or at least I thought I did – and I hoped that if the baby came it would patch things up. Like a plaster over a relationship that was clearly falling to pieces. But it was all too late.'

Grace watched her, her forehead creased. 'And? What

happened?'

Anna let out a puff of air and inhaled deeply. 'It was all so predictable in the end, I'm afraid to say. I found a bra under our bed. A bra that was two sizes too big for me. I wondered briefly whether Dan was dressing as a woman, and to be honest that would have been preferable. But really, I knew. He was having an affair. And worse than that, he was doing it in our house, in our bed. I could have forgiven him most things, but not that.'

'No. No, I don't suppose you could have done.' Grace clasped her hands in her lap. 'So, you threw him out?'

Anna shook her head. 'No, I left, that night.'

'Why didn't you make him leave?'

Anna squirmed, uncomfortable with this part of the story, even now. 'I just couldn't face the fight.'

Grace nodded, saying nothing.

'Anyway. Dan made a half-arsed attempt to deny it but we both knew there was no point. He didn't want to be there anymore and it was obvious. It was me who left, but in the end neither of us wanted to be in the house we'd bought together so we've been trying to sell it ever since. That was eighteen months ago.'

'I'm sorry. It's a long time since I felt anything like that, but seeing you talking about it now – well, it brings it all back like it was yesterday.'

The two women fell into silence for a moment and all that could be heard was the ticking of the carriage clock on the mantelpiece.

'Gosh, look at the time,' Anna said, glancing at it. An hour had passed since she'd arrived.

'You'd better be off – I'm sure you've got much more interesting things to be doing on a Friday night than sitting with a silly old woman.'

'Not really. Just a few drinks at the Ship.'

'Where's that?'

'Just down the road. It's nothing special, just a few drinks after work.'

'Well, go on then, off you go. You never know, there might be a nice young man waiting for you.'

'Ha, not likely in Lowestoft.'

'You can't be too sure. You haven't met them all yet.'

'That's true. But I'm really not interested in meeting a man at the moment. I'm quite happy on my own.'

'I'm sure you are. But just remember, you never know when Mr Right will come along so you have to keep your eyes open at all times, just in case.'

'OK, if you say so.' Anna stood, eager to change the subject. 'Anyway, I'm meant to be working and I've hardly done anything for you apart from make you a sandwich. Is there anything else you want me to do?'

'No, no, you've done quite enough. It's the company I'm after more than anything, I told you.'

'But – please, let me do something at least. I'll hoover upstairs.'

'It doesn't need hoovering.'

But Anna wasn't listening, and seconds later she was dragging the Henry up the stairs to the landing and pushing it into all the nooks and crannies, determined to show Grace she was doing her job properly. By the time she'd finished it was time to leave. Downstairs she found the box of photos packed away on the dining table, but no sign of Grace, so she headed into the front room where she found her, stick propped up against the chair, eyes closed, snoring gently.

Keen not to wake her, Anna crept out and, as she kick-started her bike and pulled out onto the road, she couldn't help thinking how lucky she was to have met Grace.

Chapter Three

'So, tell us about this Grace,' said Anna's mum, Angie, plonking two oversized mugs of tea on the low coffee table. A splash of dark brown liquid escaped from one, staining the wood and soaking into the pages of a magazine. Anna leaned forward and pushed the magazine out of the way, wiping the remains of the tea with her sleeve, as her mum settled onto the chair opposite.

'She's great, Mum, you'd love her. She's so funny and cheeky, and has some amazing stories to tell. She reminds me of Grandma in some ways.'

'Oh, love. You miss her, don't you?'

'I really do. I can hardly believe it's been two years since she went.'

'I know, me neither. She'd have been proud of you though.'

'Proud? What, of a broken marriage?'

'Don't be silly, Annie. She was always proud of everything you did, and she'd be especially proud of the way you've handled yourself through all of this.' She waved her hand around the room to indicate a general sense of ill-ease, then picked up one of the mugs and handed it to Anna. 'And you should be too.'

Anna took a sip of her tea, hoping the rising steam would hide the tears that threatened to spill down her cheeks. She might seem as though she was getting on OK, but the truth was that Daniel's betrayal still hurt if she thought about it too much. It wasn't just the fact that he'd ripped away the future she always thought they'd have – although there was that, of course – but it was also that she felt so humiliated by it all. How many people had known what was going on and chosen not to tell her about his sordid little affair? How could she trust her friends now, not knowing who knew and who didn't? It was, if she was honest, the part she struggled with the most and the reason she didn't really see any of their joint friends anymore.

Her thoughts were interrupted by the ringing of the door-bell. Angie stood and went to answer it, and seconds later two little balls of energy exploded into the room and bundled into Anna's arms.

'Aunty Nanna!' they cried, one little mop of blonde hair dressed in a princess dress, the other more sedate in jeans and a lemon T-shirt.

'Hello, you two,' she said, as her brother, Adam, walked into the room looking exhausted.

'Hey, Annie,' he sighed, slumping into the chair their mum had been sitting in. He had dark smudges under his eyes and his clothes were covered in brick dust and who knew what else from his job as a brickie.

'You look done in.'

'I can't even begin to tell you,' he said, lifting his lips into the beginnings of a smile. 'Josie, Bee, get off your aunty and let her finish her tea.'

The two girls peeled themselves away and went and sat on the sofa wedged into the bay window. Anna adored her nieces but she found them exhausting, even in short bursts – like little fireballs whose energy never seemed to wane. She didn't know how her brother did it sometimes.

Adam leaned forward and picked up the remaining mug of tea. 'Reckon Mum will mind if I nick this?' He took a big slurp and sat back.

'Bit late now.'

He grinned and for a moment Anna saw the boy he'd once been, full of beans, and cheeky, just like his daughters.

'How was work?'

Adam shrugged. 'Same old same old. We're behind and the gaffer's not happy but what can you do? We'll get there in the end.'

'Jo not coming?'

'No, she's got caught up at school. Some inspection coming up, I think.' Adam's wife, Jo, was the headteacher at their local primary school and often worked late. Adam nodded towards the two girls, currently huddled round an iPad they'd found tucked down the side of the sofa. It was keeping them quiet at least. 'Hence why I've got these two this afternoon.'

'You staying for tea, Ads?' Angie said, coming back into the room.

'What you having?'

'Steak-and-kidney pie and mash. The girls can have fish fingers if they want.'

'Please, Mum.'

Angie saluted and walked back out to the kitchen to peel some more potatoes.

'So, how's work for you? Going OK?'

'Yeah, it is actually. I've just started with a new client, Grace. She's great. Reminds me of Grandma.'

'What, always drinking sherry and pretending it's tea?'

'Ha! No, not that bit. More like the never-ending supply of cardigans.' She grinned. 'You'd love her.'

'Sounds great.' He sniffed. 'Any news on the house?'

He said the words carefully, like he always did when mentioning anything about the house Anna had bought with Daniel. Everyone did, knowing how sensitive she was about it. She'd loved that house, which they'd bought for a song when they first got married. It had been a wreck then, and they'd slowly done it up over the years. But the interior wasn't the thing that had made Anna fall in love with the place, it was the views. There was a window on the landing where she'd always loved to stand, drink in hand, and watch the white tips of the waves way out to sea roll in towards the shore. She'd been enthralled to see the colour of the water change with the seasons – the dark-and-pale-grey stripes of bright autumn days, the angry greenish-brown of a stormy winter, the light, hopeful blues of the spring and, her favourite, the glittering white-and-blue backdrop to the comings and goings of people on the beach below during the summer months.

Now, she could hardly bear to think about the place because each time she did, all she could picture was Daniel and that woman together in the bed that Anna had chosen from a second-hand shop and lovingly restored, the two of them perhaps drinking coffee from the mugs Anna had bought, or whispering sweet nothings into each other's ears in the hallway, pressed up against the sixties-style pink-and-mint-green printed wallpaper that Anna had taken so long to pick out.

She shook her head to rid it of the memories.

'No, no news,' she said. 'We've had a few viewings but no

offers. I just want to get rid of the place and buy somewhere new now. Start afresh.'

'Get out of that depressing flat as well, I should think.'

'Yes, that too. Although it's not that bad.'

'S'pose not, if you like living in a bland cardboard box.'

'Well, it's not for much longer, I hope.'

'You could come and stay with us, you know – the offer still stands.'

'I know, and it's lovely of you, but your house isn't big enough for the four of you, let alone with me getting in the way as well. It's fine, the flat. I'll be gone soon.'

'All right, if you're sure.'

'I am.'

She was glad she and her little brother were so close. They always had been, had never been the sort of siblings to fight, and even if they disagreed over something it never lasted long. She really didn't know what she'd do without him around.

Adam looked towards the door. 'Where's Dad? Don't tell me he's out – wonders will never cease.'

'He's upstairs getting dressed, apparently.'

'Getting dressed? It's gone five.'

'Oh, he *was* dressed, but it's darts night at the pub and he wants to look his best so he's getting *re*-dressed.'

Adam grinned. 'This from the man who used to walk to the paper shop in his PJs and slippers?'

'Yup, one and the same.' Anna grinned back at him. He was a lost cause sometimes, their dad. Retired early from his job at the Birds Eye factory because of a bad back, he spent most of his time these days getting under their mum's feet, and not – as she complained – getting any of the jobs done on the house that he'd always promised he would but, rather, just mooching around, being more of a hindrance than a help. Anna always smiled when her mum made this accusation, knowing that, despite it all, Angie and Bill adored each other and always had.

As if on cue Bill came into the room, his face shiny, his checked shirt buttoned right up to the top and his still-thick grey hair swept back off his face.

'All right, you two?' he said, his London accent still strong despite him having spent the last fifty years in Lowestoft.

'Hey, Dad,' Anna and Adam said in unison.

'Grandad!' the girls squealed from where they were still installed on the sofa. He stuck his tongue out at them and they giggled again.

'Looking very dapper, Dad,' Anna said.

'Thanks, love.' He adjusted his collar self-consciously. 'It's a big tournament tonight, against Great Yarmouth. Win this one and we're through to the finals. Can't go in any old scruffy jeans and T-shirt now, can I? Gotta show 'em we mean business.'

'No, I suppose you can't.'

'You look nice as well, love. You going out 'n' all?'

Anna glanced down at her jeans and jumper and wondered what her dad saw when he looked at her. 'Thanks, Dad, but no. Not tonight.'

'Shame. I thought you might have had a date at last.'

'Dad.' Adam's voice was firm.

'What? I was only saying.'

'Only saying what, love?' Angie asked, pecking Bill on the cheek as she came back into the room.

'I was just saying how nice it would be to see our Annie on a date for once.'

Mum rolled her eyes. 'Come on, Bill, you know she's not ready, she's told you enough times. Can't you leave it, just this once?'

Anna gave a weak smile and blinked back the tears that

tried once more to put in an appearance. She knew her dad meant well but every time he mentioned her lack of a love life she felt like even more of a letdown. The trouble was, there was nothing she could do about it. She just wasn't interested in meeting anyone else. She didn't know if she ever would be.

Eager to change the subject, Angie clapped her hands together. 'Now, who's coming through to eat? I'm just about to serve up.'

'Ooh, smashing, love, I'm starving,' Bill said, hot on the heels of Angie as she headed for the tiny dining room. The others followed, the girls trailing behind.

'Ignore Dad,' Adam said as they filed along the hallway. 'He means well.'

'I know.' She looked at her little brother's face. 'You know me. The queen of bottling things up, same as him. I'd just prefer not to talk about it every time we come round, that's all.'

'Well, you've got my vote on that one. I'd be happy if we never talked about that arsehole ever again.'

Anna grinned. She could always rely on Adam's support in everything, and the business with Daniel was no different. The two men had always got on fine when they'd been together even though they'd both made it clear they would never be friends if it wasn't for Anna – but that had been enough for her. Now, though, Adam was so furious with her soon-to-be-ex-husband for what he'd done to her, it almost seemed he was more upset about it than she was.

'Thanks, Ads. Love you.'

As they chatted over dinner Anna couldn't help but notice a feeling of satisfaction settling over her. She was lucky, really. She had all these people that she cared about and who cared about her. And now she had Grace too, who was fast becoming an important part of her life.

She didn't need Daniel, and she definitely didn't need a replacement for him, whatever her dad, or anyone else, might think.

Perhaps, at last, she was finally starting to feel happy again – on her own terms.

Chapter Four

'I've got an idea, Grace,' Anna said as she put the cutlery away in the dresser drawer.

'What's that?'

'I wondered if you fancied a day out.'

'Out where?'

Anna shrugged. 'Somewhere local. A stroll along the seafront, something like that. I thought it might be nice.'

Anna had been spending much more time with Grace than she was being paid for over the last few weeks and something Grace had said a couple of days ago had stuck in her head and made her suggest this outing. Anna hadn't said much in reply at the time, but Grace's words had been playing on her mind ever since: 'It's a trick, you know, ageing,' she'd said. 'You still feel like the same person you've always been – you've got the same arms and legs, the same mind. But your body doesn't seem to realise it and, one bit at a time, stops letting you do the things you've always loved, until you can hardly even get out of the chair without an enormous effort. You know, I used to be so busy I hardly had time to go for walks. But I've got all the time in the world now, only I'm too tired to take those walks – and anyway, I couldn't get very far on these ancient old legs even if I wanted to.' She'd sighed heavily. 'It's not fair, Anna.'

Grace was fitter than most people in their nineties; she was able to walk on her own, and further with the aid of a stick. It seemed cruel that she was stuck in her home all day, every day. Which was why Anna had come up with the idea of taking her somewhere.

She waited for Grace's response.

'Do you really think we could manage it?'

Anna looked at Grace now and saw the excitement shining in her eyes. 'I reckon we could. We don't have to go far, but it would be fun – get you out of the house for a while.'

Grace nodded, then she frowned. 'But how would we get all the way down to the seafront? I can hardly cock my leg over the back of your bike, can I?'

'I don't see why not.'

'But –' Grace stopped, her eyebrows raised so high they were almost in her hairline. 'Oh, very funny, young lady.'

'Sorry,' Anna said, grinning. 'No, we won't go on my bike. But we could get a taxi.'

Grace thought for a moment. 'I could ask Tom to take us.'

'Your nephew?'

'Great-nephew. I'm sure he wouldn't mind.'

'If you like. But I was thinking a taxi would be fine. It's not very far, a couple of miles.'

Grace nodded again. 'Yes, all right, let's do that. We can always ask Tom another time. You'd like him. He's a gardener, runs his own business. Teaches little kiddies how to swim during the summer down on the beach as well. Lovely boy.'

Anna nodded, not really listening. 'Great, well, that's that sorted then. I'll book a taxi and pick you up.'

'I'd like you to meet him, you know.'

Confused, Anna turned to face Grace. 'Meet who?'

'Tom.'

'Oh, right.' Grace had mentioned her great-nephew several times over the last few days and Anna hadn't really paid much attention. But now, Grace had a glint in her eye that suggested she was up to something.

'I think you'd really like him.'

'Uh-huh.'

'Maybe he could take you out for a drink one day.'

'What? No! No way!'

'But why?' Grace's voice had risen a few notches to become almost a whine.

'Because…' Anna stopped and took a deep breath, determined not to shout. 'Because I don't want to go for a drink with Tom. I don't want to go for a drink with anyone. I'm not interested, OK?' Her voice came out firmer than she'd intended and she saw Grace's face fall.

'All right, dear, there's no need to be cross. It was only an idea.'

Sitting down, Anna rested her elbows on her knees and leaned forward. 'I'm sorry, Grace. Really. I'm not cross. I just –' She sighed. 'Everyone seems to want to set me up all the time and I'm just not there yet. I'm not ready to meet someone new. What happened with Daniel still hurts, and I'm still licking my wounds. I just need to be on my own for now, that's all. It's going to be some time before I can learn to trust someone again.'

Grace was silent for a moment and Anna was worried she'd really offended her. But then she spoke, her words so soft Anna had to strain to hear them.

'I am sorry, Anna. Truly.' She looked up, her eyes rheumy behind her glasses. 'I should have known better.'

Anna shook her head. 'You weren't to know, Grace. I'm the one who should be sorry.'

'No. It was my fault. I should have known better because I know how it feels, because everyone kept doing it to me too, after Arthur left. But you can't force it, and in the end it just becomes annoying when all your friends keep on bringing up the subject. My mother was the worst, always asking if I had a date, if I was courting anyone. It drove me mad until I lost my temper with her one day and it took her a week to forgive me.' She reached out and clasped her hands round Anna's. 'So, I'm sorry. Will you forgive a silly old woman?'

'Of course I will. But it really is fine, honestly.'

'Thank you, Anna.'

* * *

After Anna had left for the day, Grace's mind was still racing. She could have kicked herself for being so insensitive earlier. She knew from experience how upsetting it was when people kept expecting you to be ready to move on, kept telling you that you should be ready to find someone else, as though what had happened meant nothing. As though finding someone to love you was all anyone ever lived for.

The truth was, Grace had been happy after Arthur left. Not straight away, of course. She'd been sad and depressed and mournful for months afterwards. But she'd got over it, in the end, and as she had, she'd realised there were much more important things to her than a man. That, in fact, without a man tying her down she could do whatever she wanted with her life. She could work, she could travel, she could fulfil all the dreams she'd ever had.

She could live her life for her.

Naturally, when she met Roy things had changed. But not as much as she'd feared. Because Roy was a good man. Rather than trying to change her, Roy had admired her for her career, had encouraged her to work, to be his equal. He'd looked after her when she needed it, and championed her when she needed that too. She shook her head. She hadn't fully appreciated at the time quite how special he'd been, her Roy. And now he was gone, and she missed him terribly.

Standing up, Grace shuffled over to the dining table where the forget-me-not-covered box still stood weeks later because she hadn't had the heart to pack it away again. Its lid was slightly wonky so she removed it, and then she had a thought. She picked up the first few photos – the ones she had shown Anna – and put them down on the table. Then she picked up another pile and did the same. Finally, right at the bottom of the box, she found what she was looking for.

Grabbing it with both hands, she pulled the book out of the box, sat down on a chair and opened the front cover. On the inside, in painfully familiar handwriting, it said: *Property of Grace Moran. 1941–1946. Private!*

It was her diary, from during the war. She'd written it faithfully, while Arthur had been away fighting, as she'd waited for him to return, as she'd lived through the horrors and the daily grind of the Second World War and its devastating effect on the town she loved so much. Writing had always given her such pleasure, helped her understand the world by getting her thoughts and feelings down. It was no wonder she'd ended up doing it as a living for so many years.

But she hadn't looked at this diary for a long, long time – not once while she'd been with Roy. She hadn't needed to, and somehow she had always felt as though she'd be betraying him if she so much as glanced at it. But in the six months since Roy had died, and now that Anna had come into her life, so many memories had been stirred up and Grace felt a sudden urge to read it all over again.

And so, turning the page, she started at the beginning, at the words she'd written more than seventy years before.

4 February 1941

In exactly one week's time it will be a whole year since Arthur and I fell in love. I can hardly believe it. And now he's off fighting and isn't even here to share a kiss with!

I keep thinking about that night when I first saw him. It was 11 February and the air was bitingly cold. My nylons had a hole in them and I had no desire or time to mend them so I decided to brave the cold in my bare legs, tie an old belt round the waist of my favourite dress, which had faded so much in the three years since I'd bought it, to try and make it look a bit more exciting, and thread a ribbon round my hair. Father had other ideas of course, and when I came downstairs he told me I was far too young to go out looking like that, and that he wouldn't allow it. I remember thinking, we're at war for goodness' sake, what does a bit of bare leg matter?

But it mattered to Father and in the end he insisted, and I had to borrow a pair of Mother's nylons – ones without holes in them.

I was glad as it turned out, of course, because it really was bitterly cold outside so I was thankful for the thin layer of fabric against my skin as I walked arm in arm to the dance hall with Joanie and Susan.

'Let's hope the blasted sirens don't go off again tonight,' Susan said, but I told her I was going to the dance hall sirens or no sirens. I'd been looking forward to it for weeks. Joanie agreed with me too. She said it had taken her ages to make her dress. It looked like a couple of old tea towels sewn together to me, but I didn't like to tell her. Mind you, maybe it was…

Chapter Five

A few days later Grace and Anna found themselves ambling up the esplanade along Lowestoft seafront. The day was bright and breezy – a proper East Anglian summer's day – the sun warm but the air cooled by a forceful wind that was determined to push them backwards as they walked.

'I love it here,' Grace said, holding onto the stick she'd brought along 'just in case'.

'Me too.' Anna tilted her face skyward, feeling the warmth on her skin.

They carried on along the promenade. To their left the beach was heaving with people seeking out the early summer sun. Brightly striped wind breakers flapped in the breeze, small children ran around, ice cream dripping down their arms, while groups of teens preened and posed and giggled in bikinis and shorts, their lean bodies a patchwork of reds, pinks and browns. To their right they passed the lush green of the gardens, then a shop selling buckets and spades, plastic spinning windmills, sticks of rock and all manner of beach paraphernalia overflowing onto the path. When – after a brief stop so they could people-watch for a bit and Grace could get her walking legs back – they reached the Claremont Pier with its flashing lights and kiss-me-quick hats, they dropped onto the lower promenade and passed the bright beach huts all lined up in a row, families on matching deckchairs spilling out of the open doors and passing round boxes of gritty sandwiches.

'Shall we stop and have a sit down?' Anna asked as they reached a bank of benches overlooking the beach. The tide was out and the sand stretched away from the sunbathers so that they had to navigate several metres of wet, hard sand to reach the icy water.

'I used to love going in the sea,' Grace said as she slowly lowered herself onto the black plastic bench.

'Oh, so did I,' said Anna. 'Me and my brother Adam always used to come down here during the summer holidays with Mum while Dad was at work and we'd spend the whole day on the beach. We were clearly much hardier then because we'd splash around in that freezing water for hours on end. Although I never actually learnt to swim, can you believe it?'

'Really? I thought everyone who spent their childhood at the seaside could swim almost before they could walk.'

Anna shrugged. 'Not me. It just never seemed to matter, and Adam was always happy to stay in the shallow water with me.'

Grace looked out across the beach. 'I wish I could go in there now. We used to be in there all the time too as youngsters, Ernest and I. We had a beach hut, just over there –' She pointed back in the direction of the pier. 'Spent most of the summer there, come rain or shine – the weather never stopped us.' She sighed. 'Course, it belongs to Tom now. He's done it up, made ever such a good job of it. He runs the children's swimming lessons from there.'

Anna nodded vaguely, trying to ignore Grace's references to Tom, keen not to upset her.

'I remember the days when you couldn't go on the beach at all,' Grace said suddenly.

'Really? How come?'

'Because of all the bombing during the war. For years afterwards we were told not to go on the sand because of the danger of unexploded bombs buried underneath. You were always hearing stories about kids being blown up digging a sandcastle. It was horrifying.'

'Good grief!'

'Quite.'

They were silent for a few moments, watching the black outlines of birds flapping overhead, others gliding easily on the slipstream, and listening to their squawks. Then Grace spoke again.

'I found my old diary the other day, from when I was a teenager.'

Anna looked round. 'Did you?'

'Yes. It was quite a revelation.' Grace paused for a moment, apparently deep in thought.

'Are you going to tell me more?'

'I was just thinking it's funny, you see, because the first page was all about the day I met Arthur, and right here is exactly where it happened.'

'Ooh, how exciting.' Anna felt a thrill at the thought that she might hear more about Grace and the mysterious Arthur.

Grace nodded. 'It was, really.' She pointed up at the clifftop, where scaffolding surrounded an old building. 'Just up there, where they're doing all that work, was The Grand Hotel. During the war it stayed open and I used to go with the girls – my best friend Susan and her cousin Joanie – once a week or so to dance with the soldiers. We were only young –

fifteen, sixteen – but we'd put on our nylons and our best dresses and we'd head off to have some fun.

'This one night – 11 February 1940 it was – I was sixteen and headed out with the girls as usual. It was funny reading about it, it all came back as though it was only yesterday.' She smiled as she recounted to Anna the saga of the hole in her nylons and her father going mad about her bare legs.

'I was secretly glad later that he'd made me wear an old pair of Mother's nylons – freezing it was. Well, you know how bitter the wind can get, especially along the seafront. We walked hand in hand all the way along, hoping the sirens didn't go off. Not that it would have stopped us even if they had – we loved our dancing.' She paused, still smiling. 'I'd remembered Joanie's dress that night too, even before I read about it again in the diary. It looked like two tea towels sewn together, hardly anything to it. Come to think of it, it probably was. We made do with anything in those days.'

Anna glanced at Grace and saw she was miles away, decades away, lost in the memory of that long-ago night.

'Anyway, when we arrived at The Grand the dancefloor was empty so we found a table at the edge where we could see everyone coming and going. It was about twenty minutes later that this man walked in and I couldn't take my eyes off him. He was wearing a smart suit, smarter than what most of the other lads had managed to cobble together, and the spotlights shone on his dark slicked-back hair. I watched him as he smiled at something his friend said to him, then the whole group of them walked right past our table without even a glance to sit at another table quite some distance away. I pretended not to look at him, but Joanie had noticed me gawping like a goldfish and told me to go and talk to him.

'I didn't, of course. I wouldn't think twice now, but I wasn't so brave in those days. I'd love to go and tell my teenage self to stop being such a limp lettuce. But in the end it didn't matter because a while later, after I'd danced with a couple of perfectly nice young chaps, he came and stood at the side of our table, held out his hand and asked me to dance.

'And that was that, Anna. I was ever so flustered, thought I was going to trip over my own two feet as I walked onto the dancefloor, I was that nervous. But I didn't, and I can remember clear as day how it felt to be spinning around with Arthur's arm slipped around my waist and thinking I'd never been happier in my whole life than I was at that very moment. That was love, right there, and I knew it.'

Grace stopped for a moment, her eyes watering in the wind.

'And do you know what, Anna?'

Anna shook her head, afraid that speaking might break the spell.

'That was one of the best nights of my life. Never mind what happened afterwards, I knew right then that if I could have bottled that feeling, I'd never need worry again. I felt happiness again when I met Roy, but by then I was older, wiser. More cynical. This, Anna, was my one fairy-tale meeting, and I've never forgotten it.'

'What happened after that dance?'

'Well, we danced a while longer, I know that. And I remember walking along the seafront with him in the bitter, bitter wind, my toes and face numb. But I didn't even care about the cold because all I could think about was the feeling of Arthur's hand in mine. Oh, I was so silly, Anna, you wouldn't have believed it.'

'I bet I would, Grace. Surely we've all felt like that at some point.'

'Have you?'

Anna thought for a moment. There had been boyfriends

when she was younger, but she couldn't say she'd ever truly felt the way Grace had just described. If she was honest, Dan was the first man she'd ever truly loved, and by the time she met him she was well past the fairy-tale stage.

'Only with Daniel, I suppose,' she said, her voice wobbling.

Grace studied her for a moment, leaving Anna feeling exposed. 'I'm sorry, Anna, I shouldn't have reminded you of all that again.'

'It's all right. It would probably be good for me to talk some more about him. I try to avoid it normally.'

Grace nodded. 'So, how did you meet him?'

Anna stared out at the sea, watching the cotton-wool peaks of the distant waves, the kids splashing on the shoreline, and she took a deep breath.

'It was just along from here, actually, near the South Pier. I was twenty-seven, so it was about twelve years ago. It was a sunny day, late spring, and I'd gone with a couple of colleagues down to the beach after work one evening. We sat down with our towels in front of a group of lads playing frisbee and suddenly there was a massive whack to my head and an explosion of pain. One of the lads – Daniel, it turned out – came over and apologised over and over again, said he hadn't meant to throw it near me, he was sorry – even asked if I needed to go to hospital.

'To be honest, after the initial shock of the pain it was my pride that was hurt more than my head, and I kept telling him I was all right. He started to get on my nerves after a while and in the end one of my friends, Chloe, told him to shut up and just sit down. So he did.

'We chatted after that, us and the four boys – well, men really. Dan was twenty-five, two years younger than me, and he was funny. Before they left Dan gave me his phone number and asked for mine. I didn't think he'd ever ring, but a couple of days later he did – an actual phone call, not just a text message. He asked if I fancied going out and I said yes. He wasn't the most handsome man in the world, but there had been something about him that made me feel there was a connection – he had a nice smile and a cheeky laugh, and gave off a kind of warmth. That probably sounds daft, doesn't it?'

'Not at all, dear. Arthur was never the handsomest man in Lowestoft, but his eyes held all the secrets of the world, and he intrigued me. Neither was Roy, truth be told, but he was the best man I ever met, and you just need something to spark, don't you? The rest takes care of itself.'

Anna nodded. 'Exactly. Well, we had a few dates and sort of fell into seeing each other. I mean, I was twenty-seven, most of my friends were married or getting married, or thinking about having children, and I was miles away from that. It wasn't just that Dan came along at the right time, though. I believed he was the right *man* at the right time. He was solid, funny, and he had a mischievous side that I needed in my life. I could see myself growing old with him.' Anna paused, twisting her fingers round each other. 'Six months later we moved in together. I had a lovely little house that I'd bought when I was twenty-one and had been doing up. He had a flat, too, and we sold them both and bought a beautiful big town-house down by the seafront. You'll know where I mean – up on the hill towards Pakefield cliffs. The views were amazing, and sometimes I just used to stand staring out of the top window on the landing struggling to believe how lucky I'd been, finding Dan when I did. Finding this place.'

Anna glanced at Grace but the old woman's face was unreadable.

'I've already told you about how we tried for a baby and how Daniel started staying out late and drinking. In the end, our first round of IVF is what doomed things, I think. We'd had to wait ages for it and by then we were hardly even speaking to each other, let alone anything else, and the stress of it was all just too much when it didn't work. I shouldn't have been surprised when I found that bra.'

She stopped and a silence fell. Anna watched as a seagull wheeled on a current of air in front of her.

'I'm sorry, Anna,' Grace said quietly. You deserve better than that.'

Anna nodded. 'It's taken me a while, but I think I'm slowly starting to realise that too.' She stood and held out her hand. 'Shall we walk back to the South Pier and get a cup of tea and a slice of cake? I think we need it after all that exertion.'

'Excellent idea,' Grace said, using her stick to push herself to her feet. 'Lead the way.'

They walked slowly back the way they had come – past the imposing Victorian terraces; past the beach huts, where Grace pointed out the pretty blue-and-white-striped one that belonged to Tom; past the ice-cream and candy-floss vendors; past the small children whizzing about on bikes and scooters.

'You know, Roy hated to dance,' said Grace, her voice almost whipped away by the wind so that Anna was unsure whether she'd heard her right.

'Did he?' she said, hoping it was the right response.

'Yes. Said he had two left feet. And yet he always came with me, to The Grand, years after I met Arthur there. Of course, it was different then – the music had changed, and we were all older – but I still loved to dance, even then. And even though Roy hated it, he came anyway. Just for me.'

Anna didn't say anything, just listened to the sound of their footsteps along the esplanade, hers slow and steady,

Grace's faster, softer, and accompanied by the gentle tap of the walking stick.

'That's what you need. Someone like Roy. Someone who loves you no matter what, who loves the bits of you that other people find annoying, the bits even you don't like, and who will dance with you even when he'd rather be doing anything else in the world than that.'

'I need a Roy,' Anna said matter-of-factly.

Grace's mouth broke into a smile as she turned to look at Anna. 'Yes, dear, that's exactly it. Everyone needs a Roy.'

Chapter Six

Anna woke early the next morning and climbed out of bed. She'd had a fitful sleep, going over her conversation with Grace on the seafront, thinking about Dan's betrayal all over again.

It was still only just after six o'clock but she felt restless. She'd always loved running, but had stopped doing it after everything that had happened with Daniel. It had been her release, her time to clear her head, think things through or just switch her mind off completely and concentrate on the steady in-out of her breath, the thump of her heart and the pounding of her feet on the pavement. But since the failed IVF and all that had come afterwards, it hadn't occurred to her to run. Her trainers had been moved from the house they'd shared together to her flat and had never even seen the light of day.

Now, she had the urge to get out there. She rummaged in the drawer for her old running gear, then dug her trainers out of the box they'd been sitting in ever since she'd moved. She downed a glass of water, slipped on the shoes and left the house.

It was light but the sun was still fighting valiantly with a thick bank of cloud and the air had an early morning chill to it. Turning right out of her block of flats, she headed in the direction of the sea. Gulls flapped overhead and she listened to the roar of her breath as her lungs, un-used to exercise for so long, screamed for air. She slowed her pace and sucked in deep lungfuls until she felt she had it under control. Her legs felt stiff and her arms pumped at her sides, propelling her along the path, until finally, at the end of the road, she turned right again onto the seafront, where she was hit by a sheet of wind that almost knocked her over and whipped her breath away. She stopped and walked slowly over to the wall facing the South Beach. This early in the morning there was just one lone dog walker traipsing through the firm sand by the water's edge, the dog splashing and barking alongside. To her left the pier looked forlorn with paint peeling from the windows, doors all locked up awaiting the influx of tourists later that day. Down here the easterly wind from which her flat was sheltered was so strong that it was impossible to hear anything else and Anna stood and let it whip round her body, closing her eyes and holding onto the wall.

Moments later, her breath back under control, she turned and started along the esplanade at a slow jog. She enjoyed the feeling of having the wide pavement to herself this morning; there were no children getting under her feet, no groups of teenagers showing off to each other, no holidaymakers out seeking the best spot on the beach, no tearaways zipping about on scooters. It was just her and the odd dog walker, nodding at each other as they passed.

Reaching the end of the prom, she stopped, lungs burning, and stepped down onto the beach. Her feet sank into the soft sand as she marched towards the sea, the grains slowly becoming more compact as she got closer and closer to the water. A few pebbles were scattered at the shoreline but otherwise the beach, from here, looked pristine. Forget Thailand, Barbados, Australia. Why would she want to be anywhere else when she had this slice of paradise on her doorstep? No, Lowestoft wasn't perfect, but who could deny the beauty of this? She stood for a moment breathing in the fresh sea air, letting it bluster and dither round her body, buffeting her from all sides. In front of her the surf quietly shushed onto the sand, tiny, apologetic waves arriving from distant shores.

She recalled her grandma's words as they had once stood hand in hand right where she was now, letting the cool water lap over their sandy feet: 'You realise how endless the possibilities are for you when you stand here. And it also makes you realise how small and insignificant you really are.' Back then Anna had merely nodded, letting her grandma have her moment, lost in her own thoughts. But now, as she stared out before her, she saw how right she had been. The blue-grey peaks of the sea stretched out beyond her line of sight, the clouds reflecting back in them morosely, and she tried to imagine the lives of people carrying on way beyond the horizon – were they happy, sad; were they having a good day, a bad day? Had they lost someone, or were they celebrating a birthday, a christening, a new baby?

Up high, the sun was beginning to win its battle and a shaft of light poured out through the rapidly separating clouds and sliced across the water, transforming it from a dull grey to a silver ribbon of sparkle. It was all in the way you looked at things, wasn't it? When something bad happened, you could let it stop you in your tracks. Or you could pick yourself up and carry on, make the most of the time you had left.

That, she realised, was exactly what she wanted to do. It was time to put Dan behind her and get on with living. And perhaps that was the reason Grace had been brought into her life – to help her see that.

Smiling, she set off back up the beach towards the bank of red, blue, yellow and striped beach huts and jogged home, back the way she had come. She had another suggestion for Grace, and she hoped her new friend would like it.

* * *

A few days later Anna and Grace were all packed and ready to go on their second day out. Grace was jittery, excited. Anna, though, was feeling cross.

And that was all thanks to the man sitting at the dining-room table with a face like thunder.

Grace's great-nephew Tom, about whom Anna had heard so many wonderful things, had come along to try to put a spanner in the works. And despite the fact that Grace had insisted they were going out anyway, Anna was still fuming.

He was already there when she arrived earlier that morning. She'd parked her bike in the drive and let herself in as usual, calling out to Grace as she did, but had almost cried out in shock when a dark figure loomed towards the doorway from the hall, heading straight for her.

'You must be Anna,' the figure had demanded, crossing his arms over his chest.

'Yes,' she'd said, confused. 'And you are?'

'Tom.' He hadn't offered any more information than that, and hadn't held out his hand for her to shake so Anna didn't offer hers either.

'Hello,' she'd said instead, slipping off her shoes and placing her helmet on the side. When she moved towards the door where Tom was standing, he finally, grudgingly, moved out of the way and let her through. He followed close behind

– so close she could almost feel his breath on the back of her neck, as though he wanted her to be completely aware of his presence.

'Morning, Grace,' she'd said as she walked into the room.

Grace's face had lit up. 'Oh, hello,' she beamed, clapping her hands together like a little girl. 'Are we ready to go already?'

'You're still going then, are you?' Tom's voice from behind her was low.

Anna turned. 'Yes, why on earth wouldn't we? It's been planned for days.'

'Tom here doesn't think it's a good idea for us to go out together today,' Grace said.

Anna whipped her head round. 'Really? Why ever not?'

Tom shrugged, a belligerent child. 'I just don't understand why you'd want to. I mean, it's not your job.'

Anna turned and faced him, pulling herself up to her full height. He was tall, and she was determined not to feel cowed by her lack of stature. 'No, it's not my job. But Grace and I thought it would be nice to have a day out together.'

'If you say so.'

Anna had felt the blood rising in her face then. 'I do say so, yes. And to be honest, I really have no idea why you'd object to that.'

'I think Tom finds it odd that someone your age would want to hang out with an old biddy like me,' Grace said, a cheeky glint in her eyes. 'I think he suspects you have an ulterior motive or something.'

'It's not that,' Tom had said. 'I just don't understand why you'd want to spend time with a client when you're not being paid. Haven't you got friends your own age you'd prefer to be seeing?' His eyes glowed dark in his tanned face.

'Grace *is* my friend,' Anna said through pursed lips and

didn't miss the smile of delight on Grace's face. 'Why have you got such a problem with this? Do you think I'm going to kidnap her or something?'

Tom's eyes rolled. 'It just seems weird, that's all.'

'I don't know why it's weird – but if you're so worried, why don't you come with us?'

'Yes, Tom, why don't you?' Grace had said.

Tom shook his head. 'I can't today, I'm working. But I just think you'd be better off staying here.'

'We're only going down to the Sparrows Nest for a wander and a bite to eat, Thomas, we're not going skiing in the Alps or jumping out of an aeroplane. I think we'll be all right.'

'Well, how are you getting there? You can hardly go on Anna's motorbike.'

'We're getting a taxi,' Anna said. 'It's not very far.'

'And I suppose Aunty Grace is paying for that, is she?'

Grace had objected then. 'Oh, don't be so ridiculous, Tom. It doesn't matter who's paying for the taxi. Anna suggested a day out and I want to go – that's all there is to it. Now go on, get yourself to work. Those kiddies won't teach themselves to swim.'

Tom shook his head and stalked out of the room. They'd heard the clattering of plates in the kitchen and then footsteps into the dining room. Anna sat down on the armchair next to Grace.

'I –' Anna started. She was too upset to speak.

'I'm sorry, Anna,' Grace said, turning and placing her papery hand on Anna's arm. 'He's not normally so rude; I don't know what's got into him. In fact, he's such a kind boy, does so much for me. I wonder whether he feels as though you're treading on his toes a bit.'

'Do *you* think that?'

'Not at all. I love having you around, and there's room for

both of you in my life. Tom's the only one of Ernest's grand-children that I see regularly, and he really does help me out – not just the gardening; he goes shopping, pops round as often as he can to keep me company. In the summer, though, he's always so much busier with his gardening business and the kiddies' swimming, and I think he feels guilty. Although he shouldn't.'

'There's no need to take it out on me, though. In fact, he should be glad I'm here to keep you company.'

'I know that and you know that, dear, but he's a stubborn old thing when he wants to be. He'll come round, and then you'll get on together like a house on fire. Why wouldn't you?'

Anna doubted that, but bit her tongue. Tom obviously meant a lot to Grace and was clearly kind to her. Anna telling her just what she thought of him wouldn't do her any favours, she knew. Instead, she stood up.

'Well, if you still want to go, shall we get moving?'

'Yes, let's,' Grace had said, pulling herself from her chair with a bit of effort. 'I'll just get my bag and stick, then I'll be with you.'

Anna had walked through to the kitchen. She could see Tom, now, from the corner of her eye, sitting at the dining table and staring out of the window. He didn't glance at her as she passed so she said nothing. And when she and Grace left the house a few minutes later he left too, disappearing off to work.

* * *

As the taxi made its way down the ravine towards the sea Grace felt the excitement building in her. When she was a little girl this ravine had always felt so thrilling, like some-where magical creatures might live, somewhere fairy tales could happen. It was always dark and cool down here no matter what the weather, and above the road the trees hung like dark curtains, knitted together over the years. When she came down here the thought had always occurred that it felt like a theatre – the curtains were drawn, and as you reached the bottom they parted to reveal the extravaganza of the sea and the huge sky painted above, the scenery that had been concealed on the journey down.

It was funny how those feelings lingered even as your body and mind aged, thought Grace as they reached the bottom and pulled into the car park opposite Sparrows Nest Park, right opposite the town's North Beach.

She'd read some more of her diary last night and she had something else she wanted to tell Anna today. It wasn't about Arthur or even Roy, but she knew Anna found stories about Lowestoft fascinating. The beginning floated into her mind as they walked up the path towards the café.

13 January 1942

Such terrible news today. I was leaving work and I popped into Wallers to see Susan – she's been working there for the last few months and I'm ever so jealous, it seems much more interesting than my job at the Co-op. Anyway, it was about two-thirty – I know that because for some reason I checked the time on my wristwatch just before I arrived. I wanted to know if she was free to go for a walk later, before it got dark. She said couldn't though, because her wretched boss had asked her to work late, so we agreed to do it tomorrow instead.

So I left her there and walked home. As I walked down London Road I couldn't help glancing at the piles of rubble where buildings had once stood. It's awful how the devastation has all become so normal to me that I barely even notice it anymore. Even though there's rarely any bombing during the day, I spend most evenings sitting at home listening out for the crump and bang of bombs, or waiting for the siren to peal, telling us all to race to the safety of our shelters. But I did hear of someone who almost got shot by the Jerries the other day as they walked home in the middle of the afternoon, so I never like to dawdle.

I'd barely been home ten minutes when there was a loud crunching sound, followed by three more. They had sounded like bombs dropping some distance away, and I felt sick. I stood still for a moment, listening, wondering where they had dropped.

But a few minutes passed and I heard nothing more, so I went into the kitchen to find Mother peeling some tiny, shrivelled potatoes. I offered to help her chop some cabbage and she said yes even though I'm probably the worst cook that's ever lived. Mother despairs of me sometimes.

Anyway, I'm getting away from the point. Just minutes after I'd started on the cabbage, the peace and quiet was interrupted by the most awful sound, like machine-gun fire. It took me a moment to realise it was someone hammering on our front door, so I wiped my hands on my pinny and went to answer it. It was Mrs Beaumont and she was as white as a sheet. But it was what she said next that made my blood run cold.

'You've got to come,' she said. 'It's Harold. It's Wallers – there's been a bomb. Oh, please come…'

'I do love the feel of the sun on my face,' Grace said as they sat on a bench overlooking the flowerbeds. The roses and the primroses were in full bloom and although the air had a slight chill to it, even Anna had to admit this was exactly what she'd needed today.

The bandstand, where concerts were played during summer evenings, stood empty at this time of the day and small children ran around inside it, laughing and shrieking as young mothers half-watched them, chatting to friends, since the walled gardens were set away from the dangers of both the sea and the road. Although Anna doubted Grace could manage the steep climb up through the paths to the top of the park, they were happy sitting down here at the bottom, next to the children's play park and the café, with the distant view of the sea.

Anna watched a seagull glide overhead and thought about the times she'd been here as a child, when it was her and Adam running around in the bandstand, or begging for an ice cream or to go to the beach, and driving their mum crazy.

'It's just always felt so safe here, don't you think?' said Grace. 'So far removed from the rest of the town.'

'You're right, Grace, it does feel safe.'

Grace sighed. 'This place saved my friend's life, you know.'

'Really? How?'

'Are you sure you want to hear another old story? Tell me if I'm boring you, won't you? I don't get to talk about these things very often, and I'm feeling a bit sentimental at the moment for some reason – perhaps because you remind me of myself at your age.'

'You're not boring me at all, Grace. I love hearing about the past, about the way the town was before I was born.'

Grace was silent for quite a while and Anna briefly wondered whether she'd fallen asleep. But then she spoke, so quietly that Anna had to lean towards her to catch her words before they were snatched away by the breeze.

'It was January 1942 and Arthur had been off at war for

some time. Apart from a surprise visit home a few months before, I hadn't seen him for so long that I was starting to forget what he looked like. Anyway, I spent most of my time, when I wasn't at work, with my friend Susan – remember, I told you about her before. We were thick as thieves in those days. If ever you needed someone to cheer you up, she was the one for the job. So, one day, on my way home from work, I stopped by to see Susan at Wallers – that was a big restaurant in the town centre, right where Starbucks is now – to see if she wanted to go for a walk. She couldn't, though, she said, because she'd been told to stay and work some extra hours until five-thirty, so there wouldn't be time before the curfew. She was pretty fed up about it, as I recall.' Grace cleared her throat.

'I went home and didn't think too much more about it. It was strange walking around town in those days because although we knew there were bombs – how could we not, they were all around us – we still had to get on with our lives. Someone once told me that if you heard the *rat-tat-tat* of a bomber above your head then you were safe because they'd already dropped their bombs behind them, but I never fancied hanging around to find out whether that was true.

'But that day I'd only been home a few minutes when there was an almighty crunching sound, followed by three more. It sounded like bombs dropping some distance away and although I was worried, when a few minutes had passed with nothing more I tried to put it out of my mind and helped Mother get on with preparing the dinner.

'Then Mrs Beaumont from across the road hammered on our door. She was hysterical, shouting things we could barely make out. In the end we worked out that her husband, Harold, had been at Wallers and she'd just found out that was what had been bombed. My blood ran cold. That's where Susan was.

'I ran down the road with Mother and Mrs Beaumont, all the way to town. The whole way we could see an ominous plume of dark grey smoke snaking into the sky ahead of us, and there was this terrible, acrid smell filling the air. My heart pounded so hard from the running and from fear that I could hardly breathe, but I couldn't stop. I had to find out whether Susan was all right.' Grace's voice broke, and she cleared her throat again.

'When we arrived at the scene it was worse than any of us had imagined. The entire street was filled with smoke, and half of it was flattened. Sirens wailed, people ran around screaming, and the injured sat sobbing, or being treated by any doctors who'd already got there. Oh, it was terrible, Anna. I just stood and stared at the gaping hole where Wallers had been; where I had been talking to Susan just half an hour before.

'The whole thing had gone. Where there had been people enjoying tea, and life and happiness and friendship and laughter and love, now there was nothing. As I said, Susan had been working late. She should have been at home, safe. Instead, she'd been here. I knew there was no way she could have survived.

'As Mrs Beaumont and Mother fussed about, trying to find out what had happened to Mr Beaumont, I sat on a wall nearby and sobbed. I couldn't believe my best friend in all the world had gone, just like that.' Grace glanced up at Anna, and a small smile crept onto her face.

'Well, you'll never believe it, but a few moments later I felt a hand on my shoulder. I expected it to be Mother, come to console me, but when I looked up I thought I was looking at a ghost – because there stood Susan, alive and unharmed.'

Anna gasped. 'No! How did she survive?'

'Well, it turned out the Navy boys had been planning some sort of do right here at the Sparrows Nest where they were stationed and Susan had been asked to take some spare chairs down for them to use. And that was what saved her life. It felt like a miracle, to be honest, amid all the horror. It felt as though we'd both been given a second chance.'

Grace stopped suddenly, slightly breathless, and coughed long and deep.

'Grace, are you all right?' Anna asked, placing her hand gently on Grace's shoulders.

Some moments later the coughing subsided and Grace sat up. 'Yes, yes, I'm absolutely fine. Nothing to worry about, just a little tickle.'

Anna wasn't so sure it was just a tickle but right now, after Grace's outpouring, it didn't seem like the time to probe further.

'That's an amazing story, Grace,' she said instead.

Grace nodded. 'I know. I often think about how lucky we both were. If I'd have popped in to see her just fifteen minutes later, we'd both have been goners.' She shook her head. 'The world's a funny old place sometimes. I mean, why did it save Susan and me when it killed so many other people?'

'I don't know, Grace. But I'm glad it did.'

Grace smiled. 'So am I. Otherwise, I'd never have met Roy, and then what would have become of him, without me to annoy him for the rest of his life?'

The sun dipped behind a cloud and the air turned fresh. Anna shivered. 'Shall we get some lunch now? We could try the café over there, or the restaurant if you prefer.'

'The café will be just perfect,' Grace said, standing. 'I could murder a cup of tea and a toasted teacake.'

As they walked slowly up the gentle slope to the café, Grace spoke again.

'I am sorry about the way Tom spoke to you, you know.'

'It's not your fault.'

'No, I know it's not, but I feel responsible. I hadn't told him about you until today and I think he was a bit surprised. As far as he was concerned you were just my new carer, and I suppose he thought it seemed odd that we were doing something else together. It doesn't excuse his rudeness, though.'

'Are you this close to all your brother's grandchildren?' Anna asked, curious.

'No, dear, not in the slightest. There's just always been something special about Tom. He was the only child of Ernest's daughter Louisa. She never said as much, but I think she struggled to have any more. Anyway, Louisa and her husband Andrew lived not far from here and used to come and see me regularly, every time they visited Ernest. They always brought Tom and he was such a kind, thoughtful little boy. He used to go out in the garden to pick me flowers and would come in with a fistful of daffodils and dandelions and tulips and daisies. I never had the heart to tell him that Grandad Roy had spent ages planting some of those bulbs and that the rest were weeds, because he looked so pleased with himself.' She sighed. 'Louisa comes to see me from time to time now, but since Ernest passed away the visits have dropped off. Tom's the only one who still comes regularly.'

'It's nice that you've got him,' Anna said. 'I suppose I can understand why he might be suspicious of me. I mean, he doesn't know me from Adam, does he? I could be after your money for all he knows.'

'You'll be lucky, there's not much of that left,' Grace said, chuckling. 'Besides, Tom should know he means the world to me, and just because I'm spending time with you, that doesn't change.'

'Maybe he's just upset because he couldn't come with us. We could make sure we pick a day he can come too next time.'

'Ooh, are we planning another outing already? How exciting.'

'If you'd like to, Grace, I'd love to.'

Grace went quiet and when Anna turned to face her, she looked serious.

'What is it, Grace?'

'Well, it's just that I do know what Tom means.'

'You think I'm after your money as well?'

'Don't be daft. I just do sometimes wonder why on earth you'd choose to spend so much time with a silly old fool like me. Don't you have other people you'd prefer to be socialising with?'

'Of course I have other people to see, and I do see them. My parents, my brother and his girls, my best friend Julia, my friends from work. But, well, I don't know, Grace. I haven't felt this close to any of the other people I look after. There was just something special about you from the moment we met. I like you, Grace. You're my friend.'

They walked into the café and the warm air hit them, and as they settled at the nearest table, Anna saw tears shining in Grace's eyes.

'Are you OK?'

'Yes, sorry. It's just, that was such a lovely thing to say. It's been a long time since I made a new friend, and most of my old friends have died off over the years. It's quite lonely being ninety-four, you know. Yes, I have Tom, and Good Old Gerald, and whichever carer they send me – you, now – but it's never been quite the same as just having people who are there because they're my friends. And it's nice. It's nice to have someone to call a friend at my age.' She wiped her cheek. 'Thank you, Anna.'

'Don't thank me, Grace. It's my pleasure, and I'm looking forward to spending much more time with you.' She held up her empty glass and waited for Grace to do the same. They clinked them together and Anna said, 'To Us. To new friends.'

'To new friends.'

* * *

The sun was high in the sky as Grace and Anna strolled arm in arm along the North Sea wall, Grace's stick tapping rhythmically on the ground. The waves were rougher here, caught by the wind, and the beach was stony, less inviting. A few people were dotted about, perched on blankets and towels, but it had a totally different feel to the South Beach with its swathes of soft golden sand.

They'd come for a short walk after their lunch at Grace's insistence. 'Are you sure you're not too tired?' Anna had worried, aware she was responsible for Grace even though she wasn't officially her carer today. 'I'm absolutely exhausted,' Grace had replied, 'but I'm having such a lovely time I don't want it to end. Just a little walk, I'll be fine. These ancient legs aren't completely done in yet.'

So Anna had agreed, and now she was glad she had. She loved it up here, away from the crowds. 'This is my favourite beach,' she said, as the cliff rose up to their left. Among the gorse bushes and heather you could see the odd pillbox peeking through, symbols of the past long since gone to ruin.

'It's lovely, isn't it?' Grace said. 'Roy and I always used to walk along here. He'd bring his binoculars and I'd sulk about coming second to the birds, and we'd spend the day pretending to be cross with each other. But we both knew the other one wasn't going anywhere, because we just loved to be together. Besides, like I said before, what's love if it's not about doing things you hate for the other person?'

'Dan would never have done that for me.'

'And that's precisely why you're better off without him, no matter what you think.'

The wind had died down slightly now, making it easier to walk without having to battle against the constant breeze, as well as easier to talk.

Grace continued. 'People change, that's what you have to remember, Anna.'

'I know. It's just that, actually, I don't think Dan changed at all. I think he was always like that but I chose not to see it.'

Grace shrugged. 'Maybe. But maybe it was not being able to have a baby that changed him. Maybe it changed you both so that you didn't fit together anymore. Things like that happen all the time.' She gestured up to the cliffs.

'I remember a day many, many moons ago, right up there, when I realised that Arthur had changed almost beyond recognition. Unfortunately I chose to ignore it too, but looking back, I knew it, even then.' She glanced at Anna. 'Do you want to hear about this? I'm aware I've already bored you with one story today.'

'Course I do, Grace. You know I love your stories.'

Grace nodded. 'All right, if you're sure.' She took a deep, rattly breath as she looked out towards the slate-grey of the North Sea.

'Well, Arthur hadn't long been back from the war and we'd come for a walk just up there, along the top of the cliffs. It was bitterly cold, and as we walked hand in hand along the seafront, I ignored my freezing toes and the fact that my cheeks had turned numb with the cold. All that mattered was that Arthur was there by my side.

'I remember the gorse bushes were thick with snow; the pillboxes had snow roofs and the slits looked like dark eyes gazing out to sea. Ooh, that's quite poetic, isn't it? Anyway, as we stood there watching the water rise and fall in angry peaks, I felt absolutely certain that he was going to ask me to marry him. I felt sick with excitement and nerves.

'But do you know what, Anna?' She kept her gaze on the horizon.

'What?'

Grace shrugged. 'Nothing happened. Not a sausage. Instead, when I looked over at him I got the strong suspicion he wasn't even really there with me. Oh, his body was there all right, on the edge of a freezing cliff in Lowestoft, but it was obvious his mind was somewhere else entirely. Somewhere terrifying, if the look on his face was anything to go by, and when I called his name he looked petrified, as though he'd woken up from a sleepwalk.

'He was apologetic of course, kept telling me he didn't know what had happened and that he was happy to be back here with me. But something in him had changed, and that was the day I realised it. My brave, funny, carefree Arthur had gone, abandoned somewhere on a battlefield in France, and in his place was this sad, slightly detached, scared man. I didn't know if I'd ever see the old Arthur again.'

She shook her head, the wind ruffling her white curls. Anna stayed silent, not wanting to intrude on Grace's memories.

'Over the next few weeks things didn't change. We went dancing and he always stood stiffly, just far enough away from me that our bodies didn't touch. Or we'd go for afternoon tea and he'd spend most of the time staring out of the window rather than looking at me. I knew he was moving away from me, a little bit more each day, but I didn't know what to do about it and so I pretended it wasn't happening.

'But then Arthur asked me to marry him. It had been what I'd been waiting for the entire time he'd been away. Bombs had dropped and families had been destroyed, but all the while I'd been dreaming of being Mrs Arthur Robb like the silly teenager I was. And so, of course, I said yes, even though the deepest part of me knew it would be wrong, things being the way they were. I suppose I hoped it would somehow repair our damaged courtship.' She looked at Anna now. 'A bit like you and Daniel.'

Anna nodded as they turned round to walk back the way they had come after Grace finally admitted she'd had quite enough for one day.

'You're right, Grace.'

Grace shrugged. 'I usually am.'

Anna smiled at her and the pair continued in silence at a slow pace.

'One day you'll find your Roy and then you'll know you've found the right one,' Grace said suddenly.

'I'm happy as I am, Grace.'

'Oh, I don't doubt that you are, Anna. I was too, for a long time. But you know what – meeting Roy made me properly happy again, and I'd never have thought that could happen after Arthur.' She took a deep breath. 'Just never say never. The next love of your life could be just around the corner and you don't want to miss your chance at happiness because you were too busy looking backwards.'

Chapter Seven

'Honestly, he was so bloody rude, I wanted to smack his smug face off his shoulders and watch it roll across the kitchen floor.' Anna tipped her head back and drained the last of the wine from the bottom of her glass.

'Just ignore him, it doesn't matter what he thinks,' Julia said.

'Maybe not, but he matters to Grace so it does matter to me.'

'Fair point. But it sounds as though Grace isn't taking any notice anyway, so why should you?'

Anna shrugged, despondent.

'Come on, Annie, don't let a bloody man get you down. Since when do we ever listen to them?'

'Oh, thanks very much,' muttered Al, Julia's husband, from the kitchen area, where he was chopping vegetables on the island.

'Not you, darling, of course,' Julia said, blowing him a kiss. He pretended to catch it and gave her a wink.

'I really don't think you should worry about him, Annie. Either he'll come round or he won't, but either way, Grace will still be your friend.'

'That's why I love you, Jules, you always talk sense,' Anna said, clinking her glass against her friend's and slumping back against the sofa. She could hear laughter coming from the other room, where Julia's children were watching inane YouTube videos.

'You're staying here tonight, right?' Julia asked with concern, indicating the empty bottle of wine on the coffee table in front of them.

'I'd better – I don't think I should be riding my bike.'

'You definitely shouldn't.'

Anna smiled. Julia had always been the sensible one, even when they were young children and teenagers. If Anna had wanted to climb a tree that was too tall, Julia would talk her down. When, drunk one night, she'd tried to jump off the pier into the sea, it had been Julia who'd stopped her; when she'd been determined to have a perm, it was Julia who'd vetoed it, telling her she'd look like Deirdre from *Coronation Street*. All the bad decisions she'd avoided in her life had been thanks to Julia. The ones she'd gone ahead with were entirely her fault.

Tonight, still fuming about the way Tom had spoken to her earlier, Julia's sensible head was exactly what Anna needed to calm her down. The wine was just a bonus.

'So, when do I get to meet this Grace, then? Sounds to me like she needs the best-friend seal of approval.'

'Why don't you come over one day? Or, no, I know – why don't I bring her here? We're planning some days out over the next few weeks while the weather's nice; maybe we could come over to Beccles to see you?'

'I'd love that.' She took a sip of her wine. 'It sounds to me as though you're her pet project.'

'What do you mean?'

Julia raised her eyebrows. 'You know, all these stories she's telling you about the past. Don't you think she's trying to make you feel better about what's happened with You Know Who?'

Anna smiled. She loved the fact that Julia was so protective of her that she wouldn't even say Dan's name, as though merely speaking it would invoke evil in her presence, like Voldemort.

'I think that's exactly what she's doing,' Anna agreed. 'And, actually, I'm really enjoying hearing all about it. What I went through was awful at the time, but you know what? I'll get over it. I am getting over it, slowly. But I just can't imagine how she must have felt, to be left standing at the altar and then never to have found out what happened. She never even saw him again.'

Julia shook her head. 'Poor Grace. I don't think I could have coped with that. I'd have been like a dog with a bone, chewing and chewing away at it until I got the answers I wanted. I mean, she must have spent her whole life wondering what she did wrong.'

'I know. I think she has, in a way, although she plays it down. And she's had a good life since. But I can't stop thinking about it. About Arthur.'

'That's our natural nosiness, Annie. Remember when that boy mysteriously turned up at school and no one knew where he'd come from, or why? Me and you were like bloody Sherlock Holmes, trying to find clues and work it out. I don't know what great secret we thought we were going to uncover.'

'I'd forgotten about that.' Anna grinned at the memory. 'But you're right. I am nosy, and I just don't think I could have let it lie, if I'd been her.'

'Then don't.'

'What do you mean?'

'Well…Grace might not have wanted to know what happened to Arthur, but it doesn't mean you can't try to find out.' At this, Al raised his eyebrows but said nothing, trying to ignore the women's conversation while he carried on cooking.

'Grace would never want me to start digging around in the past like that.'

'You don't have to tell her.'

'I can't do that!'

'Why not, Annie? What harm would it do? Besides, if you don't, I'm going to have to. I don't think I can bear not knowing.'

'Don't you bloody dare!'

Julia laughed. 'All right, all right! I was only saying. A little Google search wouldn't do any harm, though. You probably won't find anything, but if you do then you can decide whether to tell Grace or not.'

Anna shrugged. 'I don't know, Julia. I'll think about it.'

'Well, make sure you tell me all the juicy details if you do find anything.'

'I wouldn't dare not.'

Julia stood up. 'Do you need any help with dinner, love?'

Al held up the pot of vegetable chilli. 'Nice timing – it's all done.'

'Oh, you're an angel.' She went to the fridge and pulled out another bottle of white wine, plonking it on the coffee table in front of Anna. 'As you're staying, you can open this while I try to get the horrors to bed.'

'Don't listen to her,' Al said as Julia left the room.

'What about?' asked Anna as she unscrewed the top from the wine bottle and topped up the two glasses. The half a bottle she'd already drunk had settled in her stomach and she felt relaxed, if a bit light-headed.

'This Grace, and Arthur. If you don't feel comfortable going behind your friend's back, ignore Julia. You know what she's like. Head screwed on, but a terrible influence sometimes.'

'I know. But she is right – I *do* want to know.'

Al poured rice into a pan and added water, setting it to boil. 'Well, then do it. But don't let that one bully you into anything.'

'Who's bullying who?' Julia demanded, walking back into the room.

'No one, dear,' Al said, smacking Julia's bottom as she passed. Anna couldn't help feeling a small pang of jealousy at their easy intimacy. She'd never really had that with Dan, now she looked back. She'd always felt a little on edge, a little bit as though he was judging her in whatever she did. But she definitely missed the physical closeness they'd once had. Julia was lucky. She'd been with Al since she was twenty-one, just home from university with this funny long-haired boy in tow who seemed to worship her. Now, eighteen years later, Al had lost most of his hair, but a cycling habit kept him trim and he still adored Julia as much as ever. The feeling was clearly mutual.

Anna's thoughts were interrupted by two loud voices. 'Night, Aunty Anna!' they cried, and suddenly she was almost barrelled off the sofa by nine-year-old Finley and seven-year-old Rufus.

'Night, you two,' she said, squeezing them hard. 'Be good.'

'Ha, yeah, right,' said Finley as he pulled himself up and walked towards the stairs.

'Well, be as good as you can be then,' Anna called after them. She was answered by the clatter of feet as they scrambled up the stairs, Julia following closely behind.

Al slumped into the armchair opposite Anna and sighed heavily.

'Everything all right?' she said, leaning back and tucking her feet underneath her. There weren't many men she felt this comfortable around.

'Yeah, just knackered,' he said, tipping his head back and drinking from his can of cider. 'Did thirty miles this morning and I think I'm getting a bit old for it.'

'Rubbish, you're fit as anything.'

'Not anymore.' He rubbed his hand across a tiny mound of belly, barely visible beneath his T-shirt. 'I'm getting a paunch, look. As if it's not bad enough I'm going bald, now Julia's got to put up with me getting fat as well.'

Anna laughed. 'Don't be daft, Julia would love you if you gained ten stone and never left the sofa again.'

He shook his head. 'I'm not so sure, you know.' He turned to her and she saw his expression was suddenly serious. He looked awkward and kept glancing towards the door. 'Do you –' He stopped, looked down at his hands.

'Al, what's up?' Anna had never seen him like this before, so unsure of himself.

He shrugged. 'Oh, I don't know. I'm probably just being stupid but – well, sometimes these days I worry that Julia might just stop fancying me and bugger off and find someone else.'

'She'd never do that!'

He looked at her, held her gaze. 'Really? You honestly don't think she would?'

Anna shuffled round to properly face him. 'I can't believe you of all people are asking me this. You and Julia are the happiest couple I know. Well, joint with my mum and dad.'

He squirmed. 'Well, maybe. But I just worry. You know, after everything…' He trailed off, his face flaming.

'You mean after what happened to me?'

He shrugged again. 'Kind of. Sorry, Anna. But it's not just you and Dan –' he caught himself – 'I mean You Know Who. It's everyone. Everyone I work with seems to be having some sort of marriage crisis, or getting divorced, or having an affair, and I just – I worry. About Julia.' He swept his hand down himself. 'I mean, she's still hot and I'm – well, I'm middle-aged, Anna.'

Anna shook her head and gave a small smile. 'Oh, Al. I'm sorry to laugh but you have got to be kidding me. There's absolutely no way Julia would ever look for anyone else – she adores you.' She leaned over and poked him in the belly. 'Even if you are getting a bit porky these days.'

'Oi!' A grin spread across his face and he rubbed his hands across it. 'It's just so hard though, isn't it, when you see everyone else falling apart around you and you just think – it'll be me next?'

'What'll be you next, love?' Julia breezed into the room, her hair piled on top of her head.

'God, woman! You've got to stop creeping up on us like that – can't anyone have a private conversation around here?'

'Nope, definitely not without me in it.' She flopped down next to Anna and crossed her legs. 'So come on, out with it.'

Anna looked at Al and raised her eyebrows as if to say *over to you.*

'Really, it was nothing, love. We were just talking about this business with Grace and Arthur and I was telling Anna not to listen to you if she doesn't want to.'

'Oh, well, course she doesn't *have* to listen to me.' She grinned at Anna cheekily. 'But you must know that if you don't, I'll have to kill you.'

Anna held her hands up in surrender. 'OK, OK, I'll do it, if only to shut you up.'

'Good.' Julia smiled. 'Now, let's eat. I'm starving. And pass me that wine.'

* * *

Early the next morning, back at her own flat, Anna made herself a cup of coffee and opened her laptop. Julia's words had been playing on her mind since last night, about Arthur. Grace might insist she didn't want to know what had happened to him all those years ago, but Anna couldn't help wondering. She knew it was unlikely that she'd find anything after all this time, but to satisfy her own curiosity she needed to at least have a look, see if she could piece anything together.

Unsure where to start, she simply opened up Google and typed in Arthur's name: *Arthur Robb.*

Almost instantly a list of Arthur Robbs appeared. There were thousands of results, and none of them seemed obviously helpful. She peered at the top one, an obituary of a man called Arthur Robb who had recently died in New Zealand. She clicked on it and seconds later the page was filled with the life story of a man who had been a farmer for many years and left behind three children, a wife and six grandchildren. There was a small photo attached. She squinted. He didn't look old enough. But she'd only seen one photo of him; would she really know what he looked like?

She sighed. She supposed it could be him. After all, she didn't have any idea of where he'd gone after leaving Lowestoft all those years ago. He could quite literally be anywhere in the world, if he was even still alive.

The magnitude of the task hit her. What was she doing? Did she really think she'd be able to find out what had happened to Arthur when nobody else had managed to do so? And even if she did, what was she going to do with that information? She didn't think Grace would be very open to hearing about it.

And yet.

She took a sip of her coffee and rubbed her face. She'd try a few more things and then call it a day, for now.

She clicked back to the results page and scrolled down. There was an Arthur Robb who was a music teacher; a photographer from Scunthorpe; a retired lawyer from Florida; a landscape gardener from Seattle.

Then one caught her eye: *Arthur Robb, Boat builder.* The picture was tiny and the man on it looked too young, but who knew how long ago the photo was taken? She couldn't dismiss anything at this stage. She clicked on the link and was taken to a website dedicated to boat building. Images of yachts filled the screen, and in the top-right corner was a photo of a man beaming out from what she guessed to be his own boat. He looked about thirty-five and ruddy. The picture didn't seem old enough to have been Arthur sixty years before.

Clicking back to the search page, she added *Lowestoft* into the search. This time the screen threw up some of the same results, as well as dozens of entries about the history of Lowestoft, and many, many seemingly unrelated listings. She shook her head and added in *disappeared* to the search. A few different entries popped up, and she scanned them quickly. Nothing useful, as far as she could see.

She sighed again, feeling at a bit of a loss. She was no expert in these sorts of things. Was there a website where you could go to look for lost people? But then again, Arthur wasn't lost, technically, so she guessed he wouldn't show up on there anyway.

In desperation she typed a few more things into the search engine – any combinations of words she could think of – in the blind hope something might just pop up: *Arthur Robb missing; Arthur Robb married; Arthur Robb Second World War; Arthur Robb died.*

Nothing.

This was hopeless. Downing the dregs of her coffee, she checked her watch and stood up. It was almost time to leave for work, so she'd have to continue the search another time. And, in the meantime, she might have to see if she could somehow get some more information from Grace about Arthur – although how she was going to do that without raising suspicion she had no idea.

* * *

Clicking her knitting needles together furiously, Grace felt her mind wandering. She was making another cardigan for the babies in the hospital prem ward. She'd made so many over the last few months she could do it with her eyes closed – in fact, sometimes she did. It had given her something to do after Roy died, something to fill her time and plug the enormous gaping void that was his absence.

She stopped clicking for a moment and glanced across at the armchair next to hers, the one where Roy used to sit every evening reading a book in the dim light of the standard lamp, glasses perched on the end of his nose, the paperback getting closer and closer to his face as the years passed and his eyesight deteriorated. Sometimes he had put the paperback face-down on the arm of the chair and she had stopped watching whatever programme she'd been tuned into and turned to look at him, returning the smile she knew she'd find upon his face. And then she'd reach over and clasp his hand in hers and Roy would say 'I love you, Gracie'. Every time. Just those words. And Grace would feel a wave of happiness surge through her, even as her own eyesight dimmed, as her body aged and as the wrinkles on her face deepened. She knew without a doubt that Roy loved her, and she loved him too.

The thing she struggled with the most now that he was gone was the silence of the house. She'd never noticed before how the radiators clicked, or the boiler roared, or how the wind howled through invisible gaps in the window frames. Now, though, she could hear every little sound because there was nothing to mask it.

She used to sit here, in this very armchair, and hear Roy clattering about in the kitchen as he made dinner. He'd always done that job, because she was such a useless cook. He'd never said as much, of course. He was too kind. But when he'd suggested she might prefer to do the tidying up afterwards and leave the cooking to him, they both knew what he meant, and she was grateful. Her meals were awful – great lumps of bland mashed potato, heaps of overcooked carrots, pork chops that were burnt on the outside and almost raw in the middle. She just never seemed to improve.

If Roy wasn't in the kitchen, he would be in the dining room listening to Radio 4, or sitting rustling a newspaper and commenting every now and then on some story that angered or tickled him. And then later, when he was ill, when their doctor had delivered the news that Roy's heart was so weak he didn't have long left, there was the heaving of the ventilator all through the night, or the gravelly sound of Roy's breathing, the desperate wheezing in and out as he struggled to fill his lungs with enough air to keep him alive for one more hour, one more day.

She'd brought him food then. Tins of soup warmed in a pan – even she hadn't been able to mess that up; cakes from the bakers – lemon drizzle, his favourite, when they had it; endless cups of milky tea, and Ovaltine at bedtime. The way he'd always done for her. Then she'd sat by his bedside and held his hand until he fell asleep, or stroked his arm, his thinning hair, his pale, grey face – the face that had always been so full of life, love and laughter but now looked like a shadow of its former self. And yet she could still see her Roy in there, the same man she'd met all those years ago with the sparkling eyes and the loud, infectious laugh. He was still there.

And then he was gone. The house felt empty, forlorn, but Grace couldn't bear to leave it. She didn't want anyone else there either, invading the space that had been hers and Roy's for so long. But after a few weeks the loneliness became too much and she started letting people back in again – Tom, of course, and Gerald from next door. She was persuaded to accept visits from a carer and so there had been a succession of those, but they'd all just made her feel worse and Grace had sent them away. And then Anna had come into her life and something in Grace had changed. Anna had somehow made Grace stop wanting to shut everything out and start thinking about the things that had happened in her life. Good and bad. And she wanted to help Anna, too. She wanted to help her be happy again – as happy as Grace had been when she'd finally met Roy.

What she was furious about now, though, was the other memories that had unexpectedly crept up on her, the memories she hadn't felt the need to let in during all of her years with Roy. The memories, specifically, of Arthur. Why was she thinking of him all these years later when it was Roy who had filled her life, who had made her happy? She felt treacherous, as though she were betraying the love of her life merely by thinking about what had happened all those years ago.

And, yet, now she'd started – reading her diary, looking at old photographs, going out with Anna and remembering things, little details she was surprised she hadn't long since forgotten – she couldn't seem to stop. It seemed as though it was almost some kind of therapy for her. And the more the memories came, the more she found she wanted them to come.

She reached her hand out and laid it on the arm of the chair next to hers, imagining Roy's hand beneath her own, the way it had always been. 'I'm sorry, Roy,' she said, her voice barely more than a whisper. 'I'm so sorry, my love.'

Chapter Eight

'We're going out,' Grace announced the minute Anna walked into the room.

'Out? Where?'

Anna almost jumped out of her skin as a voice came from behind her. 'I'm taking Aunty Grace out for dinner and she wants you to come too.' Anna's heart sank as she turned to find Tom standing there, his arms crossed over his chest, looking as pleased to see her as she was to see him.

'Oh.' She turned back to Grace, a question on her face.

'Tom said he wanted to take me out for dinner for my birthday, which is a lovely thing to do,' Grace said, 'but I told him I didn't want to go without you. If you want to come, of course.'

'Goodness, is it your birthday today?'

'It is. Ninety-five. Who'd ever have imagined I'd live this long, eh?'

'Oh, Grace, why didn't you tell me?' Why hadn't she checked Grace's notes, more like?

'When you've had as many birthdays as I have you don't

tend to bother making a fuss about them anymore,' Grace said, grinning. 'But for some reason Tom thinks being so ancient is something to celebrate. So, will you come?'

'Where are you going?'

'My favourite, The Victoria.' Anna knew it – the hotel and restaurant on the clifftop at the top end of town had been a favourite of her grandma's when she'd been alive.

It was clear Tom was hoping she'd say no and his presence was making her feel inclined to do just that. How much fun would she have if she had to endure his sullen face for the duration of a meal? But Grace looked so excited she couldn't bring herself to refuse.

'That would be lovely, Grace, thank you.'

'The table's booked for seven so you might not have time to get home and change.' Tom's voice was flat.

'I'm sure it will be fine,' Anna said, picking up an empty teacup from the table and moving towards the kitchen. 'I'll be gone by five-thirty and I don't live far from The Victoria, so I can meet you there.'

'Excellent!' Grace said, clapping her hands together the way Anna saw her niece Bee do when she got her own way. Tom didn't speak and Anna walked out of the room without giving him another glance. Let him be moody; she didn't have to speak to him. Besides, she was going for Grace, not for him.

After tidying up and trying to ignore Tom's lurking presence, Anna was done. There was no sandwich to make this evening since they were going out to eat, and Grace insisted Anna leave early to get herself ready.

'She hasn't done half an hour yet,' Tom objected.

'It doesn't matter, you go,' Grace said.

'But what's the point in paying for someone if they don't even do what they're paid for?'

'Thomas, don't be rude, I've told her to go.'

'No, it's fine, he's right. What else do you need?' Anna asked, straightening out the antimacassars on the backs of the armchairs.

'Absolutely nothing. Now, please, go and get ready and I'll see you at dinner.' Grace's voice was stern, icy even. Anna had never heard her cross before. She picked up her helmet, slipped her shoes on and left, not waiting to hear what Grace had to say to Tom. She knew what she'd like to say but, for Grace's sake, she'd bite her tongue. For now.

On the way home Anna grabbed a birthday card and some flowers from the local Tesco, then raced back to her flat to get changed. As she pulled a dress over her head and flicked mascara across her eyelashes, she couldn't dislodge a feeling of unease about the night ahead. She loved spending time with Grace, but Tom really seemed to have something against her. She understood that he might feel a little put out that she saw as much of Grace as he did, and that maybe he felt she was intruding, but if it made Grace happy then she really didn't understand why he cared.

She thought about him standing there filling the doorway with his presence, trying to intimidate her, and felt conflicted. Grace had said so many glowing things about Tom: how he ran his own business, how he taught children to swim, how he looked after her garden and took care of her when he could. On paper, he sounded like the ideal great-nephew. Even the ideal man.

And yet. All he'd done so far was be rude to Anna and make her feel uncomfortable.

She inhaled deeply. She'd get through tonight for Grace,

but if he continued to behave the way he was doing she'd have to speak to him, tell him she didn't mean any harm. That all she wanted was to be Grace's friend.

Grabbing her keys and bag, she headed out of the door and into the warm evening air. The wind had subsided and it was still light, and as she walked briskly along the seafront towards The Victoria, she filled her lungs. She always found the sound of the sea soothing and, now, she felt the anger seep out of her, leaving her calm in preparation for the night ahead.

It was just after seven when she ran up the steps to the entrance and made her way inside. It had been almost two years since she was last here – at her grandma's wake – and the place was barely recognisable. Where tables and chairs had once been, now there were booths painted in cheerful blue-and-green stripes to look like beach huts. The once-old-fashioned bar had neon lighting and rows of drinks back-lit at the rear. She wondered what her grandma would have made of it.

Spotting Grace and Tom in the corner, she made her way over. Grace was facing the window with its view out to sea – the same seat her grandma had always chosen. Tom was next to her, so Anna walked round the table to sit opposite Grace, diagonally across from Tom.

'Evening, all,' she said as she sat down and handed Grace the card and flowers. 'Sorry it's nothing much, but *somebody* didn't tell me it was their birthday.'

'Oooh, thank you, they're lovely,' Grace said, burying her nose in the bouquet. 'Yellow's my favourite colour.'

'You're welcome.' Anna looked Tom directly in the face. 'Hello, Tom.'

He nodded. 'Hello, glad you made it. We thought we'd wait for you before ordering.'

Was she imagining it or was Tom's voice softer now, less clipped? Perhaps he really had endured a telling off from

Grace after Anna had left. Whatever had caused the change, she welcomed it. She hadn't been looking forward to a night of sullen grunts.

Tom tilted his head up to look out of the window. The sun was setting behind the building, to the west, creating sparkles of light on the waves far out to sea that glittered as they reflected back in at them, giving Tom's face an orange glow and making his dark hair shine. Anna had never really looked at him before and she was annoyed to realise he was actually quite handsome. It didn't mean she had to like him any more, though.

'So, are we getting a bottle of wine?' Tom asked his great-aunt.

'Yes, I rather think I'd like that. Can we have red?'

'You can have whatever you want, Aunty Grace,' he said. 'You're the birthday girl.'

Drinks and dinner ordered, they studied the view from the window. The sea was flat this evening, just a few gentle ripples denting the stretch of pale blue and the regular splash of waves breaking far out in the distance.

'I love it when the sea's like this,' Anna said. 'It makes me glad to be on the coast.'

'I prefer it when it's wild,' Grace said. 'When the waves are huge, and it's a dark iron-grey and it feels as though it could swallow you up at any moment. It makes you feel small and vulnerable.'

'I agree,' Tom said, twirling his wine glass between his fingers. 'More people drown when it's calm than when it's wild because they think it's safe. People get complacent.'

'Tom's a qualified lifeguard; he sometimes helps out when they need him during the summer,' Grace explained.

Anna had to refrain from rolling her eyes. Was there anything Saint Tom didn't do?

'I don't have as much time these days, the gardening's so busy,' Tom said.

'And yet you still find time to do mine for me.'

'Anything for you, Aunty Grace.'

'That's really kind,' Anna said, pushing any sarcastic comments to the back of her mind. 'Grace's garden is lovely.'

Tom nodded. 'I do what I can. Aunty Grace means the world to me.'

Perhaps Tom wasn't being so friendly with her now after all. He was clearly trying to make a point, and Anna was damned if she was going to react. Instead, she thought about the last time she was here, after her grandma had died. She had been the last one of her grandparents to go, and Anna had adored her. As everyone had gathered in this room eating triangular sandwiches and making small talk, sharing memories, Anna had stood right here at this window admiring the view her grandma had treasured the most in the world.

Her thoughts were interrupted by the arrival of dinner and, as they settled into eating, a silence fell over the table for a while until Grace said suddenly, 'This is where Arthur proposed, you know.'

'Is it?' Anna asked.

Tom rolled his eyes. 'Not Arthur again, Aunty Grace. Why are you talking about him all of a sudden?'

'I don't know, Thomas. Since your uncle Roy died, I've been feeling more and more nostalgic. Plus, I found my old diary, of course, and then all these places that Anna's been taking me to have stirred up old memories even more. There are ghosts of everyone I've ever loved all over this town, hiding in places you'd never expect.'

'I hope it hasn't made it harder for you,' Anna said.

'Well, she's never spoken about this Arthur before.' Tom's voice was sharp.

'No, I haven't, Tom, but that's nothing to do with Anna. I loved your uncle Roy more than anything in the world, as you well know. But Arthur was part of my life too, and I have to admit it's felt good for me to think about what happened after all this time. A bit – what's the word? Cathartic? Yes, that. I've buried it all away for so long, it's about time some of those ghosts are laid to rest.'

'Tell us about it then, this proposal,' Anna said, ignoring Tom. 'It was right here in this hotel?'

Grace nodded, a smile playing on her lips. 'In this very room, in fact,' she said. 'I remember it came as a surprise, though, after everything that had happened since he'd got back from the war.' She looked first at Anna and then at Tom. 'Remember I told you how he'd changed?'

Anna nodded.

'Well, things got worse. It felt as though he was drifting further and further away from me and I was at a loss. I was desperate to hold on to him, but I didn't feel I knew him anymore. I didn't know what he was thinking, what he wanted. I didn't even know where he went most of the time. He felt like a stranger.

'But then occasionally, just when I was thinking I'd lost him, I'd be rewarded for not giving up on him – his eyes would light up when he saw me, or he would smile at a joke I made. Then I felt sure the Arthur I loved was still in there somewhere and that he still loved me.'

She stopped and took a mouthful of fish, chewing it slowly, then swallowed.

'And then it happened. We'd arranged to have an early dinner here. It was a grey day, cold, I remember, with a mist hanging over the sea, not bright like it is today. The room was packed, full of couples, conversations buzzing round, and as I took my coat off and sat down opposite Arthur, I felt happier than I had in ages.

'We sat here for a while and I tried to work out what was going on behind his closed face, but it was impossible. He never spoke about the war and what had happened to him even though I had hoped he might confide in me one day. I suppose these days he would have been diagnosed with post-traumatic stress or some such thing but back then people were just expected to pick themselves up and get on with it.' She shook her head. 'There were a lot of problems because of that.

'Anyway. He started fussing with the menu, smoothing down non-existent stray hairs, playing with his collar. And then he reached over and took hold of both of my hands. He seemed nervous.

'The waitress came and took our order – meat pie, I think we had; there wasn't much choice, what with rationing still – and he seemed to freeze. And then he said he had a question to ask me.' She paused, took a sip of water. Tom carried on eating as he listened to his great-aunt's story, keeping his eyes fixed on his plate.

'Well, after the way he'd been over the previous few months it didn't even occur to me that he might be asking me to marry him. So when he did, I nearly fell off my chair right here in the middle of the dining room.' A smile spread across her face, creating folds in her cheeks and making her eyes almost disappear behind her glasses.

'How did he ask, can you remember?' Anna said, leaning forward, gripping onto every word.

'He just flittered about a bit, licking his lips and scratching his ear and darting his eyes around the room, and then he simply said "Will you marry me?". Just like that.'

'And did you say yes straight away?'

'I think I froze for a minute, not sure if I'd heard him properly. But I soon recovered and of course you both know I said yes. His cheeks went pink and the couple on the table next to us noticed what was happening and started clapping, which made us both go bright red. Once, Arthur would have loved that – being the centre of attention, having people congratulate him. But that day he just looked awkward and uncomfortable.

'He produced his grandmother's ring, and when he slipped it on my finger I felt like the happiest woman alive. And although he didn't seem as excited as I might have hoped, I chose not to dwell on it and just put it down to him so recently being back from the war. I told myself he'd get better, in time, now we were getting married.'

She sighed, tired out by the telling of the story.

'Are you all right, Aunty Grace? Do you need some water?' Tom shot Anna a look, as if it were her fault Grace was struggling.

She shook her head. 'No, I'm fine, just a little worn out. I hadn't thought about that day for a very long time until I read my diary the other day. I haven't felt the need to, with Roy by my side. I just – I don't know. The memories seem to be coming thick and fast at the moment.'

Anna reached out her hand and laid it on Grace's frail forearm. She was reminded how tiny the old woman was beneath the smart pink blouse she'd put on for the occasion. She noticed now how Grace's hair was perfectly styled and that she'd even applied a little lipstick to come out for dinner and she felt a surge of love for this woman in front of her who'd lived her life and was still making an effort, even now. She hoped she too would be the sort of woman to never give up when she was Grace's age.

'Your dinner's gone cold,' Grace said, pointing at the plate of congealed pasta in front of Anna.

'Oops. I must have got a bit too caught up in your story,' Anna said.

'Well, Aunty Grace hasn't eaten hers either,' Tom said disapprovingly.

'It's all right, Tom, I can eat it cold. It won't kill me.' Grace grinned cheekily as she speared the longest chip on her plate and popped it into her mouth.

'I don't think it's doing you any good, all this dwelling on the past,' Tom said, scraping the last bit of sauce up with his fork. 'And I don't think it's a good idea to encourage it either,' he added, fixing his gaze on Anna.

'Oh, Tom, stop being such a stick-in-the-mud. This is nothing to do with Anna. We're just enjoying spending time together, and we talk, that's all. There's nothing more to it. I don't know why you've got such a bee in your bonnet about it.'

'I haven't –' he started to say, his face like thunder, but Grace interrupted him.

'I don't know why you think Anna's got some sort of secret plan. I can assure you she hasn't, have you, Anna?' Grace looked at Anna, who shook her head. 'As far as I'm aware she's simply my friend, and quite honestly, Thomas, it's rather an insult if you think there's some other reason for her being here than the fact that she just thinks I'm quite marvellous.' Anna hid a smirk behind her hand.

'That's not what I meant, Aunty Grace,' he said, his face flushing. 'I just – it's just – well, I just thought it was strange that someone Anna's age would choose to spend so much time with someone your age. That's all.' He held his hands up. 'But if you say there's nothing more to it then that's fine. I'll back off.'

'Really, Tom, you have nothing to worry about,' Anna said. 'I'm not here to step on anyone's toes, or try to take

Grace away from you. I just like her, that's all. We're friends, aren't we, Grace?'

Grace's face lit up and her lips spilt into a grin. 'Yes, we are. That's exactly what we are. Friends.'

Unsure what else to say, Tom stayed quiet and Anna felt the urge to say something to break the awkward silence. But it didn't feel like the right time to mention Arthur again, and it most definitely wasn't the right time to bring up the fact she'd been trying to find him.

'My grandma loved it here too,' she said instead. 'In fact, both of my grandparents on my mum's side did. We came here all the time for birthdays, anniversaries – any excuse really.'

'I didn't know that,' Grace said.

Anna nodded. 'It was one of their favourite places in the world, which is why we put a bench in the garden with their names on it. It doesn't quite overlook the sea as it's too low down, but it's got a lovely view of the gardens, and the sea is just beyond the wall so you still know it's there.'

'Can we go and see it?'

'Now? It'll be dark soon.'

'It'll be all right if we go right away.'

'OK, if you like.'

Anna stood and helped Grace to her feet.

'Are you coming?' Grace asked Tom, but he shook his head.

'I'd better stay here in case they think we're trying to do a runner without paying.'

'I hardly think they're going to suspect me of running anywhere,' she chuckled, 'but suit yourself.'

As Tom pulled his phone from his pocket Anna took Grace's arm and they made their way down in the lift and out of the back door into the garden. There, in the falling light of the evening, sat a bench with two plaques. They moved towards it and bent to read the inscriptions.

The one on the left read:

In loving memory of Gordon, much-loved father, grandfather and great-grandfather, who loved it here.
1928–2015

And, next to it, the other read:

In loving memory of Cora, beloved mother, grandmother and great-grandmother, who has joined her beloved Gordon.
1929–2017

'Oh, that's lovely, Anna,' Grace said.

'I do miss them.' Anna sat on the bench and leaned back, looking out over the small garden. The hedges were neatly trimmed, the flowerbeds immaculate and weed-free. In the dusk the plants formed strange silhouettes and the flowers dulled to varying shades of grey but it was still easy to see their beauty. Above Grace and Anna's heads gulls wheeled, and they could just make out the sound of the sea splashing gently on the shore as the tide made its slow creep inwards.

Grace sat down too, hands on her thighs, knees pressed together primly. 'I expect you do. And I'm sure they know that.'

'I hope so.' Anna slid a look at Grace. 'You'll think I'm mad but sometimes I come down here just to sit and talk to them. I tell them both everything that's happened since they died, and when Dan left me it felt good to come and sit here and speak to them.'

'I don't think you're mad at all. In fact, I'd be surprised if you didn't do that since they meant so much to you.'

'They really did. They were just always there, all through my childhood. If we went out for the day it was always me, Adam, Mum and Dad, and Grandma and Grandad. And we spent hours at theirs, watching TV, eating snacks we weren't allowed to eat at home. They meant as much to me as Mum and Dad.'

'You must have found it hard when they died.'

'I did. But it's the way it's meant to be, isn't it? The old die before the young, on and on forever. It's only ever a tragedy when the young die first. It doesn't stop it hurting any less though.'

'I wasn't as close to my father as you obviously were to your grandparents, but I missed him terribly when he died.'

'How old were you?'

'Only twenty-five. He never met Roy. He never spoke to me about what happened with Arthur but I knew he was furious with him on my behalf. He was a very traditional man though, stiff upper lip.'

'How did he die?'

'Lung cancer, I think, although no one ever said it back then. He'd smoked a pipe for as long as I could remember. But even though we weren't close, I often think about him and wonder what he would have made of my life. I wish I could have had somewhere to come and talk to him.'

They sat for a few more minutes, listening to the sounds of the sea, voices passing by every now and then just above their heads.

'I do feel guilty, you know,' Grace said.

'What about?'

Grace shrugged. 'About Arthur.'

Anna turned to face Grace. 'What do you mean?'

Grace looked down at her hands, clasped in her lap, and licked her lips. 'I thought about Arthur a lot after he left. I always wondered whether it was something I did that made him leave. But when I met Roy I took the decision not to think about Arthur ever again. It felt like a betrayal.' She sighed. 'Roy was a good man. One of the best. But I never really forgot about Arthur, and now, talking about him makes me feel as though I'm betraying my Roy all over again.'

'Oh, Grace, don't be daft.' Anna reached out and gently took Grace's hand in hers. It was cold to the touch. 'It's not a betrayal. Arthur was a part of your life as much as anyone. But it's obvious how much you loved Roy.'

'But then why do I need to think about it all over again?'

'Who knows. Minds work in mysterious ways. Maybe you just need to know for certain that it wasn't your fault.'

Grace shrugged again. 'Maybe. But as I'm never going to find out, what's the point now?'

Anna let the words settle between them for a minute, but decided now wasn't the time to mention her fledgling search. Not until she had something more concrete to offer Grace – if, indeed, she ever did.

'Maybe there doesn't have to be a point, Grace. Maybe it's OK to just reminisce about someone and not let it mean anything.' She stood. 'Now, let's go back inside, it's getting chilly.' Grace stood too and, slowly, they made their way back to the table, where Tom was paying the bill.

'Oh, thank you, Tom, you didn't have to do that.'

'I said it was my treat, Aunty Grace,' he said, smiling at her.

'Let me pay you for mine,' Anna said, keen not to take any favours from him.

'No, it's fine, really. It's paid now.'

She was about to insist when she saw a flash of something pass across his face that made her change her mind. Was that anger, or something else?

'Well, then thank you, Tom.'

'It's my pleasure.'

She held an arm out for Grace to take, and then Tom took Grace's arm on the other side. Anna knew she didn't need them both to help her but she wasn't about to tell Tom that – she didn't need to give him any more reason to dislike her.

As they made their way to Tom's car, Anna thought of something to take Grace's mind off Arthur.

'If Arthur proposed here, where did Roy propose?'

'Roy? He didn't propose, dear.'

'But you were married, weren't you?'

'Quite right. I asked him to marry me.' There was more than a hint of pride in Grace's voice.

'Did you, Aunty Grace? I don't think I ever knew that.'

'Didn't you? Well, it was all so long ago, and when you're married as long as Roy and I were you do forget things.'

'It sounds very forward-thinking of you,' Anna said as Grace climbed into the front seat of Tom's battered old Volkswagen Passat.

'Well, get in, dear, and I'll tell you all about it.'

'But I only live round the corner.'

'Oh, come on, come and have a glass of wine with a silly old woman on her birthday. Please?'

'Is that OK with you?' she asked Tom as he opened his own door.

'Yes, if you like.' She wondered if he was finding it hard to maintain a veneer of politeness.

Eager to hear the rest of Grace's story, Anna climbed onto the back seat and took her place next to some pink and blue swimming noodles and a bag of compost, leaning through the gap to carry on their chat.

Grace continued her story, clearly pleased to be thinking about Roy again. 'I suppose it was quite modern of me, but it just seemed like the right thing to do at the time. I'd messed him about quite a lot, you see. I'd already said no to him twice so I couldn't very well expect him to ask me again, could I?'

'So, what happened? I do enjoy a good love story.' Anna ducked down as Tom concentrated on reversing out of the parking space and then pulling out of the car park.

'Well, as I mentioned, I'd said no to him twice before, because – well, because of Arthur. Once bitten, twice shy is what they say, isn't it? I just didn't see the point in getting married and ruining what we had. But then I got scared he'd leave me if I kept saying no forever, and I knew I didn't want that.' She glanced back at Anna. 'So, I decided to ask him myself, in case he never asked me again.'

'Oh, how romantic. Tell me more.'

'It was far from being romantic. We were at home and I was attempting to cook a shepherd's pie. I remember it was cloudy and grey outside and Roy was reading the newspaper in the dining room. Even though I was a hopeless cook, I'd offered this time because he was always the one having to make dinner. I think he thought I'd been taken ill.' She smiled at the memory.

'I was listening to him sighing and chuckling at whatever stories he was reading, and the rustle of paper as he turned the pages. Then he seemed to finish, so I left the mince bubbling away on the stove and the potatoes cooking in the pan, wiped my hands on a tea towel and went through to see him.

'He was looking out the window at his beloved garden and I stood behind him with my hands on his shoulders. The roses he'd planted were in hiding, waiting for the first warmth of spring; the branches of the trees were still bare. It felt as though everything was holding its breath, waiting for something to happen. It felt like the right time.'

Beside Grace, Tom tutted as the traffic lights turned red again. The one-way system was designed to make people angry, Anna had decided a long time ago.

Grace continued. 'I went over to the dresser drawer and found the box I'd been hiding in there for a while, waiting for the time to be right. And then I walked back across the room and told Roy I needed to talk to him. Well, I've never seen anyone look so frightened. I think he thought I was about to tell him I'd set fire to the kitchen or something. So before he could say anything, I whipped out the box and opened it up for him to see. I dropped to my knee and said "I think we should get married".

'It wasn't the most romantic way I could have phrased it, but he looked like he'd won the pools. A few weeks later we ran away to Gretna Green. This time there was no long white dress, no veil, no trailing flowers. There were no bridesmaids or guests or any kind of a reception. It was just me in a smart green suit with a white collar, Roy in his Sunday best, the registrar and a witness. We said our vows, and then we kissed, and that was that. And I was the happiest I've ever been in my life.'

A moment of silence fell inside the car as a few fat drops of rain smattered against the windscreen and the wipers scratched back and forth, leaving behind trails of smudge.

'That's so lovely,' Anna said with a sigh. 'It must be amazing to have someone who adores you.'

'It was, but I adored him too. He was such a lovely man. Big and strong but gentle too, always thinking about everyone else.' A tear slid down the side of her face, leaving a track mark in her make-up. 'I miss him a lot, every day.'

They pulled up outside Grace's house and Tom stopped the engine. 'I miss him too,' Tom said, his voice quiet.

Grace turned and put her hand gently on his arm. 'I know you do, sweetheart. He had a lot of time for all Ernest's grandchildren, but especially you.'

Anna opened the door and climbed out, keen to let them have their moment together lost in memories of someone she'd never known and would never get the chance to meet.

After a short time Tom got out and helped Grace out, and Anna stood aside and let him. If allowing him do things for Grace without her intervention was what it took to get him to like her, then that's what she'd do.

* * *

A half-empty bottle of claret and three empty glasses stood on the table. The TV was on in the corner but nobody was watching it. Instead, they were poring over some newspaper cuttings that Grace had asked Tom to drag out from under the bed.

'This article was one of my favourites,' Grace said, picking up a fragile piece of newspaper. It was yellowed and the edges had crumbled slightly.

Floods Halt North Sea Fishing Boats
  By Grace Moran

'This was the first thing I ever wrote for the newspaper,' Grace said, placing it on the felt table topping and smoothing it down. The three of them huddled round the table to get a better look. 'I was so proud to see my name in print for the very first time.'

'This is amazing,' Anna said, leaning over to read the first few lines in the dim light. The subject matter wasn't thrilling but Anna understood what it must feel like to fulfil an ambition, which was something she'd never had the chance to do.

'Well, it's a boring old story but, still, I was lucky to have such opportunities, especially in those days.'

'How did you get into being a journalist? Anna asked Grace, sitting back and watching her in the lamplight.

'It was my aunt Val,' Grace said. 'She knew I'd always wanted to be a writer, and she knew someone who worked at the newspaper offices and so arranged for me to go and try out. At first it was just typing up letters, learning shorthand, arranging meetings for Samuel, the editor, but – well, I soon realised I was good at it, and within a few months I was writing news stories along with all the men in the newsroom. I was the only woman there for a long time.'

'That must have been strange,' said Anna.

'I didn't think much of it at the time, truth be told. They mostly left me alone, although that's not to say some of the old hacks didn't try it on sometimes. But – well. Let's just say I had a special friendship with the editor.'

'Aunty Grace!' Tom said, his cheeks flaming.

'What? I was a young woman, working in a man's world – it was good to have someone looking out for me. But enough of that, I don't want to embarrass poor old Tom. Perhaps I'll tell you all about that another time. But it was wonderful. I loved every minute of it.'

'You were so lucky,' Anna said, picking up another yellowed piece of paper.

'I was. But the one thing it taught me, Anna, is that if

there's something you really want to do, you have to grab it with both hands and give it a go.'

Anna nodded, aware that Grace was studying her. She kept her eyes fixed on the story in front of her, not reading it.

'I have a question for you,' said Grace, as Tom sifted through the rest of the cuttings.

'What's that?'

'What do you want to do with your life?'

'Wow. A big question then. Not just, can I have another cup of tea, please, Anna? Or what do you think of my cardigan, Anna? You're going straight to the big guns.'

'Are you trying to avoid answering it?'

'Maybe. A bit.'

'Come on, there must have been something you always wanted to do. Look at Tom – he always wanted to be a gardener, and that's exactly what he went and did. Well, after he got over wanting to be a burglar, of course, but we didn't encourage that one.' That got a grin from Tom, and Anna tried not to notice how attractive he looked when he wasn't scowling. 'And don't tell me it was to look after old farts like me for the rest of your life, Anna, because I know that can't be true.'

Anna smiled as Tom stood to refill their wine glasses. She hesitated a moment, her mind whirring, the words on the tip of her tongue. She loved her job as a carer but it hadn't been her dream when she was a child. When she was young, all the girls wanted to be a vet, a doctor, an air stewardess. What most of them ended up becoming was a shelf-stacker, a secretary or a housewife. Artistic dreams, creative dreams, such as the one Anna harboured, weren't understood, at least not at her school – or even in her house, much as her parents had tried. And, so, she'd become used to never talking about it, never daring to even dream about it, and to just stick to studying, the same as everyone else. But the urge had never quite left her.

'I wanted to be a painter.'

Grace raised her eyebrows, her mouth forming a perfect 'o'.

'And did you paint much?'

'I used to. As a teenager. I asked for an easel and canvas and paints for my fourteenth birthday and when I got them I couldn't believe it. I kept them in my bedroom, hidden away from everyone else. They were my pride and joy.'

'And did you ever get the chance to use them?'

'Most nights.'

'Were you any good?'

'I think so. At least, my art teacher, Mr Rowsley, told me I was. He even asked to speak to my mum and dad about it when I was a bit older, suggested I apply for art college.'

'But you didn't?'

Anna shook her head, remembering. 'No. Mum and Dad didn't really understand why I'd want to go to college to study something that wouldn't get me a job. It was so far off their radar that it might as well have been in space. But, really, they just couldn't afford for me to stay in education any longer, so I left and got a job at sixteen.' She sighed, remembering when Julia had left to go to university. Quite apart from the fact that she'd missed her best friend desperately, she'd been jealous too. Julia was getting to do what she wanted, but Anna had been forced to stay here, earn money. It had seemed so unfair.

Grace nodded thoughtfully. 'So, what happened to your painting?'

'I don't know. I suppose I started going out, having fun, meeting new people. I started temping, and then – well, then everything just got packed away, forgotten about.'

Grace nodded. 'And did you never want to start again, later?'

Anna frowned, thinking. 'I suppose I did, sometimes. Painting had always been a release for me. If I felt sad or worried, I painted. If I was happy about something, I painted. It was the way I expressed myself, and when I stopped, I did miss it. I missed the feel of the paintbrush in my hand, of the brush against the canvas, the satisfaction of something coming to life beneath my fingers.'

'And where are they now, the paintings you did?'

Anna smiled. Grace's journalistic instinct for asking too many questions had obviously never left her. 'I think Mum and Dad kept them in their loft, but I'm not sure.'

'I'd like to see them.'

'Would you?'

Grace nodded. 'I'd love to, if you'd like to show them to me.'

At that point Tom stood up, yawning. 'Sorry, I've got an early start tomorrow, I'd better get going.'

'OK, Thomas dear, see you tomorrow,' Grace said.

'Bye, Aunty Grace. Bye, Anna.'

Anna waited for him to leave before responding to Grace's suggestion.

'I don't know, Grace. I haven't seen the paintings in such a long time. They're probably awful.'

'And so what if they are?'

'I really don't know. I just don't think I'm ready to revisit all that again.'

Grace studied her for a moment, her frail hands clasped under her chin. 'I think you should show me some.'

'It's in the past now. What's the point, at my age?'

'Your age? Anna, you're a baby! You've got most of your life still ahead of you.'

Anna shrugged. 'I'm not sure.'

'Think about it. Think about how it used to make you feel when you painted. You said it yourself, you got a feeling of release as you brushed strokes onto the canvas. Why wouldn't you want that again?'

'But I haven't done it for so long. I don't think I'd know how to paint anymore.'

'I'm not suggesting you should run before you can walk. I'd just like to see some of these paintings of yours. Can't you indulge an old woman?'

Anna thought about it. She hadn't looked at her paintings for years. She'd forgotten about them mostly, tucked them up in the corner of her mind in the same way they'd been tucked away in a dusty corner of her parents' loft. Maybe she could dig them out, have a look at them, try to remember the Anna she used to be. The Anna who painted them before life got in the way. What could be the harm?

'OK. I'll go and see if I can find them and bring a couple over next time I come.'

'Thank you, Anna.'

* * *

Grace hadn't meant to push Anna as much as she did, but it had seemed important at the time. Now, with Tom and Anna both gone for the night, she sat in her favourite chair by the patio doors and looked out into the darkness of the garden wondering whether she'd done the right thing.

She'd always been like this. Pushy, her mother had called her. Determined was how she liked to think of it, but she knew she'd alienated people thanks to her stubborn streak. She hoped she hadn't done the same with Anna.

Outside the window the shadowy trees in the churchyard

beyond swayed in a gentle breeze, their black edges blurred against the navy night sky. As she stared out, mulling things over, a familiar tightness began in her chest and she closed her eyes, leaning her head back against the headrest. She tried to draw in air through her nose and down into her lungs but she couldn't seem to get enough, and soon her body crumpled forward and she let out an enormous hacking wheeze. As huge, agonising coughs wracked her body she thought how relieved she was that this hadn't happened when Anna and Tom were here. She knew they were both concerned about her, but she didn't want them to be. She just wanted to spend time with them both, before it was too late, and she had no desire for that time to be tainted by pity.

Finally the coughing subsided and, despite the lingering pain in her chest, Grace knew it was all over for now. She could breathe easily again.

Her thoughts turned to Anna and Tom. She'd had high hopes, tonight, that they might start to like each other at last. It would be good for them to have each other, when she was gone, and she'd hoped that being forced together over dinner might have broken down the wall that seemed to exist between them. But it hadn't worked. If anything, things seemed even more strained between them than they had been before. She just didn't understand it. How could two people she cared about so much dislike each other so intensely? It made no sense.

She did feel cross with Tom, though. She'd heard the way he spoke to Anna, the shortness of his answers, his curt, clipped tones every time he addressed her. It just wasn't him – he was usually so warm and open. She needed to get to the bottom of it, find out what he was playing at. Perhaps, if she could just convince him to be nice, Anna would begin to see what Grace saw in him and the two could finally start to be friends.

Or more?

Stop it, Grace. She knew Anna didn't want that, and she also knew that if Anna had even an inkling that she was thinking about it, she'd back off even more.

No, she'd just have to keep trying – and see if she could make them both see it for themselves.

In fact, she had an even better idea brewing. She just needed to convince the pair of them to join her.

Chapter Nine

Anna sighed. She knew Grace had been up to something – she'd been grinning at her ever since she arrived twenty minutes earlier. And then Tom had turned up and she'd finally revealed her plan.

'It's been an age since I went out of Lowestoft,' Grace said, looking from Tom to Anna and then back again from the comfort of her armchair throne. Her eyes were wide and innocent behind her glasses. 'Your uncle Roy and I used to love going to visit gardens before he got ill and I wondered whether you'd take me to one. Well, take us both to one – Anna and me.'

The corner of Tom's mouth curled up in a half-smile.

'How do you know I'm not working today, Aunty Grace?'

'Well, I don't. I'm just hoping you might be free.' She clasped her hands together under her chin to reveal her perfectly straight row of false teeth. 'Pleeeease? It's such a perfect day for it.' Anna had to hand it to her, she was crafty.

Tom shook his head in defeat. 'All right, Aunty Grace. I

was meant to be at work this afternoon but I'll call the guys. I'm sure they can cope without me for once.'

'Oh, thank you, Tom.' As Tom disappeared outside with his mobile clamped to his ear, Grace turned to Anna. 'And you will come too, won't you?'

'Do I have any choice?'

Grace straightened up indignantly. 'Of course you do. I just thought it might be nice.' Her voice sounded wounded and Anna relented.

'Well, you're in luck, Grace, because I don't have anyone else to see today so I'm free and I'd love to come.'

'Hurray!' Grace clapped her hands together like a child. In truth, she'd chosen today because she'd known they were both likely to be available, but it had still been a risk not to check with them first. She'd just been hoping that, being put on the spot, neither of them would feel able to refuse. It had worked like a dream.

Tom came back into the room. 'So, where do you want to go? Were you thinking of somewhere in particular?'

'I don't really mind, Thomas. You're the gardener, where's nice at this time of year?'

'Hmm, early July. I'd say our best bet would be Helmingham – but it's quite a drive. Do you think it might be too far?'

'Oooh, no, I love it there. What do you think, Anna? Fancy it?'

'If Tom says it's a good choice then I'm happy. I've never been.'

'Really? You've missed a treat. It's always beautiful – but the roses are my favourite.'

'Right, well, I'll just go and clear the rubbish out of the back of the car and we'll get going, shall we?' Tom said. He was still directing his words to Grace but Anna was sure she could detect a slight thawing towards her since they'd been out for Grace's birthday. He hadn't refused this outing, so that was a start at least.

'Shall I make some sandwiches?' Anna said, moving towards the kitchen.

'Oh, no, let's eat there. We don't want a load of sweaty rolls in the bottom of our bags, do we? My treat, of course.'

'If you're sure.'

'Sure about what?' Tom said as he came back into the room clutching two bags of tools and a pink rubber ring. Anna tried not to grin.

'Me treating you both to lunch today to say thank you.'

Tom raised his eyebrows. 'And whose idea was that?'

'Mine, dear, why? Who else's would it be?'

Tom gave a nod but didn't reply. Anna knew what he'd imagined – he thought she was after a free ride again. Well, she'd make sure she paid her own way today, whatever Grace said.

Twenty minutes later they were on the road. The sun streamed through the windscreen and in the back of Tom's car Anna wound the window down and let the warm air brush across her skin. She refused to let Tom's snarky attitude ruin her day. He needed to get over himself and accept that she and Grace were friends and that it meant nothing more than that.

Almost ninety minutes later they were parking the car, taking bags and Grace's stick out of the boot, and making their way into the gardens of Helmingham Hall. The sunshine had brought out the crowds and Anna and Tom stood either side of Grace, holding her elbows so she didn't get jostled about.

'I don't think we'll bother visiting the house in this weather, will we?' Grace said, rummaging around in her bag for her purse.

'No, I'd say the gardens are plenty for today,' Anna said. 'But I'll pay.'

'No, no, I insist. It was my idea, so it's my treat.'

Aware of Tom's eyes on her face, Anna shook her head. 'No, let me pay for us to get in. You can still buy lunch. Deal?'

Grace rolled her eyes. 'You are a stubborn little thing, aren't you?' she said. 'All right then, it's a deal. Thank you, Anna.'

Anna stepped forward to pay for the three of them. Suddenly Tom grabbed her elbow.

'You don't need to pay for me.'

She turned to face him. 'It's fine, Tom. You paid for dinner on Grace's birthday. I insist.'

Tom stood still for a moment, his eyes burning into hers as though he was trying to see right inside her mind. She felt her face turn pink but she refused to be the first to look away. If he was trying to intimidate her, it wasn't working.

Finally, he looked away and nodded. 'OK then. Thank you, Anna.' For the first time he smiled directly at her and she felt her face go from pink to red as she noticed again how handsome he was. What was *wrong* with her?

Inside the grounds the pathways were full of people, strolling, admiring the beautiful colours of the well-maintained gardens. Grace stopped for a moment, her hand on her chest.

'Oh!'

'Grace, what's wrong?' Anna felt her pulse quicken. Perhaps this was going to be too much for her after all.

'Nothing. Nothing at all,' Grace said, and Anna noticed she had a smile on her face. 'It's just – the last time I came here was with my Roy, and it's brought back a wonderful memory.'

'Uncle Roy really loved it here, didn't he?' Tom said. 'Do

you remember the time we came a few years ago and it poured with rain but even though we were drenched to the bone he refused to leave until he'd seen absolutely everything?'

'Oh, yes,' Grace said, her eyes damp. 'He was a silly old thing sometimes.'

'He was,' Tom agreed, grinning.

'So, where shall we go?' Anna peered at the map she'd been handed at the gate.

'Can we go and see the rose garden?' asked Grace.

'Yes, let's do that first,' Tom said, taking hold of her hand gently. Anna walked on the other side of Grace, ready to support her if she needed it. The tap of Grace's stick was muffled on the grassy paths.

'Oh, it's just as wonderful as I remember,' Grace sighed as they stepped inside.

'It really is beautiful,' Anna said, looking around in awe. In every direction she could see a riot of colour – purples and red and yellows and pinks, all different shades, bursting proudly from immaculate flowerbeds. Tom's face lit up as they stepped forward.

'This place was built in 1965,' he said, looking around in excitement. 'There are so many different species of rose here, including these Hybrid Perpetuals.' He pointed at a bright pink bloom and touched it gently, cradling it in his palm. He released it with care and turned to another one. 'This is a David Austin rose, I think, and look here –' He pointed at the flowers jostling for space in between the roses. 'These are foxgloves, and these ones here are Madonna lilies.' He smiled as something else caught his eye. 'Oh, look, they've got forget-me-nots too, Aunty Grace – you love those, don't you?'

'Ooh, I do, Tom, and how pretty they are!' Grace was so happy, but it was Tom that Anna was watching. She studied his face as he pointed out the flowers and saw in it a pleasure she hadn't witnessed in him up to now. He really was in his element here, in the gardens, among the flowers, and, clearly, he was not only knowledgeable but also passionate about his line of work. For the first time since they'd met, she found herself enjoying his company.

As they strolled round the rest of the garden Tom pointed out all his favourites until, finally, Grace announced that she was too exhausted to go any further.

'Can we go and get something to eat now?'

'Yes, let's get to the tea rooms before it gets too close to lunchtime and we can't get a seat,' Tom said, taking a gentle hold of Grace's elbow. Anna walked on Grace's other side, letting Tom take charge.

They made their way through the knot garden – 'This was built so you could see it properly from inside the house, from above,' Tom said, consulting his guidebook. He shook his head in wonder. 'The hours they must spend maintaining this place.'

'Imagine if you had a garden this big to work on,' Anna said as they entered the tea rooms. 'What would you change?'

Tom looked at her and frowned. 'I honestly don't know,' he said thoughtfully. 'It's pretty spectacular as it is; I don't think I'd ever be so bold as to want to change anything. But it would be fun to try.' He grinned and Anna smiled back, glad to have something to talk with him about for once.

As they ate their lunch Anna listened to the conversations around them and tried not to stare at Tom too much. It was early days, but today she thought she might just be beginning see what Grace had been on about all this time. Because today was the first time she'd had a conversation with Tom that wasn't awkward or strained, and she could see that, in fact, he could actually be quite pleasant.

Grace might have had an ulterior motive in getting them

together today, and while Anna wasn't interested in anything like that – and she was absolutely certain that Tom wasn't either – at least tensions had eased and the atmosphere between the two of them had thawed at last. And that, for one day, was enough of a success.

* * *

Back at home, as she pulled her nightdress over her head and climbed into bed, Grace couldn't help smiling to herself. She was pretty clever, even if she said so herself.

All right, so Tom and Anna had always been unlikely to fall wildly in love with each other over the rose bushes in just one day. No, Grace knew that these things took time. But she was playing the long game, and as far as she was concerned, today had been a roaring success. Finally, Tom had stopped behaving like the grumpy boy he always seemed to be around Anna, which meant that Anna could see for herself what Grace had been trying to tell her all this time.

And she'd noticed how Anna had looked at Tom as he'd shown them the flowers and shrubs around the garden. That had been her plan all along – to get Tom in a place that made him happy, that made him come alive, where he wouldn't be able to help himself.

And it had worked.

Chapter Ten

Standing at the top of the cliff by the North Beach, Anna let the wind whip her hair round her face like tentacles. The bracken swayed in the breeze but her body was rooted to the spot, her arms clenched tightly to her sides. The sea was slate-grey today and the sky almost as dark too as clouds gathered, racing each other across the huge open expanse. It felt wild up here, more like late autumn than the July day it was, and for the first time in as long as she could remember, her fingers itched to paint the scene in front of her. Grace had stirred up something that had lain dormant inside her for a very long time.

She'd run up here and now, looking out over the sea, she inhaled deeply to steady her breathing. She shivered, her light-weight jacket no defence against the brisk north-easterly coming off the sea. The run had cleared her mind after a restless night's sleep. She'd spent ages lying awake last night, thinking about Grace, and about Tom. She'd had a lovely day at the gardens with the pair of them even though she'd felt dread at spending all that time with Tom when Grace had made the suggestion. But she'd found she had enjoyed seeing him in his element, and it was true that she'd seen a different side of him at last.

But it was also true that he still seemed to believe that there was some hidden reason for her friendship with Grace other than the fact that they simply liked each other. There had still been the comments about her paying for things, or about Grace paying for her, and she couldn't forget them. It was also still clear that he wasn't keen on her looking after Grace when he was around, that he felt it was his job, not hers.

After getting home last night she'd wondered whether maybe she ought to take a step back and let Tom see that she wasn't trying to tread on his, or anyone else's, toes. But now she wasn't so sure if that was the right thing to do either.

Perhaps what she needed to do was step away completely. Maybe Tom was right. Maybe it *was* weird to strike up such a close friendship with someone so much older than her. Perhaps people were looking at the pair of them and wondering what on earth either of them was getting out of it.

She thought about her other friends. There was Julia, who she'd known since they were at primary school together and who she'd trust with her life. Julia was the one who'd lied for her when she almost got expelled for getting locked in the cellar of the school. She was the one who'd sprayed pink hairspray all over the boy who dumped her when they were in 4FG because he said her breath smelt funny, the one who'd brought her magazines and sweets when she broke her leg falling off the trampoline, who'd supported her when she was trying for IVF and her marriage was going down the drain. And there was Jenny, her best friend from work, with whom she'd spent many Friday nights out drinking cheap white wine and who seemed to lurch from one boyfriend crisis to another.

There were plenty of others, of course, but these were the people she counted among her closest, most important, friends. And she got everything she needed from them – along with her family.

But now there was Grace. How did she fit into all this? Anna hadn't expected to find a new friend at this stage in her life who meant so much, and she would bet everything she owned that Grace hadn't either. It had always felt as though the most important friendships were forged earlier in life, at important times – when you started school, when you got a new job. But perhaps that was just it. Perhaps she needed something more. Perhaps she needed what Grace had to offer. And the truth was, she couldn't imagine her life without Grace in it.

Lifting her arms above her head and breathing in deeply, Anna bent forward and stretched out her hamstrings. Why was life always so complicated? Why did it have to even be an issue that she wanted to be friends with someone who was more than fifty years her senior? Why should it matter?

As she started running back the way she'd come, back along the seafront towards home, she thought about Tom again. Until yesterday she'd just seen him as an irritant, someone to put up with if she wanted to spend time with Grace. But she'd already noticed how he was with Grace – so kind and thoughtful – and how much Grace thought of him, and she'd known there must be more to him. And yesterday, on their day out, she'd finally seen that for herself.

But there was something else too. Something she'd been trying to ignore, and possibly part of the reason she was so keen to make him like her – or at least dislike her a bit less. Tom was pretty good-looking. Not so drop-dead gorgeous you'd stop in the middle of the street and stare at him, but there was something in the tilt of his head when he spoke, the crease of his mouth when he smiled, the wonkiness of his eyebrows when he was cross that made her look twice.

She concentrated on her breathing – in, out, in, out – as she pounded the pavements, leaving the bracken-covered cliffs behind and passing houses now, running on past the water fountains next to the pavilion that were still at this time of day, just tiny pinpricks in the ground. It was still early, and as she reached the South Pier she decided to make a detour.

Taking a right turn just past the gardens, she ran at a right angle to the sea and along the familiar route, a route she'd been taking for as long as she could remember, and a few minutes later she arrived. She raised her hand to rap on the door and within seconds, as though she'd been standing on the other side waiting for her, her mum appeared.

'Oh, hello, love,' she said. 'Why didn't you use your key?'

'I've been out running, I don't have it.'

She nodded and stepped aside to let Anna in, then closed the door behind her. Anna followed her down the dark, narrow hallway to the kitchen, where the smell of bacon cooking made Anna's mouth water.

'You're just in time for breakfast, if you want some?'

'Please, I'm starving.'

Anna sat at the small table in 'her' chair – still hers even though she hadn't lived at home for almost twenty years. She studied the familiar kitchen as Angie scuttled around, pouring water into the teapot, cracking eggs into a pan, chopping mushrooms. The wooden cupboards that had been the height of fashion when they were installed in the nineteen-eighties were outdated, their brass handles tarnished and the worktop scratched. Considering how much her mum loved to cook, the kitchen was tiny. Anna couldn't help thinking about the huge kitchen she and Dan had in their empty house, and felt a pang of regret.

'Do you want a hand?' she asked, knowing her mum hated anyone getting in her way.

'No thanks, love, I'm fine,' she said, checking the bacon that was sizzling under the grill.

'Where's Dad?'

'I'm here.' Anna turned just as Bill reached out to ruffle her hair, a gesture that was meant as a sign of affection but had always infuriated her. 'What are you doing here at the crack of dawn, love?'

'It's almost nine o'clock, Dad.'

Bill shrugged, wrapping his dressing gown tighter round his belly and smoothing his thinning hair down. 'That's early when you're retired. Isn't it, love?' He ruffled Angie's hair too, then moved away quickly when she tried to swat his hand with the fish slice. It was a well-practised move and Anna grinned at the familiarity.

'Get out of my kitchen, William Snow.'

'Sorry, love,' Bill said, swiping a mushroom from the pan and making his exit before he could get swatted again.

'He gets right on my nerves these days,' Angie complained as she started serving bacon and eggs onto three plates. 'He's always under my feet.'

'Oh, come on, Mum, you love having him around more.'

Angie turned, her hair stuck to her face in the heat from the cooker. 'I most certainly do not! He's always just *here*, getting in my way. Forty years we've been married and I've always just got on with it, had my own routine. Now, if I want to go anywhere it's like twenty flippin' questions – where am I going, who with, how long will I be, can he come with me?' She sighed, sticking slightly undercooked toast in the toast rack and placing it on the table in front of Anna. 'You know I love him, but he's driving me mad.'

'Do you want me to take him out for the day?'

'Don't you spend enough time with old people?'

'Dad's not old! Well, not as old as the people I look after anyway. I can if you want. I'll ask him.'

'Yes, if you like, love. I doubt he'll go though. He spends most of his time either watching TV in his dressing gown or sitting at his computer buying endless rubbish off eBay. We've got a shed full of old bits of motorbike, broken lawn-mowers, rusty tools, spare bike tyres and Lord only knows what other junk. He needs a hobby apart from darts – something to keep him occupied during the day.' She plonked the three plates of bacon, egg and mushrooms on the table, along with bottles of ketchup and brown sauce. 'Bill, breakfast!'

Anna tucked in greedily, the kitchen alive with the sounds of tea being slurped and butter being spread. Bill arrived moments later and sat opposite her.

'How's work, love?' he asked her through a mouthful of bacon.

'Great thanks, Dad.'

'And how's it going with your friend Grace? Still seeing her a lot, are you?'

Anna nodded, her mouth full of toast. 'Mmmm. We've been on a few days out. And she's told me loads more of her amazing stories.'

'Oh? Like what?'

'All sorts. Her life during the war, her friends. A man she used to love. She's fascinating, you'd both love her.'

Her mum looked across at her. 'And is it just the two of you going on these trips? I mean, can you cope all right? She's pretty old, isn't she?'

'She's ninety-five, Mum, but you wouldn't know it. She's pretty sprightly for her age. But no, it's not always just the two of us. Sometimes her great-nephew comes along too. Tom.'

She felt her face flush as she said his name and took a sip of scalding-hot tea to mask it.

Too late. Bill had noticed and he gave Angie a look Anna didn't miss.

'Tom, eh? And what's he like, love?' said her Mum, trying to sound casual.

Anna shrugged. 'He's all right.'

'Just all right? Why?'

She sighed. 'Oh, I don't know. He seemed to take an instant dislike to me, seems to think I've got some sort of plan to take Grace away from him, stop her seeing him. They've always been really close. He's pretty rude to me most of the time actually.'

'Well, that just seems damn childish if you ask me,' Bill said, battling with a piece of bacon on his plate. He popped it in his mouth and chewed. 'Hope you've told him that.'

'Not really. It's a bit awkward. But Grace has made it clear she won't stand for it, so that's something.'

Bill nodded approvingly. 'Shame though – when you mentioned a young man you were hanging out with I was hoping he might be new boyfriend potential.'

'Bill!'

'What?' Bill looked back and forth between them both, a puzzled look on his face. 'I was only saying.'

'Anna's perfectly happy as she is, aren't you?'

'Yes, Mum, I am.'

'Although…' Angie paused, twisting a piece of toast round with her fingers. 'It would be nice if you did meet someone.'

'Oh, for goodness' sake, you two,' Anna said, her cutlery landing with a clatter on her plate. 'It's not even been two years. I'm hardly an old spinster. You both make it sound as though I've been hung out to dry.'

'I know, I know, we're sorry – aren't we, Bill?' Angie said, her words tumbling from her mouth. Bill nodded, his mouth stuffed with toast. 'I was just saying. Your dad and me – well, we just want what's best for you.'

'She's right. We do.' Bill swallowed. 'I'm sorry too though. I just heard the name Tom and I thought – well, you know what I thought. Never mind, ignore me.'

'OK, I will.' Deciding not to say anything more to save an argument, Anna drained her tea from her Arsenal mug – her dad's favourite, having never lost his love for his native London – and stood up. She'd been about to leave but then a thought occurred to her.

'I don't suppose my old paintings are still up in the loft, are they?'

'Of course they are, love, I'd never get rid of them.' Her mum peered at her. 'Why do you ask?'

'I just thought I might dig a couple out.'

'I packaged them all up in bubble wrap and brown paper because I was worried they were going to get damaged, so you'll have a job knowing which one's which.'

'I'll go and have a look.' Anna made her way upstairs and pulled down the stairs to the loft, then climbed up. The paintings were easy to spot, stacked in a row at the far end of the dimly lit space. She pulled a few out and started unwrapping them carefully. She wasn't sure which ones she wanted to show Grace. It had been so long since she'd looked at these paintings she couldn't picture them clearly anymore, but she hoped the right ones would leap out at her when she saw them.

An hour later she emerged with two hastily rewrapped paintings.

'Got what you need, love?' her mum asked from the kitchen doorway, an apron tied around her waist. The smell of scones filled the house, her mum seemingly unable to get through a single day without baking something.

'I think so.' She indicated the paintings. 'I forgot how many there were.'

'You loved painting when you were younger. Shame you never carried on.'

Anna nodded. She'd never criticised her parents for their lack of encouragement because they'd be heartbroken if they knew how it had affected her.

'I'm showing a couple to Grace – she asked to see them.'

'Oh, that's nice. I'm sure she'll love them.'

Angie paused, wrapping the tea towel she was holding round her hands. 'She obviously means a lot to you.'

Anna nodded. 'She really does, Mum.'

'Just promise me something.'

'What?'

'Don't get too attached. I mean, she won't be around forever and I'd hate to see you get your heart broken again.'

From the moment they'd met, Anna had tried not to think about Grace dying. Even though she was ninety-five, she was so full of life that it didn't seem possible all her vitality could be snuffed out just like that. But the thought was always lurking, like a ghost.

'Don't worry. Grace isn't going anywhere any time soon. And when she does – well, I'll be fine. I'll miss her but I'll always be glad I had her in my life, even if it wasn't for very long.'

Angie stepped forward and wrapped her arms around Anna. 'Now, let me give you some of these scones to take with you, otherwise your dad will scoff the lot.'

Ten minutes later Anna walked towards the front door, two paintings tucked under one arm and a plastic tub of still-warm scones in the other hand.

'Bye, Dad!' she called.

'Bye, love,' came her dad's voice over the theme tune of *This Morning*.

'Don't let him drive you too mad,' Anna said, kissing her mum on the cheek. 'And let me know when you want to get rid of him for the day and I'll take him out for you.'

And then she left, thinking about Grace and hoping she'd like the paintings Anna had picked out to show her.

* * *

'Screw him and the boat he sailed in on.' Julia's voice echoed round the flat as Anna clicked her onto speakerphone and propped the mobile on the table. She grinned. She could always count on Julia to spring to her defence.

'I knew you'd say that.' Anna tugged on her work trousers and slipped on her shirt.

'Well, it's true. You can't stop being friends with Grace just because Tom doesn't like it. He just needs to get over himself.'

'You're right, he does.'

'Anyway, what on earth does he think you're going to do, steal all Grace's money? Try to bump her off in her sleep?'

'Probably both of those things and more. You should see the way he looks at me sometimes, as though he's furious I'm even daring to be in the same room as him.'

'But he paid for your dinner at least, so he can't hate you that much.'

'I suppose so. And he was much nicer to me when we went to that garden. Almost friendly.'

'Are you sure he's not just secretly in love with you?'

'Well, who wouldn't be?' Anna felt her face flush at the suggestion and was glad Julia couldn't see her. She didn't even like this man; why was she blushing every time someone mentioned him?

'You never know,' Julia said now. 'People can be weird sometimes.'

'Being in love with me wouldn't be that weird, would it?'

'You know what I mean. Maybe he's just rubbish at chat-up lines.'

'That's an understatement.'

Julia chuckled. 'So, how's your search for Arthur going? You have started, right?'

'Of course. I wouldn't have dared ignore my instructions.'

'Good. So, what have you got to report?'

'Not much. I don't really know enough about him, so it's hard to know where to start.' She pulled her boots on. 'Anyway, I don't know what I'd do with the information if I did find anything out.'

'You'd tell Grace, wouldn't you?' Julia's voice sounded surprised.

'Well, no. I'm not sure that I would.'

'Why ever not? I was only kidding when I said you should do it behind Grace's back. You *have* to tell her if you find anything.'

'I'm only really doing this for me. And you, of course. But Grace has made it perfectly clear that she doesn't want to know anything about him, and I have to respect her wishes.'

'But that's probably just because she thinks there's no way of finding anything out. I bet she doesn't use the internet, does she?'

'Not that I've seen, no.'

'Well then.'

'Well then what?'

'Well, it's obvious, isn't it? You look, and probably find nothing. But if you do find something, you just tell her what you've found and explain you thought it was worth a go because things are easier these days.'

'She'd still be angry though. She told me she feels like she'd be betraying her late husband, Roy. I don't want to alienate her.'

'Well, it's up to you. My guess is that she'd be pleased, in the end. But it's not even worth worrying about until there's something to worry about.' Julia giggled. 'You know what I mean.'

'Not really, but I'll let it go.' Anna picked her phone up from the side. 'Listen, I need to go to work now. Are you still on for meeting us next week?'

'Definitely, it sounds great. Let me know when you'll be here.'

'Will do.'

Anna hung up and thought about the plans they'd made for next week. She was excited but nervous at the same time because she was taking Grace to meet Julia and she desperately hoped these two women who were both so important to her would get on brilliantly with each other.

Chapter Eleven

Anna took a sip of coffee and rubbed her eyes. Having exhausted all the possibilities in the search for Arthur the last time she'd tried, she was struggling to think where to start now, as she sat with her laptop open at the kitchen table. But she wanted at least to give it one last try.

Over the last few days, she'd been thinking about Arthur a lot, trying to imagine how she would feel if she'd been Grace – if she'd been left at the altar, humiliated. What Anna had gone through with Dan had been bad enough, but at least she knew what had happened. She knew where she stood. Poor old Grace had spent seventy years never knowing whether she was dumped because of something she'd done wrong or if there was another reason entirely that had been completely out of her hands. And it was that thought that had fuelled this one last late-night attempt to find out what had happened to Arthur.

Whether Grace would actually want to know was another matter entirely, but, in any case, Anna doubted that she'd even be able to find him; the chances of his being alive were minuscule. But there had to be something somewhere that would give her an indication of what might have happened to him at least. Because even though Grace's many years of being married to Roy had stamped down her curiosity about the past, it was clear to Anna that the memories were coming back strongly to Grace now, and she wanted to do something that might help give her friend some peace.

With that in mind, Anna pulled up some local newspaper websites. Unsure whether she'd have access to ancient archives, she again typed in the name *Arthur Robb* along with various search terms, including *Lowestoft, boats, Second World War, Grace Moran, St Peter and Paul Church* and *disappeared*. But still nothing. The trouble was, nobody seemed to have any idea where Arthur might have gone after he disappeared. The only thing Grace had said she was certain of was that he hadn't stayed in Lowestoft.

Anna frowned, trying to think back to the conversation she'd had with Grace about what had happened after the wedding that never was. She'd told Anna that she hadn't tried to find Arthur but that there had been a period of a few days, maybe more, when she'd been furious and had demanded answers from anyone and everyone. Anna closed her eyes and tried to tease out the memory, the seed of information she knew must be in there somewhere. Grace had stomped round to Arthur's parents' house, convinced they must know more about his whereabouts than she did. They didn't, but what had she discovered during those visits? She thought hard, sifting through the many stories Grace had told her over the last few weeks. What had Arthur's parents said? Had they said anything? She was sure they had, that there was something she'd forgotten. If only she could pin it down.

She poured herself a glass of wine, hoping the distraction would jog her memory.

And then, suddenly, realisation dawned.

It hadn't been Arthur's parents who'd said anything more – it had been one of his friends. She remembered, now, what Grace has said: '...*but apart from one person who said maybe he'd gone home to the North East...*'. The North East. Of England? Presumably. So that was where – Newcastle, Durham, Sunderland, Middlesbrough? Chances were it would be another dead end. But it had to be worth a try, didn't it?

Placing her wine glass down on the table, she typed in *Arthur Robb, Newcastle upon Tyne* and clicked search. Hundreds of entries came up immediately, including a couple of news stories from New Zealand and the boat builder she'd found before. But a quick scroll revealed nothing obviously helpful.

She went back to the search box and added in *Second World War*. Seconds later the page reloaded, and this time a news story a few entries down caught her eye. It was from the *The Chronicle* and was dated just a few months ago, 15 May 2018, and it seemed to be about a group of war veterans who were raising money. She clicked on it as she took another sip of wine.

Sun Shines for VE Day Celebration!

War veterans and their families raised hundreds of pounds for local charities with a special VE Day fête last week.

Selling cakes and homemade produce donated by family members, the residents of Bartlett Care Home in Jesmond, Newcastle upon Tyne, had a lovely day out in the sunshine in Jesmond Dene, where they held games and races for the children as well as a raffle with prizes donated by generous local businesses.

One resident, Arthur Robb, 95, said: 'We wanted to mark the 73rd anniversary of VE Day. We had a lovely day and we're glad we raised so much money for a good cause.'

Arthur Robb, ninety-five…

Her heart hammered as she read the article again. She clicked on the photo and zoomed in but it just got more and more blurry. And, let's face it, she'd only seen a photo of him from more than seventy years ago so she was hardly likely to recognise him anyway. But it was the first real glimmer of a breakthrough that she'd had and she couldn't help feeling a little bit excited. What if she *had* found Grace's Arthur? What would she actually do then?

She scoured the story once again. It really didn't tell her much at all, but it did at least give her somewhere to start. Taking a few notes – she hadn't bothered to get a printer set up in this flat – and emailing the story to herself, she smiled. This was quite thrilling.

She was about to close the laptop when she had another thought. There was someone else she had an urge to find out more about as well.

With a sense that she was doing something she ought not to be, she opened up Facebook and typed a name into the search box. A list appeared and her hands shook as she scrolled down, peering at the photos. There, three down, was the one she was looking for.

Tom Cross, Lowestoft.

Feeling like a naughty schoolgirl, she clicked on his profile. There was a photo of him with a little girl and she felt her heart contract. Who was she? She was sure Grace had never mentioned him having kids. In fact, no, she knew he didn't. Her heart unclenched a bit.

Why did she even care?

She scrolled down further, clicking on his photos as she went. There was a picture of him with some friends at a Norwich football match, some on the beach in his lifeguard shorts and T-shirt, one of him lined up along the sand with a group of tiny children, all beaming in the sunshine. Further down was a photo at the top of the Empire State Building dated four years ago. There were photos of gardens, and close-ups of plants, and one picture of Tom with a group of lads, arms wrapped round each other, all red in the face and grinning inanely as they held pints of beer. But there were none of him with women – at least, not women he appeared to be actually with. She smiled and sipped her wine.

What on earth was she doing? Grace might be convinced she and Tom were meant to be together, but there was absolutely no way she was anywhere near ready for anything approaching a relationship with anyone else, let alone with a man who so clearly seemed to dislike her, whatever Grace said in his defence.

She was about to close the page when a name caught her eye in the comments. She peered more closely at it and almost gasped. They had a mutual friend – Jenny! How did Jenny know Tom? Oh god, don't say they'd been out together. She wracked her brains, trying to remember what she'd told her colleague about Tom. Not much. Just that he was Grace's nephew and he wasn't very friendly. Jenny would never have known who she was talking about.

Filled with a sudden urge to know how well Jenny knew him, she typed out a text.

How do you know Tom Cross?

The message was read straight away and seconds later a reply popped up.

Tom? I don't really, he's just a friend of my brother's. Why?!!! J x

What should she say? How could she explain that she was cyberstalking someone she didn't even really like? Jenny would never believe her.

He's Grace's great-nephew – the one I told you about who doesn't like me. I had a nose at his profile on Facebook and saw you were friends.

A reply came back almost straight away.

Checking him out, were you?! You could do worse. Tom's a nice bloke. J x

Oh, great. Now Jenny thought she liked him too.

No, I don't like him! I was just being nosy – and DON'T tell him I asked!

She hoped Jenny believed her. The last thing she needed was for her to start going on about how wonderful he was too.

Closing the page and turning her mobile to silent, Anna grabbed her glass of wine and stalked through to the bathroom to run a long, hot bath and try to think about something other than Tom bloomin' Cross.

Chapter Twelve

The bell above the door tinkled as Anna pushed it open, and a wave of warm, doughy air hit her face.

'And Iiiiiiiii-I will always love yooooouuuuuu.' The singing was coming from behind the counter but Anna couldn't see anyone there.

'Hello?'

Suddenly a woman appeared like a jack-in-the-box from behind the doughnuts and pastries, her round face pink, strands of wiry hair poking out from beneath her hairnet.

'Oh, hello,' she said, her face splitting into a grin. ''Scuse my singing – I always get a bit carried away when I think no one's listening.' She leaned over and turned Whitney down a notch. 'What can I get you?'

Anna peered through the glass at the display of cakes and pastries, pies and buns. They all looked delicious.

'I'll take two blueberry and two chocolate muffins, please.'

She watched as the woman pinched the cakes with a pair of tongs and placed them into a paper bag. 'Anything else?'

'No, that's it,' Anna said, handing over her fiver.

'Well, thank you then, dear, hope to see you soon,' the woman said as Anna pulled the door open and left to the sound of the tinging bell and Shakin' Stevens being turned up.

Making her way back along the street to her motorbike, Anna found she was looking forward to their trip today and was relieved the sun had decided to shine on them.

She recalled Grace's pessimism as they'd discussed where they should go for their next outing – 'The trouble with this country is you can never plan anything because more often than not it gets rained off,' she'd said; 'I can't count the number of times I've stood shivering in a freezing, wet field over the years pretending to be having a good time.' 'Let's just risk it,' Anna had replied. 'Maybe we'll be lucky this time.' And Grace had had the last word with 'All right, but don't say I didn't warn you.'

Now, the sun was putting a smile on Anna's face, and she hoped Grace would be just as pleased, despite being proved wrong.

Hopping on her bike, she stowed the muffins in her rucksack and made her way to Grace's house, weaving carefully through the heavy traffic. During the winter you could get from one side of Lowestoft to the other in about fifteen minutes, but during the summer, when holidaymakers swarmed to the town, it took forever to get anywhere.

Finally, after a stop to wait for the swing bridge and a ten-minute queue at yet another set of traffic lights, she pulled up outside Grace's house and parked just inside the gates. She was surprised to see Tom's battered Passat sitting on the drive and tried to pretend she wasn't pleased about it as she walked into the kitchen.

'Sorry I'm late,' she called. 'The traffic was terrible.'

She was about to walk to the front room where she usually

found Grace, but a movement caught her eye as she passed the dining room and she paused and turned.

'Hello,' Grace said, flashing a lipsticked smile. Anna's heart melted. Grace was wearing a pale yellow blouse and a darker mustard jacket with navy blue trousers, and had tied a blue-and-yellow scarf round her neck. She'd obviously made an effort for their day out as her hair was set, and on her face she'd pressed some powder that was getting caught in all the crevices.

'You look lovely,' Anna said, planting a kiss on Grace's cheek as she went in.

'Thank you, dear, so do you. Doesn't she, Tom?'

Tom was sitting in the armchair by the window watching a chaffinch peck at the bird feeder. He turned his head slowly and nodded. 'She does.' Then he turned back to the window.

Grace raised her eyes to the ceiling. 'Are we ready to go? I've been so looking forward to this.'

Tom stood and picked his car keys from the table. 'I'm ready.' Oh, so he was joining them then.

'Me too.' Anna tried not to look at Tom as they walked to the car. What if he could tell from his Facebook page that she'd been looking at his profile? Or, worse, what if Jenny had told him she was asking about him? She'd look like some kind of stalker. Besides, she wouldn't want him to think she was even the slightest bit interested in anything he was doing.

Tom helped Grace into the front passenger seat and Anna climbed into the back again, next to the gardening paraphernalia. She moved a trowel out of the way before it poked her in the bottom, took Grace's stick from Tom, and then a minute later they were pulling out of the drive and setting off into the busy traffic once more.

'What time is the boat ride booked for?' Grace said over her shoulder.

'Ten,' Anna replied, glancing at the clock.

'Oh, we should be fine then. Shouldn't we, Tom?'

Tom peered at his sat nav. 'Yeah, we've got plenty of time.'

Satisfied, Grace sat back in her seat and watched the world go by. Anna did the same. It was preferable to attempting conversation with Tom, who seemed to have forgotten the nice time they'd had the other day and had gone back to being his usual sullen self. *Could* he have found out she'd been checking him out online? Surely not.

Feeling her face flame at the thought, she stared out of the window. People eager to stake their piece of sunshine before the crowds arrived were already making their way from B&B to beach laden down with mats, towels, buckets, spades and rubber rings. One poor man, dressed in shorts, socks and sandals, looked as though he needed a small donkey to carry everything while his unburdened wife hustled a gang of children along behind him. The town came to life on days like this, but Anna had to admit she preferred it when it was quieter, when the air was cooler and people stayed away. And then there were the days when the clouds hung over the beach like enormous chandeliers, when she felt as though she was the only person left here, as though she had the town to herself. Those were the days she liked best.

Forty minutes later they pulled up at Everitt Park. There was still half an hour before they needed to board the boat so they made their way past the playground and coffee shop to the bank of benches lined up along the waterfront, Grace's stick tapping on the concrete path like a metronome keeping time.

'Who'd like a muffin?' Anna offered as they sat down, pulling the slightly battered-looking paper bag from her rucksack.

'Ooh, me,' Grace said, picking out a blueberry one. She

took a bite and then frowned. 'What are these things?' she demanded, holding it up for inspection.

'They're blueberries, Grace. Surely you've had a blueberry before?'

'Well, of course I have, but never in a *cake*. Who'd do that?'

'Don't you like it?'

'I'm not sure yet, I'll need to have another bite.'

Anna grinned and passed the bag along to Tom, who chose a chocolate-chip muffin and took a huge bite as though he hadn't eaten for a week. The three of them sat in a row and watched the seagulls flap across the choppy water and the boats come and go behind the bank of reeds that danced in the breeze directly in front of them, not saying a word.

Half an hour later they were on the boat, swaying gently as they prepared to depart. Grace was sitting at the front next to Tom, and Anna was just across the aisle. The sun streamed through the window, making it feel slightly too hot. Anna shuffled uncomfortably.

'I can't wait to meet Julia,' Grace said.

'She can't wait to meet you either. I've told her so much about you.'

'Have you? I can't imagine there's very much to tell.'

'Oh, there's plenty, Grace, don't you worry.'

Beside Grace, Tom was still ignoring Anna, so she decided to annoy him by speaking to him directly.

'Was it hard to get the day off, Tom?' she said.

He turned slowly to face her. 'Not really. One of the joys of working for yourself – you can pay other people to do the work for you sometimes.'

'And no kids to teach?'

'No. That's only a couple of times a week.'

'Well, it's great that you could come with us,' Anna said, not meaning a single word. With him in this mood she would've much preferred it to have just been her and Grace, as they'd planned. Tom's presence was making her feel on edge. It was almost as though the day at Helmingham Hall Gardens had never happened.

'I thought it would be nice to spend the day with Aunty Grace,' he said. 'I didn't realise we were meeting your friend.'

'I told you about that all along,' Grace said, giving his thigh a gentle slap.

'Well, I must have forgotten.'

'You'll like her, she's lovely,' Anna said. 'Lovelier than me, anyway.'

'I doubt that,' Grace said, while Tom said nothing. Oh, screw him and the boat he came in on, Anna thought, grinning as she remembered Julia's words from the other day. She couldn't wait to see what her feisty friend would make of him.

Finally the boat pulled away from the quay and started chugging its way across the Broad. Anna looked out over the estuary as they drifted along, the sound of the engine and the chatter of people around them making it unnecessary to make idle small talk. The sun was still shining bright, with only the odd puff of cloud in the sky, and it sparkled on the water like diamonds. Every now and then a bird dived down just beneath the surface and swooped back up with its catch, soaring high into the azure sky. Anna was glad they'd decided to take this trip and she was determined, even if Tom continued to be rude and sullen, that she was going to enjoy it.

Behind them Anna heard the cry of a baby, and a repetitive thumping on the wooden floor as a toddler, presumably, ran up and down the aisle. A movement at Anna's elbow made her turn. A small boy in a red T-shirt and blue welly boots was holding out a bag to her.

'Want a seetie?'

'Oh, thank you, sweetheart, but you keep them,' Anna said. She turned to see his mother watching them, shaking her head. 'Sorry, he likes to chat to everyone,' she said. 'Come here, Oscar.'

The boy toddled back to his mum and Anna's eyes lingered on him as he went.

She jumped at the warmth of a hand on her arm and turned to find Grace looking at her.

'Everything all right, Grace?' she said.

'I'm fine. Are you?'

'Me? Yes, I'm good. Why?'

Grace shrugged and gave her arm a light squeeze before pulling her hand away. 'I was just watching you, with that little boy.'

'Oh?'

'After what happened with Daniel, do you feel sad – about not having children?'

'Oh,' Anna said again, taken aback at the blunt question. Most people skirted round the issue with her, knowing instinctively that it was a subject to be avoided. And she was glad, usually. But something about Grace's manner made her feel differently, and she found herself not minding at all.

'Yes, I do sometimes. But I usually try not to worry about it too much because there's nothing I can do about it anyway.'

Grace nodded and continued to study her. Anna avoided her gaze, staring down at her hands in her lap. She didn't know what else to say.

'I understand perfectly. It's tough, when the decision is taken out of your hands, isn't it?'

Anna looked up, confused. 'Did you ever want children then, Grace?' Anna had always assumed that Grace's choice not to have children was something she and Roy had decided together rather than something that had been decided for her.

'Yes, I did, once. But it wasn't to be.'

Unsure whether to push her, Anna waited. Eventually Grace looked up and turned to Tom, who'd been ignoring the conversation up till now. 'You won't know this either, but your uncle Roy and I always wanted children of our own. But something happened when I was younger that meant it could never be.'

'Really?' Tom said, angling his body round so he was facing them both. 'What?'

Grace sighed and looked out of the window, her mind clearly stuck somewhere in the past. Tom was staring at Anna now, she noticed, but when she caught his eye he looked away quickly. She wondered what he'd been thinking, whether he was blaming her once again for making Grace recall these painful memories.

After a long few moments, Grace started to speak. 'As you know, I worked at *The Lowestoft Journal*, and I loved that job. I started out just typing up letters and making cups of tea, answering the phone, but soon I started doing more and more for the editor, Samuel Harding. Oh, he was a lovely man, Samuel. Tall and broad, with wild red curls, always wore his waistcoat undone, and polished his shoes to the highest shine.' She smiled. 'It was one of the first things I noticed about him, actually.' Anna recalled Grace mentioning this editor once before and hinting at some kind of 'special friendship', but she kept quiet and waited for her to carry on talking.

'Anyway, I sat just outside his office and watched the reporters running around the newsroom, cigarettes dangling from their mouths, notepads in hands as they chased stories, and I desperately wanted to be doing their job. I was pretty sure I could do it better than most of them too.'

She continued, straining to make herself heard over the noise of the engine. 'Then, one day, I got my chance. And it was all thanks to Samuel. He called me into his office and I thought he was just going to give me some pages to type up or ask me to dictate a letter. But he told me he'd been observing me and thought I'd make a fine reporter. Well, you can imagine how thrilled I was – this was the chance I'd been waiting for!

'He gave me my first story – the one I showed you, about the terrible flooding that was going on that year – and I spent hours on that thing, chopping and changing it, fretting as I tried to perfect it. I so desperately wanted to impress him, to prove to him that he'd been right to take a chance on me.

'I worried myself silly about that story, but it was all for nothing as it turned out, because was so happy with it he ran it word for word, and he gave me more and more stories from then on.

'Some of the lads in the office weren't best pleased – they didn't think it was the sort of job a woman should be doing, I suspect – but I didn't care. I'd got the job of my dreams, writing stories. I never once suspected there was anything more to Samuel giving me the job than the fact he thought I was capable. And, to be honest, I was damn good at it – better than most of the old hacks who'd been doing it for years and had got lazy, if I say so myself.'

Grace stopped, her voice catching in her throat, and coughed violently. Her shoulders shuddered back and forth with each cough that shook her body until she seemed to be turning in on herself with the effort.

Anna looked to Tom for help but he just shrugged, a look of panic on his face.

Slowly, Grace's coughing started to subside and Tom wrapped his arm around her shoulders, pulling her towards him gently.

'Aunty Grace, how long has your cough been this bad?'

Grace shook her head. 'Oh, it's nothing, just a tickle.'

'That's more than a tickle,' Anna said leaning forward. 'Please tell me you've been to the doctor's about it?'

'No, no, it's fine. It's nothing to make a fuss about, really.' She pushed herself away from Tom and sat bolt upright as if to prove she was right as rain.

'Aunty Grace, it sounded terrible. You have to go and see the doctor about it. Promise me you will.'

'Yes, all right, don't nag. I will go, but I already know what he'll say – it's just a little chest infection. I get them all the time and they go, in the end.' She held up her hand to stop any objections. 'But I'll call him, I promise.'

She wiped her eye with a tissue and tucked it back into the sleeve of her blouse, then clasped her hands in her lap. 'Now, where was I?'

'You were just telling us about your job as a reporter,' Anna said.

'Oh yes. Well, anyway. As I was saying, I was good at the job, and happy doing it. I loved seeing people's faces when they noticed a woman doing what they considered to be a man's job.

'Then, one evening, about a month later, after everyone else had gone home, Samuel called me into his office. He asked me to sit down and offered me a drink. I was surprised, to say the least, but accepted his glass of whisky without questioning it. Well, you didn't, did you?'

Anna leaned forward again, wondering where this was going and what it had to do with Grace not being able to have children. But it almost didn't matter. She loved hearing

Grace's stories and could have listened to her telling them all day.

'Then something most unexpected happened. He gave me my drink and then, rather than return to the other side of the desk, he perched on the desk right in front of me and brushed his leg against mine. I felt ever so uncomfortable, wondering what he was up to.

'He told me he thought I was doing a sterling job, and then he leaned forward and breathed whisky on me. He smelt like Father, warm and familiar. He was so close I could see the bright green of his eyes, and the tiny veins that had broken out on his nose. And then he kissed me.' She glanced at Tom to see his reaction but he was just as engrossed in the story as Anna and didn't even flinch.

'I should have pushed my chair away, run out of the office screaming. But I didn't. It actually felt quite nice, and I was flattered. I won't go into too much detail because you wouldn't want to hear all that, but suffice to say we became close that day, and over the next few weeks we had more late-night meetings, and became closer.' She looked at Anna coyly. 'You know what I mean?'

Anna nodded, eager for Grace to continue.

'Well, it went on for several months. He was married, of course, so we kept it secret, although I'm sure there were more than a few people who suspected there was something going on between us. But for the first time since Arthur had jilted me, I was happy.' She sighed.

'And then something happened.'

She paused, pain etched on her face. Anna held her breath.

'I missed my monthly. And then another one. I started throwing up in the toilets every morning before work. I was scared. How could I tell Samuel I was pregnant? But I had to. And I suppose I hoped deep down that he'd tell me he'd leave his wife and marry me, or at the very least help me out, be there for me.

'So, I told him, right there and then in the office. I'll never forget the look on his face. He went white as a sheet and stood still for several seconds, not speaking. And then he just said "I'll help you deal with it". I knew exactly what he meant, and my heart felt as though it had snapped in two. He meant he'd help me get rid of it, as though it was some irritant you could just pretend had never happened.

'It wasn't what I wanted but I didn't have any choice. Without Samuel's support, without my job, I wouldn't be able to bring up a baby on my own. Not to mention the disgrace of it.' She looked at Anna, her eyes seeming to plead for forgiveness. 'So, I agreed.'

Silence fell for a few moments, only disturbed by the odd rustle of sandwich wrappers and the quiet mumble of voices as the boat chugged along. Outside the window the horizon rose and fell, rose and fell, and inside the seconds ticked by.

'So, you see, that's what happened. Samuel paid for me to have an abortion – which, as I'm sure you know, was not all that in those days. They were awful, actually, brutal. But I survived, and a few days later I was back at work.

'I felt empty for weeks afterwards. For months. The thought of the baby I'd got rid of never deserted me, and I was left with a terrible pain every single month that almost sent me to my bed. But it was what it was. I couldn't change it, so I tried to forget about it and just get on with things. I worked hard, and Samuel even offered me a promotion, which I took. I knew he felt guilty – he wasn't a bad man – but he was never going to leave his wife, and that was that.

'It wasn't until a few years later, when I met Roy and we married and started trying for a baby, that I realised how much that decision had changed my life. A pregnancy never happened for us, and in the end we just stopped thinking about it and got on with our lives without a child.' She shrugged. 'What else can you do?'

Anna let out a breath of air and wiped away a tear. She could imagine what Grace had been through. She'd been unable to have a child herself – but it must have been even worse for Grace, never knowing whether it was something she had done to herself that ruined her chances or whether it would never have happened anyway. How could she not blame herself?

'Oh, Grace, I'm so sorry,' Anna said, taking hold of her papery hand.

'It's all right, dear, it was a long time ago.' She turned to Tom. 'Besides, I'm lucky that I've got such a lovely big family anyway. I don't need children of my own to feel happy – I had Roy, and my nieces and nephews, and great-nieces and-nephews. I had everything I needed, in the end.' She held Tom's hand with her free one and the three of them sat like that, linked together, thinking about Grace's words, until the silence was broken by an announcement over the tannoy: 'We will be arriving in Beccles in approximately ten minutes' time.'

'Oh, good grief, look at me talking all this time. I've hardly even looked out of the window,' Grace said.

'It's all right, Aunty Grace, we've still got the way back. Anyway, I'm glad you shared that story. I've never heard it before.'

'Well, no, it's not something I talk about much, as you can imagine. But for some reason I'm being bombarded by memories wherever I go at the moment.'

'Well, just don't go making yourself feel too sad,' Anna said, standing as the boat came into dock. 'These days out are meant to be making you happy, not morose.'

'Don't you worry about me, I'm fine. Besides, it's good to

talk about the past sometimes – especially when you know you haven't got much of the future left.'

'Aunty Grace, don't be so morbid!'

'Oh, it's all right. When you're both as ancient as me you'll find you've completely come to terms with dying. It is what it is.' She sneaked a look around her. 'Besides, I'll probably outlive some of these old duffers on here.'

The three of them chuckled as they made their way off the boat and onto the quayside. The sun was warm now and Anna felt hot in her denim jacket. She pushed her sleeves up and slid her sunglasses down from her head. From behind the safety of them she watched Tom as he helped Grace walk up the path towards the restaurant where they'd agreed to meet Julia. He was so gentle with her, so patient. She'd seen the concern on his face as Grace was telling them her story. Maybe there really was more to him than she'd seen so far. And maybe today was the day she'd find out for sure.

* * *

'Julia, this is Grace; Grace, this is my best and oldest friend Julia,' Anna said as they arrived to find Julia already waiting for them at a table overlooking Beccles Quay.

'Julia, it's absolutely lovely to meet you,' Grace said, holding out her hand. 'Although I'm afraid Anna's wrong, because I'm most definitely her oldest friend by a country mile, I'd say.'

'Lovely to finally meet you too, Grace,' Julia said, standing and taking hold of Grace's hand for a moment. 'And I'm more than happy to let you have that honour.'

Julia remained standing as everyone sat down, then turned towards Tom and stuck out her hand, bracelets rattling on her wrist. 'You must be Tom,' she said smiling. 'Anna's told me lots about you too.'

Anna felt herself blushing, fully aware that Tom would know exactly what she might have said about him to her closest friend. She watched nervously as Tom took hold of Julia's hand and shook it.

'Nice to meet you,' Tom said, then dropped her hand and turned his attention to the menu in front of him.

Julia caught Anna's eye and gave her a wink as she sat down and picked up her own menu. Anna grinned back.

With lunch ordered, a silence fell upon the table. Sun streamed through the huge windows and high up a wasp buzzed determinedly, trying to get back outside into the fresh air. Julia swatted at it lazily every time it came near.

'So,' she said, turning to Grace. 'I hear you've been spending more time with my best friend than I have recently.'

Grace's eyes opened wide. 'Have I? Oh…' she trailed off.

'I'm only kidding,' Julia said. 'And, actually, it's good because you can tell me how she is – she hardly ever remembers to ring me these days.' She cast a glance over at Anna, who stuck her tongue out. Opposite Anna, Tom sat watching a boat scull slowly past on the River Waveney, leaving a ripple in its wake.

'Oh, I'm sure that's not true, dear,' Grace said, taking a sip of water and patting her lipsticked mouth with the napkin. 'Anna's told me all about you, and I must say it sounds as though you have a marvellous friendship. It makes me realise how much I miss all my old friends.' She sighed. 'They're all dead now, of course.'

'I'm so sorry, that must be awful. I can't imagine what it's like when your friends start dying on you.'

'Well, it's very inconsiderate, that's what it is.' Grace smiled, a trace of pink lipstick on her teeth. 'But I'm lucky that I found Anna when I did and that you're happy to share her with me. Quite frankly, I don't know what I'd do without her.'

Beside Grace, Tom cleared his throat and turned back to the table. 'You've always got me too, Aunty Grace.'

'Of course I have, Thomas dear,' Grace said, laying her hand gently on Tom's bare forearm. Anna noticed the fine hairs that shone golden in the sun and looked away quickly, but not before Julia saw her looking and raised her eyebrows at her across the table. 'But it's always nice to have a friend as well as family to call special, particularly at my age. I'm lucky to have you both.'

'Thank you, Grace. I'm lucky to have you too,' Anna said, her heart swelling at Grace's words.

Grace cleared her throat and looked around. 'Now, what does a woman have to do to get a glass of wine around here? I'm parched.'

'Allow me,' Julia said, filling Grace's glass up with sauvignon blanc from the bottle they'd ordered that had been sitting untouched on the table. Anna kept her eyes fixed on her friend as she poured out the drinks, desperate not to catch Tom's eye. She'd picked up on the undertone of his remark just now and she didn't want him to think for one moment that she was trying to replace him. She also hoped he hadn't noticed her staring at him before.

Grace's voice interrupted her thoughts as she held her glass high in the air.

'Thank you to both of you,' she said, looking from Tom to Anna. 'You've been my rocks. Cheers.'

They all clinked their glasses together and Anna realised, as the sun rose higher in the sky and the clouds scudded across the pale heavens, that this was the happiest she'd been in a long time.

And it was mainly thanks to the ninety-five-year-old woman sitting across the table from her.

* * *

As she slowly chewed her piece of fish, Grace couldn't help a feeling of satisfaction wash over her.

She was pleased that Anna and Tom were getting on a bit better. They were hardly love's big dream, but it was clear they both liked each other – at least, it was to her, and she was fairly sure Julia thought the same too. She'd seen the way she'd raised her eyebrows at Anna just now, and she'd certainly seen Anna staring at Tom with that look in her eye, even though she thought no one had noticed.

She also liked Julia a lot. She was a sharp girl, that one. And she might just be a good ally to have too.

She took another sip of wine and tuned back in to listen to Julia telling her about her husband, Al. Maybe there was hope after all, with Julia on side.

* * *

Dinner eaten, they headed out to the nearby park to get some fresh air. As they passed the playground, Grace lowered herself onto a bench.

'I'm pooped,' she said, resting her stick against the wooden seat. 'You lot carry on; I'll just wait here for you. Legs this ancient don't like to walk too far.'

'Are you sure, Grace?' Anna asked.

'It's all right, I'll stay with you,' Tom said, sitting next to her and stretching out his long legs in front of him. The bottom of his legs, exposed below his cargo shorts, were tanned, Anna noticed, then wondered why she had. She looked away.

'We could go back if you like,' she suggested.

But before anyone could answer, Julia linked her arm through Anna's. 'Do you mind if we just take a little stroll along here and back, work off a bit of that lunch?'

'Of course not. Take your time, we're all right here, aren't we, Thomas?'

'Course we are.'

'There you are then – off you go.' Grace shooed them away and, as they walked off, Anna felt like a rebellious schoolgirl escaping from the grown-ups.

'I'm glad I've got you on your own for a few minutes,' Julia said as they strode arm in arm along the riverbank. A small boy was feeding the ducks, throwing in huge chunks that floated on the surface for them to peck at.

'Why's that?'

'A number of things.' Anna could hear the smile in her friend's voice and turned to look at her.

'What's wrong with you, Julia?'

'Oh, I don't know. Could it be something to do with a certain man who joined us today?'

'Tom? What about him?'

Julia stopped dead, pulling Anna back by the arm. 'You didn't tell me he was so good-looking,' she hissed.

'What? What are you on about?'

'Don't act all innocent with me, young lady. And don't pretend you haven't noticed that he's tall, dark and handsome.'

'Oh, come on, Jules! I've told you how rude he's been to me and how he's made me reconsider my whole friendship with Grace because he's been such an arse, and now, just because you think he's good looking, all that doesn't matter?'

Julia linked her arm back through Anna's and dragged her

further along the path. 'I'm not saying it doesn't matter. I'm just saying it changes things a bit, that's all.'

'Why – because if he was an arse that looked like Quasimodo then he would definitely be an arse, but someone with a handsome face and nice legs can't be rude and arrogant?'

'Aha, so you do think he's handsome.'

'Oh, shut up. You know what I'm saying.'

'I do. And do you know what else? I think there's more to this than meets the eye.'

'You do, do you?'

'Yup. That's my professional opinion.'

'Professional what – busybody?'

'No, matchmaker.'

'Oh, come off it, Jules. I'm not interested in Tom bloody Cross and he's certainly not interested in me. He's made it perfectly clear he can hardly stand to be in the same room as me.'

'Ah, but that's where I think you're wrong, you see. I think that shows that he absolutely does like you.'

Anna rolled her eyes and didn't answer.

'I know you're rolling your eyes, Annie, but it's true. I saw him looking at you over lunch, and it definitely wasn't hatred in those eyes of his. And anyway, didn't you say he was much nicer to you when you went to that garden the other day? You're obviously starting to have an effect on him.'

'I don't think that's true at all, Jules. I think it was more that he was so happy in the gardens showing off his knowledge. I doubt his good mood that day had anything to do with me being there. Quite the opposite, in fact.'

'Don't be so daft. You'll see.' She stopped again and turned them both back the way they'd just come, the sun now shining in their eyes. 'I bet you've Googled him, haven't you?'

Anna felt her face flush and looked away.

'I knew it! So, come on then, spill – what did you find?'

'Not much. On Facebook there were some pictures of him with friends. He likes holidays and he spends a lot of time on the beach. That was about it.'

'And there was no girlfriend, no wife, I take it.'

Anna shook her head. 'Grace already told me he was single. She's as bad as you.'

'It's only because we care,' Julia said. 'Anyway, you've proved it now.'

'Proved what?'

'That you like him. You don't go looking people up on Facebook if you're not at least a little bit interested in their lives.'

'It's only because he's so important to Grace.'

'Yeah, right. I've known you for a long time, remember.'

'How could I forget?'

They strolled along a little further, boats slipping by on the river beside them.

'Oh, I forgot to tell you, me and Al are renewing our wedding vows,' Julia said.

'Jules, that's brilliant!'

She shrugged. 'I think it's a bit silly, really. I mean, he knows I love him – I don't know why we need to prove it to anyone. But we've been married for ten years now and Al was really keen.'

'I think it's a lovely idea. When's it happening?'

'A few weeks. I'm not sure.' She turned to Anna, a smile twitching the corner of mouth. 'Maybe you could bring Tom.'

'Julia!'

'Sorry.' She smirked as they continued along the riverside path. Ahead, Grace and Tom were still sitting on the bench where they'd left them, tiny specks slowly getting closer and closer.

Suddenly Anna stopped and pulled her arm away. 'I've just remembered something else I need to talk to you about before we get back.'

'What? Is it about boys again?' Julia grinned.

'Shush. No, it's about a man. A very old man, actually. I think I might have found Arthur.'

'What? No way! And he's still alive?'

'Well, I don't know, but if it is him then he was definitely still alive in May because he was quoted in a newspaper article.'

'And?'

'And what?'

'Have you tried to actually find him?'

'Well, no, not yet. That's what I wanted to talk to you about.'

'Go on.'

'He lives in a care home in Newcastle.'

'Up north Newcastle?'

'Yep.'

'So, what's the problem?'

'Well, I don't know whether I should. Try to find him, I mean.'

'After finding him alive? I'd say that the fact a ninety-something-year-old man that you're looking for is still living and breathing is a sign you most definitely should try to find him!'

'I knew you'd say that.'

'Well then, glad to be of service.' She gave a little bow.

'But that's not the point. What would I be trying to achieve, if I actually managed to speak to him? It's not as though Grace even asked me to find him. So, what, I find him and say "I know a woman you jilted more than seventy years ago. Oh, but she doesn't want to talk to you"?'

'You can decide that if you get that far. But you *have* to at least give it a go, don't you?'

'You're only saying that because you're so nosy.'

'So? Are you saying you're not?'

'Well, no. I would like to speak to him, find out what happened. But what then? Would I tell Grace? Or would I have to keep it a secret from her for the rest of her life?'

'I don't know, Anna, only you can decide that. But promise me you'll at least give it a go.'

Anna sighed. 'I don't know, Jules. I might. I'll think about it.'

She linked her arm back through Julia's and they continued on towards Grace and Tom.

Grace beamed when she saw them approach. 'Hello, you two. Nice walk?'

'Lovely, thanks,' they both said together.

'We were just watching the ducks,' Grace said, pointing at the ducklings waddling across the grass behind their mother like a regiment of soldiers.

'Well, I was watching them. Aunty Grace was watching the backs of her eyelids.'

'Oi, Thomas, don't give me away,' Grace said, tapping him on the arm. 'I was just resting my eyes.'

'Let's get back to Lowestoft before we all fall asleep,' Anna said, holding her arm out for Grace to take.

'Good idea.' Grace pulled herself upright and picked up her stick. 'It was so wonderful to meet you,' she said clasping Julia's hand between her own tiny ones. 'You remind me of my best friend Susan, although you've got much better hair – hers was always so frizzy, looked like a loo brush every time it rained.'

'Bet she didn't have such good products as me,' Julia said, pulling the old woman gently into a hug. 'You should see me without my straighteners.' She pulled away and held both of Grace's hands. 'I can see why Anna thinks so much of you.'

'I could say the same about you.'

And then Anna, Grace and Tom walked off, leaving Julia to wave them goodbye as their boat pulled away from the quayside and headed back towards Oulton Broad.

Chapter Thirteen

The sunset was spectacular from Anna's tiny kitchen window, streaks of pink, orange and yellow creating silhouettes of buildings and trees and settling a sodium glow across the town. She drummed her fingers on the table, a cup of tea cooling next to her. Her head hurt and she was exhausted but she felt happy after a lovely day out.

Grace had fallen asleep on the boat back to Lowestoft, so when they arrived Anna and Tom had agreed that he should take her straight home and Anna go back to her flat – she had to go and freshen up anyway as she'd arranged to meet Jenny and the others at the pub later.

'Thanks for a wonderful day,' Anna had said, planting a kiss on Grace's sleepy cheek.

'Thank you both,' Grace said with a yawn as she climbed into the car, leaving Tom and Anna standing in the car park.

'Thanks for arranging this,' Tom said, staring at his feet. 'I think Aunty Grace enjoyed herself.'

'No problem. Thanks for driving us.'

Tom nodded, then ducked into the driver's seat and drove

off with Grace already sound asleep in the passenger seat beside him.

Anna had walked home from the car park, enjoying the warmth of the late-afternoon sun on her face and the cool breeze from the North Sea. As she walked, she'd thought about what Julia had said, about looking for Arthur. She still wasn't sure it was a good idea. What would be the point? But the trouble was, Julia was right – she *was* nosy and she did really want to see if she could find out what had happened all those years ago, because she cared a lot for Grace and knew that she had been dwelling on the past lately. And now Anna might just have a chance to put her mind at rest.

As she'd got nearer to home, twisting down streets of Victorian houses and getting closer to the sea, her thoughts had turned to Tom. She couldn't help replaying in her head what Julia had said about him watching her, about how he hadn't looked as though he hated her but rather as though he might quite like her. She'd been trying very hard not to think about how handsome he'd looked as he'd driven away, or the slight smell of salt water he gave off whenever he was near. Because what would be the point in that either?

And now, she was poised, laptop open, trying to decide what to do. Should she email the care home where Arthur lived to find out whether it was indeed Grace's Arthur, or should she just leave it?

Sipping her cooling tea, she started typing a letter to the care home's manager, who she'd found out was called Margaret.

Dear Margaret,

My name is Anna and I'm researching my family tree. I've discovered that I'm related to a man called Arthur Robb and I believe he might be a resident at your care home. I wondered whether I might speak to him, or send him a letter to explain a little bit more.

I'd appreciate any help you might be able to offer.
Many thanks,
Anna Snow

It was only a small white lie, but she was more likely to receive the help she needed if they thought she might be a long-lost granddaughter so she buried the pinch of guilt and pressed send before she could change her mind.

Then she closed the laptop and packed it away in her bag to help her resist the temptation to press 'refresh' every few minutes.

Anna was still thinking about her email and whether she'd have a response yet when she arrived at the pub later that evening. It was already full and as she approached, the sound of voices and music spilled out onto the pavement every time the door swung open.

Going through the door herself, she looked around the place and saw Jenny at the bar.

'Anna!' Jenny said the minute she spotted her. 'You're about three drinks behind everyone!'

'Sorry I'm so late, I had a few things to do,' Anna said, leaning in to give her friend a hug.

'Well, you're here now. Wine or shots? I'm having both.'

'Then I will too,' Anna said, trying not to think about the hangover she'd have in the morning.

'So, what was that important you had to do it tonight?'

Jenny asked as they picked up their drinks and weaved their way to where their colleagues were sitting.

'Oh, nothing much, just a couple of emails to se – oh!' Anna stopped, drinks balanced in her hands, mid-sentence.

'What?' Jenny wheeled round, looking for the source of Anna's surprise.

'It's just –' Anna stammered, as a familiar man walked towards her carrying two empty pint glasses. He almost bumped into her before he realised she was standing right in front of him.

'Oh god, I'm so sorry,' he said, grabbing her elbow to stop her from falling over. And then he stopped too and stared at her for a second. 'Oh, hello again, Anna.'

'Hi, Tom,' Anna said, straightening up.

'Well, hello, Tom Cross,' Jenny said, coming to stand beside them both. 'Long time no see.'

'Jenny, hi.' He looked from Jenny to Anna and back again, confused. 'How do you two –' He waved the glasses in his hands from side to side.

'We work together,' Jenny said. Beside her, Anna felt her face turn red as she willed Jenny not to let slip that she'd asked about him.

'Oh, right. How's John? I haven't seen him for months.'

'Oh, you know my brother, same as always – working too hard, smoking too much.' She smiled and took a step back. 'Anyway, I'd better get back to everyone, I guess I'll see you in a minute, will I?' she said, giving Anna a pointed look. Anna hoped her face said *please don't leave me*, but if it did, Jenny chose to ignore it and left her standing there with the man she'd been pretending not to think about since she'd said goodbye to him that afternoon.

'So, today was lovely, wasn't it?' Nice one, Anna, really exciting.

'Yeah. Yeah, it was.' Tom nodded. He looked round and Anna wondered if he was looking for someone or just looking for a way out.

'Well, I've only just got here so I'd better go and find my friends,' Anna said, indicating over to the other side of the pub with her head.

'Oh, yeah. Right. Me too.' He held up the empty glasses. 'My round.'

'Well, OK then. Nice to see you.'

'You too.' Tom hurried towards the bar looking like a man who'd just been told he didn't have a terminal illness after all. Why was he so desperate to get away from her?

'What are you doing back here already?' Jenny said, a look of fury on her face as Anna arrived at their table.

'I can't believe you left me with him.' Anna took a huge gulp of her wine. 'That was so awkward.'

'Why? Tom's a lovely bloke, I thought you'd want a bit of time together. He definitely looked like he wanted a bit of time with you.'

'No! And please promise me you won't tell him I asked about him the other night.'

'I won't. But on one condition.'

'What?'

'Admit you like him.'

'I do *not* like him!'

'Oh, come on, Anna. Tom Cross is hot – you can't tell me you haven't even given it a thought.'

'Absolutely not. I don't even really like him. He's been so rude to me since I met him.' Even to her own ears the words lacked conviction so she couldn't blame Jenny for the smirk on her face.

'Uh-huh.'

'It's true.'

'Well, let's hope that he's not coming over to insult you right now then.'

'What do you mean?'

She turned at a movement at her side to find Tom placing his hand on her elbow. She tried to ignore the warmth that radiated from his skin to hers and the familiar salty smell.

'Oh, hello again.'

Tom thrust a glass of what looked like gin and tonic towards her. 'I wasn't sure what you were drinking so I guessed. I hope it's all right.'

'Oh. Thanks.' Anna took the glass from him, careful not to touch his hand. She wasn't sure what was going on but she was feeling decidedly odd in the company of a man she'd been sure couldn't stand her. Suddenly she was beginning to wonder whether there was any truth in what Julia and Jenny had said after all, not to mention the numerous times Grace had brought it up; maybe he did like her more than she'd believed. They all seemed pretty determined that Tom was a bit of a catch.

Tom hovered for a moment, then stepped back. 'Right, well, I'd better get back to the lads.' He pointed over his shoulder in the vague direction of the bar. Anna glanced across to where a group of four or five men about Tom's age were drinking pints and laughing at something.

'Yes. Right.' She held the glass up. 'Well, thank you again.'

'Pleasure.' Tom turned to walk away. But before he could take a step he was accosted by Jenny.

'Hey, you're not going already, are you?'

Tom turned back. 'Well, yes.'

'Oh, come on, at least stay and have one drink with us. I didn't even know Anna knew you, and I haven't seen you for ages.' She looked at Anna pointedly again and Anna's heart sank. Jenny was more drunk than she'd realised and she wasn't going to let this go.

'Actually, I really do have to get back over there.' He gestured towards his mates again, slopping beer over the edge of his glass. 'But why don't you come back with me and say hello?' He was looking at Anna now. 'It's Simon's birthday and we're trying to get him a bit drunk.'

'Oh…er –'

'We'd love to,' Jenny said, turning to grab Anna's sleeve. 'Wouldn't we, Anna?'

'What? Oh, yeah. Course.'

'Come on then,' Jenny persisted.

They followed Tom across the pub and, from behind, Anna couldn't help noticing for the first time how the curls at the back of his head rested lightly on the collar of his T-shirt.

As they approached the group of Tom's friends a couple of them turned to greet them, and grinned knowingly.

'All right, Tom, been picking up the ladies, have we?' one slurred.

'Ah, yes, this is Si,' Tom said apologetically. 'It looks as though the plan to get him pissed is going pretty well after all.' He winked at them as his friend swayed, then righted himself by grabbing onto a nearby table.

Simon held his pint in the air. 'It's my birthday,' he said, his words merging into each other.

'Happy birthday,' Anna and Jenny said in unison, and he grinned back at them.

Tom then introduced them to the rest of his friends, fortunately none of them as drunk as Simon.

'How do you know Tom then?' It was a man Tom had introduced as Stu.

'He's Anna's friend,' Jenny said, swaying a little as she waved her glass around.

'Is he now?' Stu smirked, and nudged Tom in the ribs.

'We don't know each other that well,' Tom said. 'Anna's been looking after my Aunty Grace, that's all.'

Anna tried to hide her disappointment at the dismissal and plastered a smile on her face. 'And what about you? How do you two know each other?'

'I'm a lifeguard down at the beach.' Stu nodded at Tom. 'Tom sometimes helps us out, but we also see him when he's teaching the kids' swimming lessons. He's pretty good – don't know how he does it myself, it would do my head in.'

Tom shrugged. 'It's fun. The kids love it and it's good to know I'm helping to keep them safe.'

'Yeah, well, rather you than me, mate.' Stu turned to Jenny, who'd been hanging on his every word. 'And where do you fit into all this then?'

'Tom knows my brother, but mainly I'm Anna's friend, Jenny.'

'Are you now?' Stu stuck his hand out to shake hers. 'Nice to meet you, Anna's friend Jenny.' As Stu and Jenny got drawn into conversation Anna and Tom were left to stand alone, Tom looking just as awkward as Anna felt.

'I wish my nieces would learn to swim,' Anna said eventually. 'Adam – my brother – is always worrying about them getting into trouble when they're at the beach but they're stubborn and won't be taught by him.'

'They can't swim? They must learn, it's so important.' Anna could hear the urgency in Tom's voice, could hear how important it was to him. 'It's dangerous living by the sea and being unable to swim.'

'Yeah, well, I've always been all right.'

'What? You can't swim either?'

Anna shook her head, suddenly ashamed. 'Not really. I mean, I can sort of flail around a bit and I reckon I'd be OK if

I fell in. But I've just never properly learnt to swim; I just stuck to the shoreline when we were at the beach as kids.' She shrugged. 'Seems mad, really, when I say it now, but the sea scares me a bit, if I go any deeper than this.' She indicated her waist.

Tom didn't say anything else, just watched her, and Anna was keen to take the attention away from herself.

'Anyway, your friends seem nice.'

'Yeah, they are, mostly.' He dropped his voice. 'Simon's not normally this raucous. I think we should probably stop buying him drinks for a while before he throws up.'

Anna glanced over to where Simon was knocking back a shot of clear liquid and grimacing at the aftertaste. He looked a bit green. 'I think it's possibly too late for that.'

'I think you might be right.'

Silence fell again and Anna glanced round the pub to avoid Tom's gaze. But all she could think about was his presence beside her, and the warmth she could feel from his arm that was pressed lightly against hers in the crowded space.

'Have you got any more trips planned with Aunty Grace?' Tom's voice made her jump and she flushed.

'Oh, no. Not yet. I'm am popping round soon though to show her those paintings I told her about.'

'Ah yes, I remember. They're good, are they?'

'Well, I don't know about that. I painted them years ago. I haven't really thought about them in ages to be honest but Grace – well, you heard her, she insisted she really wanted to see them. I think she hopes it might encourage me to start painting again.'

Tom nodded knowingly. 'She's like that, Aunty Grace. Sweet as anything, but knows how to wrap you round her little finger to get what she wants.' He grinned. 'She rarely fails either – not with me, anyway.'

'Ah, but you love it, don't you?'

'I do. I'd do anything for her, really. She's always been special to me. Her and Uncle Roy. I had quite a lonely childhood – just me and my mum and dad – and I loved going to visit them. When my grandad died – that's Grace's brother Ernest – my mum stopped going to visit as often, but I carried on.'

'That's so lovely.'

'I don't know about that. I don't do it because I think I should, I do it because I want to. Aunty Grace means a lot to me.'

Anna looked up and found Tom's gaze boring into her. Was he trying to get her to understand that she could never come between them? Was he trying to tell her to back off? Or had he just had a little bit too much to drink? It was difficult to tell.

She turned to look for Jenny, but her friend was still caught up talking to Stu. They were standing very close, their mouths almost brushing each other's ears as they spoke above the music.

'It looks as if those two are getting on pretty well,' Anna said, nodding her head in their direction.

'He's a good one, Stu,' Tom said.

'Jenny's pretty nice too,' Anna said as they watched their friends flirting with each other. Anna felt a pang of jealousy at the ease with which Jenny could talk to Stu, who she'd only just met, while she still felt so ill at ease with Tom, who she'd known for some time. Why did it have to be so difficult? Why couldn't she be a bit more like Jenny?

And why couldn't Tom be more like Stu?

Suddenly there was a crash and everyone jumped back. There, on the floor in front of them, was Simon. He was lying on his back in a puddle of spilt beer laughing hysterically.

'Oh god, I think I'd better get him outside,' Tom said, stepping forward to lift his friend up. Slowly, with Stu's help, they got him back on his feet again and supported him from either side.

'I'm really sorry, Anna, but I think we're going to have to take him home,' Tom said.

'Yeah, sorry Jen,' said Stu, leaning over and planting a kiss on her lips. Jenny beamed back at him. 'See you soon?'

'Yeah, I'll text you.'

Anna watched as the three men made their way back through the pub and out of the front door, Simon clinging onto his friends' shoulders for dear life. Suddenly Jenny was at Anna's side again.

'You two were getting on pretty well,' Anna said.

'Yeah, he's lovely,' Jenny sighed, a lopsided grin on her face. Anna tried not to roll her eyes. Jenny was always falling madly in love and then getting her heart broken. She hoped Tom was right about what a good bloke Stu was and that it wasn't about to happen to her all over again.

'Anyway, what's with you and Tom? I thought you said you didn't fancy him.'

'What? I don't!'

'Yeah, right, Anna. Your tongue was practically hanging out.'

'It was not!'

'Well, maybe not quite, but he's hot. You can't tell me you don't fancy him at all.'

'Well, he's all right, I s'pose.' She grinned. 'But I don't think he's interested in me so it doesn't really matter.'

'I reckon he is.'

Anna shook her head. 'No, he's made it quite clear. But it's OK because I don't need a man in my life. In fact, I don't want one.'

'If you say so.'

'I do. Anyway, that's enough about men. Here's to us and having a great night out tonight – cheers!'

'Cheers!'

And they downed their glasses together.

It wasn't until later that night as she lay in bed staring at the ceiling spinning above her head and trying not to think about Tom Cross that Anna realised she hadn't checked her emails to see whether anything had come through from Arthur's care home.

Oh well. It would just have to wait until the morning because she was far too drunk to care right now…

Chapter Fourteen

As Anna pulled onto Grace's driveway her heart thumped wildly. Tom's car was there, and she hadn't seen him since their night in the pub. She wondered how things were going to be between them now.

She pushed the back door open and called out Grace's name.

'In here!'

Anna found her sitting in her usual armchair. Tom was on the sofa opposite and he stood as she came in.

'Hello, Anna,' he said, leaning towards her. For a panicky moment she wondered if he was going to hug her, but then he touched her elbow lightly and pressed his lips to her cheek. Her heart hammered harder and her cheek burned from his touch and she hoped Grace hadn't noticed how flustered she was feeling.

'Hi, Tom.' She turned to Grace and tried to get her voice back under control.

'Ooh, have you brought me those paintings?' Grace said.

'I've just brought a couple of the smaller ones as I'm on

the bike, but I'll go and get them now if you'd like to see them.'

'Yes please – how exciting.'

Anna turned and scurried out to her bike, returning moments later with two square parcels wrapped in brown paper tucked under her arm.

Her heart thumped in her chest and she found herself fumbling to get the Sellotape off the brown paper. She hadn't shown these paintings to anyone for years. Dan had never been interested in her hobby so it had never occurred to her to show him any of them. Now, her palms were damp at the prospect of not just Grace seeing them but Tom as well. She was surprised by how much she cared about both of their opinions.

She prised the last piece of bubble wrap and brown paper off the back of the first canvas and turned it round. She remembered painting this one. She'd been about sixteen and had just got back from a holiday in the north of France some-where. She didn't remember much about the holiday apart from the fact that she'd spent most of the time either mucking about with Adam on the beach or sulking in her room because she missed her friends. But there had been one memorable day on the beach. It was late in the evening and the sun had started to dip by the time they arrived. The sea glowed red and gold while the sunset streaked pinks and yellows and purples across the sky like Neapolitan ice cream and it had taken her breath away.

She'd snapped a few photos with her ancient camera and when she got home to Lowestoft she'd got them developed and stuck them to her bedroom wall and had spent the next few weeks desperately trying to recreate that sunset, that dazzling kaleidoscope of colour. It had taken numerous attempts, but eventually she'd done it. And this was the result.

'Here,' she said now, holding the canvas up to show Grace and Tom. She found she was holding her breath as they both studied it, their faces giving nothing away. Then Grace's eyes fixed on Anna.

'Anna, it's absolutely beautiful,' she said. 'I love it.'

'You do?'

Grace nodded, her gaze returning to the canvas. 'I saw some sunsets like this during my travels,' she said. 'I could never quite remember them afterwards, but at the time they took my breath away, quite literally. This,' she pointed at the picture, 'this is exactly it. This captures those sunsets perfectly.' She turned to Tom. 'Don't you agree, Tom?'

Tom kept his eyes trained on the painting, his face unreadable. Anna felt her hands shaking as she waited for his appraisal. Finally, he lifted his eyes up to meet hers.

'It's stunning, Anna,' he said.

'Oh, thank you,' she managed to utter. She hadn't expected him to be rude about it but she hadn't expected that either. Her face flushed.

She turned back to Grace. 'Do you want to see the other one?'

'Without a doubt.'

Anna propped the first painting against the sofa and picked up the other one she'd chosen to bring. This was completely different, and she wondered whether it would have the same effect on Grace, whether she'd understand what it was Anna had been trying to do.

Anna turned it round and Grace gasped. 'Oh, Anna!'

'Do you like it?'

'It's astonishing.'

For a few moments the three of them studied the picture together. Anna could remember the individual strokes of the brush as she'd painstakingly tried to capture the essence of the land along the length of the Acle Straight, the road that ran between Great Yarmouth and Norwich. It was like nowhere else she'd been before or since; the earth was so flat you could see for miles around, and the sky so enormous you felt it could cover the whole earth like a blanket. This time, though, instead of trying to capture the sunset, she'd painted the scene on a stormy day, the black clouds gathering, threatening, making the cows and horses recoil, the grass whipping wildly back and forth, the colours dark and moody and gothic. She'd felt really proud of the way it turned out.

'You're so talented, Anna. Why did you ever stop?' said Grace, and Tom nodded.

'I told you. Life.' Anna shrugged, unsure now as she looked at these again why she had ever stopped painting. She could recall the release she'd felt as she brushed each stroke across the canvas, the scene taking shape deftly beneath her hands, the frustration when it went wrong, the elation when she got it right. She missed it.

'What do you think, Tom?'

There was a pause and then Tom looked up.

'I think she'd love them.'

Anna frowned, confused. What were they talking about? Who was *she*?

Before Anna could say anything, Grace explained.

'I hope you don't mind, but Tom had an idea and I thought it might be rather wonderful.'

Anna waited for her to continue, but it was Tom who spoke next.

'I've got a friend – Emily,' he said, reaching out for the smaller painting in front of him, the sunset one, and studying it. 'She owns a gallery in Norwich. She's always looking for new local talent and I think she'd be really impressed with these.'

'But –' Anna started, unsure what to say. She felt conflicted; part of her was angry that they'd hatched this plan without speaking to her first, but the other part felt proud that Grace had so much faith in her. And that Tom had, too, come to think of it.

'You're not cross, are you?' Grace said now. 'We don't have to show them to Emily. I just – *we* just – thought it might be a nice idea.'

'I don't know.' Anna looked at their expectant faces and took a deep breath. 'The thing is, I haven't even looked at these paintings for years. I have no idea whether they're any good at all. I – I just never expected them to see the light of day again, let alone be shown to anyone else…' she trailed off.

'But they're brilliant, Anna,' Tom said. 'At least, I think they are. And I'm willing to bet that Emily will like them too. This is exactly the sort of thing she exhibits.'

Anna briefly found herself wondering how well Tom and Emily knew each other, then stopped herself. That wasn't what mattered right now. What mattered was that she needed to decide whether to show these paintings to an actual gallery owner. It was a bit of a shock, to say the least.

'I think you should, Anna,' Grace said. 'What have you got to lose?'

Grace was right. What *did* she have to lose? If she showed her paintings to this Emily and she liked them then that would be amazing. And if she didn't – well, she hadn't lost anything at all, had she?

'OK,' she said.

'Hooray!' Grace said, clasping her hands together. 'You won't regret it, Anna, I'm sure of it. Your paintings really are wonderful.'

'I have one condition though, before you both get too excited,' Anna said holding her hands up.

'Anything.'

Anna looked Grace in the eye. 'I'd really like you to have one of these paintings, Grace. If you'd like one.'

Grace's eyes were wide behind her glasses. 'You can't give me one of these. What about the gallery? And Emily?'

'I can still show them to her and she can decide whether she wants them. But whatever happens, she won't keep them forever – and one of them will always be reserved for you. So, will you have one?'

Grace scrutinsed the two paintings, her eyes flitting back and forth between them.

'Well, I would really love the Acle Straight one,' she said finally, pointing a tremulous finger at the second painting Anna had unwrapped.

Anna picked it up and held it out in front of her. 'Then it's yours.'

'Are you sure? It's so beautiful.'

'Absolutely positive,' Anna said. 'It would mean the world to me to know you were enjoying it.'

Grace nodded. 'Wow. Thank you.'

'That's very kind, Anna.' Tom said.

Anna shrugged. 'It's the least I can do after the kindness Grace has shown me.'

Tom stood, brushing imaginary crumbs from his jeans. 'Well, I'd better be going, I've got a class of six-year-olds at midday. But I'll speak to Emily and let you know when we can go over there. How does that sound?'

'Great, thank you.' A thought occurred to Anna then. 'How many more will we need to take over? We can't just take these two.'

'How many have you got?'

'Quite a lot. I'm not exactly sure.'

'I'll ask Emily then and let you know.'

And he picked up his bag and left, closing the back door quietly behind him. Anna breathed in the scent he left behind, then silently scolded herself for being so ridiculous.

'You know, you could always get the paints out and paint some more, just in case,' Grace said as Anna stood to make a cup of tea.

'Pardon?'

'You heard me. You could always paint some more before we go and see Emily. See what happens. You just never know.'

Anna stopped, trying to hold back a smile. She might have known Grace was up to something.

'Was this all a ploy to get me painting again?'

Grace shrugged. 'We all need something in our lives to hold on to that we love, and this is definitely your thing. I mean, anyone would only need to look at your paintings to see that straight away. So, yes, I think you should start painting again.' She nodded her head vigorously.

Anna sighed. 'I think you're right.'

'You do?'

'Don't sound so shocked – you're the one who suggested it!'

'I know, but I thought you might shout at me,' Grace said. 'I didn't think you'd be this easy to convince.'

'Well, maybe you've done a good job on me then, Grace. Maybe it's your influence.'

'I'd certainly like to think so,' Grace said with a satisfied smile. 'I'd like to think I've done something useful with my life.'

'Oh, come on, Grace, you've done so much. Don't start feeling sorry for yourself now.'

'No, I don't feel sorry for myself. I'm just pleased I can still do something to help.'

'Well, let's not get ahead of ourselves. Emily might not even like them.'

'Of course she will. How could she not?' Grace tapped her fingers lightly on the arm of the chair. 'Although of course there is a chance she might not want to take them on, if she thinks there's something going on between you and Tom.'

'What? Why on earth would she think that?'

Grace looked at her. 'I know you two don't always see eye to eye, but he does like you, you know.'

'Who, Tom?'

'No, Desmond Tutu. Of course Tom!'

'Oh, Grace, I love you, but you're completely wrong on this one. Tom isn't bothered about me one way or the other. I'm not even sure he likes me that much.'

Grace raised her eyebrows so high on her forehead they almost disappeared beneath her cloud of hair. 'Don't be daft. I know he seems grumpy but it's only because he's protective of me.' She shook her head. 'But I know him, and I can tell he really likes you. He's just being stubborn.'

'But –'

Grace held her hand up to stop Anna from saying any more. 'No, it's true, Anna. Of course it is. Why else would he have come round here to see your paintings today?'

'I assume because you asked him to.'

'No, dear, it wasn't that at all. I told him you were popping over with the paintings and he insisted on coming over too. It was all entirely his idea.'

'Oh.' This was all such a turnaround Anna didn't know what to say. But then she remembered something Grace had just said. 'What did you mean, when you said Emily might not like me?'

'Well, she's Tom's ex, you see, dear, and I get the impression she's still rather sweet on him.'

'Oh,' Anna said again, stuck for words a second time. 'Well, I don't think she's got anything to worry about.'

Grace steepled her fingers underneath her chin and studied Anna. 'Hasn't she?'

'No! Of course not.'

'Tom told me you met him in the pub the other night. Sounds as though you had a lovely time.'

'I –' Anna stammered. 'Yes. Yes, it was nice. But it wasn't planned, we just bumped into each other, and it doesn't mean Tom fancies me or I fancy him. You're barking up the wrong tree here, Grace. Tom's made it clear he doesn't like me that much, and I'm miles off being ready to be with anyone else. I thought I'd told you that.'

'Yes, you have, dear, and I hear what you're saying. But I still think you're wrong about Tom. I've known the boy his whole life and if he didn't like you then I'd know about it. He's never been very confident with girls. His girlfriends have always been people he was friends with first.' She looked at Anna, one side of her mouth curling up into a grin. 'He's not courting at the moment, though. Hasn't been for a while.' Grace held her hands up defensively. 'I'm just saying, that's all.'

Anna nodded, unsure what she was meant to say next. Instead, she stood up and starting collecting empty plates and cups and taking them through to the kitchen.

Standing at the sink, she took a deep breath and looked out at the roses and the rows of neat shrubs in the garden that Tom obviously worked so hard on for Grace. She thought about how kind and generous Tom was when it came to his great-aunt; he obviously cared a great deal about her. He was good with the kids he taught to swim as well, if his friend's account was anything to go by. And she couldn't deny how attractive he was in appearance too.

Snapping out of her reverie, she rinsed the dishes and left them to dry on the side and then made her way back into the front room, where Grace was sitting with a book in her hands. She looked up when Anna came in, a strange look on her face.

'What's happened?' Anna said, her heart thumping. What could possibly have happened in those few moments she'd been out of the room? Had Grace fallen ill?

Grace held the book up. 'I wanted to read you some of this.'

'What is it?'

'It's my diary. The one I was telling you about that I found a few weeks ago when we were looking through those photographs.'

Anna sat down in the armchair beside Grace's. She could see her painting in the corner of her vision as she dried her hands on a tea towel she'd brought through with her and waited for Grace to say more.

'It's quite strange reading it. It's like I'm reading about someone else's life entirely.' Grace sighed. 'I was so *young*, Anna. So naive.'

Anna shuffled in her seat. 'So, what was it you wanted to read to me?'

Grace opened the diary. 'This bit.' She stretched a gnarled finger across the page. 'About meeting Roy.'

'Oh, about when he swept you off your feet?'

'He wasn't really the sweeping kind, dear, more the pick-you-up-and-carry-you-along-safely kind.' She smiled. 'But it struck me as I was rereading this that I'd quite like to tell you about it, and I might as well just read it out loud – if you'd like to hear it.'

'Absolutely, yes please.'

Grace placed the book on her lap and smoothed the yellowed pages out, worrying them over and over. Anna could see the tightly packed handwriting, the loops and swirls inscribed onto the thin paper all those years ago, and felt a deep longing to know what was contained within those pages – the fears, the hopes, the dreams of the young Grace who wrote it all down long before her life had unfurled before her.

She sat quietly now, waiting for Grace to begin.

6 March 1954

It's been a while since I wrote in here, but today I have a very good reason. You see, dear diary, I'm in love.

Yes, you read that correctly. After vowing never to trust a man again, I, Grace Winifred Moran, have fallen in love. Whoever would have thought it?

It all happened when we went for some drinks one night after work. It was an ordinary Friday night and I was only planning to have one quick drink to celebrate the end of the week. Samuel came along and he brought a friend. He said he hadn't seen him for ages. I didn't think much more of it, truth be told. But then, just as I was finishing my Tom Collins, in walked Samuel with Roy and – well, you could have knocked me down with a feather.

It wasn't that Roy was the most handsome man in the world – his nose was slightly too big for his face and his hairline was beginning to recede. But there was something about him that made me think 'I love him'.

I didn't know what to do with myself. As they came towards me, I could hardly bear to look for fear of blushing. I was behaving like a young schoolgirl. How ridiculous.

But I suppose that's how these things go, isn't it? You're not looking for anything, and you assume you'll probably never meet anyone, and you learn to be fine with that.

And then boom! It hits you like a rocket.

I won't recount the whole of the first conversation because, to be perfectly honest, it was rather embarrassing. I sounded as though I didn't have two brain cells to rub together, and I was certain Roy would leave the moment he could.

But he didn't leave. In fact, he stayed by my side all evening, even when Samuel moved away to talk to someone else. And when I told him I needed to be leaving soon, he convinced me to stay for just a little longer.

We talked all night. From time to time Samuel would come over and join in the conversation, and at other moments I would catch him, from the corner of my eye, watching us, a puzzled expression on his face.

Roy told me about his wife, from whom he was divorced. I'd never met anyone divorced before, and it made him seem older, wiser, somehow, that he'd been through that.

And then he asked me why on earth I wasn't married. Well, there was no way I was going to tell him about Arthur, and about not trusting men as far as I could throw them after all that, and nor was I going to mention my fling with his friend Samuel. And so, I told him the only thing I could – that I'd just never met the right person.

'I find it hard to believe that you've never even been asked,' he said. 'It's not a lack of offers, it's just that I haven't wanted to be with any of them,' I said, and he threw his head back and laughed, exposing the stubble on the underside of his chin.

We clinked glasses and he told me I was wonderful and I felt as though I were floating on cloud nine. The alcohol was making me feel bolder and so, as the night wore on, I told him more about myself than I'd ever told anyone – about life during the war, about Father dying, about my job as a reporter for Samuel. And in return he told me about his experience of the war – he hadn't been called up for duty because of a slight limp in his left leg caused by a childhood illness, so he'd stayed at home in Essex. He worked as a newspaper photographer, which was how he knew Samuel, and had met his wife, Mabel, when they were both just seventeen years old. It had been a mistake from the word go, he told me. It struck me right then that Roy wasn't the sort of person to leave someone standing at the altar waiting for him. It struck me that he was a good man, and that I wanted to find out more about him.

Nothing untoward happened that night, of course – we're both far too respectable for that, and he was far too much of a gentleman. We went our separate ways at the end of the evening, sharing nothing more than a peck on the cheek, and I assumed that would be the last I saw of him.

But then the next day at work Samuel called me into his office and told me I'd had rather an effect on his friend Roy and that he'd asked him to find out whether I might be interested in seeing him again. I could tell it was taking Samuel a great deal of effort to put aside his feelings for me and ask, and I wanted to throw my arms around him and tell him how lovely he was and that I wanted him to be happy. But instead, I stood there staring at him rather gormlessly. He was very patient while I let the information sink in, and then finally I found my voice and said I'd love to meet him. To my surprise, he clapped his hands together and said he was thrilled we'd found each other. He told me there was no point his being jealous because he knew I didn't want him, and that it was the first time he'd seen his friend so happy since the divorce so I'd be doing him a favour too if I made Roy happy again.

Well, I wanted to hug him right there and then. Not many men would have been big enough to have done that. But Samuel had, and now here this opportunity was presenting itself to get to know Roy better. I knew I had to take it.

I nodded and said all right then, and then I left the room in a *daze, unable to believe what had just happened – my ex-lover was trying to set me up with a man I'd only just met and I'd agreed to it. What on earth was I doing?*

I didn't have long to fret about it though, because less than an hour later Samuel came over to my desk and handed me a folded piece of paper, then left. I opened it and it simply said: 'Ffrench's Restaurant. 7pm'.

That was it. Nothing else.

I glanced back to Samuel but he was already in his office, his blinds closed.

I had a dinner date.

I scurried home after work and got changed and put on a little lipstick, and made it to Ffrench's just in time. Roy was already there, waiting for me at a table, a candle glowing in the centre of the white tablecloth. His face lit up when he saw me and I felt my stomach drop to the floor. I felt dizzyingly in love.

That date was four weeks ago now, and Roy and I have seen each other almost every day since. I feel like a teenager all over again and it's really rather marvellous. He lives in London but he's only been home a couple of times to check on his flat and collect some more clothing. At first he was staying in a B&B on the seafront, but after two weeks I asked him if he wanted to come and stay at my house. We were snuggling together against the cold one evening and I just came right out with it and said that it seemed daft for him to be paying for a B&B when I had a perfectly good bed he could stay in. His exact words to that were 'When you put it like that, how could I resist?' I said 'You know what I mean'. I was so scared he'd say no, that he'd think me too forward.

But he didn't, of course. He said he'd love to, and then he pulled me close and gave me a long, deep kiss. He moved in the next day, and I don't mind admitting that I've never been so happy in my entire life.

Grace put the diary down and raised her head to look at Anna. Tears shone in her eyes and Anna reached out her hand and patted the sleeve of Grace's cardigan.

'I'm sorry,' Grace said, dabbing a tissue under her nose and sniffing.

'What are you apologising for?'

'I just didn't expect to get so upset, reading that again.'

'Well, I think it's beautiful.'

Grace nodded. 'Yes, it was. He was.' She sniffed again, hard. 'He was a wonderful, wonderful man, Anna. You would have loved him.'

'It sounds like I would.'

Grace closed the diary gently. 'There was a reason for reading you this to you, you know.'

'Oh?'

'Well, apart from the fact I wanted you to see just how soppy I really am,' she said with a grin, 'I wanted to show you that sometimes, life surprises you.' She swallowed. 'I hadn't been looking for love when I met Roy – far from it, in fact. I'd been convinced I didn't need anyone, and that after Arthur I didn't want to let anyone in. But sometimes life comes along and messes up your plans.'

Anna nodded, unsure what to say.

'I suppose my point is, Anna, that just because you think you're not ready for something, it doesn't mean you're right. You just need to stay open-minded and learn to trust people again.'

Anna sat for a moment, letting Grace's words sink in.

'Are you talking about Tom again?'

Grace shook her head. 'No, Anna. Not necessarily. Although of course I'd love for you two to fall in love and live happily ever after – it would make an old woman extremely happy. But I'm not going to force it.' She threaded her fingers together and fixed her eyes on Anna's face. 'I just do so want to see you happy.'

'I am happy, Grace.'

Grace shook her head. 'No, Anna. You might think you are but I can see there's still a sadness in there. And I'm making it my mission to ensure you're happy before I die.'

'You're not planning on popping off any time soon, are you?'

'No, not just yet.' She smiled. 'But I sometimes feel as though I've got my work cut out with you and, quite frankly, I haven't got time to beat about the bush.'

* * *

Grace placed the diary in the bottom of the forget-me-not box and then covered it over with the photographs. She'd ask Tom to put these memories back under the bed next time he was here. She didn't need to look at any of this again.

She stood in the dining room for a moment staring at the reflection of herself in the patio doors. The black of the garden didn't scare her the way it once did, when she used to find it creepy knowing people could see in but she couldn't see out. In fact, these days she found it strangely comforting when the darkness wrapped itself around the house like a glove. It meant she could go to sleep and try to shake off some of the tiredness that pervaded her body constantly.

It was an age thing, of course, but she did find it unsettling how your mind took so long to catch up with your body. Perhaps it was a result of all the recent reminiscing, but she felt increasingly as though her brain was still young, interested, keen, firing away, and yet her body was betraying her by galloping ahead in its years, giving up on her.

She wondered what Arthur would make of her if he could

see her now. Would he even recognise this body, shrivelled and ancient, only a whisper of the former Grace he'd known by the tilt of her head and the curl of her smile? Would she know him? His deep-blue eyes, the twist at the top of his left ear so it didn't quite match the right one, that broad smile given so freely. She doubted he'd display any of these features now – surely they'd all have been faded by the years until they were barely visible.

She sighed. She knew Anna thought she was being a busy-body, but she only hoped that, in time, she would come to understand that sometimes life could surprise you, and that Tom could be her surprise – and, most of all, she hoped that they'd give each other a chance.

Because she knew as well as anyone that time was too precious to waste.

Chapter Fifteen

Heaving the last wrapped package into the boot of his car, Tom stood and shut the door firmly.

'Right, shall we go?'

'Yes, come on,' Grace said, lowering herself cautiously into the front of the car as Anna climbed into the back seat as usual.

Anna was feeling anxious about today. She'd spent the last couple of days rummaging around in her parents' loft sorting through her old paintings and bringing down ones she thought were the most suitable to show a gallery owner. Not that she had any clue what this Emily was like, but a quick Google search of her gallery had shown Anna that, in fact, Tom had been right. These were exactly the sort of paintings Emily liked, and she was a huge champion of local artists. Anna was surprised by how much she wanted to impress this woman.

They pulled out of Grace's driveway and within minutes were on the A146 northwards towards Norwich. Grace was sound asleep before they even reached Beccles, and was snoring gently. Anna sat back and listened to the sounds of the radio and the gentle hum of the tyres as the road slipped beneath them. She watched the clouds as they floated by and wondered what it would be like to paint them – how it would feel to hold a paintbrush between her fingers and create something from a blank canvas once again, to express herself through nothing more than a palette of paint and a brush. The long-forgotten itch was beginning to return, and she liked it.

After about forty minutes they arrived at the gallery and, as Tom pulled up outside, Anna's heart rate quickened. What if Emily hated her paintings? What if she hated Anna?

What if, when Tom saw Emily again, he realised that he still loved her?

More to the point, why did she care?

Between them they hauled the ten paintings out of the back of the car and propped them up against the wall they'd parked alongside.

'I'll just ring and let her know we're here,' Tom said. Anna tried not to listen as Tom spoke to Emily, and a few minutes later a figure appeared at the door.

'Hi!' Emily said as she came out to greet them. She hugged Tom tightly and planted a kiss on his cheek, then stood back to examine him like a grandma would do. 'You don't change at all, do you, Tom Cross?' she said, a smile playing on her lips.

Tom shrugged. 'It's not been that long.'

She shook her head. 'No, I suppose not. It feels like it though.'

A loaded silence fell between them before Emily seemed to remember about Anna and why she was there and promptly switched on what Anna could only presume was her business smile. She threw her hands out, clamping them round the tops of Anna's arms, and kissed the air either side of her face, the two women nearly bumping noses in the process. Anna had to stop herself from rolling her eyes. Where did she think she was, Paris?

'You must be Anna,' Emily said, studying her intently.

'I am,' Anna said, folding her arms across her chest.

'It's lovely to meet you. I'm looking forward to seeing your paintings.'

'Thank you.'

Emily clapped her hands together. 'Right, let's get these inside then,' she said, picking up the two smallest paintings and walking through the door with them, Anna following immediately behind Emily, and Tom behind her – they'd left Grace in the car for the moment while they were to-ing and fro-ing – and Emily talked incessantly as they walked.

'Tom's told me all about you and your paintings,' she said, placing them down on the floor as they arrived now in the main part of the gallery. Anna looked around at the artwork that hung on the walls already – a mixture of landscape paintings, portraits and more abstract pieces, as well as sculptures mounted on plinths and some extravagant-looking jewellery in a cabinet at the back. The space was bright and open and felt inviting.

'This is amazing,' Anna said.

'Thank you. It was always my dream to open a gallery of my own, and it's early days, but – well, it's here. And I do love it.' Emily paused, laid a hand on Anna's arm. 'I'm always looking for new artists to showcase, especially ones from East Anglia, so I was excited when Tom rang me.' She looked at him through lowered lids, which Anna supposed was meant to look seductive. 'Totally out of the blue it was; he hasn't rung me for ages so I knew he must want something, hey, Tom?'

Tom gave a curt nod and for the first time Anna felt a pang of sympathy for Emily. She'd also been on the receiving end of more than one of those curt nods and knew it didn't feel good. 'I'll just go and get the rest,' he said, making his escape and leaving Anna alone with Emily.

A moment of silence fell and then Emily clapped her hands together again dramatically. 'Right, let's have a look at these then, shall we?'

Anna's hands shook as she started removing the brown paper and bubble wrap from her paintings. This was a big moment for her. Nobody apart from Grace and Tom had seen these paintings for many years, and Anna realised now she was here how much this meant to her – getting the approval of someone who had no reason to tell her how great she was.

'So, how do you know Tom then?' Emily asked as she waited patiently.

'Oh, I – through Grace,' Anna said, feeling her face flame.

'Oh? How do you know Grace? Friend of the family, is she?'

'No, I was her carer. I am her carer, I mean. But we became friends and – well, here we are.'

'Oh, right. That's a bit odd, isn't it? Becoming friends with someone that old that you're meant to be looking after. Is it even allowed?'

Anna bristled at Emily's tone. She wasn't sure what she was getting at but she didn't like it.

'Grace is lovely and we have lots in common. We like each other, there's nothing more to it than that.'

'Hmmm.'

Anna felt herself tense up with irritation but said nothing else as she finally got the paper off the first painting and turned it round. It was the sunset one she'd first shown Grace, and Emily gasped.

'Oh!' she said, drawing her hands to her face. She bent down to study it more closely, then lifted it and held it up to the light. She squinted her eyes and tipped her head to the side, then nodded.

'Yes, this is lovely. Really special.'

Anna felt her chest swell with pride, especially as Tom had just arrived with two more of her paintings. She caught his eye and her face flushed. She looked away to see Emily watching them both, her face suddenly stern.

'Is that all of them?' Emily said, her toned clipped.

'No, I'll just go and get the last two and bring Aunty Grace in too,' Tom said, clearly oblivious. 'She'll want to hear what you think about them – it's her that championed Anna all along.'

Emily gave a curt nod of her own as Tom left, and picked up the next painting that Anna had unwrapped, the Acle Straight one. Despite any feelings Emily might have had about Anna and Tom, Anna could tell immediately that she loved the work as much as Grace had.

Emily picked up the next one, and the next and the next, until she'd seen all ten of them. She didn't say a word until she put down the final one, and then she turned to face Anna, Tom and Grace, who were all now lined up on chairs along the edge of the gallery.

'Well, that was a surprise,' Emily said, pulling out a fourth chair and sitting in front of them.

'Was it?' said Grace.

'Well, yes. I have to admit I only agreed to see them because Tom asked me to,' she said, shooting Tom a look. 'But I know he doesn't know a great deal about art so I didn't think these would be quite as wonderful as he said.'

Anna was only half listening now. The rest of her mind was trying to process what Emily had just said. Tom had told Emily her paintings were wonderful. Really? She felt her hands shake and stuck them under her thighs to keep them still. She didn't dare look at anyone except Emily as she carried on talking.

'Anyway, to cut to the chase, these are perfect for me,' she said. 'I'd love to display them for you, if you'll let me.'

Anna stared, unable to form the words. 'I –' She stopped, looked at Grace, who gave her a nod of encouragement. 'That would be amazing,' she said, her voice cracking. 'Thank you.'

Emily stood and held out her hand formally. 'Well, that's great news. I'll put together a contract with all the details of commission and so forth and we'll take it from there, shall we?'

'Yes. Yes, thank you,' Anna said, her head bobbing up and down like a nodding dog. What was wrong with her – why had she turned into such an inarticulate fool in front of this woman? Why was Emily putting her so much on edge?

It didn't matter. It didn't matter what she thought of Emily, or what Emily thought of her. All that mattered right now was that she was offering to sell some of Anna's paintings. She realised Emily was still speaking. 'And, of course, if you do paint any more in the meantime, I'd love to see them first. I'm sure these will fly out of the door.'

'Of course, thank you.'

And before she knew what was happening, Anna, Tom and Grace were being escorted back to the car, her paintings still in the gallery.

It wasn't until they were in the car on the way home that Anna felt the power of speech coming back to her. 'Well, that was unexpected.'

Tom turned his head to face her as they slowed at some traffic lights. 'Was it? Why?'

'Well, I don't know. I didn't think she'd like them that much.'

'What, you didn't trust our opinion?'

'No! I —' Anna said, horrified. Then she noticed the smirk on Tom's face.

'I'm only kidding,' he said, catching her eye in the rear-view mirror. 'I mean, I knew I liked them but Emily was right in that respect — I don't know anything about art. But I do know what I like to look at, and your paintings are definitely up there.'

'Thank you.'

'I agree,' Grace said. 'There's something breathtaking about them from the very first moment you clap eyes on them. You're a very talented young lady, Anna, and Emily would have been a fool to ignore that just because she's still in love with Tom.'

'What?' Anna and Tom spoke in unison.

'Of course she is,' Grace said, placing her hand gently on Tom's leg. 'And she clearly thought Anna was your girlfriend and was hoping that her paintings were going to be rubbish. Any fool could have seen that. The look on her face when she saw how good they were — I wish I could have taken a picture.'

'Don't be mean, Aunty Grace. You always liked Emily.'

'Oh, she was all right. I tolerated her. But all those dramatics over every little thing; it does get a bit wearing after a while.' She shot Anna a glance. 'He's well rid of her, you know.'

In the mirror Anna saw Tom roll his eyes and grin. Neither of them said anything in response, and Grace took the chance to have another nap as they drove the rest of the way home in silence. Anna didn't like to try guessing what might be on Tom's mind.

Chapter Sixteen

Dear Anna,

Thank you for your email. I'm afraid I can't give out any details of residents at the home, but if you would like to send me your phone number then I can certainly pass it on to Mr Robb and if he would like to speak to you, he can call you himself.

I'm sorry I can't be of any further assistance, but as I'm sure you can understand, we have to protect the privacy of our residents.

All the best in your search.
Margaret Turner
Manager, Bartlett Care Home

Oh. The email had been sent while she was out at the gallery, and Anna stared at it for a few moments now, disappointment flooding her body. Even though it had always been a long shot, she'd allowed herself to get her hopes up that she'd found Arthur. Stupidly, it hadn't occurred to her that Margaret wouldn't just be able to pass his details on to any Tom, Dick or Harry.

She went into the kitchen and flicked on the coffee machine. After everything that had happened so far today and the bottle of wine she'd just celebrated with by herself as soon as she'd got home, she needed strong coffee, and lots of it, to deal with anything else right now.

She sat at the kitchen table, head in her hands. There was so much to think about but her brain was struggling to function properly.

First things first. Arthur. She needed to email Margaret back with her phone number. That, at least, was something positive she could be doing. Flipping her laptop back open, she went into her emails and replied to the manager, giving her phone number. Then she closed the lid again and tried to put it out of her mind.

Anna picked up her coffee and wandered into the bedroom. Her covers were still scrunched up at the bottom of the bed, the sheet twisted and pillows on the floor. It looked, she thought, like a bed that had seen some passion the night before rather than the sleeping place of a single woman who'd just drunk too much cheap white wine on the sofa alone. A wave of self-pity washed over her and then she felt hot as an image forced itself into her mind: her and Tom, tangled together in the sheets. She could picture his tanned, toned body, his dark curls spread across the pillow… Oh god, what was her problem? Maybe it was the alcohol mixed with the excitement of the day that was pickling her brain.

Shaking the image from her mind, she clambered into bed, pulled the covers over her head and tried to sleep, hoping to push all thoughts of Tom, of Emily, of Arthur out of her mind.

* * *

Anna was still half asleep when she realised it was actually her phone ringing next to her bed and not the one in the dream she'd been having. Fumbling around the bedside table, she picked it up and held it to her ear without checking who it was.

'Hello?' Her voice was groggy and she cleared her throat, so missed the first words on the other end. 'Sorry, I didn't hear that. Who's this?'

'Is that Anna Snow?' said a tremulous voice.

'Yes. Speaking.' Anna sat up, glancing at the clock as she did. Eleven o'clock – she'd slept in really late.

'Hello.' A pause so long Anna began to wonder whether he'd hung up. Then a wheezing cough, followed by: 'My name is Arthur Robb. I was told you might be looking for me.'

Arthur!

Wide awake now, Anna sat up, her heart beating rapidly in her chest.

'Oh, hello, Mr Robb.' She stopped, unsure what to say. She hadn't actually imagined that Arthur might ring her back – certainly not this soon – and she felt flustered, panicky.

'Are you still there, dear?'

'Yes, sorry, I am.' She cleared her throat. 'Thank you for calling me back.' Her palms were sweaty now as she searched her mind for what to say.

'Margaret told me you'd rung. Said something about you being related to me, but I'm fairly sure that isn't right.' He chuckled, his breath raspy in his throat.

'Ah, no, sorry about that. I might have fibbed a little bit.' She listened to Arthur's breathing again for a moment. 'The thing is –' She stopped again, took a breath. 'The thing is, I think I might know someone who knew you once and I thought…I thought it would be nice…' She trailed off again.

'Nice to what? And what do you mean you know someone who knew me once? Is this some kind of prank?'

'No, honestly, it isn't. I – I do know someone you used to know. At least I think so.'

'Well, who is it then?'

'Grace Winterton.'

'Grace Winterton…' There was a clicking noise that gave Anna the impression of a brain turning over but which she suspected might be false teeth. 'No. No, I don't think I do know her, dear, sorry. You must have the wrong person.'

Anna's heart plummeted. But then a thought occurred to her.

'Oh! You would have known her as Moran. Grace Moran.'

This time there was such a long pause that Anna began to wonder whether he'd cut her off. But she could still hear the sounds of the TV in the background and, if she listened carefully, the whistle of air in and out of his nose. She waited.

'Well, I didn't expect that,' was what he eventually said.

'So, you know her?'

'Oh yes, I do. Or at least I did, many, many years ago. But I suspect, if you know her, then you know that already, don't you?'

'Yes. At least, I hoped it was you.'

His teeth clicked again and she heard a puff of air being expelled. 'How did you find me? It's been a long, long time.'

'I searched on the internet. It wasn't very difficult in the end, although I wasn't certain I had the right Arthur Robb.'

'No, I don't suppose I look anything like I did in those days.' He gave a small chuckle. 'So, what do you want then?'

'Well, I –' She stopped. What should she say? That she didn't know what she wanted, that Grace didn't even know she'd been looking for him, that she'd probably be furious if she did? 'I'm not really sure.'

'Oh.'

Aware she needed to say something else, Anna tried to explain why she'd contacted him. 'The thing is, I've known Grace for a few months now. I – we're friends. She means a lot to me. And she's told me lots of stories, things that have happened to her over the years, and she told me about you and, and her, and…'

The whistling breathing continued and Anna wondered whether Arthur would say anything else.

'I don't suppose I came out of it all very well, did I?'

'Well, no, not really.'

'And I assume she doesn't know you've contacted me.'

'No.'

'So, why have you?'

'I'm not sure. I just wanted to know – I needed to know why.' She took a deep breath, determined to explain herself. 'Grace told me what happened, about you leaving her on what was meant to be your wedding day. She told me she tried to find you, tried to find out what had happened, but nobody seemed to know the answer, or where you'd gone – or at least, they weren't telling her. So, she gave up. But she always wondered, you know. She always wondered whether it was her fault and I – I suppose I wanted to find you to ask you whether it was actually something she did or something else entirely that made you leave. Because if it was – something else – I think that would help her. At least, I hope it would.'

Arthur let out a long, shaky breath.

'I see. Well, Miss Snow, I could tell you to mind your own business. I probably should.' He coughed again. 'But I'm not of a mind to do that. You know, I loved Grace, once. Many, many moons ago. I thought she was the most wonderful woman. She was beautiful, so strong, so independent. I wanted nothing more than to marry her. But things changed.' He stopped, his breath wheezy now. Then a rustling sound like someone covering the mouthpiece, and muffled voices in the background.

Moments later Arthur's voice came back on the line. 'I'm sorry, dear, I'm going to have to go now. I'm in trouble – been told I've got to have a rest.' He clicked his teeth again. 'But give me your address and I'll write to you.'

'I –' she started, but then there was more rustling and the voice of a young-sounding woman with a strong Geordie accent came on the line.

'Hello, Miss –?'

'Snow. Anna.'

'Miss Snow. I'm Mr Robb's nurse and I'm afraid he's exhausted. But he's asked me to take down your address for him.'

Anna reeled it off and thanked the nurse. After she hung up, she sat for a moment, propped up on her pillows, stunned. She watched seagulls swoop past the window in formation as she tried to digest what had just happened.

Poor old Arthur – what a shock he must have had when she admitted why she'd contacted him. She hoped she'd done the right thing.

Now, she just had to wait and see whether Arthur would contact her again.

* * *

'Tell me again what happened,' Julia said, applying mascara in the adjacent mirror as they spoke on FaceTime.

After her conversation with Arthur, Anna had needed someone to talk to so had rung Julia. Whenever Anna floundered, or didn't know what to do, her oldest friend was always the voice of reason. Surely she'd know what to do this time too.

'Well, it was him, and he remembered Grace. And he said he was going to write to me. Or maybe he meant to Grace.'

'That's good, isn't it?'

'Yes, I suppose so. But the thing is, do I tell Grace?'

Julia looked back at the camera, her eyes wide. 'Of *course* you have to tell her. This is massive.'

'But what if she's angry?'

'What if she is? She'll get over it.' Julia sniffed. 'Listen. Why did you start looking for Arthur in the first place?'

'Because you told me to.'

Julia rolled her eyes. 'Apart from that.'

'Because I wanted to see if I could find out why he left. Whether there was anything reported, and whether he was still alive.'

Julia nodded. 'Exactly. And because you're nosy and you can't help yourself.'

'That too.'

'But the main point remains. You wanted to know what had happened to him – and you thought Grace wanted to know as well, right?'

'Well, that's just it. Do I know that? I mean, Grace has never actually said as much.'

'But she's obviously been thinking about Arthur or else why would she have told you all those stories about him? And she tried to find him herself once, to ask him why he'd left, didn't she? How could she know how much easier it is to track people down these days? Plus, you said yourself that it must be hard for her since Roy died. She's on her own a lot and has all that time to think about the past.' She shrugged. 'I reckon this would give her closure, as the Americans say.'

'Hmmmm.'

'What do you mean *hmmm*? I'm right, aren't I? You can't get this far down the line and then not tell Grace about it. I mean, what would be the point of that?'

'I suppose.'

'Think about it. If it was you, would you want to know?'

'Yes, but I'm not Grace.'

'Oh, come on, Annie, you know what I mean. You *have* to tell her. How can you not?'

'OK, OK,' Anna said, holding her hands up. 'Consider her told – but I'll just wait and see what comes from Arthur first.'

Julia rolled her eyes. 'Any excuse to put off the confrontation, eh?'

Anna was about to object but realised Julia was right. She always hated confrontation and would do anything she could to avoid it – which was probably why she'd stuck with Daniel so long despite all her suspicions about him – so she changed the subject instead.

'Anyway, where are you off to?'

'Oh, just some boring work do. Room full of solicitors banging on about property prices, I expect.' She picked up her lipstick and looked away into the mirror again. Smacking her lips together, she turned back. 'Heard from the lovely Tom?'

'What?!'

Julia cackled loudly. 'I knew you'd get all indignant if I mentioned him. So, have you?'

'I might have done.'

Julia pressed her face close to the monitor until all Anna could see was her left eye. 'Anna Snow, are you blushing?'

'No.'

Julia gasped. 'You *have* seen him!'

Anna shrugged.

'Young lady, you tell me what's happened right now or I'm going to come over there and kick your arse from here to next week.'

'I've seen him a couple of times.'

'A couple?'

'Well, I saw him the other night at the pub. He was with some mates and he bought me a drink and – we chatted.'

'And?'

'And that's it, end of story.'

'But he bought you a drink.'

'I just said that.'

'And when else?'

'He took me to a gallery his ex-girlfriend owns to see if she wanted to take any of my paintings.'

'Wait, *what?* How have you not told me any of this? I've just been talking to you about some old man for ten minutes and now I find out all this has been going on just before I have to leave to get my taxi? How could you do this to me?'

'There's nothing to tell really. He saw my paintings when I showed them to Grace, and asked if it was OK to show them to his friend Emily. And then we went over there and she liked them. She didn't seem too keen on me though.'

'And this Emily, she's his ex-girlfriend, is she?'

'Uh-huh.'

'You're bloody lucky she agreed to take your paintings then.'

'What do you mean?'

'Oh, come on, Anna, think about it. If Dan asked for a favour for his new girlfriend, you wouldn't be too keen, would you?'

'That's hardly the same. I hate Dan. They don't hate each other.'

'But does she still like him?'

Anna paused. 'Yes, I'm pretty sure she does.'

'And yet she still took the paintings. You must be bloody good, Anna Snow.'

'But Tom's not my boyfriend either.'

'She doesn't know that though, does she?'

'I suppose not.'

On the screen Julia shook her head. 'I can't believe you're only just telling me all this, Anna. You're such a dark horse sometimes.'

'I'm not being mysterious, I promise. It just all happened so quickly.'

'Too quickly for you to pick up the phone to your poor old best friend and tell her all the gossip?'

'There is no gossip.'

'Oh no, apart from the fact that a man you definitely don't fancy bought you a drink, took you to an art gallery run by his ex-girlfriend to get your paintings displayed and is quite clearly massively in love with you.'

'Tom is *not* in love with me!'

'Well, maybe not love, but he definitely likes you. A lot.'

'Oh, come on!' Anna shrugged. 'And anyway, so what if he does? It doesn't mean I have to like him too.'

'So, are you saying you're not interested one tiny bit in the hot gardener who teaches children to swim, is kind to old ladies and who seems to enjoy spending time with you?'

'That's exactly what I'm saying.'

Julia shrugged. 'Sometimes, Annie, I don't know what's wrong with you.'

'I –'

'Nope!' Julia held her hands up. 'I know what you're going to say, but don't. Just listen. It's almost two years since Dan did the dirty on you, and far, far longer since he started being a total arse. You deserve to be happy. You're one of the best people I know and you need to let yourself be happy again. I know you think there's no way Tom could be interested in you, but believe me when I say he does like you, and I think he likes you more than just a bit.' She smiled a lipsticked smile. 'And that's all I have to say on the matter, I have to go now, bye!'

And before Anna could reply the screen went blank, leaving her sitting there more confused than ever.

Chapter Seventeen

'I can't believe I've agreed to this,' Anna said, shivering in nothing more than a swimming costume and a towel on the cold, hard sand at the water's edge. Beside her, her nieces Josie and Bee were jumping up and down impatiently.

'You'll be fine,' Tom said, and Anna struggled not to stare at the contours of his body in his wetsuit, which was currently only covering the bottom half of his body, the material at the top hanging down to leave his chest exposed.

It was just a week after the gallery visit and the next time Anna had gone to care for Grace, Tom had been there again.

'I'm beginning to think you're checking up on me,' she'd said, half-jokingly. Despite the very definite thaw between them, Anna still felt a little on edge when Tom was around, especially when she was working, as though he might be trying to catch her doing something wrong.

'Actually, Tom has a suggestion,' Grace had said, her eyes sparkling with mischief. She looked far too pleased with herself and that had put Anna immediately on her guard.

'I've been thinking about what you told me, about your

nieces not being able to swim,' Tom had said, looking down at his feet. 'It's been bothering me, what with them living near the sea, and I thought – well, I wondered whether your brother would mind if I gave them a lesson. For free, of course.'

'Really?' Anna hadn't been able to hide her surprise. She'd forgotten she'd told him that, if she was honest, and this was the last thing she'd expected.

'I just – it's important to me, you see. If I can help people to swim then it will keep them safer around the water.'

Grace had leaned forward then. 'Tell her,' she'd said. Tom had hesitated for a moment, then turned and met Anna's eye.

'My friend's little girl, Erin, drowned a few years ago. They – they hadn't taught her to swim properly and she just got swept away and...' His voice had hitched and he'd looked down at the floor. 'The thing is, the sea's an unpredictable thing. You don't want to mess with it. You need to respect it. And learning to fend for yourself in it is an important part of that.'

'Oh, Tom, I'm so sorry.' Anna had thought back then to the photo she'd seen of him with a little girl during her Facebook stalking and had wondered whether that was the child he was talking about. 'Well, thank you. I'm sure Adam would be more than happy to let Josie and Bee do that. He's been promising to do it for ages himself anyway.'

'Great.' Tom had shuffled his feet and cleared his throat.

'Go on, ask her,' Grace had prompted him again, and Tom had looked even more mortified than he had before.

'Ask me what?'

'I don't want you to be embarrassed,' he'd said, and her body had flooded with panic. What on earth was he about to say?

'How would you feel about me teaching you to swim too?'

'Me?'

Tom had nodded, hitting his stride. 'I know you said you can swim a bit, but it's the same as it is for the kids. If you can't swim, you're not safe, not round here. Maybe you could all come together, for a lesson.'

She'd stared at him for a moment, letting his words sink in. The truth was she could think of nothing more humiliating than having Tom teach her to swim. But he was being so generous and earnest about it – how could she have turned him down?

'Thank you, Tom, that's very kind,' she'd replied, feeling she had no choice.

And that was how she now found herself here, shivering on the shoreline, building up to removing her towel and revealing her pasty white thighs. How she wished she'd slapped on some fake tan at the very least. She glanced up at the clouds building above and gave a silent prayer of thanks to the weather gods. At least it wasn't sunny, which meant fewer people down here to witness her humiliation.

'Come *on*, Aunty Nanna, hurry up,' Josie said, tugging at her towel.

'All right, all right, I'm coming,' Anna said, flinging the towel down to one side. A gust of wind brushed her body, making her skin dimple. She hugged herself tightly.

'Right, come on, you three, let's get in here.'

Anna glanced back at the blue-and-white beach hut from where Tom ran his business to see the tiny outline of Grace, sitting outside on a deckchair with a blanket over her knees and a lovely warm cup of tea. Anna had been surprised by how high-tech the hut was with all its mod cons, including a kettle and a heater – which was all she could think about right now as she shivered again at the water's edge.

She still couldn't believe Grace had roped her into this.

Tom had been right when he'd said his great-aunt could convince anyone to do anything. The water was freezing around her ankles and she squealed as it lapped over her calves and up to her knees. She grabbed hold of her nieces, one with each hand, and together they ventured into the icy-cold waves, jumping every time a swell threatened to push them back towards the shore.

Finally, when Josie and Bee were in the water up to their waists and Anna found the cold gripping her thighs, Tom stopped wading out.

'OK, you two,' he said pointing at the girls. 'Show me what you can do.'

Immediately they plunged themselves into the water head-first, arms flailing around wildly, heads bobbing under the surface and popping back up again. Seconds later they both stood up, laughing hysterically, water pouring down their faces and plastering their hair to their heads.

'See, we can swim,' Bee announced proudly.

'Yes, I can see that,' Tom said, a smile playing round his lips. 'I tell you what. Why don't you run up the beach to the hut – you see where Aunty Grace is sitting – and get yourself a couple of floats each? And maybe have a little drink while you're there.'

'Ohhhhh,' Bee cried. 'But what about our lesson?'

'It's all right, you're still having your lesson. I just need to see what your aunty Anna can do, and I don't think she'd like you to see that she's not as good as the both of you.'

'OK!' they yelled, and raced off, splashing through the waves and back up the sand to the beach hut.

'Right, let's see what you can do now then,' Tom said.

'I –' Anna hesitated. She wasn't keen on putting her face underwater, and it had been a long time since she'd been anywhere near out of her depth. What was she thinking, showing Tom how pathetic she was?

'Come on, don't be a wuss,' he said, and then she jumped as he grabbed her hand in his and pulled her further out to sea. As the water reached her waist, and then her chest, she held her breath, terrified that she was about to be carried away on the tide.

'Don't look so scared,' Tom said. 'I'm here and I promise not to let go.'

She nodded stiffly.

'OK, all I want you to do is lean backwards into the water, tip your head back and let your feet come off the floor.'

'But –'

'Don't worry, nothing's going to happen. I'll have my hands under you and the salty water will help keep you afloat even if I wasn't doing that. But you've got to trust me. Can you do that?'

Despite her fear, Anna found herself nodding. There was something about Tom's manner in the water, the confidence he oozed, the patience he had, that eased some of her fears. She could see why he made such a good teacher.

'OK, good. So, look, my hands are right here.' He waggled them around so she could see. 'When you're ready, just let yourself go.'

Anna squeezed her eyes shut and breathed in and out deeply. Her skin had gone numb from the cold and she was no longer shivering. She bobbed around self-consciously for a moment, feeling the motion of the water around her body. Then she took a deep breath and picked her feet off the floor and leaned back.

Suddenly, halfway there, she felt her body stiffen and she started to sink below the water. She waved her legs around and planted her feet firmly back on the ground, her breath coming in bursts, her heart pounding in her chest. She turned to face Tom, who was watching her.

'Sorry, I panicked.'

'It's OK. But look. Look at me.' Anna lifted her gaze to meet Tom's eyes. 'There's nothing to worry about. You won't sink, you won't drown and you won't float out to sea and be lost forever. I'm here, and I've got you. Do you believe me?'

Anna gave a tight nod and turned back around, her breathing finally back under control.

'Right, when you're ready…'

Before she could think about it any longer, she picked her feet up and tipped right back, trying not to panic as her head hit the icy cold of the water and waves splashed around her face. She felt herself floating, untethered, and at the thought of it she felt her body tense again. And then suddenly there was the solidity of Tom's hands beneath her, barely even touching her, just resting lightly on the backs of her thighs and her shoulder blades, and she felt herself relax. She'd done it. She'd trusted him and now he'd got her, held her so she was safe, and now she was floating.

She screwed her eyes up to shut out the pale grey of the sky, to shut out Tom's face, the clouds, the water, everything, and just listened to the sound of her heart beating in her ears, the lap of the water as it bounced around her face, and she felt all the tension seep out of her body. She was floating. She was doing it.

And then she realised. Tom's hands weren't touching her anymore. She opened her eyes and saw him standing next to her, his arms by his sides, ready to catch her if she needed him. And it hit her that just knowing he was there was enough.

Just like that, she'd conquered her fear.

She tipped herself forward again and planted her feet back on the sand. Tom was smiling at her.

'Well done,' he said. 'That was really great.'

She looked at him, at the pride on his face, and she felt a rush of something. She wasn't sure what. She knew she liked this man standing in front of her in the freezing-cold water. She knew, with a jolt, that he was the first man she'd been able to trust for a long, long time – since well before Dan had betrayed her.

She rubbed her hands over her face and smiled. 'Thank you, Tom.'

'Hey, it's my job,' he said. 'We'll get you swimming in no time.'

And Anna believed him.

The moment was interrupted by the arrival of Bee and Josie, splashing beside them.

'Aunty Nanna, you did it,' Josie cried.

'I did, didn't I?' Anna grinned. 'I suppose you two want your turn now, do you?'

'Yes-yes-yes!' Josie jumped up and down while Bee gripped Anna's hand and peered up at Tom shyly.

'All right then, you two, let's go closer to the shore and start there,' Tom commanded, holding out his hands for them to take one each. Josie grabbed one excitedly, while Bee extricated her hand from Anna's and took hold of Tom's other hand more cautiously.

Anna stood for a moment and watched the three of them as they splashed through the water, and then as Tom explained what they were going to do. From a distance she couldn't hear his words, but she could see that the two girls were rapt; Tom had their complete attention. Even Josie was listening, and Anna smiled as the pair of them leaned forward into the water and doggy-paddled their way towards Tom in perfect sync. He clearly had the knack, somehow, of getting them to do what they were told – and Anna knew from experience how lively these two could be.

'Are you coming to join us?' Tom called, as the girls stood up looking pleased with themselves.

'Of course I am,' Anna called back, pushing her legs through the water and making her way towards them. 'But you'd better not show me up, you two,' she said, ruffling Bee's hair as she reached her.

'Don't worry, Aunty Nanna, we'll let you catch up with us,' Bee said solemnly, and Anna caught Tom's eye and smiled.

Maybe, she thought, this wasn't going to be quite so bad after all.

Chapter Eighteen

One glance out of the small kitchen window told Anna she was going to get wet on her bike today. So much for it never raining on the island, she thought – although technically her flat wasn't actually on the island itself but a few streets away on the other side of the bridge. Rivers of rain tumbled down the dirty glass leaving the world outside smudgy and indistinct – a bit like Anna's head today, which was full of conflicting thoughts about Grace, about Arthur and about Tom. But she didn't want to think about any of that right now.

Walking towards the kitchen to get some breakfast, she saw the post had arrived. She picked up the pile of mainly junk and dropped it on the table while she switched on the coffee machine and pushed some bread into the toaster. Outside, the rain pattered on the glass, the odd gust making it hammer for a few seconds and obliterate all other sounds before returning once more to a gentler rhythm.

She flicked through the small pile of leaflets and brown envelopes. But then her eyes fell on a small lilac envelope, the sort from a writing set that hardly anyone owned these days, made from thick, good-quality paper and with her name and address scrawled on the front in spidery writing. She stared at it for a moment, her hand shaking. This had to be from Arthur.

She tucked her finger under the flap and prised it open, trying to steady her hands. All this time – and now Grace might finally get some answers. But would she like them?

She pulled out the contents and unfolded them, seeing that there were two letters inside. The top one was addressed to her and this time the writing was round, neat. She sat down to read it.

2 August 2018

Dear Anna Snow,

This is Arthur Robb, although someone else is doing the writing for me because my hands are too weak to make a pen do what I want it to do these days.

It was rather a shock to hear from you, I must say. I hadn't been expecting that.

However, after we spoke, I thought long and hard about what I should do, if anything. I hadn't thought about Grace Moran in a very long time, and the more I thought about her and all that happened, the more it occurred to me that maybe, even after all this time – especially after all this time – I do owe her some sort of explanation.

So, I've given her one, for what it's worth. It's enclosed with this letter. You're free to read it first and decide whether or not to give it to her, but I do hope you decide to do so. It's less than she deserves but all that I can give her, I'm afraid. It would be nice to do something that makes someone happy before I leave this earth for good.

All best wishes,
Arthur Robb

Holding her breath, Anna placed the top sheet on the table and started reading the letter Arthur had written to Grace.

After she'd read it through twice – once at speed and then again more slowly, taking it all in – Anna dropped the letter on the table. Around her the world had shrunk so that there was only her, the letter, and Arthur's words spinning round in her head.

He had loved Grace. She hadn't done anything wrong. All these years of wondering whether it was her, something she did, that had scared him away.

Surely Grace needed to know this.

Or were there some things that were best left in the past?

A burning smell permeated her senses, jolting her back to her flat, and she hurried to the toaster, where two slices of cold, blackened toast stuck out of the top. She threw them in the bin and made a cup of coffee, then walked, zombie-like, back to the table. Sipping her hot drink, she tried to order her thoughts, to work out what to do for the best.

Julia thought she should tell Grace, and that was even before this letter had arrived. But she didn't know Grace well. She could have no idea of the possible ramifications of this letter on Grace's life.

But there was one person who knew her even better than Anna did. Someone who cared for Grace and might be able to help Anna work out what to do.

She knew who she had to ask.

* * *

Anna stared at the number scribbled on a piece of paper in her hand and took a deep breath. Grace had been curious about why she'd needed Tom's number so Anna had just had to pretend it was to organise another swimming lesson for the girls.

She dialled, and waited, half-hoping it would go to answerphone and she could leave a message. But after three rings, a voice came on the line.

'Hello?'

'Hi, Tom?'

'Speaking.' His voice was formal, suspicious.

'Tom, it's Anna. Snow.'

'Oh. Hello, Anna.'

He didn't sound thrilled to hear from her.

'Is now a good time?'

'Yes. It's fine. Hang on.'

A few bangs and a scrape floated down the phone and then he was back, slightly out of breath.

'Sorry, I was up a ladder. Is everything all right with Aunty Grace?'

'What? Oh yes, sorry, everything's fine.'

'Oh, right. So, how can I help you then?'

Anna picked up the letter in her free hand and glanced at the words, letting them blur into one. How was she going to break this news without making Tom furious? It had taken a long time for him to get over his distrust of her, and this certainly wasn't going to help her cause. She took a deep breath.

'I need to ask your advice.'

A pause, then: 'Go on.'

'You've got to promise not to get angry.'

'I can't promise that before I know what you're going to say. And now I'm getting worried, so come on, what is it?'

'It's about Grace.' She paused, started again. 'The thing is, after she started telling me all these stories about the past, I realised it seemed as though she'd never really got over what happened with Arthur all those years ago. I mean, I know she was happily married to your uncle Roy and everything, but it was clear she never really understood what had happened and I thought she might blame herself for it.' She knew she was gabbling but she was desperate to get the story out before Tom got cross.

'Right…' If Tom hadn't sounded suspicious before then he certainly did now.

'So, anyway, I tried to find out what had happened. And I found him.'

'You found who?'

Anna cleared her throat. 'Arthur.'

Tom said nothing for a moment, and Anna thought maybe she'd lost connection.

Then: 'You're kidding.'

'No, I'm not. He's still alive and living in Newcastle and he's written me a letter explaining everything, which he wants me to give to Grace, and I don't know what to do.' It was better to get it all out in one go, wasn't it?

Again, Tom didn't reply instantly, and Anna wondered what was going through his mind. This was a lot to take in, all in one go. If it was this hard to tell Tom, she couldn't imagine how she was ever going to tell Grace.

'Why in God's name would you do that?' Tom's voice was icy.

'I – I just wanted to do something for Grace. She's helped me so much and I…' She stopped, aware it sounded lame. The truth was she'd really started looking for Arthur out of her own interest. She'd never truly imagined she was actually going to find him, so it had all been pretty academic, at first, just a bit of a challenge to see if she could actually get any answers. But now she'd found him, it had all got a bit more serious.

'How could you think for one moment she'd want to hear from that man after all this time?' It was clear he was struggling to keep his anger in check.

'I thought it might help her.'

'Help her? Why on earth would it help her? She loved Uncle Roy and she hadn't thought about this Arthur bloke for more than – what? – seventy-odd years before she met you.'

'Not that you know of.'

'What?'

'She hadn't told you maybe, but it doesn't mean she didn't think about him.'

'Of course she didn't.'

'And how do you know that?'

'Because she was happy. And now you've come along and stirred it all up again.'

'I haven't stirred anything up. We merely got talking and she told me stories – about her, about Roy, and some of them about Arthur. I think she's enjoyed having someone to talk to, to remember some of the things that have happened in her life with. I think she's trying to make sense of it.'

'Before she dies, you mean. Oh, that's lovely.'

'Oh, come on, Tom. I know you love Grace, and I do too, but she's ninety-five. She's told me herself she's OK with dying, with the fact that's it's nearly the end of her life. But I think, from some of the things she's said, that there are parts of her life she never got closure from, and getting that would probably bring her the peace she deserves.'

'Closure? What is this, an episode of Oprah?'

'No, Tom, it's not, but just because you don't agree with something doesn't make it wrong.' Anna stopped. 'You know what, forget it. I rang to ask your advice but if all you're going to do is be rude, I don't know why I bothered.'

She pulled the phone away from her face and was about to press 'end' when she heard a voice shout. She put it back to her ear.

'Did you say something?'

'Yes. I said wait.'

'OK.'

Tom let out a huge breath of air and she imagined his cheeks puffing out like balloons.

'I'm sorry.'

Anna waited for him to carry on.

'I didn't know anything about this and it's a bit of a shock, that's all.'

'I know, and I'm sorry about that. I know you love Grace, but this is nothing to do with that. Maybe I shouldn't have gone behind Grace's back to look for Arthur, but to be honest, I never in a million years thought I'd actually find him, or that he'd still be alive. But I did, and he is, and I feel as though maybe that's a sign that Grace does need to know. That she deserves to know.'

'You're right.'

'I am?'

'Yes. Maybe I didn't know about this Arthur before but it's easy to forget that Aunty Grace was young once, that she had a life years before I came along, that she was as feisty and independent then as she is now.' He stopped. 'Aunty Grace knows her mind, and I think she'd want to be told about this.'

'Blimey.'

'What?'

'It's just – that was a bit of a turnaround.'

'Yeah. I know. I do that – get cross and then realise I'm being an arse.'

Anna couldn't help grinning. 'Well, Cross by name, cross by nature.' Tom didn't reply and Anna hoped she hadn't insulted him. 'I'm only kidding.'

'I know. It's just –' He stopped, and Anna waited, holding her breath.

'I'm sorry I've been so awful to you.'

'Oh!'

'I was rude to you from the moment we met and I didn't mean it. Well, I did to start with, but as I said, that's what I do. Get angry first, think later. But now I know you're not trying to do anything to hurt Aunty Grace and I'm happy she's found you. She's been so sad since Uncle Roy died, like a lost little girl. But since she met you, she's been like a new woman. She's got some of her old spark back.'

Anna didn't know what to say. She'd hoped for Tom's support, but she'd never dreamt he'd apologise for the way he'd treated her.

'Thank you, Tom. Really. I do think the world of Grace, and I've loved having her in my life. Does that mean you and I can be friends now too?'

'Yes. I'd like that.'

Anna felt a heat spread from her cheeks to her hairline and all the way down her chest and she was glad Tom couldn't see her.

'Well, I would shake your hand but – you know,' Tom teased.

'Next time you see me.'

'Definitely.'

'So, you're OK if I tell Grace about this, then?'

'Yes. Just one thing.'

'What?'

'Can we do it together? I think it will be better coming from both of us.'

'Won't she feel as if we've ganged up on her?'

'Possibly, but I think she'll be more likely to come round to the idea. I can wrap her round my little finger when I need to.'

'I think it's the other way round, but OK, let's do it.'

A few minutes later, when Anna ended the conversation, she couldn't help smiling to herself. She'd made that phone call expecting the worst. She hadn't expected for one minute that Tom would be pleased with what she'd done – and she certainly hadn't expected him to help her hatch a plan to tell Grace about it.

But now maybe, just maybe, they could convince Grace that meeting Arthur would be a good idea. Together.

Chapter Nineteen

'Are we nearly there? I need the loo.'

'You sound like my niece and she's only five,' Anna said.

'I can't help it if I need a wee. You wait till you're my age, young lady – your bladder won't hold out for long either.' She looked at Tom, who was smirking behind his hand. 'And you can stop it, too. You cheeky bloody pair.'

'Sorry. But we're nearly there, I promise. Five minutes, and I'll try to park near the pier so you can go to the loo straight away.'

True to his word, Tom pulled into a parking space right by the seafront a few minutes later.

'I'm glad we came early, it's getting busy already,' Grace said as she climbed out of the passenger seat and looped her stick over her arm. Anna raced round to help her.

The sun was warm even though it was still only a little after nine. When they'd suggested this day out, Grace had warned: 'Southwold gets packed when the sun's out, you'll have no chance of finding a space if we leave it any later than nine.' And it looked as though she was right, Anna thought, as the three of them made their way towards the pier, Anna on one side of Grace, Tom on the other. Already bodies dotted the sandy beach as far as the eye could see; people hammered in wind breakers, struggling to control them as the breeze sent the fabric dancing wildly beneath their grip; the sun lit up the sea until the bright blue turned a sparkling white, while wisps of cloud floated casually past like puffs of smoke. It was going to be a beautiful day.

Toilet stop done, they headed along the pier. The wind was stronger as they walked further out over the sea.

'I might blow away in a minute,' Grace said, wobbling as a gust made her lose her footing. Tom and Anna instantly grabbed an arm each and righted her again. 'I used to come here all time with Roy,' she said, reaching past Tom to take hold of the railing to her right and looking out across the waves to the beach and the blue-and-white-striped beach huts in the distance. 'We always talked about getting a beach hut here but then all the London people started buying them for the price of a house and we decided not to bother. Made do with the one we had in Lowestoft instead.'

They stood and watched the world go by for a minute.

'Shall we go a bit further on?' suggested Grace.

'Are you sure you'll be OK?' Anna asked.

'Certain. Besides, you can't come all the way to Southwold and not go to the end of the pier.'

They carried on past the little shop selling sticks of rock, bracelets and postcards until they reached a sign advertising *The Under the Pier Show*.

'Ooh, can we go in here?' Grace said, and before either Tom or Anna could answer she'd pushed the door open and gone inside.

'Look at this!' Grace laughed as she sat inside the Booth of Truth. 'The mystic balls read your hand and deliver an accurate assessment of your character,' she read out. She rummaged in her purse for 40 pence, inserted it, then stuck her hand inside the machine. 'Ooh, it tickles,' she giggled. Music started playing, then a soft voice said: 'You do not like change…You have a tendency to think well of others…There was a chance in your past that you regret not taking…' Tom returned Anna's meaningful glance. 'Your reading is now complete. Thank you for using the Booth of Truth.'

'Gosh, that was funny,' Grace said, removing her hands from the machine and leaving the booth. 'Although I don't know what it means by a chance I wish I'd taken. What a load of old nonsense.' Anna raised her eyebrows at Tom and he smiled.

After several more minutes inside the curious arcade, they left and walked further along the pier and reached the water clock.

'Ooh, can we wait and see them piddling?' Grace said, stopping in front of the quirky clock. 'I think they do it every half hour or so.'

Sure enough, a few minutes later the two figures performed their act and Grace giggled. 'I don't know why I've always found that so funny,' she said with a smirk.

The three of them continued right to the end of the pier, where they stood letting the wind push and pull them around. Grace gripped the railing, her stick hanging loosely from her wrist.

'You know what, it's ever so nice to see you two getting on at last,' Grace said, a smile playing at her lips, 'although I can't help feeling as though you're up to something – you both look decidedly shifty.'

Anna glanced at Tom and widened her eyes. Should they tell Grace about the letter now? Tom gave a barely perceptible shake of his head.

'Tom's just feeling guilty about being so mean to me before because he's finally realised that I'm actually pretty great,' Anna said instead, looping her arm through Grace's. 'Isn't that right, Tom?'

'Afraid so.'

'Well, I don't know why it took him so long – I saw it straight away.'

They turned and walked back the way they had come, progressing slowly along the seafront before hooking right towards the town centre.

'There's a tea shop up here I always used to love coming to. Can we see if it's still there?' Grace asked.

'Of course,' said Anna. 'I could murder a cuppa.'

The high street was packed – holidaymakers were stocking up in the Co-op for a day on the beach; people were wandering all over the road, getting in the way of the traffic.

'Look, there it is,' Grace said excitedly, waving her stick across the road. 'Shall we go in?'

Moments later they were settled sipping tea at a table in the back. Grace had an enormous slice of coffee-and-walnut cake in front of her, which she'd hardly touched.

'Thank you for bringing me here today, it's been years.'

'You're welcome,' Anna said. 'I love Southwold but I never make time to come.'

'Me too,' added Tom, pinching a piece of cake from Grace's plate and shoving it in his mouth.

'Thomas, manners,' Grace scolded, and Tom gave a lopsided grin, cake crumbs spilling out of one side of his mouth.

Anna grinned too. It was hard to believe this was the same man who used to grimace at her every time he saw her. Since their chat on the phone the air seemed to have not only cleared but changed beyond all recognition. The Tom sitting in front of her now was funny and cheeky, and she was finally beginning to see for herself that he was just as handsome as Julia and Jenny both kept telling her.

She looked away before he caught her ogling him.

'The last time I came here was with Roy. It must have been seven or eight years ago, long before he got ill.' Grace broke off a small piece of cake with her fork and popped it in her mouth, chewing slowly. 'I do miss him terribly, you know.'

'Oh, Aunty Grace,' Tom said, wrapping his arm around her shoulders. She looked like a small child next to him. Tears shone in her eyes.

'It's funny because I've been fine until recently. But as you know, I've been thinking about the past more and more in the last few months.' She gave Tom a stern look. 'And don't go blaming Anna here for it again. It's not her fault, it's just one of those things that happens when you get old.'

Tom held his hands up in defence. 'I wouldn't dream of it.'

'No, well.' Grace pressed a napkin to her lips, leaving a smudge of peach lipstick on the thin white paper. 'The thing is, it's been good for me, thinking about the happy times. It's just the rest that's been a bit harder.'

'All the stuff from before, you mean – with Arthur?' Anna ventured.

Grace looked up sharply. 'Yes. You see, I hadn't thought about those days for a long, long time. At least, not properly. I suppose it was always there, lurking, but when I was happy and had my Roy, it stayed away. Now, though, it's all coming back – the good bits and the bad.' She put her fork down and placed her hands in her lap. 'I suppose it's my brain trying to make sense of everything before I go.'

'Oh, please don't say that.' Anna gave Tom a look. Was this the right time? He nodded.

Grace persisted. 'It's true, though. I don't have long left.'

Anna took a deep breath. 'And do you ever wish you did know?'

'Did know what?'

'What happened with Arthur. Why he left, I mean.' Anna was aware of Tom watching them both and she kept her gaze fixed on Grace.

'I suppose I do sometimes wonder,' she said. 'Not that it ever did me any good.'

'But do you – do you think you'd feel differently about it if you knew that it wasn't your fault that he left?'

Grace gave her a quizzical look. 'I don't know. Maybe, but I don't dwell on it.' She stopped, a frown creasing her forehead even more. 'Why are you asking me all these questions?'

Tom took hold of Grace's hand. 'Listen, Aunty Grace, we've got something to tell you.'

Grace's eyes were huge behind her glasses and she looked from Tom to Anna, then back again. 'What on earth is going on, you two? What have you done?'

'I've found Arthur.' The words shot out of Anna's mouth like bullets, as though saying them quickly would lessen the blow.

Grace's eyes widened even more and her mouth hung open. She didn't say anything for a moment, just sat staring from one to the other.

'Aunty Grace, are you all right?'

'I –' She stopped. 'Well, I don't know. That depends on what you mean when you say you've found Arthur.'

Tom took over. 'You see, it's much easier to find people these days than it used to be, and Anna thought it might be interesting to see if she could find out a bit more about Arthur. Maybe find a story about him, see if she could find something to tell you.'

Anna nodded, carried on. 'Yes, and the thing is, I didn't expect to find much – or anything. I just thought it would be fun, at first. I was just being nosy, I suppose. Well. Anyway.' She paused, cleared her throat. 'I found him, and then – well, we chatted. Me and Arthur. And he sent me a letter. For you.'

Grace's body seemed to fold in on itself and her face turned the colour of porridge.

Anna was worried. 'Grace, are you OK?'

She shook her head slowly. 'I don't understand why you've done this.' Her voice was a whisper, the words raspy. She coughed.

'Are you angry?' Anna asked.

Grace gave a small shrug. 'I have no idea how I feel.' She pulled herself up straight again and puffed her chest out. Her hands were visibly shaking in her lap. 'Arthur Robb.' She shook her head.

'Would you like to see the letter?' Anna rummaged in her bag and pulled out the familiar lilac envelope. It was slightly creased at the corners after being in her bag for a few days. She held it out but Grace made no move to take it.

'Have you read it?' Her words were clipped.

'Yes.'

'And you?'

Tom shook his head. 'Not yet, but Anna's told me what's in it.'

She regarded the letter for a moment, her eyes half-closed. 'And do I want to read it, Anna?'

Anna had thought about nothing but this since the letter had arrived. On the one hand, what actual good would it do her? But on the other hand, it could put to bed some long-unanswered questions – and that, surely, would not do her any harm.

Finally, she said: 'Yes, I think you should.'

She laid it out on the white tablecloth in front of Grace, next to her fork. In the background plates clattered, teacups rattled and the bell above the door of the adjoining sweetshop tinkled regularly. But at this little table in the corner, the three of them heard none of it; they just stared at this ordinary-looking letter as though, if they eyed it hard enough, it might give up all of its secrets.

Slowly, Grace lifted her hand and placed it on top of the envelope and wrapped her fingers round its edges. She looked dislodged, out of place, as though the world had shifted imperceptibly for her in the last few minutes. Then in one movement she flipped the envelope over and pulled the letter out and held it up in front of her face, peering at it through her glasses.

'My hands are shaking too much to read it,' she said, placing it back down on the table.

'Do you want me to read it to you?' Tom offered.

'If you wouldn't mind. I don't know if I can do it. I feel as though a hand has reached through the decades and is trying to strangle me.' Her voice shook as Tom closed his fingers around the letter.

* * *

In the warmth of the teashop, in the middle of a busy morning, Tom read the words Grace hadn't even realised she'd been waiting so long to hear.

Dear Grace,

This is a letter I never imagined I would write, but here I am now, at the grand old age of ninety-five, explaining myself at last. It's about time, I know.

It's hard to know where to start, so I'll go back to the beginning, to the day we met. Forgive me if this wanders around a bit, I'm dictating it to a lovely girl called Eloise who looks after me so wonderfully here, and my memory isn't what it used to be, as I'm sure you'll understand.

But I'll do my very best.

When we met, we were both very young – barely seventeen, and silly and naive. I remember walking into that dance at The Grand and spotting you straight away – your beautiful yellow dress, your nylons, your hair swept off your face with a ribbon – and I thought you were the most exquisite woman I'd ever seen. You see, I remember the details, even now.

That night was wonderful. Dancing under the lights, walking in the freezing cold to take you home. I felt as though I'd never been happier. I want you to know that, Grace. I was happy.

To start with, at least.

When I went away to war I missed you terribly, to begin with, and I lived for the arrival of your letters, which were so full of hope and love and happiness, as well as those short moments of leave when I got to see you, and to fall in love with you all over again each time.

But the visits were always too short, and as the war continued, I began to find it harder and harder to come home.

It's difficult to explain, Grace, what you see when you're fighting. I've never forgotten some of the things that happened all those years ago, and at the time, of course, they were fresh in my mind. These days I suppose we would have been treated for post-traumatic stress disorder, but back then we were just expected to put up and shut up, and get on as though nothing had happened.

But that was the problem, you see, Grace.

Something had happened. And it had changed me, forever.

I won't tell you the details of the war. I wouldn't want to horrify you with the memories that have haunted me all this time.

But the truth is, when I finally returned for the final time, back to Lowestoft and my life, I wasn't the same man I had been before, and I knew I never would be again.

I was still fond of you. More than fond of you, I suspect. But it didn't seem to matter. Nothing seemed to matter.

As you know, I struggled to find a job at first and I felt so worthless. Mother and Father tried to be understanding, but how could they truly understand? I doubted I would have done in their position.

I knew I had changed and I knew that you could see I had changed. But there seemed to be nothing I could do about it.

Some days were better than others, and on those days I tried to make things good between us. And it was on one of those days that I asked you to marry me. I was sure, on that particular day, that it was the right thing to do, that we could be happy.

But that feeling didn't last long.

I would have made you desperately unhappy, Grace. I could see that I was already doing that.

I felt myself spiralling, in the end. I would wake up in the morning and see no reason to get out of bed, no reason to be alive. Days would pass without me noticing, and I felt as though everything had been put on hold. I was numb.

At the time I wasn't as aware of this, of course. It's only after many years of thinking about it and getting the help I should have had back then that I can see clearly that I had been depressed.

I should have spoken to you about it. I should have explained, told you I didn't think we should get married, at least not yet, that I was unhappy and that it wasn't your fault – of course I should have. But depression is a selfish thing, and so I didn't, and in the end I just didn't know what to do about it. I felt trapped.

So I ran.

There was no other reason. It was nothing that you did. You hadn't changed, and you were still as lovely as you had ever been.

But I knew neither of us could be happy the way things were, and I didn't know how to tell you. And so, I did what, at the time, in my unstable state of mind, seemed like the kindest thing to do.

I realise of course, now, that leaving on the day you're supposed to be getting married is one of the cruellest things a person can do. But I'd tried and failed to leave before that, in the days and weeks leading up to the wedding – I just hadn't been able to bring myself to do it – and this, in my mind, was my last opportunity. My last chance of escape.

I've thought about my actions many times over the years. I've tried not to think about you standing outside the church waiting for me. I've tried not to think about how hurt you must have been, and just kept telling myself that you'd have got over it quickly and that I had done it for all the best reasons.

But I was a coward, Grace, and for that I will always be sorry.

I hope that now, though, you have the answer you need, and that you finally understand that it wasn't your fault. I did love you, and I think I would have continued to love you for the rest of my life had I not gone off to war.

I knew I couldn't stay in Lowestoft. It would have been wrong and cruel – and, selfishly, I didn't want to have to face you, face your questions and your accusations. I needed to get away.

And so I hitched a lift. I had no plan, I just went wherever I was taken, wherever the next driver was going. And that's how I ended up, a week or so later, up north in Newcastle, where by chance I had some family I hadn't seen for many years. And that's where I stayed, for more than seventy years.

I admit I considered coming to find you more than once. I even started the journey once, but turned round and went home after half a day of travelling, sure you'd never want to clap eyes on me again. I was a coward, of course, the same as I'd always been.

For a time I wondered whether you'd try to find me. But

when a few years had passed and you didn't, I had to learn to accept what I'd lost, and I tried to block out the past entirely and pretend it had never happened.

I felt guilty about leaving everyone. Mother and Father didn't know where I'd gone either, not for many months, until I finally sent them a letter to tell them I was alive. But I didn't tell them where I was for several more years and so it was a long time before I saw them again.

I won't tell you all about my life. I'm sure you don't want or need to know any of that, and that isn't what this letter is for. Maybe I can tell you in person – if you're interested, that is.

I'd like to see you, if you can make it. I'm too weak to travel but I can only hope you're not. But I do realise it's an awfully long way, especially at our age.

So, all that remains to be said is that I hope I've explained myself well enough, and that you can find it in your heart to finally forgive me.

I hope you have been happy, Grace. You deserve to be.

Yours,

Arthur

* * *

In the car on the way home, Grace felt utterly floored. It was as though she'd been visited by a ghost – some sort of vision sent from the past to throw her life entirely off course just when she thought she'd almost made it through to the end unscathed.

She was furious, quite frankly. What Anna had thought she was doing looking for Arthur Robb she had absolutely no idea.

Yes, she'd told her a few stories about him. And, yes, since she'd found those diaries she had been thinking about him more than she'd done for many, many years.

But that did *not* mean that she wanted to find him. Why on earth would she? What good could it possibly do anyone?

Not to mention Roy. She'd adored Roy. She'd loved him more than she'd ever loved anyone. He was the kindest person she'd ever met and from the moment she first saw him he'd made her forget her past and all the bad things that had happened – the war, her father's death, Arthur's betrayal, her lost baby – and be happy again. Properly happy.

Oh, Roy.

But most of all she felt furious at the pair of them for sneaking around behind her back. Oh yes, Anna had tried to make out it was all her doing, nothing to do with Tom. But he wasn't discouraging her, was he?

There she'd been, happily getting things in order, helping Anna and Tom find love – together, if possible – getting Anna's paintings seen so she realised how talented she was, as well as trying to make sure all her own affairs were sorted out for when she finally went. And all this time things had been going on behind her back of which she'd known absolutely nothing.

Arthur Robb.

It was a name so familiar yet so far removed from her current life that it could be that of a film star, once idolised but now long-forgotten. Only this one had played a part in her life that she'd really rather hadn't been played at all.

Then again, maybe if Arthur hadn't left her at the altar she would never have been the person she became. Perhaps she would never have been strong enough to have done the job she loved so much for so many years, or to have got together with the man she adored for the rest of her life.

Maybe it had all happened for a reason.

Only now, here these two were telling her she should consider going to meet Arthur. What were they thinking? If it was some sort of explanation they somehow believed she needed, surely she had it already. Surely the fact that she'd listened to his letter was enough. She'd heard the words and now she understood that Arthur hadn't left her because of anything she'd done but because of what had happened to him.

And it was good to hear, she supposed.

But why would she want to meet him? What more could he *possibly* have to say that would make any difference after all this time?

And yet.

She couldn't help feeling intrigued.

But right now, she did wish they'd shut up, the pair of them. They didn't half harp on sometimes.

She closed her eyes and tried to block them out, letting images of Roy fill her mind and take her away to another time entirely.

Chapter Twenty

Grace was sulking. Anna could tell because she was folded into the armchair by the window in the dining room staring out of the patio doors, her face pulled into a frown as deep as the ravine down to the seafront, her arms crossed over her chest. She was closed off to Anna, and she wanted her to know it.

Refusing to play silly games with a ninety-five-year-old woman, Anna ignored her and went back into the kitchen to make a sandwich. She pulled a farmhouse loaf from the bread bin, butter from the fridge and a tin of tuna from the cupboard and started putting it all together. Sandwich made, she poured tea from the pot into a cup, placed it on a saucer and took everything through to the table. Grace still didn't look round. Instead, she pulled her cardigan tighter around her body and turned another couple of inches away.

'Tea's ready, Grace.'

Grace lifted her a chin an inch or so higher and closed her eyes.

'It's so nice to be able to have such a mature conversation

with you,' Anna said in an attempt to lighten the frosty atmosphere.

Grace's head snapped round, her lips pursed tightly. 'Well, what do you expect?'

Anna sighed. Tom had warned her Grace would probably be like this: 'She might seem all right now, but when she's had a chance to think about what's happened she'll be really cross with you. With both of us. Be prepared for a bit of sulking,' he had said.

And he hadn't been wrong. This was the first time Anna had seen Grace since their trip to Southwold two days before and it appeared that over those couple of days the old woman had been simmering with resentment – culminating in a refusal to even speak to Anna now.

Anna decided she'd have to try to break the ice some other way. 'Listen, I'm sorry, Grace. Assuming this is about Arthur, I thought you were happy about it. You seemed to be when we were in Southwold.'

'Yes, well. I was in shock then.' She pushed her glasses up her nose and coughed. 'I've had lots of time to think about it and I've read the letter again and – well, I can't believe you've done this to me.'

Anna pulled out a dining chair, placed it next to Grace's armchair and sat down facing her.

'I meant it well, Grace.'

Grace lifted her shoulders and looked down at her hands, which were twisting over and over in her lap.

'Perhaps you did. But –' She stopped.

'What is it? What's wrong?'

'I –' Her voice caught in her throat and a single tear slid down the side of her face.

'Oh, please don't get upset. We can forget all about it if it's going to upset you this much. None of it matters.'

Grace wiped her cheek and looked at Anna, her glasses magnifying her eyes so they looked twice their usual size. 'It's not that. It's just that I feel so guilty.'

'Guilty? What on earth about?'

Grace shook her head. Her hands were twisting faster than ever in her lap now, her knuckles white. 'About Roy.' The words were so quiet, as though she'd used all her effort to push them out, that Anna wasn't sure whether she'd heard them correctly.

'Roy?'

Grace gave a small nod.

'But why?'

'Because –' She paused again, took a deep breath. 'Because he was the love of my life, Anna. Because he made me so happy, and we had so many wonderful years together. And now here I am, just a few months after losing him, thinking about another man entirely.'

'Oh, Grace,' Anna said, sliding herself off the chair and kneeling down next to Grace to wrap her arms around her. She pulled her close, breathing in her talcum-powder scent, feeling the scratch of over-sprayed hair against her cheek. A feeling of love overwhelmed Anna as she felt the frailty of Grace's body in her embrace.

Finally, Grace pulled away. 'I'm sorry, Anna, I know you probably think I'm being silly –'

'I don't. I don't at all.' She sat back on her chair but kept hold of Grace's hand. 'But you do know, don't you, that this has nothing to do with how much you loved Roy? This is about you.' She squeezed her hand. 'From the moment I met you it was clear how much you missed Roy, how much you loved him and he loved you. How much you still love him. But something about losing him and then meeting me shortly after seems to have triggered a flood of memories for you, and it was obvious to me that some of those memories were happier than others.'

Grace was silent so Anna continued. 'Although I told you it was my nosiness that first made me start looking for Arthur, all along I did really want to help you, however misguided that might have been. I just couldn't imagine how hard it must have been for you – never knowing what had happened, or why Arthur had left.' She sighed. 'I suppose I just thought that if I could find out something to tell you, it might make you feel better.' She shrugged. 'But then I found him.'

'How?'

'How what?'

'How did you find him? I never had any luck all those years ago; how did you manage to stumble across him so many decades later?'

'Luck, really. I remembered you'd mentioned he was from the North East, and I searched his name on Google and added in *Newcastle upon Tyne*, and a newspaper cutting came up, where he was quoted.'

'Oh my. Who would have thought, back then, that you could trace someone as easily as you can write a shopping list?'

'I know. And that's what made me think of doing it. It seemed too easy not to.' Anna cleared her throat. 'Anyway, I left my number with the care home and a few days later Arthur rang me and told me he was going to send that letter. And the rest you know.'

Grace shook her head, the creases in her neck switching from side to side with each slow movement. 'I can't believe it.'

'What, that I found him?'

She pursed her lips and looked angry all of a sudden. 'No. That after seventy-four years he thinks that a two-page explanation will cut the custard.'

Anna grinned. 'It's mustard, Grace.'

'What's mustard? What are you talking about now?' She glanced at her sandwich, going dry on the table, its edges curling.

'Never mind. If it makes you feel any better, I think it was as big a shock to him as it was to you. In fact, I know it was. I don't think he knew what else to do.'

'Hmm, well.'

'Doesn't it help a little bit, to hear what he has to say?'

Grace shrugged, sticking her bottom lip out like a grumpy six-year-old.

Her voice sounded pensive when she next spoke. 'I don't know.' She looked up at Anna again. 'I don't know what to do.'

'About what?'

'Well, he says he'd like to see me, and you and Tom seem to think it's a good idea. And even though I've been feeling so guilty and worrying what Roy would think, there's a small part of me that does keep wondering what he'd be like.'

Anna felt her heart race with excitement. Was Grace saying she'd like to go up and meet Arthur? Oh, how she'd love this so much. Trying not to put her off by being too enthusiastic, she said: 'Maybe we could go, together?'

Grace snapped her head round. 'Don't be daft, Anna. I couldn't do that.'

'Why not?'

'Well, quite apart from the obvious, which is that it would be entirely inappropriate, how do you suggest we get up there? Should I stick a helmet on and sling my leg over the back of your bike?'

Anna grinned. 'We could try side-saddle if you prefer.'

'I think those days are long gone sadly,' Grace said.

Then Anna had an idea. 'We could ask Tom. He might be able to take a few days off and drive us up there.'

Grace didn't look convinced. 'It still doesn't solve the other problem – that it wouldn't exactly be proper for me to be chasing round the countryside after a man who I haven't seen for more than seventy years. Not to mention that I've never chased after a man in my life and I don't intend to start now.'

'Oh, Grace, this isn't about chasing after someone. It's about getting answers before –' She stopped.

'Before I kark it, you mean.'

'I didn't mean that.'

'It's all right, I'm perfectly ready for it, as you well know.' She ran her fingers over the creped skin of her face. 'But I suppose you do have a point. About getting answers, I mean.' She glanced over at the photo of her and Roy on the mantelpiece. 'Roy was everything to me but I can't pretend that what happened with Arthur didn't affect me. Look how many times I turned Roy down before we got married because I was convinced it was all going to go wrong.

'Thinking about everything again has been strange for me. But good, too. And I think maybe you're right. This is the only thing I never quite came to terms with in my life. I never really got over it, I just shoved it under the bed and pretended it wasn't there. But it was. It still is.'

'So, what are you saying?'

'I think what I'm trying to say is that maybe I should go and see Arthur one last time. I've got an answer, of sorts, in the letter, but seeing him is an entirely different thing.' She grinned, her eyes twinkling. 'Why else would he still be alive if someone up there' – she pointed skywards – 'didn't want me to see him, even if it's only to give him a damn good piece of my mind?'

'You don't believe in anything up there,' Anna said laughing.

'Beside the point entirely, dear. What I mean is I think it's a sign.'

'All right then. Let's do it. Do you want me to ask Tom?'

Grace looked at her and raised her eyebrows. 'This is a turn-up for the books, you and Tom getting on so well. Is there something I should know?'

'No! He's just – we're friends now. Thanks to you.'

Grace rubbed her chin and tilted her head, studying Anna. Then she nodded her head. 'If you say so. I can't say I'd be disappointed if you did fall for each other, though.'

Feeling herself going red, Anna stood up and let her hair fall across her cheeks. This was ridiculous, behaving like a schoolgirl at the mere mention of a boy. 'Let me make you another cuppa, this one's stone cold,' she said quickly, scooping up the cup and saucer and almost running into the kitchen to escape Grace's scrutiny.

As she waited for the kettle to boil, she stared out at the garden and thought about Tom. Talking about this very garden was the first time she'd heard his name, and Grace had made him sound like such a golden boy – the way he looked after her, came to visit, sorted out her garden – that when she met him and he turned out to be sullen and rude, she'd been more disappointed than she cared to admit. In fact, it had made her angry.

But as the weeks had gone by she'd noticed a change in him, and in her attitude towards him. Julia's teasing and then Jenny's had annoyed her at the time, but afterwards it had given her pause for thought: *was* it possible that Tom liked her? And, more importantly, might she actually like him?

Before meeting Grace she'd been happily single but closed off entirely to the possibility of meeting anyone new after Daniel's betrayal. She didn't need anyone else; she wasn't looking and she was unlikely to be for a very long time. But then she'd met Grace and Tom, and slowly things had changed. Grace had made her understand that things happen for a reason – that what might seem like a hammer blow to the heart at the time, something from which you'll never recover, can lead to something even better in the end. If Arthur hadn't left Grace at the altar, she would never have met Roy. If Daniel hadn't cheated on her, Anna would never even have given Tom a second glance.

She liked Tom. The thought of him gave her a warm glow. She liked the way his lips were slightly crooked when he smiled, the way he looked at his feet when he was embarrassed, the way he cared so much about his great-aunt. The trouble was, she didn't know what to do about it.

'Have you gone to China for the tea?' Grace's voice cut through her thoughts and brought her back to the kitchen. She hastily made the tea and took it through, placing it on the table next to the remnants of the sandwich, which Grace was now chewing her way through.

'Sorry, Grace, I got distracted.'

'That's all right. I'm sorry if I embarrassed you with all that talk about Tom.'

'It's OK.'

Grace laid her hand on Anna's. 'If you like him, dear, don't ignore it. I know Daniel broke your heart but it doesn't mean Tom will. Just remember that.'

Anna pulled her hand away and started clearing up, picking up newspapers and tucking away a pair of slippers, dusting around the ornaments that lined the mantelpiece, in the hope that Grace would change the subject.

'Would you like to see some more photos?'

Anna looked at Grace, who was watching her intently.

'I'd love to.'

And so for the rest of the afternoon the pair sat going through old photographs – black-and-white snaps, curled at the corners, the edges blurred and indistinct – of a younger Grace. In one she was huddled on the steps of a wooden beach hut wearing a knee-length white dress, her face locked in a smile of pure happiness, her toes curled into the sand; beside her in a deckchair sat a man in a shirt with the sleeves rolled up and a neatly trimmed moustache, a woman with neatly set dark hair and a wispy smile, and a younger boy with a mop of fair hair, only a slice of his face visible. 'This is Mother and Father, and this is Ernest,' Grace said, a spindly finger pointing at the back of the young boy's head. 'Here we are at what is now Tom's beach hut, look. We went down there in all weathers.' She smiled wistfully at the memory. In another photo Grace's parents – called Charles and Cecilia, she told Anna – stood stiffly together staring at the camera uneasily; another was of Grace and Ernest digging a hole in the sand, the pier just visible in the background.

And then, finally, there were the photos of Grace and Roy: standing at the end of a pier, hair blowing wildly in the wind; holding hands on a beach, Grace in the shortest shorts Anna had ever seen; the pair of them on their wedding day, the simplicity of their outfits only serving to highlight how much in love they were.

She sighed. Maybe Grace was right after all. Did she really want to let her stupid pride get in the way of finding a love like that for herself?

* * *

Ever since she was a little girl Anna had hated speaking to people on the phone. There was something about the dislocation of not being able to see someone's face or their expression as they spoke that made her feel awkward, anxious about saying something wrong, or misunderstanding someone. Email, for her, had been a godsend. But now she had to make a call that had been niggling at the back of her mind all afternoon.

With shaking hands, she dialled the number that she'd scribbled on a scrap of paper a few days before. As it rang and rang on the other end of the line, she wondered what sort of a reception she was going to get.

Just as she was about to give up, there was a scrabbling sound and some muttering.

'Hello? Mr Robb? Arthur?'

More scrabbling as though the phone was in a pocket somewhere, then, finally, a shaky voice. 'Hello? Hello, who's there?'

'Arthur? It's Anna Snow. We spoke the other day.'

'Is that Grace's friend?'

'Yes, yes that's me!' she said, louder than she intended.

'No need to shout, dear, I'm old, not deaf.'

'Sorry.'

A pause while he cleared his throat, then: 'You showed her the letter, then?'

'Yes.'

'And?'

'She'd like to come up and see you, if you'll let her.'

'And she can, can she?'

'Can what?'

'Get all the way up here. I assume she still lives in Lowestoft.'

'Well, yes, we're hoping so.'

'Who's we? I can't have the world and his wife descending on me, not at my age.'

'Me, and my friend Tom – he's Grace's great-nephew and he's ever so nice, he won't cause you any problems.'

'I see.'

'Is that OK?'

'I suppose so.'

'So, when can we come?'

'Whenever you like, I'm not going anywhere. Couldn't even if I wanted to.'

'No, no, course not. Well, how about next week? Tuesday? Wednesday?'

'Either is fine. You decide and let me know.'

'OK, well, let's say Wednesday. I'll ring you when we're on our way, shall I?'

'No, I hardly ever have my phone switched on. You were lucky to catch me today only my grandson's just been and sorted it out for me, told me the whole point of a mobile phone is to have it with you and switched on so people can get hold of you. The thing he seems to be missing is that I don't really want people to get hold of me.'

'No, well, quite. So, we'll see you next week then, shall we?'

'Yes, all right. See you then. I shall look forward to it.'

'Thank you, Arthur.'

The line was silent for a moment and she wondered whether he'd hung up. But then she heard the clicking sound she'd heard last time, like false teeth clattering, and Arthur said, so quietly she had to strain to hear it: 'Has she had a happy life, Anna?'

'You'll have to ask her that, Arthur.'

More silence and then, without a reply, the line went dead. Anna couldn't help smiling to herself. Arthur was blunt but she didn't think it was down to rudeness. She suspected it was more to do with a fear of the mobile phone. Her grandma had been just the same, leaving messages that sounded like a formal letter, ending with 'Love Grandma'.

She realised her hand was shaking. After all this time, Grace was going to see Arthur.

Now all she needed to do was work out how to get a ninety-five-year-old woman halfway across the country.

Chapter Twenty-One

Anna's mobile beeped, and when she saw who it was she felt her stomach flip over with excitement.

We're just leaving, we'll be with you in about 15 minutes. Tom x

She tried not to think too much about what the kiss at the end meant. He was probably one of those people who put a kiss at the end of every text. But she couldn't help thinking how much she'd enjoyed all the time they'd been spending together over the last few days, planning this trip.

First, she'd had to tell Grace that Arthur had agreed to a visit, and she had prayed Grace wouldn't change her mind about going when she heard. When Anna had arrived at Grace's house to break the news last week she'd been relieved to see Tom's car in the driveway, glad of the moral support. But when she'd walked into the room and seen him sprawled on the sofa she'd found herself blushing furiously. Tom had stood up to give Anna a peck on the cheek and she'd tried not to linger on the warm, woody smell as he leaned in close, or the touch of his hand on her elbow that seemed to burn through her sleeve. Instead, she had greeted him simply and then turned to Grace, who'd been watching them with what looked like a smile of satisfaction. Grace had greeted Anna then and told her Tom had just popped over to say hello, and he had explained that he'd wanted to check on the garden – 'make sure Aunty Grace hasn't let it go to pot,' he'd said, before flopping back onto the sofa.

That's when Anna had come right out with her announcement:

'Well, I'm glad you're here because I've got some news,' she said, shrugging her coat off and hanging it at the bottom of the stairs, trying to sound efficient and businesslike.

'Oh?'

'Arthur's agreed to see you.'

Grace went so pale Anna was worried she was going to pass out. 'Oh,' she said again, this time her voice barely a whisper. 'Oh dear.'

Anna glanced at Tom for help.

He shrugged helplessly at first but then stepped up. 'Aunty Grace, aren't you pleased?' he said, his voice low.

'What, dear?' Grace looked at them both, her lower jaw hanging slightly, her deeply lined face almost grey.

'Aren't you pleased that you're going to get the chance to see Arthur after all these years?'

Anna leaned over then and took Grace's hand gently in hers as she waited for the old woman to take in the news.

Finally, Grace looked at her, her eyes wide behind her thick lenses. 'Are we definitely going to go, then?' Her voice was pleading and Anna wasn't sure what to say. All these years of not knowing, of wondering what she might have done wrong – of not even knowing whether Arthur was still alive – and now this. How could Anna tell Grace what to do?

'Listen, Grace.' She closed her other hand round Grace's and held it firmly. 'You don't have to do anything you don't want to do. I know this is hard for you, it's bound to be. But I will say this. Several weeks ago you told me you'd always wondered what had happened – whether it was your fault that Arthur left, what you might have done wrong. And now you have the chance to find out a bit more – if you want to.' She paused. 'Not many people get that chance.'

'No, I don't suppose they do, do they?' Grace looked at Anna, then at Tom. 'All right. I'll do it. But don't leave me on my own with him, will you? Either of you.'

'We won't leave your side,' Tom said, his voice warm.

'Thank you.' Grace coughed, her chest rattly. 'So, when do we go?'

And, now, here they were, about to set off.

Anna checked her reflection in the bedroom mirror, conscious she hadn't even thought about what she looked like for such a long time. She was relieved to see her normally unruly hair was behaving today, and she hoped her make-up was subtle enough to look as though she hadn't made an effort. She didn't want Tom to think it was for his benefit – but, more than that, she really didn't want Grace to feel too smug about her matchmaking skills. Nothing was actually going on with Tom yet, but it didn't mean she couldn't look presentable.

The buzzer made her jump and she grabbed her overnight bag and ran down the stairs. Tom was peering through the glass, and when he saw her his face lit up.

'Hello, you,' he said, pressing his lips to her cheek when she opened the door. 'You look nice.'

She felt her face flush. 'Thanks. How's Grace?'

'A bag of nerves,' he said as they made their way to his car. 'I thought she was going to change her mind about the whole thing this morning but I managed to coax her into the car eventually.' Tom opened the back door. 'I hope you don't mind but I've put Grace in the front.'

'That's fine,' she said, ignoring the sinking feeling that she wasn't going to be sitting next to Tom. Of course Grace should sit in the front.

Clambering in, and noticing that Tom had tidied the back for her so she didn't have to sit among his gardening tools for hundreds of miles, she buckled up as Tom pulled out of the car park.

Grace twisted round in her seat a little. 'You look lovely,' she said, smiling to reveal the characteristic smudge of lipstick on her teeth.

'Thank you, Grace. How are you feeling?'

'Oh, you know. Sick with nerves but I'm sure I'll be all right once we're on our way.'

'And have you thought about what you might say to Arthur, when you see him?'

'I've thought about nothing else, dear.'

'And?'

'I still have absolutely no idea.'

Anna smiled and rubbed Grace's shoulder. 'You'll think of something, I'm sure.'

'Let's hope so, because I'll look like a right lemon other-wise, won't I?'

Anna settled back into her seat and watched the familiar houses pass by out of the window. As they drove further inland the air changed, the light became duller and the land-scape flattened out. She followed the patchwork of green and yellow fields with her eyes as they stretched away to meet the sky, a bank of dark grey clouds lurking in the distance and threatening rain. Leaning her head back and closing her eyes, she listened to the hum of the car, the rustle of sweet wrappers and the gentle buzz of conversation coming from the front.

Suddenly the feeling of motion stopped and Anna sat up, rubbing her eyes. They were in a car park.

'Wakey-wakey, sleepyhead,' a voice said and she saw Tom peering at her through the gap between the front seats.

'Oh god, sorry, did I fall asleep?' she said, pushing herself upright.

'Yes, but it's all right because I didn't.' He grinned at his joke as he unplugged his seatbelt.

'Sorry, we're stopping for a wee already,' Grace said. 'Bladder's not what it used to be.'

Anna glanced at the clock. They'd only been going an hour. This could take some time.

'That's all right, we could do with stretching our legs a bit, couldn't we, Anna?' Tom said.

'Yes, and I could murder a coffee.'

Anna climbed out of the car and opened Grace's door. She held out her hand. 'Have you got your stick?'

'I'm all right without it,' Grace said, taking hold of her extended hand and tugging herself to standing.

'But won't it be easier to have it? The loo might be miles from the door.'

'Don't fuss, I'll be fine. Anyway, I've got you two, and I know you'll look after me, won't you?'

'Course we will,' Tom said, appearing at Anna's side and taking hold of Grace's other elbow. 'Now, let's go.'

The unscheduled stop took longer than expected and by the time they finally got going again fat raindrops were falling from the sky, turning the road into a paddling pool and blurring the view so it looked as though the world beyond the windscreen had melted. Tom slowed right down and crawled along in the slow lane.

'My grandma always used to say it never rained on the island because it had exhausted itself by the time it got that far,' Anna told them over the roar of the rain, smiling as she thought once again about her grandma's favourite sayings about the local weather.

'She was right, dear,' Grace said. 'It hardly ever rains in Lowestoft.' She peered up at the sky. 'Although I must say, this doesn't show any sign of slowing down before it gets there. It's quite ferocious, isn't it?'

'It really is,' Tom said, his face screwed up in concentration.

'Do you think you should stop for a bit?' Anna asked, leaning between the seats.

'Maybe we should. I can't really see.'

Clicking the indicator on, he slowly pulled over to the side of the road and came to a gentle stop behind someone else's brake lights. The windscreen wipers were going crazy so he flicked them off and the window immediately filled with streaks of water, running off it like rivers. It felt as though the three of them were cocooned in their own private world.

'This journey could take longer than we thought,' Tom said, opening the weather app on his phone. He turned it round to show them. 'It says it's going to be like this for at least another couple of hours.'

'Oh dear.' Grace was gripping her handbag on her lap.

'We'll be OK,' Anna reassured her.

'But what if we don't get there on time?'

'Well then we'll have to rearrange. I don't think Arthur will be going very far.'

'No, I don't suppose he will.' She coughed and clutched her chest. 'Oooh.' It came out as a small grunt.

'Grace! Are you all right?' Anna felt her heart rate quicken and didn't miss the concern etched on Tom's face.

'I'm fine, nothing to worry about. Just the usual chest infection, that's all.'

'You should have told us it was getting worse. We could have come another time.' The steady drum of raindrops on the roof beat in time with Anna's heart.

'I know, and that's exactly why I didn't mention it.' Grace turned slightly in her seat. 'I couldn't bear to put this off any longer. I know it's been seventy years and that a few more days shouldn't make much difference. But to be honest, at my age every day counts. It was now or never.' Grace coughed again, a weak sound that made her chest rattle.

'Well, OK. But you still should have told us. It's us two that are responsible for you, you know.'

'I'm not a child, Anna,' Grace snapped.

'Anna knows that,' said Tom soothingly. 'She just means that we're both here to make sure this all goes smoothly, and if you go getting ill on us we're going to feel terrible.'

'I'm fine, honestly. I'll shake it off, I always do.'

'Well, if you're sure. We're not too far away to turn round and start again another day.'

'Absolutely not. I need to do this now.'

Tom glanced at Anna and she gave a small nod.

'All right then. But if you get any worse, I'm taking you home. No arguments. Deal?'

'OK, bossy breeches,' Grace said sulkily. 'Whatever you say.' She folded her arms across her chest and sat facing the front of the car, staring moodily at the smudged world in front of her. A smile played on Tom's lips and Anna felt herself grinning too. They'd been well and truly told off.

They sat a while longer, listening to the rain pound the car as wheels swished past slowly, headlights picking out the puddles as vehicles made their way cautiously along the road. The windows steamed up and above the racket came a gentle snoring sound as Grace nodded off.

Anna pulled herself forward and leaned between the front seats again.

'Do you think she'll be OK?' she mouthed.

Tom looked across at Grace and they both listened to the gentle rattle of her breath catching each time she drew in air. He shrugged.

'Honestly, I've got no idea,' he whispered. 'But she's determined to go, so my call is that we carry on and play it by ear.' He twisted round to face her and his mouth was just inches from hers. Anna felt the warmth of his breath on her nose. 'I don't think she'll ever forgive us if we don't.'

Anna nodded. 'But I do worry. She's ninety-five years old. What if something happens to her?'

'Then I guess we'll just have to deal with it.'

Tom turned back round to face the front and Anna sighed. 'If we ever get there.'

'You're as bad as Grace, being all sulky,' Tom said, catching her eye in the rear-view mirror.

'Sorry. It just feels as though we're doomed,' she continued in hushed tones. 'I mean, we've been going two hours and we're only about forty miles from home. Maybe someone's trying to tell us this is a bad idea.'

'What, you think Arthur did some kind of rain dance to make this happen?'

'Ha ha, hilarious.' She giggled. 'To be honest, I don't think he'll be in any fit state to do any kind of dance – he tired himself out just talking to me on the phone.'

'Is he older than Grace?'

'Only by a few months.' She sighed. 'It's sad really, isn't it?'

'What is?'

'This. Both of them nearly at the end of their lives, and they've still got all these regrets.'

'I suppose so. But at least they're getting the chance to try and sort this one out.'

'You're right. We have to get her there, whatever it takes, don't we?'

'I think we do.'

Several more minutes passed before the rain eased enough for them to carry on, and even then the pace was much slower than planned thanks to all the water streaming down the road. Anna watched the back-and-forth motion of the windscreen wipers, listened to Grace's gentle snoring and smiled. They were an unlikely bunch, but she felt happy to be here with them both. And she felt excited about what the rest of the day might bring.

An hour later they pulled into another service station. As the engine cut out, Grace murmured and opened her eyes.

'Where are we?'

'We're just stopping for petrol,' Tom said.

'Is it still raining?'

'Not much.'

'Oh good.' Grace rubbed her face. 'Oooh, I'm peckish. Are we having lunch?'

'We can if you like,' said Anna, 'but it's only midday. We might be better to keep going a bit longer, get some miles under our belt.'

Grace did the sticking out her bottom lip thing again. 'All right.' She opened her bag and pulled out a foil-wrapped package. 'Just as well I brought some sandwiches then, isn't it?'

'Did you make those yourself?'

'I'm not entirely incapable, you know,' she said, holding out a slightly squashed ham roll behind her. 'Want one?'

'Thanks,' Anna said, and took an enormous bite. She hadn't realised how hungry she was too.

The car all fuelled up, they were off again, and this time Grace was clearly in the mood to talk.

'So, you two seem to be getting on well,' she said, mischief glinting in her eyes.

'Why wouldn't we be? Anna's lovely,' Tom said, catching Anna's eye in the mirror and smiling. She beamed back.

'Oh, I know she is,' Grace agreed, brushing crumbs from her skirt. 'But it didn't half take you a long time to realise.'

Anna was sure she saw Tom's reflection redden as he stared straight ahead at the road. 'Yes, well. The less said about that the better.' He glanced across at Grace. 'Anyway, you of all people know what a pain I can be sometimes.'

'I did tell Anna that.'

'Oi!'

Grace shrugged. 'If the cap fits, Thomas.'

The car hummed on, the road slipping steadily by beneath it now the rain had eased.

'So, does this mean you like each other now?' Grace said outright, a playful expression lighting up her face.

Anna jumped in. 'Er…yes. I think it means I have a new friend in my life now.' She wondered whether Tom was going to answer too, but before he had the chance, Grace piped up again.

'A friend, eh?' Grace grinned. 'Well, that's a good start anyway.'

Anna was watching Tom closely in the mirror for a reaction; he rolled his eyes and changed the subject. 'So, how are you feeling about today, having read Arthur's letter again?' he said.

Grace picked at her skirt, suddenly thoughtful. 'I'm not sure. I was angry at first. I mean, who does he think he is, sending me a two-page letter and thinking that's enough to make up for everything? But then I thought about it and realised that it wasn't entirely his fault. Oh, I don't mean breaking my heart – that definitely *was* his fault. But the not being in touch afterwards. I mean, he was ill, wasn't he? He couldn't help it.'

'That's true,' Tom agreed. 'It's still a lot to take in, though.'

'It is.' All of a sudden her body jolted forward and she doubled over in a cough, her breath wheezy as she sucked in air after each bout. Tom and Anna waited silently for her to finish. Finally, the coughing subsided.

'Do we need to be going home?' Tom said, his voice stern.

'Absolutely not. It was just a little cough, that's all. Must have got a bit of sandwich stuck.'

Anna nodded doubtfully. It was impossible to know whether Grace was telling the truth or whether she was just trying not to worry them. If she was anything like Anna's late grandmother, she'd be a martyr until the very end, insist there was nothing wrong even as she took her last breath.

God, please don't let her take her last breath any time soon.

Shaking the thought away, Anna reached into her bag for a packet of wine gums. 'Want one?' she offered, waving it around towards the front of the car.

'Ooh, I haven't had these for ages,' Grace said, delving straight in. 'Oh, but they might pull my dentures out.'

'They might pull all my fillings out too but I'm going to live life on the edge and eat some anyway,' Tom said, sticking his spare hand into the packet and shoving three or four in his mouth at once.

'You pig!' Anna laughed as Tom spluttered in amusement through a mouthful of sticky sugar.

'Hiii hike hine hums,' he said, his mouth masticating like

a cow chewing grass.

'You'll have no teeth left if you eat like that,' said Grace, popping one delicately into her mouth and chewing slowly.

A few minutes passed, then Tom said, 'Come on, Aunty Grace, tell us about Arthur.'

'What about him?'

'Well, what do you think you might say to him when you see him for the first time after all these years?'

'I don't know. I might not recognise him.'

'That reminds me,' Anna said, pulling a printed sheet of paper from her coat pocket. 'I found a photo – it was part of the news story that helped me track him down in the first place.'

'And you're only just telling me this now?'

'Well, yes. I don't have a printer so I had to print it out at the library. Sorry.'

Grace took the piece of paper with trembling hands and unfolded it. The picture was grainy and she pulled it close to her face and studied it in silence for a moment. After a while she spoke. 'I might have known.' She folded the paper up again and placed it in her lap. 'He hasn't changed at all.'

'So, you recognise him then?'

'Yes. I'd know those eyes anywhere,' she said, her voice tinged with sadness.

'Well, that's great news,' Tom said. 'It means you won't start talking to the wrong person and demanding answers.' He grinned at Anna. 'Can you imagine it, some poor old sod sitting there getting abuse from Grace and not having a clue what's going on?'

'Terrifying,' Anna agreed, laughing.

'Very funny, you two,' Grace said. 'For your information, I was never actually worried I wouldn't recognise him. I just – couldn't quite picture him, old. And now I can.'

'Well, good.' Anna leaned forward again. 'So, have you thought any more about what you're actually going to say to him?'

Grace sighed heavily. 'I have absolutely no idea. I mean, where do I start?' She looked round, her rheumy eyes wide. 'You really do promise you'll come in with me, won't you? Both of you. You won't leave me to go in there on my own? I don't think I could do it.'

'Of course we'll stay with you, won't we, Tom?'

'You don't think we're coming all this way to miss out on all the fun, do you?'

'Ooh, I'm going to throw something at you in a minute, young man!' Grace launched a piece of scrunched-up foil across the car, causing Tom to duck and swerve the steering slightly.

'Shit!'

'Oh dear, sorry,' Grace murmured.

'It's fine. No harm done,' Tom said, straightening up. 'But I mean it, Aunty Grace. We're not bringing you all this way just to dump you the minute we get there. We're in this together.'

'Thank you, Tom, thank you, Anna.' She cleared her throat. 'I might sound ungrateful sometimes but I do really appreciate this, you know. I know neither of you had to do this for me.'

'We wanted to,' Anna said. 'It might sound soppy but you've come to mean a lot to me over the last few months.' She reached her hand forward and gave Grace's shoulder a little squeeze.

'You mean a lot to me, too.' Grace patted Anna's hand gently, her skin feeling warm and dry to the touch. A single tear made its way down the side of Grace's face.

'Oh, don't cry,' Anna said.

'I'm sorry, I'm being so silly.'

'You're not being silly but we don't want to see you sad. What's making you cry?'

'It's just – I don't know. I keep thinking about how different my life would have been if I'd married Arthur. I mean, who's to say it would have been a good life? I would probably have settled down to be the dutiful wife, maybe even had a baby, and I never would have done all the wonderful things I did in my life. I certainly would never have met my darling Roy.' She sniffed. 'I hope he wouldn't have been cross at me for doing this.'

'He wouldn't,' Tom said. 'Uncle Roy was the kindest man in the world and he loved you so much. He knew you loved him too, but he would have wanted you to find some answers from all those years ago if you got the chance. He would have been the first one to tell you to do this.'

'You're right. He would have been.' She sighed. 'I've had a good life, you know. Despite everything. It could end at any moment and nobody could say it was a tragedy. But you're right that I'm doing this for me, not anyone else. If I can talk to Arthur again, get some proper answers about what happened back then – more than just this letter – then I suppose I'll have peace. And that's all you need at the end of your life, isn't it? Peace. And love – but I've had plenty of that. I'm one of the lucky ones.'

They all fell into a silence for a moment after Grace's words. Anna wasn't ready to lose her friend just yet, not when she'd only just found her. But she thought about what Grace had said about being lucky. Some people never found love, never found someone to make them feel special. What was the saying – it was better to have loved and lost than never to have loved at all? Something like that anyway. Anna wasn't sure about that – losing love was pretty painful, as she knew from experience. But she was lucky that she had people in her life who loved her: her mum and dad, Julia, and now, she liked to think, Grace too. She tried not to wonder whether the man sitting in front of her could ever think of her that way, but she knew beyond a shadow of a doubt that whatever happened in her life from now on, meeting Grace had changed it in more ways than she might possibly ever realise.

* * *

What on earth was she doing, agreeing to this journey? Her back hurt and her legs ached and, to be quite frank, she wasn't sure whether this was such a good idea after all. Oh, she was a silly old woman sometimes. What did she think she was going to achieve by seeing Arthur after all these years?

But Grace couldn't deny she felt a little bit excited too. There was this constant fluttering in her tummy, and every time she tried to imagine setting eyes on Arthur again she felt tingly with anticipation. What on earth was she going to say to him after all these years?

She rolled her eyes at herself, and listened to the rumble of the tyres. She liked pretending to be asleep sometimes, because it meant she could earwig on Tom and Anna's conversations when they thought she wasn't listening. She was so glad they seemed to be getting on these days. It seemed as though this whole Arthur thing had brought them closer together for whatever reason. So, if nothing else, it had been worth it for that.

Closing her eyes and leaning back against the headrest, she let the hum of the engine send her towards sleep again. All the excitement was making her feel exhausted. If she could just get a little bit of shut-eye…

Chapter Twenty-Two

'Can we stop again?' Grace demanded. 'I could do with another wee.'

'Me too, actually,' Tom said, squinting at the approaching sign. 'Five miles to the next services – let's stop there.'

The stop, as usual, turned into a much longer break than expected, and by the time they piled back into the car having eaten a second lunch of sandwiches – Pret this time – another two hours had passed.

'How much longer until we get there?' Grace asked, sighing as she rested her head against the back of the seat.

Anna checked Google Maps. The A1 looked busy all the way up. 'It says another two and a half hours, but if we stop again it will be much longer.' She glanced at the clock. It was already gone two o'clock. 'We're going to be very late for Arthur. We said we'd be there before three.'

'Well, let's get going and see how we get on,' Tom said, starting up the engine.

'Can we have some music?' Grace asked as he pulled onto the motorway.

'What would you like?'

'Oh, I don't know about all this modern stuff – I like a bit of Cliff Richard. Why don't you surprise me?'

Tom passed his phone to Anna in the back seat. 'Can you find something on here?' he said.

Anna scrolled through Tom's Spotify playlist. You could tell a lot about someone by their taste in music and she was worried about what she might find. What if he was a secret Justin Bieber fan, or he had every album Neil Diamond had ever made?

Relieved to find his taste in music was really quite normal, if a little on the bland side, she selected Adele, hoping Grace might approve.

'Ooh, I like this one,' Grace remarked as the rich tones of 'Someone Like You' rang out.

Feeling content, Anna closed her eyes and let the rhythmic pulse of the music and the rumble of the car tyres send her off into another snooze.

She came to with a realisation that they were no longer moving and glanced out of the window expecting to see the car park of yet another service station. But there was nothing outside the car except lines of traffic, vehicles queuing as far as the eye could see on either side of them, engines idling. Someone was standing on the grass verge talking on a mobile phone; a few people were wandering around trying to peer into the distance to see if they could work out what was causing the hold-up.

'Where are we?' she asked, her voice a croak.

'Somewhere between York and Darlington,' Tom said. 'We've been sitting here for a good twenty minutes already and there's no sign of any movement yet.'

'Accident?'

He nodded. 'I think so.'

She sighed. In the past she would have felt angry, frustrated at the delay and the inconvenience it was causing her, cross about the ruined plans. But something about the mission they were on, the reason they were even in the car in the first place, made her take stock. Life was a series of random events, good and bad, and if you were to let the things you couldn't control get under your skin you'd drive yourself mad. Besides, as least they weren't in the actual incident ahead, whatever had happened. They were safe.

'It doesn't look as though we're going to get there in time to see Arthur today,' Tom said, indicating the clock. It was already four-thirty. 'Do you think you should ring him?'

'Yes, I probably should,' Anna agreed. 'Do you think it will be tomorrow now?'

'I should think so. We're going to have to go straight to the hotel when we get there. If we ever get there.' He grinned. 'I don't fancy sleeping in the car.'

Anna nodded, distracted by the thought of staying in a hotel with Tom. She found her phone in the bottom of her bag and called Arthur's number but it went straight through to answerphone. She called the care-home number and left a message.

'They should let him know,' she said, hanging up.

'Who'll let who know what?' Grace had woken up.

'The care home,' Tom said. 'We don't think we're going to make it to see Arthur today, so Anna was just letting them know.'

'Why ever not?'

Tom motioned out of the window and Grace followed his gaze, a look of surprise on her face.

'Oh, we're stuck.'

'We are and we have been for some time,' Tom said. They

fell into silence as an ambulance screamed past down the hard shoulder, lights flashing.

'Oh no,' Grace mumbled.

'Quite,' Tom said, chewing his bottom lip. Anna found herself staring at him and had to force herself to turn away.

'I need to get out,' Grace said suddenly, pushing open the passenger door and starting to climb out.

'What are you doing?' Anna and Tom said in unison.

'I just need to –' She stopped, doubled over on the edge of her seat, legs outside the car, as enormous hacking coughs wracked her body once again. Anna leapt out of the back seat and stood by Grace as her body convulsed, afraid she was going to fall and smack her head on the tarmac.

Minutes passed before the coughing slowly subsided. Anna crouched down beside her and rubbed her back gently. Grace's face was white, ghostly, and she looked frightened.

'Grace, I'm really worried about you, this is getting worse,' Anna said.

Grace shook her head. 'I'm all right, really,' she said, rubbing her chest gently. 'It's just a cough.'

'I think it's a little bit more than that, don't you?'

'I'll be fine. I've had it before and I lived to tell the tale. Besides, I'm not letting a pesky cough stop me from seeing Arthur, not now I've come all this way.'

Over the top of Grace's head Anna glanced at Tom in the driver's seat and he shook his head and shrugged.

'Well, at least let me take you to see a doctor when we get there,' Anna said.

Grace shook her head vehemently. 'No. I don't need to see a doctor. I'm always seeing bloomin' doctors and none of it makes the blindest bit of difference. I'm fine, Anna, please don't fuss. I just want to do this and then go home.'

It was clear there was no room for argument. 'All right.

But will you at least promise me you'll go when we get back to Lowestoft?'

Grace nodded. 'Guide's honour.'

Anna bit back a smile. She despaired sometimes. 'Right, well get back in the car,' Anna said, making to shuffle Grace's legs back inside.

'But I want to get out.'

'Grace, you're too weak,' Anna said.

'I'm perfectly capable of standing up.'

Anna sighed. This was worse than trying to look after her nieces. At least you could force children into submission if you needed to. You could hardly threaten a ninety-five-year-old woman with having her Xbox taken away for a week if she didn't behave.

'Anna's right,' Tom said. 'That coughing fit really took it out of you and the last thing we need is for you to collapse on us. Imagine coming all this way and then having to go to hospital before we even got to see Arthur.'

'Will you help me then?' she pleaded.

'OK, but you have to promise to hold onto my arm and not let go.'

'All right, all right.'

'And we're only going to walk as far as that car in front and back again,' he added.

'All right.' Grace's bottom lip was sticking out and Anna again recalled the image of her as a child digging her heels in. She wondered whether you got more stubborn as you aged or if Grace had always been like this. She felt a rush of love for her.

Together, Anna and Tom helped Grace up to standing, then slowly inched away from the car and along the tarmac. By now many people had abandoned their vehicles. Two young children were kicking a football aimlessly between two cars; a couple were having a picnic on the verge; a woman was trying to console a hysterical baby. Another couple, who remained in their car, sat staring straight out of the window with stony faces. Anna wondered what they looked like, the three of them, what people would be making of them. Would they assume she and Tom were a couple, helping one of their elderly relatives? Or would they perhaps think they were brother and sister? Friends? Carers? She looked across Grace to Tom. Being huddled so closely together like this as they supported Grace was the first chance she'd had to really study Tom's face properly. His stubble was more of a beard at the moment, and it suited him. His nose was long and straight, and his eyes wide. She lingered on his strong cheekbones as she scanned her eyes over his features.

'Are you trying to remember what I look like in case you need to put together a police profile?' he said without turning his head.

'What? Oh, sorry,' Anna said, feeling the heat rise to her face.

'Well, it's understandable, I *am* very handsome.' He turned his head and flashed her a cheesy smile.

'Oh, ha ha.' Between them Anna could hear Grace wheezing gently on each out-breath. Her hand was tight round Anna's arm.

'Oh, you two,' she said, looking up at Anna then Tom. 'I knew I'd be right about you.'

'Who says you're right about anything?' Tom said, manoeuvring them round so they were facing back towards the car.

'I do,' Grace said. 'Are you telling me I'm wrong?'

'Well…' Tom said, trailing off. On Grace's other side Anna didn't say anything.

Back at the car now, they lowered Grace into the passenger seat. Halfway down she hesitated.

'What's the matter?' Anna asked.

'Why don't I sit in the back? You sit up front with Tom,' Grace said, straightening up again.

'No, don't be silly, I'm fine in the back,' Anna said.

'But I fancy another snooze so I might as well be there as up here.' Grace wasn't giving up so Anna nodded.

'All right. Let's get you in the back then.'

Anna spent a few minutes pulling the passenger seat forward, adjusting the headrest and rolling up a blanket for Grace to place under her head. Once she was convinced Grace was safely installed in the back of the car, Anna climbed into the front beside Tom. A silence fell between them as they both studiously examined the rear of the car they were pulled up behind.

'Well, this isn't quite what I had planned for the day,' Tom said eventually.

'Me neither.'

'I don't suppose you've got any more snacks in that bag, have you?'

'Nope, nothing.'

Silence descended again.

'Tell me about yourself.'

Anna whipped her head round. 'What do you want to know?'

'I don't mind – anything. Where did you grow up? Who are your family?' He paused, flicked his eyes towards her briefly. 'Have you been married? That sort of thing.'

'Oh, right.'

'I mean, you don't have to. I just thought it might pass the time, you know.' Tom's words fell over each other on the way out.

Anna shook her head. 'No, it's fine. I don't mind.' She took a deep breath. 'Well, I grew up in Lowestoft, and my mum and dad and my brother Adam and his wife and kids all live there too. I started working as a carer when I was twenty, I've never been abroad, which I realise is tragic, and I learnt to play the flute as a child.' She kept her eyes trained on the car in front. 'Now, I'm getting divorced.'

'Oh. I'm really sorry to hear that.'

'It's OK. Well, it is what it is.' She paused, unsure whether to say anything more. Did he really want to know or was he just being polite? She decided to go for it. 'Dan and I were married for twelve years. We tried for a baby, it didn't work, then he had an affair and I threw him out. That was eighteen months ago now and I haven't seen him since. Last I heard he was living with this other woman.'

'I'm so sorry, Anna.'

She heard him shuffle in his seat to face her but she couldn't bear to look at him.

'It's fine.' She shrugged. 'Well, it isn't, but it's getting there.'

Silence fell as they watched people milling about in the road ahead.

'So, what about you?' Anna said at last. She wasn't going to admit she already knew a little thanks to Grace and her Facebook searches.

He let out a lungful of air before speaking. 'God, well, there's not much to tell really. I'm an only child. I think my mum and dad struggled to have any more kids but we never talked about it. We spent holidays in France, and I spent most of my childhood on the beach, alone or with friends.' She saw him shrug. 'It wasn't an unhappy childhood but it was lonely. I think that's why I loved being on the beach so much – it just felt like a place where being alone didn't matter.' He sighed.

'Apart from that, I'm a disaster in relationships, have only had one long-term relationship and even that ended badly.'

'Emily?'

He nodded. 'She wasn't right for me anyway, so it's probably just as well.'

'But why did it end so badly?' She turned to face him now but he kept his gaze trained on the steering wheel, his jaw set.

'Honestly? I wanted kids and she ran a mile.' His face flushed. 'Most people I know have the opposite problem.'

'That's true.' She didn't know what else to say. She wanted to reach out and grab hold of his hand, but she didn't dare. What would it feel like? Soft? Rough? 'How long ago was that?' she said instead.

'A couple of years. I know, I know, that's a bloody long time. Don't I know it! Trouble is, I work all the time – the business is booming, in fact. And now here I am, sitting in the middle of the motorway telling my life story to a woman I've only known for a couple of months, taking my ninety-five-year-old great-aunt to meet the man that broke her heart over seventy years ago and wondering how on earth this all happened.'

Anna grinned. 'I think we've both been Graced, that's what's happened.'

Tom nodded. 'You're right. We have.' He looked up at her. 'But I don't think I mind too much, do you?'

She shook her head. 'No. I don't think I do.'

For a moment they sat like that, face to face across the gearstick, their hands just inches from each other. Anna kept imagining moving her fingers closer so they touched his, and wondered whether he was picturing the same. And then there was the sudden sound of car doors slamming outside, engines revving, and then cars starting inching slowly forward and all focus was jolted back to the road ahead.

Tom turned away and started the engine up, pulling on his seatbelt at the same time. 'It looks like we're off,' he said, and finally they were on the move again.

'Oh, thank goodness for that,' Anna said, her voice falsely cheerful to try to cover up the fact she was disappointed about the traffic moving again.

By the time they arrived on the outskirts of Newcastle upon Tyne it was early evening. They made their way straight to the Travelodge, five minutes from the care home. As the receptionist handed over the keys for the double room to Anna and Tom, Anna flushed.

'Oh no, I'm on my own,' Tom said, handing over the second key to Anna. 'These two are together.'

'Sorry, sir,' the receptionist said, apparently oblivious to any discomfort she'd caused.

They made their way up in the lift and at the second floor went their separate ways, Tom suggesting they meet in the bar in about ten minutes.

They didn't have much to unpack so as soon as Anna and Grace got to their room, Grace sat down on the bed. 'Oh, I'm wiped out,' she said, resting her head on the pillow.

'It's been a long day,' Anna agreed.

'I don't think I'm going anywhere for the rest of the night.'

'Oh, but you must eat, Grace.'

Grace shook her head. 'If you wouldn't mind just making me a cup of tea, that will be fine,' she said.

'If you're sure. Do you want me to stay with you?'

'Absolutely not. I want you to go out and have dinner with my lovely Thomas.'

'Do you now?'

Grace nodded. 'He likes you a lot, you know. And I think you feel the same way about him.'

'I don't know about that.'

Grace shook her head. 'Don't be coy with me, Anna, I've been around for too long to be fooled. And I know Tom very well; I can tell he's quite smitten.'

Anna smiled, beaten. She couldn't argue with Grace when she was in a mood like this, and actually she wasn't sure she really wanted to.

'Now, go and have some fun together, and don't give me another thought. And, Anna, will you make me a promise?'

'What?'

'Drop your guard. Don't let it get in the way of your happiness.'

'My –?' But the look on Grace's face told her not to persist. Besides, Anna knew exactly what she was talking about.

'I'll do my best.'

Grace placed her hand on Anna's forearm. 'Thank you. You'll make an old woman very happy.'

'See you later, Grace. We won't be late back.'

'Don't rush back for me. I'm just going to watch a bit of TV and get some sleep. I need to get some rest before tomorrow.'

'All right.' She leaned in and placed a gentle kiss on Grace's forehead. 'Night then.'

'Night, dear. Now, off you go.'

Anna didn't need telling twice.

* * *

The minute the door closed behind Anna, Grace hauled herself up to sitting. She *was* tired – it was surprising how exhausting it could be sitting in a car all day doing nothing. But the main reason she'd wanted to stay in the room was so that Anna and Tom could have the evening to themselves without her interfering. She was sure they both thought she'd done quite enough of that.

She smiled as she picked up the remote control and waited for the television to fire up. They thought she hadn't heard them talking, the pair of them, in the car earlier. Telling each other all about themselves, about lost loves. Her heart had pinched when Tom had told Anna about wanting a baby. He'd never told her that was the reason he'd split up with Emily, but it all made sense now. She was never good enough for Tom anyway, in her opinion. Far too full of herself. Anna, on the other hand… Now, even if she said so herself, she'd done a pretty good job of matchmaking there, if everything worked out. A real Cilla Black, she was.

Oh, she would be thrilled if Anna and Tom fell in love. She just hoped she'd be around to see it.

Resting her head back on the pillow, she closed her eyes and listened to the first strains of the Corrie theme tune as she drifted off towards sleep.

* * *

The evening didn't pan out quite as hoped, in the end. When Anna arrived at the bar, Tom was perched on a stool looking worried.

'What's the matter?'

Tom slid off the stool. 'I'm so sorry, Anna, but I've just listened to a message I got from work while I was driving and I've got to have an urgent look at some plans for a garden the guys are working on before the morning. It's such a pain, but it really is something only I can do.'

Anna's heart sank. She'd been so looking forward to spending the evening with Tom. But she smiled at him. 'That's OK, I'll just go on my own.' She kept her voice bright.

Tom looked around. 'Is Grace not with you?'

'No, we've tired her out, poor old thing. She says she's going to have a cup of tea and go to sleep.'

'Oh no, now I feel even worse.'

Anna patted his forearm awkwardly. 'Don't be silly – it's work. Besides, I'm quite happy on my own.'

Tom looked crestfallen. 'Oh, OK.'

'Oh! I didn't mean it like that. I just meant I'm fine on my own, that's all.' She softened her voice. 'It would have been nice to have spent some time together though.'

Tom looked at the floor. 'Yes, it would.'

'Well. You'd better go and make some calls then,' she said, shooing him out of the room.

He disappeared towards the lift, leaving Anna alone.

'Can I get you anything, miss?' she heard the barman say.

Anna turned. 'Oh, er…yes, why not,' she said, settling onto the bar stool Tom had just vacated. 'I'll have a glass of pinot grigio, please.'

'Five-pound twenty please, pet,' he said, and she swiped her card across the machine.

This wasn't how she'd planned to spend her evening, but it didn't come as such a big surprise. It wasn't as though she wasn't used to being on her own.

Besides, with any luck, she'd have plenty of time to get to know Tom better when they got home.

In fact, she'd make sure of it.

Chapter Twenty-Three

The sun was streaming through the paper-thin curtains early the next morning, but that wasn't what woke Anna. Instead, the sound of Grace's hacking cough was what made her sit bolt upright just after six o'clock, her head pounding with exhaustion. She rubbed her eyes and tried to focus.

'Grace?'

No answer, so she waited for the coughing to stop. When it did, Grace looked up, her eyes without her glasses roving blindly round the room. Anna reached across for the glasses perched on Grace's bedside table and handed them to her.

'Good god, Grace, that sounded terrible. Don't try telling me this isn't getting worse.'

'I'm fine, don't fuss,' Grace said sharply, pushing her glasses onto her nose and blinking. She pulled herself slowly up onto the pillows and let out a shaky breath.

'Do you need anything?' Anna asked.

'I wouldn't mind a glass of water.'

Anna climbed out of bed and filled a glass with tap water, waiting while Grace sipped it. She sat carefully on the end of her bed. Grace's tiny frame was barely visible beneath the mounds of covers, and when she breathed there was no movement at all.

'Grace, I'm really worried about you.'

'I–'

Anna held her hand up. 'No, let me speak. I know you keep saying you're fine, but this is not my idea of fine. And yes, I know you're a grown-up and you don't need looking after, but the fact is I feel responsible. Tom and I both do. We're the ones who've brought you all the way up here, and it's up to us to make sure we keep you safe and well. So, with that in mind, I think you need to go and see the doctor.'

'Oh, not this again.'

'Yes, this again.' Anna sighed heavily. 'I don't understand why you're so against the idea. You've got a terrible cough and the doctor might be able to help. What's so awful about that?'

'I just don't want to go. I know what's wrong with me and going to the doctor's won't change that. As I told you yesterday, I just want to get to the care home, see Arthur, and then go home.'

Anna hesitated. 'What do you mean you know what's wrong with you?'

'What?'

'Just then. You said you know what's wrong with you.'

'Well, I do.' Grace coughed into her hand, her chest rattling. 'I've got a chest infection, haven't I? I've already told you that. But I've had it before and it will be fine. So I'm not going to the doctor's, it's nothing but a waste of time.'

'Are you going to stamp your feet and say "so there" as well?'

Grace lifted her chin. 'If I have to.'

Anna stood, defeated. 'All right. No doctors today. But I'm

keeping a close eye on you, and if I think you're getting worse, we're going straight there. Deal?'

'What happens if I say no deal?'

'Is that what you're saying?'

Grace held her gaze for a moment, then gave a small shake of her head. 'No, I'm not. Deal.'

'Good.' Anna climbed back under her duvet. 'Now, shall we try to get a bit more sleep before the day starts – otherwise we're all going to be exhausted?'

'I'm not tired, do you mind if I watch a bit of telly?'

'I suppose not.'

Grace reached for the remote and clicked the on button, and breakfast TV sprung to life. Anna rolled over and pulled the duvet tight over her head, but after fifteen minutes she realised that she was never going to get back to sleep with the sound of Piers Morgan ranting in her ear.

The day was about to begin.

* * *

Breakfasted, showered and dressed, they were all now standing in the Travelodge car park and it was still only a shade after eight-thirty. The sun was already high in the sky although it wasn't yet warm enough to take the chill off the air and Anna tugged her jacket tighter around her.

'Do you think we'll be too early if we set off now?' Tom asked as he helped Grace into the car.

'The woman I spoke to said it would be fine if we got there about nine, so we haven't got long to wait.' Anna pulled open the back door and shoved her bag inside. 'There's not much point in hanging around here.'

Tom checked his phone. 'Let's get going, then.'

'Come on, you two lovebirds, don't stand there gassing all day,' Grace teased, poking her head out of the car door.

Anna hadn't yet admitted to Grace that last night hadn't ended up being the romantic evening she'd hoped it would be. She didn't want to disappoint her today – she had enough to think about – so had just been vague when she'd asked about it.

As Tom started up the engine, Anna read out directions to the care home and, sure enough, six minutes later they pulled into the car park. The building was a two-storey redbrick and looked fairly new. A few cars were dotted around the car park and the entrance was flanked by two white pillars. Curtains hung neatly at every window, flowers bloomed in boxes and the garden was tidy and well cared for.

'This looks nice,' Tom said.

'For a prison,' Grace mumbled.

'It looks nothing like a prison!' Anna said.

'It might as well be. This is the sort of place you go to and never leave.'

'Well, then think yourself lucky you've never needed to go to one.'

Grace didn't answer but sat with her arms crossed and a furious expression on her face. Anna leaned through the centre of the front seats and placed her hand gently on Grace's shoulder. The old woman's fragile frame was shaking.

'Are you nervous, Grace?'

Grace raised her shoulders in a shrug. 'A bit.'

Tom reached across to take her hand. Her birdlike fingers were swamped by his and Anna felt her heart contract.

'You don't have to do this if you don't want to,' Tom said. 'If you've changed your mind, we're not going to be cross, are we, Anna?'

'Of course not.'

Grace sat for a moment, staring into her lap; she seemed to be holding her breath. Finally, she shook her head. 'No. I want to go in. I have to. I haven't waited all this time and come all this way to chicken out now.'

'Are you sure?' Anna asked.

'Absolutely.'

'Right, well then, let's go and find Arthur,' Tom said, opening his door and climbing out to help Grace.

With Grace flanked by Anna and Tom, the trio made their way towards the entrance. Anna's legs shook and her heart pounded in her ears. She wondered how terrified Grace must be feeling if she was as scared as this.

Inside, the building was over-warm. Slices of sun fell onto the carpet to create a patchwork of light, which they walked over as they headed for the reception desk. Leaflets and flyers were stacked on the desktop advertising mobility scooters, wheelchairs and funeral services and it struck Anna how inappropriate that was. They sat Grace down in a nearby chair as someone approached.

'Morning, how can I help?' rang out a sing-song Geordie accent.

'Oh, hello,' Anna said, turning to see a rotund woman with short bright-red-dyed hair smiling at her. 'We're here to see Arthur Robb.'

'Ah yes, you must be Anna,' the woman said, holding out her hand. 'I'm Margaret, the manager here. Lovely to meet you. Arthur's expecting you.'

'Oh good,' Anna said, shaking Margaret's hand vigorously.

'And who else do we have here?' Margaret asked.

'This is Tom, my – friend, Grace's great-nephew. And this is Grace. This is the lady who wants to see Arthur.'

'Ah, so you're Grace,' Margaret said, stepping towards Grace and extending her hand. 'Arthur's talked about you a lot since your friend Anna rang last week. He told us you used to love dancing together, before the war. It sounded very romantic.'

Grace looked stricken, her face white. She didn't reply, and didn't accept Margaret's hand.

'Grace is a little worried about seeing Arthur,' Anna interjected. 'They haven't seen each other since 1946, and – well, it's a long time...'

'Wow,' Margaret said. 'Arthur said it had been many years but I didn't realise it was that long. I wonder if you'll recognise each other.'

'I'm sure they will,' Anna said. Grace's face looked rather grey now, and Anna wondered whether she was up to this.

'Let me go and see if Arthur is ready and I'll be right back,' Margaret said, and she disappeared off down a corridor lined with doors, leaving the three of them waiting anxiously.

'Grace, are you all right?' Tom asked.

Grace gave a small nod and clutched her handbag against her chest until her knuckles turned white.

Moments later Margaret returned. 'Arthur's ready,' she announced. 'He's waiting in the lounge. I think he's looking forward to seeing you.'

Anna held her hand out for Grace to take, Tom held her on other side, and together they shuffled along the corridor behind Margaret. Anna could feel Grace quaking but she didn't dare ask her if she was OK again; she knew Grace just needed to get this moment over and done with.

The corridor stretched so far ahead of them they might as well have had a desert to cross as they inched slowly across the beige carpet towards the room where Arthur was waiting. As they passed the framed photos of residents and pictures of days out that lined the walls either side, Anna couldn't help thinking about the many stories Grace had told her. She thought about all those things that Grace had done in her life since the day Arthur had abandoned her – her job as the only woman on a newspaper, her affair with Samuel, the baby she'd lost. And, finally, her Roy, the man she'd loved for most of her life. How many of the people in these photos, behind these doors, reduced to bags of wrinkled skin, had similar stories to tell? Who knew what lives they had led, what differences they had made to the world? And soon they would be gone, leaving other people, people like her, to carry on and tell their stories. It felt overwhelming.

And, now, Grace was confronting the one thing she'd never come to terms with throughout her life. Would Arthur be able to give her the peace she deserved? Anna really hoped so.

Finally, Margaret came to a stop in front of an open doorway.

'Here we are,' she said. 'It's nice and quiet in here at the moment so you should have some privacy. Arthur's over in the corner – it's his favourite spot when it's sunny, by the big window overlooking the gardens. Shall we go in?'

Anna and Tom nodded, and between them Grace trembled. But as they started moving forwards she kept up, her ancient legs propelling her towards a conclusion her mind clearly wasn't sure she wanted. They stepped into the bright room, where chairs lined the walls and tables were covered with abandoned card and board games. One lone woman sat playing Patience and barely glanced up as they entered.

Over in the corner, in a wing-backed chair turned to face the garden, was the side profile of a man. His head was almost bald, and the little hair that remained was swept back from his face and held in place with Brylcreem. A metal walking frame stood next to him, and slippered feet poked out from the bottom of grey polyester trousers. Anna tried to reconcile this elderly man with the stories of the dashing young man Grace had fallen in love with in the dance hall all those years ago, but it was impossible. This man looked like little more than a bag of bones barely capable of walking, let alone dancing, and her heart felt like it could break.

They walked towards the chair where Arthur was sitting and as they approached, he slowly turned his head. His whole face seemed to lift as he took in the woman standing there, and it was as though seventy years had slipped away when his eyes lit up with recognition. At the same time Grace looked up, her chin raised high, defiant, and Anna felt her body stiffen beneath her touch. Pride was taking over, she knew. The two old people looked at each other for a few moments, the air between them charged with so many unspoken words.

'Hello, Arthur,' Grace said eventually, her voice clear, strong.

'Hello, Grace. It's been a while.'

Chapter Twenty-Four

Grace had read the letter from Arthur more times than she could count since it had arrived. She could have recited any part of it at the drop of a hat, had she been asked.

But now, as she stood facing the man she hadn't seen for more than seventy years, every single word of it left her mind. Every last word, every last paragraph. Every last apology.

Instead, she felt a rage boiling up inside her. A rage the like of which she'd never felt before; a rage that was the culmination of years of wondering, of blaming herself, of feeling abandoned.

She watched Arthur gesture to the chair opposite him, his hand mottled with age spots, veins so prominent they looked as though they were on the outside of his skin rather than the inside. Rather like her own, she thought sadly. She felt the squeeze of Anna's hand on her left elbow, Tom's on her right, and she felt safe.

'No thank you, I shall remain standing,' she said in a loud and formal voice. She stuck her chin out in a gesture she hoped would show him she was in control now.

'Are you sure you don't want to sit down?' Anna said beside her.

'No, Anna, I don't.' She cleared her throat and dug her feet firmly into the carpet. She felt stronger than she had for many years. 'I can hear whatever Arthur wants to say to me from here.'

The room went still for a moment, as though everyone in it was collectively holding their breath. Then Arthur spoke.

'I'm sorry, Grace. For everything.'

Grace felt her legs tremble now. Before they got here she'd had no idea what she was going to say to this man after all these years. She'd worried she might stand there gormlessly, staring at him, unable to speak. Or that he might be cold, harsh and not want to speak to her after all. What she hadn't expected was to have so many things she wanted to say that she didn't have a clue where to start. Like: *Why did you leave me? What did I do wrong? How could you have been so cruel? Why did you never try to contact me? Who did you tell?* More importantly, though, she wanted to know: *Have you been happy?* Because she wanted him to know that, despite everything, she had been.

She opened her mouth to speak. But what came out instead of the words she'd planned was a cough. And then she seemed unable to stop and she felt her body stiffen; she doubled over, her chest jerking spasmodically as her lungs tried to expel their poison. Tom pulled a chair towards them but it was too late – Grace felt her legs give way and then she was on the floor, terrible hacking coughs wracking her body until she could barely draw in breath.

* * *

'Help!' Anna yelled and within seconds Margaret was there, crouching by Grace's side.

'I'm calling an ambulance,' Tom said, pulling out his phone.

'I think that's a good idea,' Margaret agreed, holding Grace firmly in her arms.

'What's happened? What's wrong with her?' Anna felt the panic rising in her chest.

'I don't know, but we've got to get her to a hospital as soon as we can,' Margaret said. 'Has she complained of feeling ill?'

'She's had a terrible cough for a while and it did seem to be getting worse. But she insisted she didn't want to see a doctor, so I relented. I wish I hadn't now.'

'Don't worry, you weren't to know. Old people can be bloody stubborn when it comes to being ill. I should know.'

Anna shook her head. 'I should have insisted. I'm a carer – I know the drill.' She crouched down next to them as Grace's body started to relax in Margaret's arms. 'Grace, can you hear me?' she cried.

Grace didn't answer, and her eyes closed as she lay limply in Margaret's arms.

'Is she OK?' Anna murmured, terrified.

'She's fine. She's breathing.'

'Thank god!'

'Well, that was brief,' a voice said from behind and they turned to see Arthur watching them. In the panic, Anna had forgotten he was there.

'I'm so sorry, Arthur,' Anna said, pushing herself to standing and walking over to Arthur's chair.

His eyes didn't leave Grace. 'Will she be all right?'

'I hope so,' Margaret said.

He shook his head and looked down at his hands. 'All this time and now this. It's fate.'

Anna pressed her hand awkwardly to Arthur's shoulder and they all stayed silent as they waited for the ambulance to arrive.

'I'll go and wait by the door,' Tom said after a few moments, clearly keen to make himself useful.

As he left, a couple of elderly residents shuffled into the room. They stopped and stared for a moment but, presumably deciding it wasn't worth the commotion, they turned and retreated, their wondering voices carrying loudly through the air.

Minutes later Tom burst back into the room followed by two paramedics. Anna felt herself relax. At last, there was someone to take charge. How could she have worked as a carer for so long and still panic every time someone was taken ill?

She watched as the paramedics checked Grace over then lifted her fragile body onto a wheelchair and secured her tightly before wheeling her towards the door.

Tom stepped forward. 'Can we come with her?'

'Yes, that's fine,' one said.

'Are you coming too?' Tom asked, glancing at Anna.

'Shall I?'

'I'd prefer it if you did.'

Together they began to make their way out of the room. Then suddenly Anna thought about Arthur and ran back to where he was sitting, watching everything.

'I'm sorry, Arthur. We'll come back as soon as she's better, I promise.'

'That's all right, dear, I'm not going anywhere.'

'Bye, Arthur,' Anna said, then she turned and scurried after the paramedics, climbed into the back of the ambulance and they raced off towards the hospital.

* * *

The plastic seat was digging into her back and it was too hot in the waiting room at the Royal Victoria Infirmary in Newcastle. Anna and Tom had been waiting for news for two hours now and still nothing.

'I can't believe this has happened,' Anna said for perhaps the tenth time. 'I mean, I know she's old, but what a time to take ill.' She shook her head.

'I know. I suspect it was the stress. She was pretty terrified by the time we got to the care home – I thought she was going to pass out anyway.'

'You're probably right.' Anna pressed her hands into her thighs and watched her fingertips turn white. 'I wonder what she was going to say to Arthur, before she collapsed.'

'God only knows.'

They fell into silence once more. Anna's mouth was dry and she could feel her heart thumping against her chest. The truth was she felt terrible about what had happened this morning, and going over and over it wasn't making her feel any better. She knew Grace would insist it wasn't Anna's fault, would tell her she was perfectly capable of making her own decisions, but Anna still felt responsible. After all, it was her who'd suggested this whole thing in the first place, her who'd tracked down Arthur, and her who'd made Grace come.

'You're blaming yourself again, aren't you?' Tom's words cut through her thoughts and she smiled sheepishly.

'Am I that transparent?'

'Maybe I'm just getting to know you better already,' Tom said, raising his eyebrows. 'You mustn't, though, you know. Grace is a grown woman and if she hadn't wanted to come, or she was worried about her health in any way, she could have said.'

'But we should have brought her to the hospital yesterday, when it was clear her cough was getting worse.'

'Yes, and Grace made that really easy for us, didn't she?' He placed his hand on Anna's thigh and she shivered at his touch. 'Stop torturing yourself, Anna. Grace was always going to do what she wanted, and, yesterday, that was getting to Arthur, no matter what.'

Anna nodded, trying to focus on something other than the feeling of Tom's warm hand on her leg burning through her jeans into her skin.

He removed it quickly and stood up when the door swung open and the doctor who had taken care of Grace when they arrived walked in.

'Are you two Grace's relatives?' he asked, shaking each of their hands in turn.

'I'm just a friend,' Anna said.

'I'm her great-nephew.'

'I see. And does she have anyone else here?'

Anna shook her head. 'No.'

The doctor hesitated for a moment, then gave a brief nod. 'Well, then I'm going to speak to you about this.' He clasped his hands together. 'Now, I'm assuming you know about Grace's cancer.'

'What?' Anna felt her face go white and the room began to spin around her. Grace had cancer?

'Ah, you didn't know. Then I'm sorry to break it to you like this.' He indicated the chairs behind them. 'Shall we sit for a moment?'

Anna and Tom did as they were told, and waited for the doctor to explain.

'I'm afraid Grace has lung cancer. It's pretty far advanced. I've checked all her notes and she's refused treatment, which is fair enough at her age. But the truth is I don't know how much longer she has left. It could be weeks, it could be months, it could even be a couple of years. There's just no way of knowing.'

'So that's what her cough was? She told us she had a chest infection.'

The doctor nodded. 'That's what was causing it, I'm afraid, yes.'

Anna shook her head. 'Why didn't she say anything?'

The doctor continued. 'We're going to keep her in for a few days until we feel she's strong enough to travel home. Are you going to stay?'

Anna glanced at Tom. 'I don't mind staying if you need to get home,' she said.

Tom shook his head. 'No, I'll stay too.'

The doctor clapped his hands together. 'All right, good. Grace will be pleased. She seems very fond of you both.'

'She's awake?'

He shook his head. 'Not currently. But she has been. And she seemed to think she had an important appointment to get to.'

'Ah yes. We did. But that can wait.' Tom smiled.

'Good. All right, we'll keep her comfortable, but there's not much else we can do apart from let her body fight this for a bit longer. You can come and say hello once she's woken up if you like.'

'Thank you, Doctor…'

'Anderson. Jacob.' He held out his hand and shook theirs again and then hurried off to see to another patient, save another life, leaving them alone and reeling. Anna looked at Tom.

'Well, I wasn't expecting that,' he said.

'Me neither.' She shook her head. 'I can't believe she's been keeping that from me – from us – for so long. How long do you think she's known?'

Tom shrugged. 'Hard to tell. A while, I should think.'

'I can't believe she wouldn't tell us something like that.'

'It's quite common, I think,' Tom said. 'My grandad – on my dad's side, not Ernest – never told anyone when he was ill and it was only after he died that we discovered he'd had bowel cancer for three years.' He rubbed his hand across his hair. 'They don't want to admit their weaknesses, I suppose – admit that they're ill, that there's something in this world they can't fight anymore. When they've lived through the war, you can hardly blame them.'

'I suppose not.' Tears filled Anna's eyes and she wiped them away with the back of her hand.

Tom's hand landed on her thigh again and without thinking she placed hers on top of his and leaned her head on his shoulder. They sat like that for a few moments until someone else came into the room and they sprang apart.

'Right, well, we should go and get some lunch, come back later, what do you think?' Anna said, gabbling.

'Yes, good idea,' said Tom, and as they walked out of the room he reached for her hand and she let him take it, feeling its warmth against her palm as they made their way across the hospital and towards the front doors.

Sitting next to Grace's bed, holding her papery, veined hand in hers, Anna listened to the bustling sounds of the hospital as she waited for Grace to wake up. Voices mumbled and soles of shoes squeaked; trolleys rumbled and curtains snapped back. She let the noises wash over her as she studied Grace's face. She was so pale her skin was almost the colour of the pillow on which she was propped, her wispy grey hair framing her face. Her body was barely discernible beneath the blue blanket, and the rise and fall of her chest hardly even there.

Anna felt a presence behind her and turned to see Tom with two cups of coffee. He handed her one and sat down on the other side of the bed, facing her.

'How's she doing?'

'She hasn't woken up yet.' Anna took a sip of her coffee, wincing as the hot liquid burned her tongue. It was sweet and too strong but she didn't care. She longed to look at Tom but she felt suddenly too shy. They'd held hands earlier but nothing more and Anna was feeling unsure whether there was anything between them or whether it was merely the pressure and emotion of the situation.

'What are you thinking about?' Tom said, his voice low.

Anna looked up to see him watching her, his brow furrowed. 'Oh, nothing,' she said.

'That's a shame. I was hoping you were thinking about me.' Anna could hear the laughter in his voice and she looked up again. Sure enough, he was smiling at her, his teeth white and even, his thick stubble highlighting the curve of his cheek. She wondered how it would feel if she ran her hand over it.

'Well, sorry about that, Mr Ego,' she said, tearing her eyes away to look at Grace. 'But I was actually hoping that my friend might be all right and that we're not about to lose her.'

Tom didn't reply for a moment and she wondered whether she'd upset him. But then he chuckled. 'Well, that told me, didn't it?' he said, taking a long sip from his coffee cup.

She looked at him and stuck her tongue out. He burst out laughing, his eyes crinkling at the sides.

'You child!' he said.

'Well, what do you expect?' She grinned at him, and for a moment they sat there smiling at each other across the almost flat expanse of blanket.

'Hello, you two,' came a croaky voice.

'Grace!' Anna tightened her grasp on Grace's hand. 'You're awake!'

'It seems so,' she said, licking her lips. 'Can I –' She shuffled a little and pointed at the glass of water on the bedside table.

'Of course,' Anna said and held it up to Grace's mouth to let her take a sip from the straw. Her lips were cracked and dry and she drank greedily for some time before she stopped and Anna replaced the glass.

'You had us worried,' Tom said.

'Yes. I am sorry about that. It seems I was rather more poorly than I'd thought.'

'It appears you were a *lot* more poorly than you admitted to us,' Anna scolded. 'Chest infection, you said.'

'Ah. So, the doctor told you, then.' Her voice was hoarse and quiet and Anna had to strain to hear.

'About the cancer? Yes, he did.'

Grace lowered her eyes. 'I'm sorry, but I didn't want to worry either of you.'

'Well, you certainly have now,' she said, a little more harshly than she'd intended.

'I think what Anna means is that we would have preferred to have known how ill you were before this,' Tom said. 'And she feels responsible for what happened at the care home.'

Grace looked stricken. 'But you mustn't!' she said. 'This was my fault, all of it. I should never have come up here, it was silly.' She stopped and swallowed several times before continuing. 'But once you'd found Arthur it was – well, it seemed like fate. And I just couldn't *not* come.'

'Oh, Grace,' Anna said, wrapping both her hands round hers. 'I know how important this was to you but you still should have been honest with us. You had us all worried – including poor old Arthur.'

Grace rolled her eyes. 'Poor old Arthur my foot.'

'Grace! He was as shocked as we were.'

'Well then good. Serves him right.' Anna smiled and shook her head before Grace relented. 'I suppose it must have been a bit of a shock for him. Has anyone told him I'm all right?'

'I don't know. I'll find out. But you mustn't worry about anything. You just need to get yourself better.'

Grace nodded. 'Will you promise me something, though?'

'Anything.'

'When I get out of here, will you take me back to see Arthur before we leave? I can't come all this way and still not get my answers from the horse's mouth.'

Anna glanced at Tom, who shrugged.

'OK, I promise.'

'Thank you, dear,' Grace said. Her breath was laboured and she stopped to catch it.

* * *

Sitting across from each other in an Italian restaurant later that evening, a candle flickering on the table between them, it felt for all the world to Anna as though she and Tom were on a date. She was aware of her face flushing as she realised she'd really quite like that, despite the circumstances. How had that happened? Only a couple of months ago she had hardly been able to stand the sight of this man. Now she enjoyed spending time with him, and thought about him quite a lot actually.

'Poor Aunty Grace,' Tom said, taking the menu from the waiter and opening it in front of him.

'I know. I still can't believe she didn't tell us how ill she was.'

'I can. She's a stubborn old thing. I suppose it's like Margaret said, she doesn't want to admit any weakness.'

'But surely it's better if we know because then we can help her.'

Tom shrugged. 'Maybe she didn't want our sympathy. Maybe she just wanted you to be her friend, not her carer.'

Anna nodded. 'You're probably right.'

She looked down at her menu, the words blurring before her. She felt more shocked than she'd admitted to Tom about Grace's cancer diagnosis. She'd loved having Grace in her life over the last few months. And Grace had helped her so much – getting over Daniel, making her realise that life goes on, even helping her with her art work. She couldn't imagine her life without Grace in it now, but this illness meant the end was likely to be closer than she'd imagined.

'I know you'll miss her,' Tom said, seeming to read her mind, and Anna looked up. 'I will too.'

'I know. I'm sorry, Tom. I've only just met Grace, but she means the world to you.'

'It's fine, it doesn't mean you're not allowed to be sad. But you have to remember that Grace is pretty old. She's had a good life.' He spun the fork round and round with his left hand. 'We'll just have to make the most of having her around while we still can.'

'You're right.'

'Anyway, we've got lots to thank Aunty Grace for.'

'Have we?'

Tom nodded, refusing to meet her eye. He stared at the tablecloth, at the candle and over her left shoulder before he spoke again. 'If it wasn't for her, we would never have met.'

'No, I don't suppose we would have done.'

Tom finally looked into Anna's eyes. 'And I'm glad I've met you, Anna.'

'Me too.'

'Are you ready to order drinks?' The waiter's voice cut through the moment and they looked away. Anna's heart raced in her chest as she glanced down at the menu. What was happening here? Did Tom like her as much as she liked him?

Anna couldn't focus on the wine list. 'House white, please.'

'Same for me,' Tom said and the waiter went on his way.

The moment might have been broken for now but there was something Anna wanted to know.

'Why did you dislike me so much when we first met?'

Tom looked instantly ashamed. 'Oh god, I'm so sorry about that. I was so awful.'

'Yes, you were.' She grinned. 'But why? I mean it wasn't as though you knew me. You just – you just seemed to really hate me from the very first moment we met.'

Tom puffed his cheeks out, looked down at his hands on the tablecloth in front of him. 'I think –' He stopped and looked up at Anna, his eyes pleading.

'What? You mean there was a reason, and it wasn't just because you thought I was trying to steal Grace from you?'

Tom shook his head. 'No. Well, I mean, it was that, partly, as pathetic as that sounds. I felt as though you were spending so much time with Aunty Grace that she didn't have time for me anymore. But that wasn't it really. Because really I was just happy she wasn't alone all the time when I couldn't be there.'

'So, what was it then?' Anna waited, watching Tom squirm. What on earth was he going to say?

Before she could find out, the waiter arrived with their drinks and took their food order. When he'd left, they both took a sip of their wine.

'Ugh, that's awful,' Tom said, wincing.

'It's not the best,' Anna said, taking another gulp. But she didn't care about the wine. She wiped her mouth and placed her glass back down on the table. 'So, come on. What were you going to say?'

Tom shook his head again. 'It doesn't matter. It's not important.' He reached his hands out to cup them round hers and she shivered at his touch. But she couldn't let it lie, so she forced herself to pull her hands away.

'It didn't matter before but you've made it sound all serious now, so I have to know,' she persisted.

Tom sat up straight and fixed his eyes on her. 'OK then.' He shuffled in his seat, rubbed his hand over his stubbly beard. 'I thought you were only after her money.'

'What?' Anna felt her hands start to shake and all the blood drain from her body.

'I told you it doesn't matter now.'

'Oh, it matters, Tom.' Her words came out sounding as cold as she suddenly felt.

'It really doesn't because I don't think that now.'

'But you did. And I'm assuming by that you mean you thought I was hoping she'd write me into her will, and that was the only reason for me to be nice to her.'

He nodded, looking sheepish. 'At first, yes. But obviously I know that's not the case now.'

Anna shook her head, trying to grasp the full implication of what he was saying. She placed her hands flat on the table-cloth and studied her fingernails, then took a deep breath. 'But you didn't like me for quite some time, Tom. Which means you must have held that very low opinion of me for weeks. Not to mention how little you must have thought of Grace to even think that she could be taken for a fool.'

'No, that's not true.'

'Of course it is. You were rude to me for a long time after I first met Grace. I assumed it was just your manner, and I couldn't understand why Grace kept going on about how lovely you were.'

'I am lovely, Anna. Come on, you know me better now. And I know you.' His voice was pleading.

Anna nodded tightly. 'That's true.' She took another gulp of her wine, tipping her head back to drain the glass. 'But you still thought, for quite some time, that I was only after Grace's money.' She felt fury rising in her chest. 'And that, I'm afraid, I can't forgive.'

She stood, almost tipping her chair back. 'I'm sorry, Tom, but I'm going to go now.' She fumbled in her purse and placed a couple of notes on the table. 'Here's some money for my food. I wouldn't want you to think I was scrounging from you, would I?'

'Oh, come on, Anna!' Tom said, but before she could hear any more of his protestations she turned and walked away from the table, away from him, and from the restaurant.

And it wasn't until she reached the hotel a few minutes later that she allowed herself to cry. As she sank into her single bed, with Grace's empty bed next to her to remind her of everything that had happened that day and everything she might have lost, she sobbed until she fell into a fitful sleep.

Chapter Twenty-Five

Anna wasn't one for sulking or holding grudges. When she fell out with someone she was always the first person to speak to the other, to sort it out.

But not today. Today she still felt too raw, too angry, and she wasn't in the mood to be conciliatory. Not yet.

She woke up hungry, having missed dinner last night. Keen not to see Tom until she absolutely had to, she ate the two packets of shortbread biscuits from the tea tray for breakfast and made some overstrong tea with UHT milk, then got washed and dressed.

After she'd done everything else she possibly could, she checked her phone. There were two messages – only one from Tom, and it had been sent this morning, not last night. He obviously wasn't that bothered about trying to clear the air, so why should she be?

She clicked on his message first.

See you downstairs at 10 if you still want to come and see Grace this morning.

No sign off, no mention of what had happened last night. If that was how he wanted to play it then she would too.

Then she clicked on the second message. It was from Emily, the gallery owner and Tom's ex-girlfriend.

Hello Anna, it's Emily. Good news, I've sold almost every one of your paintings and wondered if you had any more?

Oh, wow. That was unexpected. Tapping out a quick reply to say she'd ring her when she got home to arrange a meeting, Anna allowed a shard of happiness to penetrate the black cloud of her bad mood. Bugger Tom. She couldn't wait to tell Grace her exciting news.

Just before ten o'clock Anna waited in reception, staring mindlessly at the leaflets for days out and museums stacked in the rack. Moments later Tom arrived looking bleary-eyed. He nodded at her and they walked out to the car without saying a word. It felt just the way it always had done between them, as though the last few weeks had never happened.

They climbed into the car in silence and Anna was relieved when Tom clicked the radio on. The sound of the Arctic Monkeys filled the car, and Anna stared out of the window at the passing traffic, at mums pushing babies in buggies, students milling around with enormous rucksacks. Her heart felt heavy, and not just because of what had happened with Tom. She'd loved having Grace as a friend and had hoped for quite a few more years yet of getting to know her better. She knew it was selfish but she wished Grace could just battle it for a bit longer.

They arrived at the hospital and made their way inside. Taking the familiar route up to the second floor and along the corridor towards Grace's ward, they walked wordlessly. Anna couldn't help thinking that Grace was going to be desperate to get out of here and go and see Arthur, and she wasn't sure how she was going to stop her. She could be pretty persuasive when she wanted to be.

They arrived at Grace's ward, Anna following so closely behind Tom that she almost walked smack into his back when he stopped dead in the doorway.

'Agh! What the hell are you doing?'

But one look at Tom's face told her there was something very wrong. Fearing what she might see, Anna looked from Tom to the bed in which they'd left Grace sleeping last night.

It was completely empty. There was nothing on the bedside table, fresh sheets were pulled taut as though ready for a new occupant.

'What –' Anna stopped, her heart thundering in her chest. She clutched the doorframe, and Tom held her elbow to steady her. 'Where's Grace?'

'Maybe –' he stammered, looking around wildly. 'She must have been moved to a different room,' Tom said, peering round the edge of the curtain to see if he could spot any clues as to her whereabouts. But there was nothing – no note, no glasses propped on the edge of the table, no handbag hanging from the back of the chair, no cardigan folded carefully over the arm of the seat. It was as though Grace had never been there at all.

'We need to go and find the doctor,' Anna said, turning and almost bumping into Dr Anderson. 'Oh!'

'Anna, Tom, I'm so glad you're here, although I wish I'd

caught you before now.' His face was serious and Anna looked round the room, bewildered.

'Where's Grace? Have you moved her?' she said.

Dr Anderson shook his head. 'No, not exactly,' he said in a gentle voice. 'I'm so sorry, Anna, Tom, but I'm afraid Grace died in the early hours of this morning.'

'I'm sorry, what?' Anna tried to push past him, although she wasn't entirely sure where she thought she was going.

'Anna,' Tom said, grabbing her arm.

'But there must be a mistake,' she protested. 'Grace was fine yesterday. We talked. She seemed *fine*.' She tugged her arm loose from Tom's grasp.

'I know, and I'm sorry this has come as such a shock,' Dr Anderson said. 'But Grace really was very poorly and her body just couldn't fight it any longer. If it's any consolation, it was very peaceful and she wasn't in any pain.'

'But…' Anna's stomach turned over. How could this have happened? Grace had been happy and laughing one minute, and now she was gone. It didn't seem real.

'Nobody rang us,' Tom said.

'No, and I'm sorry about that,' said Dr Anderson. 'I'm afraid we couldn't seem to find a number for either of you. I'm so sorry.'

Tom hesitated, then nodded. 'Yes, thank you.' Then he took Anna's elbow and led her to a bank of chairs nearby. 'I think we just need a minute.'

'Of course,' Dr Anderson said. 'Let me know if you'd like to go and say goodbye.'

'Goodbye?'

'Yes. We can arrange for you to go and see her one last time, if you'd like to.'

Anna glanced at Tom. *Would they?*

'She looks very peaceful, just like she's sleeping,' Dr Anderson said.

Tom nodded. 'Yes, all right then. Please.'

'Go and get yourselves a coffee, have a bit of time to take it all in, and I'll arrange it for you. I'll see you in half an hour or so, OK?'

Anna nodded, feeling numb, and they walked down to the cafeteria in silence. Tom ordered two coffees and they sat down facing each other across the sticky plastic table. All worries about the row they'd had the previous night were eclipsed in the face of this.

'I can't believe she's gone,' Anna said, stirring a plastic spoon round in her coffee and watching the spirals form at the top.

'Me neither.'

Anna looked up. 'She would have been happy, though, wouldn't she? When she died. I mean, she'd been given the missing piece after all those years of not knowing what really happened.'

Tom nodded and reached out his hand to cover Anna's. 'She would have been happy anyway, Anna, because she'd met you. She was very lucky to have you, and she knew that.'

'Oh, I don't know about that. I was definitely lucky to have her. She did a lot for me. She changed my life, Tom.'

'I know she did.'

'I'll miss her so much.'

'Me too.'

The cafeteria rumbled on around them, other people suffering their own dramas, their own traumas, awaiting their own news, drinking or eating in silence or talking in muffled tones. They sipped their coffees without any further words for a while. Then a voice interrupted their thoughts.

'Anna? Tom?' They looked round to find Dr Anderson by their table. 'They're ready for you.'

They stood and followed him. Anna's heart raced and, without thinking, she reached for Tom's hand. He squeezed it back. After a ride in the lift and a walk along several corridors, they arrived at a door.

'In here,' Dr Anderson said, holding it open for them.

They both walked in and Anna felt her heart contract. Grace's tiny body lay there motionless, her eyes closed. Anna stared at her, tried to imagine the life that had flowed through that body, the pain and the heartache and the joy and the happiness that those eyes had seen, that her heart had felt, the love she'd experienced throughout the ninety-five years she'd been on this earth. She put her hand out to touch Grace's, but pulled back immediately. It felt cold and stiff, nothing like the warm papery feel of Grace normally.

'Goodbye, Grace,' she whispered. 'I hope you'll be at peace now.'

She looked at Tom, who had a tear shimmering in the corner of his eye, threatening to spill down his cheek. He brushed it away self-consciously.

'Shall we go?' she asked him.

Tom nodded. 'Yes.' He reached over and pressed his hand to Grace's cheek, then leant down to plant a gentle kiss on it. 'Goodbye, Aunty Grace. I love you.'

Then he straightened, took hold of Anna's hand and, together, they walked out of the room and away from Grace forever.

* * *

After they'd left the hospital hand in hand, neither of them knowing where to go next, they walked through the town, which was thronging with people, and down the steep hill past the impressive Georgian buildings until they reached the river. The impressive steelwork of the Tyne Bridge soared above their heads and they turned left and headed along the quayside. The water, far below, flowed past them, away and out to sea. Eventually Tom steered Anna towards a bench overlooking the water and they sat down.

'Fuck, Anna.'

'I know.' She felt tears forming in her eyes and let them fall. Tom's warm palm was still pressed into hers and she could hardly believe how well it slotted into her own hand, as though it was meant to be there.

Before she knew what was happening Tom had wrapped his other arm around her opposite shoulder and pulled her towards him. With a jolt she realised his face was right in front of hers. She could feel his breath on her mouth, and his nose was just millimetres from hers. His hair brushed her forehead in the breeze and she shivered. And then he pressed his lips onto hers. They were soft and warm and tasted slightly bitter and she could think of nothing else for a few seconds.

Then he pulled away and her vision was filled with his eyes. They were warm and brown and she realised she had never seen them this close before, had never noticed the flecks of gold.

'I'm sorry for being such a dick.'

The words were such a surprise that Anna let out a laugh like a bullet. 'It's all right. I wasn't much better, storming off and sulking like that.'

He shook his head. 'It really doesn't seem important now, does it, after what's happened?'

'No.' Sadness overwhelmed her and she looked away, staring at the murky grey water through the black railings. 'I can't believe she's gone.'

'Neither can I.'

Anna thought for a moment. 'Do you think she just felt ready? That it was the right time?'

Tom shrugged. 'Who knows? But I do think getting the answers she wanted from Arthur in that letter gave her some peace. I don't think she needed anything else from him, she just wanted to see him.'

Anna sighed. 'Poor Arthur, though.' She stopped as realisation dawned. 'Shit, he doesn't know she died. We have to tell him.'

'Oh god, we do.'

'I can't believe that after all these years we found him and then they only got to say a few words to each other.'

'Maybe it was enough.'

'I hope so.'

Tom stood suddenly, pulling Anna's arm behind him so she stood up to follow him. 'We should go. We need to let Arthur know what's happened, and then we need to work out what to do next.'

'I suppose we do.'

They began walking back up Grey Street towards town and the hospital. 'You know, I think there was more to Grace feeling ready to leave than just seeing Arthur,' Tom said, his breath catching as they climbed the steep hill.

'Like what?' He stopped suddenly and she almost went into him again. 'You've got to stop doing that!'

'Sorry.' He smiled with a serious expression. 'But this is important.'

'Go on.'

'I think –' He paused and cleared his throat as people flowed past them up and down the hill. 'I think Aunty Grace was pretty happy to see us getting on so well. I think she thought perhaps her work here was done.'

'And is it?'

'What?'

'Done?' Anna held her breath as she waited for Tom to answer. He did so by taking her other hand in his and leaning in to kiss her again.

'I'd say it's getting there.'

Chapter Twenty-Six

The care home looked much the same as it had the previous day; the flower beds were tidy, the grass was neat. But this time Anna and Tom felt completely different as they approached it. Yesterday they had been full of anticipation, excitement, nerves. They had been with Grace.

Today, there was no Grace, though the nerves were still there. How were they going to break the news to Arthur?

'Ready?' Tom said.

Anna gave a small nod. 'I guess so.'

They pushed open the doors and were greeted by the distant hum of a vacuum cleaner, shouts and bursts of laughter and a pervading sense of peacefulness. Anna felt a wave of calm wash over her.

Seconds later she spotted Margaret hurrying over towards them, her hands clasped together. 'Oh, I'm so glad to see you two,' she said. 'I've been ever so worried about Grace since yesterday. How is she? Is she OK?' Concern etched her forehead and Anna took a deep breath before speaking.

'I'm afraid we've got some bad news,' she said, placing her hand gently on the older woman's arm.

Margaret looked from Anna to Tom and back again, her face bewildered. 'What on earth's happened?'

Tom took over. 'We're really sorry to have to tell you this but my Aunty Grace passed away last night.'

Margaret paused for a moment, clearly trying to articulate her thoughts. 'Oh, I'm so, so sorry,' she said eventually. A cry from one of the rooms beyond distracted her.

'Oh goodness, hang on, I've just got to go and deal with this. I'll be right back.'

Margaret shot off down the corridor, leaving Anna and Tom standing in the middle of the entrance hall.

'Are you all right?' Anna said.

Tom gave a tight nod. His face was pale. 'I think it's only just beginning to sink in that she's gone now we're telling other people.'

'I know, I was thinking that. It's going to take a while before I believe it.'

Margaret reappeared, her face etched with concern. 'Let's go somewhere more private,' she said, leading them towards an office off to the left of the reception desk. 'I truly am so sorry to hear about Grace,' she continued as they sat down around the small glass table.

'Thank you,' Tom mumbled.

'I –' She stopped, clearly at a loss. 'What happened?'

'She had lung cancer,' Tom said.

'Did she? Did you know?'

He shook his head. 'No. Nobody did, she'd kept it a secret. But it turns out she'd been ill for quite a while.'

'Oh, that's so very sad,' said Margaret. She shook her head, her lip turning up slightly at the corner. 'I'm sorry, I don't mean to be insensitive and laugh, but you wouldn't believe

how many times I've seen this, working here. I'll never understand why they feel the need to conceal their illnesses from
everyone.'

'No,' Anna said. 'Me neither. But I suppose admitting it
makes them feel more vulnerable – as though they're a
burden.'

Margaret nodded. 'You're probably right.' She suddenly
stood up. 'Oh! I must go and break the news to Arthur. He's
been asking after Grace. Do you want to come with me?'

'If you'd like us to,' Tom said.

'If you don't mind,' she said. 'I just think it might be
helpful for him to be able to talk to you, in the circumstances.'

They followed Margaret down the same corridor as
yesterday – much faster this time, without Grace – past the
same pictures, photos, drawings, until they arrived at a door
on the right, on which was taped a picture of Arthur. Margaret
rapped lightly on the wooden door.

'Yes?' came a shaky voice from inside.

Margaret shushed the door open slightly across the carpet
and poked her head round. 'Arthur, it's me, can I come in?'
Muffled words, then Margaret's voice, a bit louder: 'I've
brought Anna and Tom as well – you know, from yesterday.
Do you mind if they come in too?' More muffled words, then
Margaret opened the door wider and beckoned them inside.

'Hello, Arthur,' Anna said as they walked in. The room
was stifling and the lighting was dim, with just a small gap in
the curtains letting in the narrowest chink of sun and a
flowery bedside lamp creating a pool of light that didn't
stretch far into the room.

Arthur nodded and appeared to be looking past them as
though expecting to see someone else. He was looking for
Grace, Anna realised, and she felt her heart swell with sadness
for all of them.

'Please, sit down,' Margaret said, gesturing towards two chairs in the corner. Anna and Tom sat obediently. Margaret perched on the edge of the bed, next to the chair where Arthur was sitting. She placed her hand gently on Arthur's forearm. 'Arthur, I'm afraid we have some rather sad news.'

'Is it about Grace?' he said, looking round for her again.

'It is. It seems she was more poorly than we'd realised.' She took a breath. 'I'm afraid, Arthur, that Grace has passed away. I'm so sorry.'

Arthur's face didn't move. He sat staring at a spot on the carpet for several moments. Anna studied the deep lines of his face, the hair that had thinned over the years, the liver spots on his hands that rested in his lap, the frailness of his arms, his legs, and she thought she might cry. This was the man that Grace had loved so deeply for many, many years; this was the man that had swept her off her feet, had asked her to marry him and had, in the end, broken her heart. But Anna didn't feel any malice towards him. Quite the opposite, in fact. She knew now – and Grace had known, in the end – that he hadn't meant to hurt her. He'd been suffering himself and hadn't known what to do, where to turn, who to talk to. Things were different back then, she knew, and she felt sorry for him, for the young man she'd heard about through Grace's stories. She knew nothing about the rest of his life – whether he'd been happy, whether he'd found love again, what job he'd done, if he had a wife, children, grandchildren who cared about him. But it didn't matter. Because all that mattered now was that he was sorry, and that he had loved her friend.

Arthur turned his head towards Anna and she looked into those eyes that Grace had thought, more than seventy years before, held all the secrets of the world. They were faded now, the blue less vibrant, the sparkle almost extinguished. But as she stared into them, she could see something there – a bit of the old Arthur she'd heard so much about.

'Did she read it?' he said, his voice a croak.

He meant the letter. Anna nodded. 'Yes, she read it before we left Lowestoft.'

He nodded, licked his lips. 'Good.' He spoke again. 'Did she understand, do you think?'

'Yes, Arthur, I think she did.' Anna hesitated. Grace had been angry about the letter, she knew that. But she'd been happy about it too, in her own way. There was no point now in telling Arthur anything but that. 'I think it gave her peace, at last. So thank you, Arthur.'

He nodded again, and turned away to gaze towards the curtained window. 'Would you mind opening the curtains for me, dear?' he said to Margaret, and she leaned over and pulled them open, the daylight flooding in and making them all blink. Arthur appeared to refocus his eyes for a moment and then he looked out of the window at the large oak tree in the grounds and smiled. 'I thought about her, you know, over the years. Wondered what she'd done.'

'She was happy, Arthur,' Anna said. 'In the end.'

And then a thought occurred to her. She dug into her bag and closed her fingers around what she was looking for. Pulling it out, she held it for a moment, then extended it towards him. 'Arthur, I think you should have this.'

He turned to face her and then glanced down at what she was proffering. 'What is it?'

'It's a photo of you and Grace.'

He took it from her and peered at it for so long that Anna almost wondered if he'd fallen asleep. But then he looked up at them and tears shone in his eyes. 'She kept it, for all these years.'

'She did.'

He looked back down and then held the photo up to the light. He shook his head slowly. 'I remember this day,' he said, pointing at it with a shaky finger. 'It was just before I went off to war and we'd had a lovely day out on the seafront, sticking coins in the slot machines and having a ride on the boating lake.' He sighed. 'Can't remember what I had for breakfast this morning but I can remember this, sharp as anything.' He tapped his finger to his temple. 'Amazing what stays in here.' He looked back to Anna again. 'Are you sure you want me to have this?'

She glanced at Tom and he nodded. 'Yes, Arthur, it's yours,' he said. 'Aunty Grace would want you to have it.'

He squinted at Tom. 'Aunty Grace? So, you're old Ernest's son then, are you?'

'Almost – I'm his grandson.'

'Of course, grandson, silly me. I lose track.' He continued to look at Tom, studying his face. 'I can see Grace in you. She and little Ernest always had the same eyes.' He paused. 'Is he still alive?'

'No, he died a few years ago.'

'I'm sorry to hear that.'

Tom didn't reply and a silence filled the room.

Margaret stood up and clapped her hands together, making them all jump. 'Right, would anyone like a cup of tea? Arthur?'

'Yes please, dear.'

'Tom? Anna?'

'No thank you,' Tom said, standing up too. 'I think we probably ought to be getting off.' He turned to Arthur. 'Thank you, Arthur, for writing to Aunty Grace. I know she felt betrayed when you left her on your wedding day, but she really did find happiness again. She had a good life with my uncle, Roy. And she forgave you, in the end. She got the answers she needed.'

Anna stood too and took Arthur's bony hand. He squeezed his fingers lightly round hers for a moment.

'Take care of each other, won't you?' he said.

They glanced at each other and smiled. 'We will,' Anna said.

'And don't make the same mistake I made.'

'I won't,' Tom said.

Then, saying their last goodbyes, they turned and left Arthur and Margaret behind in the over-warm room.

* * *

The journey home was much quicker; the roads were clear and the weather was on their side.

Only this time there was a huge Grace-sized hole in the car that neither Anna nor Tom knew how to fill.

'Shall we play that Adele song she liked?' Tom suggested, and Anna guessed he was trying to create reminders of his beloved great-aunt.

'Yes,' Anna agreed, leaning forward to fiddle with the CD player, relieved to have something useful to do. The sound of 'Someone Like You' filled the car and for a few moments she was lost in memories of Grace and knew that Tom was too.

The song came to an end and for a while the only sounds Anna could hear were the rumbling of the tyres on the road, the indicator as Tom changed lanes and the whoosh of cars passing on the opposite side of the road.

'I think she knew it was time,' Anna said after a few minutes. She jumped slightly, surprised she'd said the words out loud.

Tom glanced quickly towards her and back to the road. 'Because of the letter, you mean?'

'Yes. I think she was just holding on for her answer, and once she got it, she was ready. Ready to go and be with her Roy again. She had closure, as they say.'

'You're probably right.'

'Poor Arthur, though.'

'I know. But at least they got the chance to see each other again, even if it was brief.'

Anna nodded, recalling Arthur's motionless face when they'd broken the news.

As they drove on, Anna became lost in thoughts about the short time she'd known Grace. She'd miss her, desperately. But she couldn't help thinking about all the things that had changed for the better since Grace had come into her life. She had made Anna think about what was important in life – her friends, her family, herself. She'd made her think about her artwork again for the first time in years and maybe, just maybe, there was a chance that something might come of that one day, thanks to Grace. She'd made her stop thinking about Daniel, made her realise that you could move on and be happy again and that it was OK. She'd also made her realise that age was no barrier when it came to friendships, that you could find solace in the most unlikely places. And, perhaps most importantly, there was Tom. Anna wasn't entirely sure what was happening between the pair of them, or whether anything more would come of it. But whatever happened, she had Grace to thank for bringing them together in the first place.

Now, as they sailed down the motorway towards home, Anna turned to Tom. 'Do you think I did the right thing, giving Arthur that photo? You don't think Grace would have minded, do you?'

'I think she'd have been pleased,' Tom said.

'Really? You don't think she'd have felt ashamed, letting him know she cared enough to keep it for so many years?'

Tom shook his head. 'I think you're overthinking it, Anna. Grace kept that photo for her own reasons, but none of that matters now. Arthur seemed happy to have it.'

'You're right.'

'I usually am.'

She slapped him on the leg and, for the hundredth time that day, marvelled at how quickly she'd started to feel comfortable with him, despite the argument of the previous night.

He grabbed hold of her hand and squeezed it, and she squeezed his hand back, holding it there next to him as he drove.

* * *

It was almost dark when they pulled into the car park outside Anna's flat, next to her bike, the sun dropping behind the houses on the opposite side of the road. Tom switched the engine off.

'Well, they were an eventful few days.'

'They really were.'

He sighed. 'Will you come and help when it's time to sort Grace's house out?'

'Of course I will. But won't your mum want to be there too?'

'Probably. But she can meet you then, can't she?'

Anna looked round sharply. 'Meet me?'

Tom's face flamed. 'Well, you know, she'd heard about you from Grace and…' He trailed off and they sat in silence for a moment listening to the ticking of the engine as it cooled.

'Anna?' Tom's voice was low now, uncertain. She looked up, her heart hammering as she wondered what he was going to say.

He cleared his throat, rubbed his chin. 'Can we see each other soon? I don't mean at Grace's, I mean properly.'

'You mean like a date?' Anna felt a smile spreading across her lips.

Tom flushed again. 'Yes. Yes, that's exactly what I mean.' He looked at her. 'It's not exactly been the most conventional of starts, has it? But I think you know by now that I really like you and – well, I'd like to get to know you better, properly.'

'I'd love that,' Anna said, and before she realised what was happening Tom had leant over and pressed his lips against hers and she returned his kiss greedily. His arms slid towards her and pulled her closer, and she could feel the gearstick jabbing into her thigh but she didn't care. His lips were warm and soft, and his three-day-old stubble scratched her chin red raw. She pulled away and observed the glow of his face in the orange light of the early-evening sunset.

His eyes shone as he whispered, 'Do you think Grace would approve?'

'Do you know what? I know she would,' Anna said. Then she turned away, taking hold of the door handle. 'Shall we go inside, where it's more comfortable – unless you need to be somewhere else?'

'There's nowhere else I'd rather be than here,' Tom said as he climbed out of the car and followed Anna into what, for the first time since she'd moved in, would not be a sad and empty flat.

Epilogue

Anna stretched her legs out in front of her in her stripy deckchair and wiggled her toes in the sand, which glowed like lava in the soft evening light. She let out a loud, contented sigh.

'What are you so happy about?' Tom said, unfolding a deckchair for himself next to Anna's, then fetching a blanket and placing it across her knees.

'Just this,' she said, sweeping her hand across the vista before her.

'What, Lowestoft beach?'

She smiled at him, shading her eyes from the sun with her hand. 'Among other things. It would be an amazing scene to paint, though, don't you think? Perhaps I'll bring my canvas and paints down here one evening and try to capture it. I'm sure Emily would like it.'

'No doubt,' Tom agreed. 'But I'm more interested in these other things that are making you smile.'

'Fishing for compliments, are we, Thomas?'

'A man's got to get them where he can.'

'All right then,' Anna relented. 'I'm happy about all of this. The beach, the sunset, this beach hut…' She paused. 'The company.'

He grinned at her, the orange streaks in the sky above reflecting in his eyes and making them dance. 'Me too. Although there is one thing spoiling it.'

'Oh?'

'I wish Aunty Grace was here to see us.'

'Me too. She'd have been so happy, wouldn't she?'

'She really would. About us, and about your successful career as a sought-after local artist.'

'Hardly.' Anna smiled. 'But she would be proud, wouldn't she? And it was thanks to her that it happened at all.'

'It was.' Tom sighed. 'I can't believe it's been a whole year since she died.'

'I know. I keep wanting to ring her and tell her about everything that's happened, then I remember she's not there anymore. And she never will be.'

Tom reached his hand out and wrapped his fingers round Anna's and she squeezed them gently.

'How're you both doing over there anyway?'

Anna leaned forward and reached for the cup of tea that was cooling on a foldaway table beside her. She took a sip, replaced the cup, then pressed her hand against the curve of her belly. It swelled beneath the blanket and every now and then she could feel a movement, like butterflies flapping around inside her, and it made her smile.

'Me and baby Roy are doing just fine.'

'Oh god, I do hope that name doesn't stick,' Tom laughed. 'I mean, I loved my uncle Roy very much but can you imagine the tough time this little one would get at school if we really gave him that name?'

'Ha, don't worry, I promise it's only for now.'

Tom leaned over and planted a kiss on Anna's lips. 'I don't care really. All that matters is that he'll be here in a few months, and he's going to be the most beautiful baby in the world.'

'With parents like us? Of course he is.'

Tom held his mug of coffee in the air and Anna picked up her teacup again and held it next to his.

'We've got a lot of things to thank Aunty Grace for,' said Tom, 'and this is certainly one of them.'

'It is – although I think we might have managed this bit on our own,' she winked, rubbing her belly, and Tom chuckled.

'Happy anniversary, Anna,' he said.

'Happy anniversary, Tom.'

'And here's to Aunty Grace. For interfering.'

They clinked their cups together.

'To Grace.'

Author's Note

If you enjoyed this story, please do leave a review. It makes a huge difference to us authors, and means the world.

To find out more about Clare Swatman's upcoming novels, please head to her website at:

www.clareswatmanauthor.com

Here you can sign up to her newsletter to get a free '50 Best Reads of all Time' download, as well as monthly news, reviews, recommendations and the occasional exclusive giveaway.

Twitter: www.twitter.com/clareswatman
Instagram: www.instagram.com/clareswatmanauthor
Facebook: www.facebook.com/clareswatmanauthor

Acknowledgments

Although writing a book can be a very solitary experience, the truth is, there are always more people involved in the book-writing process than just the author. And I always find that people are very kind and generous with their time, so I would like to show my gratitude to as many of them as I can.

I was keen to properly capture the essence of Lowestoft as a town. I spent a lot of time here during my childhood with my beloved grandparents, and have always loved it. But I also wanted to make sure I got the details right, both of the town as it is now, and as it was then, during the 1940s. To do this, I had help from my aunty, Jane Macardle, who, although far too young to help with the 1940s side of things, had lots of photos and anecdotes from older family members that she shared with me. My Mum was also very helpful with details. Any inaccuracies are entirely my fault.

I would have loved to have gleaned some of the details of Lowestoft during the Second World War from my grandparents themselves, but sadly they are no longer with us. However I did get some amazing help from some of the residents of

Britten Court residential home, who shared their stories of the town during the war. I'd like to thank them, as well as manager Chloe Swarbrick, for being so generous with their time. I hope I've done your memories justice.

I also have the wonderful Anne Cater to thank for always championing me, and for helping to get the word out about this book. Thank you too to all the fabulous book bloggers for all of your tireless support.

I can't leave out my wonderful editor, Katharine Walkden, who understood Dear Grace immediately, and helped to make it sparkle.

And, as always, I have to thank my very first readers, Serena and Zoe, who both loved Grace, Anna and Tom from the very first draft, and who always believed this book would one day be out in the world. Plus, of course, thank you to Tom for believing in me, supporting me, and picking me up whenever I felt like giving up. And to my boys, Jack and Harry - thanks for being awesome. Even if you do hate writing stories, I'll never give up trying to turn you into writers!

About the Author

Clare Swatman is an author and journalist. She has written for many of the women's weekly magazines for more than twenty years, and finds other people's stories endlessly fascinating.
Dear Grace is her third novel.
Clare lives in Hertfordshire with her husband and two boys. Even the cat is a boy, so she is destined to be outnumbered forever.

www.clareswatmanauthor.com

www.instagram.com/clareswatmanauthor

www.facebook.com/clareswatmanauthor

www.twitter.com/clareswatman

Printed in Great Britain
by Amazon